ANGEL EYES

"You're a very beautiful woman, Sophie," Gabriel said, his voice a whisper that brushed the back of her hand and made goose flesh rise on her arms.

She couldn't speak. The room had become thick with something deliciously seductive.

"What's your story, I wonder," he went on. "I know you won't tell me."

She shook her head the tiniest bit, and very slowly.

"But I want to know, and I will know. Someday."

Again, she shook her head. Oh, those eyes of his were wicked. They drew her like a siren's song or an angel's harp, made her feel as if all she had to do to achieve life-long peace was succumb to their lure.

She knew better.

Knowing better didn't seem to be helping at the moment. Doing so without her compliance, her face drew closer to his as if compelled by a force stronger than her. Or him. Or the both of them together.

"Sophie," he whispered.

GABRIEL'S FATE

EMMA CRAIG

LOVE SPELL   NEW YORK CITY

Dedicated to Garak Borrowdale, the Prince of Pugs,
and to his mum, Kimberly.
Garak and Kimberly are both very good birds!

A LOVE SPELL BOOK®

November 2001

Published by

Dorchester Publishing Co., Inc.
276 Fifth Avenue
New York, NY 10001

ISBN 0-505-52429-5

The name "Love Spell" and its logo are trademarks of Dorchester Publishing Co., Inc.

Printed in the United States of America.

Visit us on the web at www.dorchesterpub.com.

GABRIEL'S FATE

Chapter One

Gabriel Caine's eyebrows lifted when he caught sight of a tall blond woman striding toward the ticket counter, the handle of a large white wicker basket slung over her arm. Obviously a confident wench, she didn't bother to hide her charms. Gabriel appreciated her for it, as her charms were considerable.

Her boots made a hearty, satisfying clop against the weathered boards of the old train station. They seemed to announce her presence, like a drum beating out the entrance of a queen. No shrinking violet, she.

The peeling walls of the train depot had probably been white once. They and the decrepit wooden benches stacked against them looked as though they belonged here. She didn't. She was as out of place in Laredo, Texas, as a butterfly in a swamp full of mosquitoes. The woman was, in fact, a sight for Gabriel's sore eyes.

Although the weather was hot enough to melt wax,

she didn't show it. She held her chin high, and the flowers on her hat looked . . . perky. *Perky?* It was the only word Gabriel could think of, and it surprised him. He wasn't used to thinking of things in terms of perky. Besides, the blonde was too large and lush for so flimsy a word as *perky*. The only concessions she made to the weather were the two moist patches of perspiration under her arms as she lifted them to set her wicker basket, very carefully, on the ticket counter.

A small woman scuttled after the blonde like a puppy afraid of being left behind. Her footsteps reminded Gabriel of the mice that used to dash back and forth in the attic above his head when he was a boy visiting his grandma. He remembered those mice fondly; they'd added an almost musical accompaniment to the rhythmic rise and fall of his father's sonorous prayers.

The blonde's companion was much older than she, and a good five or six inches shorter. She too wore a flowered hat, but on her it didn't seem at all out of place. Now *she*, Gabriel decided, could be perky without half trying. She had one hand clamped onto the brim of her hat, which tilted awry on her pretty graying hair. She grabbed at the sleeve of the blonde's white shirtwaist with her other hand, delicately gloved in white kidskin. The gesture appeared timid. Gabriel got the impression no feeble sleeve-twitching was going to deter the blonde from her purpose, whatever it was. The old lady had a sweet, rather vacuous face, although it carried a worried look on it at the moment.

"But Sophie," she said, her voice diffident. "There's such an unpleasant aura about this whole business. Recollect that Nine of Swords, my dear. The cards don't lie, Sophie."

Cards? The Nine of Swords? Intrigued, Gabriel edged his hat down to hide his eyes and sidled closer to the oddly matched pair, making sure they didn't notice him. He liked the name Sophie for the blonde. It fit her somehow.

Sophie wrinkled her nose and slanted a disdainful glance at the overflowing cuspidor standing beside her. "Nine of Swords, my foot. This is Texas, Aunt Juniper. What you sense is stale sweat and cow pies. And old tobacco juice and spit."

"Sophie, no! I mean it. The Nine of Swords and the Five of Pentacles are very telling. This is a perilous journey, my dear. Listen to me!"

Plainly determined to do no such thing, Sophie smiled at the clerk, who gaped back. Gabriel didn't blame him. Sophie was quite a work of God's art. Her teeth were perfectly straight and as white as pearls; Gabriel could see them from where he stood. "Three tickets to Tucson, if you please."

"But Sophie, I don't want to go to Tucson!" The older woman, though obviously timorous around her more dynamic relative, sounded vexed. Gabriel wouldn't have been surprised to see her stamp her foot. Sophie continued to ignore her.

Tucson. Gabriel didn't go so far as to smile, but he was pleased to know he'd be able to observe this laudable specimen of nature's craft for a while longer. He aimed to go to Tucson himself, and there was only one way to get there from here.

The clerk pushed up his sleeve, snapped one of his suspenders, and shifted his toothpick to the other side of his mouth. He appreciated Sophie as much as Gabriel did; Gabriel could tell. "One way or round trip?"

"One way, please."

The older woman tugged at her niece's sleeve again. "Sophie! It wasn't just the Nine of Swords and the Five of Pentacles. Recall the Devil, if you will." Her whisper grated in the hot air and reminded Gabriel of the sound grasshoppers make when they swarm.

"In a minute, Aunt Juniper."

Sophie was adamant, and Gabriel wouldn't have given a fig for Aunt Juniper's chances of forestalling her, no matter how many minutes she managed to squeeze from Sophie's schedule. He wasn't accustomed to resolution in young females, except in pursuit of young males. They generally simpered and smirked around him. He twirled his black mustache at the thought. They did so to impress him, and he knew it. He was, after all, a very handsome man.

Poor Aunt Juniper had taken to wringing her tiny gloved hands. Gabriel decided it was time to slather on a little of his cultivated southern charm. He shoved his flat-brimmed black hat back on his head and pushed himself away from the wall. His boot heels sounded like thunder in the stifling afternoon air as he walked toward the two ladies.

Aunt Juniper jumped at the sound. When she saw him coming, she looked scared for a moment, then gave him a shy smile.

Not so Sophie. To Gabriel's amusement, she glanced at him and frowned. Her eyebrows were much darker than her hair. He wondered for a second if she dyed her hair, then decided Sophie wasn't the type to do anything calculated to attract a man's attention. Her brows drew down into a sharp vee over her nose. Because she fascinated him, he disregarded both her and her frown and tipped his hat to her aunt. He figured he'd have better luck in that direction.

"Anything the problem, ma'am? Can I help you?"

"Oh! Oh, my! Oh, I—"

"No," said Sophie, trampling over her aunt's twitters like a longhorn on a june bug. Then she said, "Thank you," sniffed imperiously, and turned back to the clerk, who almost swallowed his toothpick.

"Are there any rules about taking pets aboard the train, my good man?"

"Er—um—I—" The clerk scratched his chin and shifted his toothpick again. "Pets, ma'am?"

"Yes," said Sophie, glaring at the fellow as if she suspected him of being deliberately obtuse. "Pets."

Gabriel registered the sound of gentle snores emanating from the wicker basket. His interest in this pair increased tenfold.

Juniper tweaked Sophie's sleeve again and whispered, "Sophie!" The result she achieved this time was the same as it had ever been. Sophie didn't indicate by so much as a flicker of an eyelid that she even knew her aunt was there. Aunt Juniper looked ready to sink through the dirty floorboards.

Gabriel gave the woman a conspiratorial wink, which made her blush. He'd have thought such a reaction sweet if he weren't so hardened a cynic. Hell, women had been blushing at him for twenty years or more; it didn't mean a damned thing except that they were experts in their own ways, as he was an expert in his.

"I believe the lady has an animal she wishes to take on the train with her, Henry. You know: a pet. Like a puppy dog or a kitty cat." Gabriel used his smoothest Virginia accent, just to see if he couldn't ruffle Sophie's pretty feathers.

She gave him the same look she might have used on a frog who'd landed in her soup, and he was pleased to discover her feathers were not easily ruffled. His trip to Tucson might not be boring after all.

"Oh," said Henry around his toothpick. "You got yourself a kitty cat, ma'am?" His grin was a work of frontier art, full of crooked, tobacco-stained teeth and huge gaping spaces.

"A kitty cat?"

Gabriel wasn't sure because he didn't know her, but

13

he didn't expect Sophie could sound much more disgusted.

Aunt Juniper, diverted from her attempts to get Sophie to alter her course—which seemed to Gabriel not unlike trying to change the direction of the ocean's tides—seemed merely confused. "Tybalt?" she said. Then, rather enigmatically to Gabriel's mind, she repeated, "Tybalt?"

Gabriel had no idea what the woman was talking about, but he did begin to wonder if Aunt Juniper might not be playing with a full deck.

Without saying another word, Sophie reached into her big white wicker basket and withdrew the ugliest dog Gabriel had ever seen. The clerk behind the counter uttered a short curse and leapt back, as if he anticipated the thing's attacking him. It didn't look much like an attack animal to Gabriel. It looked like a very small pig, fawn-colored, black in the face, and with a tail that curled twice and laid flat against its haunch. It blinked at Sophie sleepily.

With a ferocious scowl, Sophie said, "This is *not* a kitty cat. This is my pet. His name is Tybalt, and he's a Chinese pug."

Then she rubbed her nose against Tybalt's, purred, "And what a sweet, sweet puppy-doggie he is, too," and Gabriel lost his heart, a circumstance that perfectly astounded him since, until that moment, he'd been sure he no longer possessed such an article.

Henry still looked scared. "That there thing's a dawg, ma'am?"

Sophie gave him a frosty look. Gabriel decided it was time for him to take over, considering interference in this instance a benevolent act. Poor Henry might not survive an encounter with Sophie without assistance.

He stepped up to the counter, therefore, presented Sophie with one of his most stunning smiles—which earned him another frown—and turned to Henry. "That is indeed a dog, Henry. A fancy one. And this lady and her aunt want to take it to Tucson with them."

As an expression of cunning crossed his face, Henry scratched his chin. "Ain't no rules about dawgs goin' to Tucson as I know about."

Gabriel had anticipated this obstructionist behavior from the phlegmatic and mercenary Henry. "Now, it seems to me that this pet of Miss—" He cocked an eyebrow at Sophie, asking silently for her name. She only glared at him and hugged her ugly dog. He got the impression she was daring him to make her tell him anything at all, and that he'd have to torture her before he'd wring her name out of her.

Undefeated and not unamused, Gabriel transferred his look of inquiry to Aunt Juniper, who blushed again. He began to think of the two ladies as a challenge. Leaning close to Aunt Juniper, he whispered into her ear, which was so hot it glowed, "What is your niece's name, ma'am? I'll just tell the gentleman here."

Aunt Juniper jumped and squeaked out a frantic, "Oh!" Gabriel continued to smile at her as if she were the only female on earth. She whispered "Oh!" again, and pressed a hand to her bosom. He sighed.

"My name is Sophie Madrigal," the blonde announced, drawing Gabriel's attention. He smiled at her again, and kept it up in the face of her fierceness. At least Tybalt seemed to like him. His curly tail wagged.

"A musical name," Gabriel murmured. Sophie continued to glare at him, but he knew he could wear her down if they spent enough time together. He wondered if a trip to Tucson would be long enough. Gabriel loved a challenge; especially if it looked like Sophie Madrigal. He'd always admired a well-grown female, and Sophie was built upon truly noble lines. He was also unused to being almost able to look one in the eye. Females generally came up to his collarbone. Sophie's head reached his nose.

He turned to Henry. "Miss Madrigal only wants to be sure that her pet has a place on the train, Henry. That's all right, isn't it?"

Henry scratched his chin again before he disappeared from sight. Gabriel leaned over the counter, wondering if Henry'd fainted in the face of so much militant femininity. He hadn't. He was scrabbling under the counter for a large volume, which he lifted and plopped on the counter. Dust fluffed up, making Tybalt sneeze. Sophie ceased frowning at Gabriel and resumed frowning at Henry.

"Ain't seen no rules about dawgs in this h'yere book."

"Oh for heaven's sake, I'll buy another passage if you're worried about me cheating the railroad." Indignation made Sophie's bosom swell. Gabriel watched it with pleasure. Sophie Madrigal had herself quite a bosom.

"Well now, ma'am, I don't know as to how another passage will fix it. I got here rules for pigs and cows and sheep and chickens and goats, but I ain't seen nothin' coverin' dawgs." Henry's dirty finger poked at a line in the open volume.

"Pigs and cows and sheep and chickens are not in any way akin to pets."

"And goats," Henry supplemented conscientiously.

Sophie huffed.

As much as he appreciated the color blooming in Sophie's cheeks, Gabriel feared poor Aunt Juniper might be about to suffer a spasm. She uttered another, "Sophie!" and paled alarmingly. He guessed he'd better fix the situation for them.

"Here, Henry. This should solve the problem." He flipped a gold piece in the air. It winked amongst the dust motes and tumbled over and over, as if it were

16

enjoying the scene, too. Henry caught it as deftly as a lizard snagging a fly.

"Why, I do declare," said Henry without so much as cracking a grin, "I see here where it says dawgs can travel with their owners on the train, no problem." His finger stabbed at the page again. "Ain't no problem a-tall."

Sophie snorted. "How convenient. Then we'll need only three one-way tickets to Tucson."

"You still need three, ma'am?" Gabriel asked sweetly. She disregarded him.

"Yes, ma'am," said Henry, all cooperation now that Gabriel's gold burned his palm. He held out three tickets and let go of them after she'd laid her cash on the counter. Sophie snatched up the tickets and stuffed Tybalt back into his wicker basket. Then she wheeled around, nearly upending her aunt, who fluttered like a sparrow before she caught her balance and came to a palpitating rest. Sophie glowered ferociously as she dug into her reticule.

"Here," she barked, holding a gold coin in her gloved palm and thrusting it at Gabriel. "Thank you very much for your help."

From her tone, she might as well have told him to go out back and shoot himself. Gabriel grinned his appreciation and tipped his hat. He didn't take the coin.

"It's nothing, ma'am. Consider it a gift."

"I do not accept gifts from strangers, sir."

"And I don't aim to take your money, ma'am, so it appears we're at a standstill here."

"Sophie!" Aunt Juniper whimpered.

Sophie grabbed Gabriel's hand so quickly his smile didn't even have a chance to vanish before she'd slapped the coin into his palm. "Here," she snapped. "I don't care what your aims are. I do not accept gifts from strangers."

Before Gabriel, in his astonishment, had thought of a suitably cutting rejoinder, a commotion from the door captured his attention. The smallest man he'd ever seen, walking like he had rheumatism in every single joint of his body, made his way across the filthy floor toward them. The fellow was clad in tan overalls and a cloth cap and reminded Gabriel of photographs he'd seen of people toiling in the turnip fields of Europe. The midget headed straight for Sophie, a circumstance that Gabriel discovered did not surprise him. He wondered if this strange trio belonged to a circus.

"There you are, Dmitri. Here's your ticket."

Dmitri—Gabriel decided his movements were akin to a mechanical man he'd once seen in a bawdy house in Dallas—took the ticket. "Thank you, Miss Sophie."

The fellow had a strange accent. Gabriel couldn't place it. He also appeared morose and didn't smile once.

Sophie seemed to like him, though. Her severe expression softened.

"You want I take Tybalt?"

"No thank you, Dmitri. Just see that our bags are properly stowed, and we'll meet you on the train. Perhaps you can arrange a place for Tybalt to do his duty in the baggage compartment."

Dmitri apparently found nothing to object to in Sophie's suggestion. He tugged at his cloth cap and departed without another word.

"Come along, Aunt Juniper." Sophie grabbed her aunt's elbow and began to haul her toward the door.

"But Sophie," Aunt Juniper cried. "You must thank that nice gentleman for helping us."

Sophie snorted. Gabriel didn't get his thanks.

He did, however, board the train to Tucson with lightness in his heart and a keen sense of anticipation.

*　　*　　*

Sophie glanced through the smudged train window and sighed when she beheld what appeared to be a sea of bone-dry desert, speckled here and there with oddly shaped plants and bleached bones, and hovered over by lazily circling buzzards. She'd heard those strange plants were some kind of cacti. They reminded her in an abstract way of men, from their thick torsos and bent arms to their long, painful-looking spines. Sophie did not admire men for the most part. Other than her father—and he only nominally—Dmitri, and one or two others, men had not been a benevolent factor in her life.

Because her thoughts were about to lead her into a depression, she stopped looking out the window and turned back to petting Tybalt. Tybalt licked the back of her hand, and Sophie's heavy heart lightened fractionally.

The railway carriage was nothing fancy, but it wasn't as bad as some she'd been in. At least she and her aunt didn't have smoke and soot and cinders billowing around their heads and threatening to ignite their clothing as they'd done in Colorado. Traveling in the Western states and territories could be an uncomfortable business.

Aunt Juniper had seated herself across from Sophie on a facing bench, upon which she'd placed a soft cushion before she'd settled her softer bottom. Now she laid a board across her lap. A little frown puckered her forehead. Sophie recognized her expression as one of intense concentration. Juniper was dealing out the cards. Sophie had no idea what she expected to learn from them, since she'd been doing the same thing for weeks now and ought to know by this time that no matter how many Devils or Nines and Tens of Swords she came up with, Sophie would not be thwarted in her purpose. She continued to stroke Tybalt absently as she added columns of figures in her head.

If Dmitri, who preferred to ride with the baggage when they traveled by train, did some discreet advertising by word of mouth and tacked up a few broadsides, she and Aunt Juniper should be able to make up their passage to Arizona Territory by reading cards and palms on the train and at the various stops between Laredo and Tucson. Even if business was bad, she still had plenty of money as long as she was frugal—and Sophie was an expert at frugality.

Anyhow, if they ran short, Sophie could always wire the bank in St. Louis. Thank heavens the general population was a gullible lot and believed in the occult and spiritual communication. The fools had made her, by this time, almost rich. She gave a soft snort of disdain and then felt guilty, knowing that if for no other reason than the fact that it provided her with a good income, she ought to respect her profession.

Besides, as much as she hated to admit it—and did so only occasionally and to herself—she'd experienced enough odd phenomena not to disbelieve altogether in the mysterious and mystical aspects of life. She hated to acknowledge it, though, and seldom did so.

At any rate, once they got to Tucson, she hoped to be able to carry out her purpose and depart without wasting any more time and money than could be helped. That all depended, of course, upon whether or not she was arrested. If the law clamped its hands on her, so be it. She was prepared to take the consequences as long as she completed the mission that had been burning her up from inside for nearly a year now. This was the first time in those long, miserable months she'd even come close to realizing it.

"Mind if I join you ladies?"

Jarred out of her thoughts, Sophie recognized the

silky voice and uttered a silent curse. Frowning, she glared at the man's elegant black vest and said, "I'm sorry, sir, we're—"

"Oh, how kind you were to help us in the station, sir!"

Sophie transferred her glare to Aunt Juniper, who turned scarlet. Apparently in one of her rare defiant moods, Juniper lifted her chin in spite of her blush and Sophie's warning glance and declared, "Well, I *am* grateful, Sophie, no matter what you are."

"Fine," said Sophie.

She turned her head again and aimed her glower higher, until it rested on the man's face. Then she looked away in a hurry. Gracious, she'd forgotten what a handsome man he was. His smile was hot enough to toast bread—not, of course, that the weather couldn't have done that on its own. He was a demoniacally good-looking fellow, though, blast him. Sophie's distrust of him trebled. Because her own embarrassment bothered her, she deliberately turned her head and stared up at him once more. She didn't care in the least if she appeared rude.

"Fine," she said again, and tried to make her facial expression as forbidding as possible.

But it wasn't fine. At all. She wanted him to go away, not the least because ever since she first set eyes on him, she'd felt a funny prickling sensation inside her. The feeling made her extremely uneasy because she'd experienced it before once or twice. She feared the pricklings boded ill for her future peace of mind, not to mention her ever-present desire to disbelieve in supernatural phenomena.

He tipped his hat and grinned a grin the likes of which must have charmed the serpent from the apple tree in Eden. He had the devil's own grin, and Sophie resented him for it. His complexion was dark and his teeth gleamed white against it. He had hair as black as

21

night, and a perfectly wicked mustache. His black coat, vest, trousers, and boots were impeccable. The only white on him, besides his perfect teeth, was his shirt. The effect was startling, and Sophie suspected he dressed the way he did because he knew he looked good. She would have scorned the affectation if he wasn't so blasted right. She pegged him for a rambler, a gambler, a rake, and a rogue—a species with which she was intimately familiar—and she hated him.

A vision so sudden she couldn't capture it flashed in her brain. She jerked slightly, as the experience was both unexpected and unsettling. When she tried to retrieve the vision, it wasn't there any longer. She had a terrible suspicion it had something to do with this man, though, and she didn't like it. At all.

Rather to her surprise, he settled himself onto the seat next to Aunt Juniper. She'd have expected him to pester her some more. Most men, particularly after they discovered her profession, attempted to get beyond her hostility in hopes of stealing a kiss if not a tumble, no matter how futile their efforts inevitably proved to be. This man clearly found Sophie's charms resistible. Well, good. He could entertain Aunt Juniper; maybe get Juniper's mind away from her worries.

On the other hand, perhaps he was being subtle and thought Sophie would soften her attitude toward him if he was kind to her aging aunt. If so, he had another think coming. She knew all about men like him. They were the ones who'd made her life miserable. Why there couldn't be more *good* men in the world, Sophie had never been able to figure out, but she didn't think it was fair at all.

Blast that vision. She wished she could recall it. Or maybe she didn't. While she'd experienced odd internal sensations occasionally, she'd never been troubled by visions before, even though they were said to run in the family. Sort of like insanity.

Gad, she had to stop thinking such things.

Because she figured he expected her to gaze at him like a moonstruck adolescent, she refused to do it. So handsome a man must be accustomed to females falling at his feet and begging him to have his way with them. If he expected Sophie to be one of those foolish females, he'd miscalculated. Out of the corner of her eye she saw him smile at Aunt Juniper as if butter wouldn't melt in his mouth. She recognized the innocent look on his face as one that had been aimed at herself from time to time by gentlemen pretending to a goodness they didn't possess. Inside, she sneered.

Politely removing his hat and settling it on his lap, he said, "My name is Gabriel Caine, ma'am. It was my pleasure to be of assistance to you in the train station in Laredo, and it's a pure delight to be riding to Tucson in the presence of two such charming ladies."

His accent was straight out of a magnolia-scented plantation summer night. It brought to Sophie's mind images of sultry evenings, mint juleps, and ladies lazily fanning themselves while gentlemen flirted at their feet. Her heart quivered like jelly for a moment or two before it settled into a solid granite block. Damn him and every man like him who preyed on innocent young women. And, she reflected, thinking of her aunt, old women.

Juniper fluttered. Sophie caught herself in time to stave off a sarcastic snort. She wouldn't give him the satisfaction of a reaction to his practiced flirtation. She despised him.

"My—my name is Juniper Madrigal, Mr. Caine. And I truly do thank you for helping us back there in the train station. Sophie is so—so—so—" Words deserted her.

Sophie suppressed the urge to swear.

"Your niece is a beautiful and resolute young woman, Mrs. Madrigal."

"Oh, I'm not married, sir," Juniper twittered. "I'm *Miss* Juniper Madrigal, you see. Sophie's father's sister."

"I'm sure you've left a score and more of broken hearts in your wake, Miss Juniper."

"Oh, la!" Aunt Juniper fanned herself with the ace of clubs.

Sophie felt her lips purse. She stroked Tybalt too hard and he grumbled, opened one eye, and frowned at her like a dog sorely abused. She would have apologized, but she didn't want Mr. Gabriel Tongue-of-Silver Caine to know he'd affected her in any way whatsoever.

"In fact, I've seldom met such a delightful pair." Gabriel shared his smile equally between Sophie and Aunt Juniper. How devilishly fair-minded of him. "You are perfectly splendid, ma'am, and your niece is—quite exquisite."

Sophie bit her tongue so she wouldn't swear at him.

"Oh, yes," cried Juniper, delighted. Sophie rolled her eyes. "She's always been so lovely. She was beautiful even when she was a baby, you know. Why, she even won a beautiful-baby contest in New York City, Mr. Caine. New York City! And her little b—*oh!*" Juniper clamped her lips together, shot Sophie a frightened glance, and pulled her legs in toward her seat and away from Sophie's boot tips.

Wishing she could tape her aunt's mouth shut, Sophie merely smiled a warning at her. Juniper, who had reason to know that smile well, looked like she might faint.

Gabriel Caine either didn't notice or chose to ignore the uncomfortable pause that erupted in the middle of Juniper's ditherings. He said, "Yes, ma'am. That doesn't surprise me at all." He gave Sophie a debonair nod; she pretended she didn't see it and gazed pointedly out the window.

Silence sprang up once more, this time because Sophie had terrified Juniper wordless. Her aunt kept shooting her apprehensive glances, and Sophie kept ignoring them and staring out the window. She neither knew nor cared what Mr. Gabriel Caine was doing or what he thought. When he spoke again, therefore, his tone as nonchalant as if he were accustomed to such overt antagonism from pretty young females, she was somewhat nonplused.

"What's that you're doing, Miss Madrigal, if I might be so bold as to inquire?"

Sophie thought sourly that the damned man could use more words to ask a simple question than anybody she'd ever met except her own father. Which, all things considered, figured. Gabriel Caine seemed to be cut of the same charming—and transitory—cloth as Martin Madrigal. Sophia heaved an internal sigh as she recalled her deceased, dynamic father.

"Oh, la, Mr. Caine," chirped Juniper. "I'm reading the Tarot."

"The Tarot, ma'am?" He sounded suitably puzzled. Tarot decks weren't easy to come by in the United States, and most people had never heard the word. Juniper had cherished her own deck for years. It had been hand-painted especially for her by Señora Esmeralda, a Gypsy woman from Spain. Today Juniper was using a plain deck of playing cards since she wasn't about to entrust her pampered Tarot deck to the questionable mercies of territorial train travel.

"The mystical cards, Mr. Caine," Juniper explained. "The Tarot. I am a medium, you see."

Although Sophie didn't turn her head to look, she could tell her aunt was blushing and bowing her head. Juniper considered her talents a gift from God, and was always humble in acknowledging them. Sophie, who figured God had better things to do with His time than confer mystical powers upon people, considered Juniper's gifts a family legacy handed down through a long line of humbugs and charlatans. Juniper irritated the life out of Sophie at times, although Sophie loved her dearly.

"Is that so?"

Gabriel Caine sounded honestly interested. Shooting him a narrow look from under her flowered bonnet, Sophie acquitted him of subterfuge, although she reserved the right to change her mind later, if she ever got to know him better. She hoped she wouldn't have the opportunity.

"Yes indeed, Mr. Caine. The gift is in the blood, you see."

Gabriel blinked at Aunt Juniper. If Sophie didn't hate him so much, she might have laughed. Nobody in the world was more sincere than Juniper.

"The Madrigals have been in the fortune-telling business for generations, Mr. Caine," Sophie said. The sound of her voice, hard and cold, surprised her, as she'd planned to ignore Gabriel Caine until he went away. She cursed herself for a fool and turned back to the window.

"Is that so? It sounds like an interesting line of work."

"Oh, it is, Mr. Caine. And when one has the gift, you know, one must use it judiciously."

"I see. And Miss Sophie Madrigal has this gift too, does she?"

Sophie figured he was aiming one of his snake-charmer's grins at her and was glad she couldn't see it. She still burned inside from the first one.

"Yes indeed. She certainly does." Aunt Juniper sounded troubled. Which made sense, as Sophie did not honor the family gift as Juniper thought she should.

Sophie honestly wished she could oblige her aunt in the matter, but her life had taught her that this so-called family gift was, for the most part, nothing but a sham. She treated it thus, hurt Juniper in the process, regretted that, and couldn't help it.

Which didn't explain away that sudden, unexpected vision she'd had. Ah, well, it was undoubtedly a momentary aberration, and wouldn't recur. If it did, Sophie would ignore it. Just because she'd been born into a family of crazy mentalists didn't mean she had to succumb to the nonsense engendered therefrom. She prided herself on her common sense, even in the face of mystical visions. Not that they were truly mystical, but . . .

Fiddlesticks. Sophie decided not to think about it anymore.

"My goodness," the man purred. "Such beauty and talent in one lovely package. My, my."

Sophie imagined the look on his face as that of a cat about to pounce on a tasty mouse. She told herself not to be fanciful.

"Oh, yes. Sophie is very talented, Mr. Caine. She's— very talented."

"I look forward to learning more about her talents one day, Miss Madrigal."

There were all sorts of subtle meanings in his tone of voice, and Sophie would have slapped him if Juniper weren't present. Juniper wouldn't understand, and Sophie felt guilty enough about her poor aunt as it was. She did nothing, therefore, and proceeded to stroke Tybalt, who snored blissfully.

"I fear," continued Gabriel, "that my own lot in life is to dwell among those uninitiated into the cabalistic arts."

Lord, the man could talk. Sophie almost admired him for it.

27

Juniper cleared her throat timidly. "Er, would you care to learn about the cards, Mr. Caine? I find them fascinating myself, and enjoy teaching people about them. I, ah, sense that you might profit from the experience."

Good Lord! Juniper only offered to teach people whom she considered blessed with the gift. Sophie couldn't even imagine why she'd consider Gabriel Caine so blessed. The man was a devil, for heaven's sake. She bit off a hot remonstrance, and stared with increased venom through the smudgy glass.

After a small pause—Sophie would have given her eyeteeth to know what he was doing but she'd die before she looked—Gabriel said, "I'd be honored, ma'am. I'd be genuinely honored. A fellow doesn't get an offer like that every day of the week."

Juniper giggled.

Thinking he'd never know how true those casual words of his were, Sophie glowered at the scenery.

Chapter Two

The dining car wasn't crowded this early in the morning, so Sophie and Juniper had their choice of tables. They opted for one in the middle of the car, and Sophie settled Tybalt's wicker basket in the chair beside her. Aunt Juniper sat across from her, her sweet face wreathed in one of her charmingly vague smiles as she surveyed the car. Juniper had, as she always did, tried to persuade Dmitri to join them for breakfast, but Dmitri preferred to dine out of the public's eye.

Juniper had tried to tell him that people didn't really stare at him, but Dmitri didn't buy it. Sophie considered that sensible of him, since she knew as well as he did that most people considered him a freak of nature because he was a midget. It wasn't fair, but life wasn't fair. Sometimes she wished she had control over life and death and the world in general; there would be many fewer people around.

Sophie had slept well on the train after an initial bout

of internal turmoil, and was glad of it. Sometimes when they traveled, she found it ridiculously difficult to get a good night's rest. The only thing that had troubled her rest last night was a recurrence of that odd vision. She wished she could capture it and study it. Or maybe she didn't.

Actually, all things considered, Sophie guessed she'd better leave the visions to Juniper, who valued them. Sophie'd as soon skip them altogether.

They ordered breakfast. Juniper folded her hands and placed them primly on the table in front of her. She cocked her head to one side the way she did when she was about to take Sophie to task for something. She reminded Sophie of a sweet little sparrow when she positioned her head thus. Sophie braced herself to endure one of her aunt's lectures, although such preparation wasn't really necessary. Her aunt's fiercest scold didn't carry a sharp enough edge to slice through butter. Aunt Juniper, unlike Sophie, was a very nice person.

"All right, Aunt Juniper, what's the matter? What have I done now?" Sophie smiled when Juniper gave a guilty start.

"Nothing is the matter, Sophie," said Juniper nervously.

"Come along now, don't fib to me. You're mad at me, Aunt Juniper. Admit it."

Juniper could no more admit to being angry than she could admit that most fortune tellers were frauds. Sophie knew it, and felt mean about teasing her. Her aunt was spared an answer when the porter brought their breakfast. Because she felt penitent about needling Juniper, Sophie smiled at the man. He smiled back, his black face shining. At once she felt better about life.

The two Madrigals sat in silence while they buttered their muffins. Sophie contemplated her breakfast with satisfaction, glad that she was able to enjoy food again. Juniper's voice startled her.

"I don't know why you were so rude to that nice Mr. Caine yesterday, Sophie." Aunt Juniper took a savage bite from her muffin, the greatest show of pique Sophie had seen from her in a long time.

As for herself, Sophie heaped jam on her own muffin and gave her aunt one of her more jaundiced squints. "That 'nice' Mr. Caine is a thorough scoundrel, Aunt Juniper. I'm surprised you couldn't tell that about him, given the family predilections and all. You, of all people, can usually tell the genuine article from the quacks." She was ashamed of herself when a stricken look crossed Juniper's face. Although she didn't think he deserved it, Sophie modified her assessment. "Although he was very nice to you, and he did help us in the train station. I'll give him credit for that."

"Oh, Sophie, I wish your unhappy experiences hadn't hardened your heart so. Not all men are bad, dear, and the world isn't really such a terrible place. Truly it isn't."

The pain she strove like a Trojan to keep under control struck Sophie's heart so suddenly and so sharply that she had to squeeze her eyes closed against it. Her muffin dropped from her fingers and she pressed them to her eyelids, as if in that way she could push the agony away. Her efforts this time, as always, were ineffective. Her other hand gripped the edge of the table hard. She felt Aunt Juniper's small hand cover hers, and she ruthlessly choked back tears.

"Oh, Sophie, I'm so sorry. I didn't mean to hurt you."

With a great effort of will, Sophie managed to withdraw her hand from her eyes, open them, and smile at her aunt. "You didn't hurt me. Don't fret, Aunt Juniper. I'm fine, I assure you. Just a touch of headache all at once."

Juniper scanned Sophie's face, trying to judge the

31

truth of her assurance. She didn't smile back. "Are you sure, dear? You know I'm always happy to consult the cards for you. Truly, Sophie, they can give you relief and hope. The cards and prayer together can't fail to bring comfort and ease the pain in your heart. God sees everything, Sophie dear. He's watching over you, even if you don't want to believe it. God is the Universal Mind, dear, whether you admit it or not. Your unhappiness and disbelief can't hurt Him, but He can give you comfort if you choose to ask for it. He knows everything and can help you so much, if you give Him a chance."

Where was God when Joshua died? Sophie wanted to scream. But she knew if she did, Juniper would first be hurt and then spout more of her endless platitudes, so she didn't. Instead, she said, "Thank you, Aunt Juniper. You already know what I think about the cards." *And the Universal Mind.* She didn't add that part. While Sophie didn't know if she really disbelieved in God, she knew from bitter experience that He didn't much care what went on down here on this planet.

Juniper shook her head sadly. "You know, Sophie dear, you do your mother and father a great disservice by speaking of them and their work as if they were fakers preying on a gullible public."

"Well?" The word popped out of Sophie's mouth before she could stop it. She and Juniper had carried this discussion around with them for years, like baggage. Neither of them would ever change the other's mind. Sophie knew it even if Juniper didn't. Because she loved Juniper very much and hated to hurt her feelings no matter what her own were, she added hastily, "I'm sorry, Juniper. I know how much these things matter to you. I didn't mean to be hateful."

Juniper shook her head again. "You're not hateful, dear. You couldn't be. But, oh, Sophie, your mother and father loved you so much. It would hurt them to hear the way you're talking now. They went through so much in order to be together."

There went the pain again, stabbing into her heart like one of her uncle Jerome's carnival knives. Sophie was prepared for it this time. She didn't so much as flinch.

"Yes, aunt, I do know it. I loved them too." She picked up her fallen muffin, prepared to enjoy her breakfast in spite of everything. "And the family is still a nest of quacks and fakers, no matter what you say." She smiled and twinkled at her aunt to pad her words' sharp spikes. "Except for you, Aunt Juniper. I know you honestly believe in all of this . . ." She waved her hand, unwilling to label Juniper's beliefs with another disparaging term and unable to think of a polite one.

Juniper tutted and gave up. "You'll learn one of these days, Sophie dear. I know you will. The cards told me so, and the cards don't lie, no matter what you *think* you believe."

"In that case, perhaps you'd best do a reading on your friend, Mr. Caine. If the cards don't lie, I'm sure they'll tell you he's a villain."

As usual, Sophie's sarcasm sailed right over Juniper's head. Her eyes were as round and shiny as gold eagles. "I already did, dear, and you're quite wrong about him."

Sophie repressed a sigh of resignation and took another bite of her muffin. She didn't say anything.

"Now, they indicate quite clearly that he lacks faith, covers his internal pain with a dry and sarcastic wit, and that his past is clouded." She frowned, as if trying to clear up the clouds in her own mind. "There may have been—improprieties."

"I'll bet." Improprieties, indeed. Sophie would lay odds that the man's past was as black as tar.

"No, really, dear. He himself is unsure of his future

path and unclear about his own merits, but if he channels the goodness inside of him, it will lead him to do great things. Heroic things."

Heroic. Sophie couldn't stand it. She nodded, declined comment, and continued to eat. Merciful heavens how had she ended up in this family?

The merciful heavens didn't deign to answer her this morning. Sophie wasn't surprised. They'd never once answered a prayer of hers. She'd come to the conclusion some months ago that if God and the heavens existed, they evidently didn't like Sophie Madrigal very much. Well, she didn't like them either, so they were even.

"And that's not all, Sophie." Juniper's voice had taken on a quality of excitement. Sophie could tell she was warming to her subject, just as she'd warmed to Gabriel Caine the prior day. Sometimes Sophie wished her aunt were more discriminating in her acquaintances. Often, in fact.

"He's well grounded in the spiritual life, Sophie. The cards said he was. He's searching for something, and he has no idea it's within himself. He has a definite gift, dear. I perceived it plainly."

"Is that so?" Good heavens. If Juniper thought that, Sophie despaired for her. If there was a spiritual bone in Gabriel Caine's entire large body, Sophie would eat Tybalt's wicker basket.

"Indeed it is. I also perceive that his future is somehow entangled intricately with—"

"Good morning, ladies."

Sophie stiffened. Wonderful. As if her aunt had conjured the devil out of the air, here he was. Sophie didn't bother to respond, or even to look at him. She could feel his smile where she sat and didn't want any part of it.

"It's a beautiful day, Miss Sophie, Miss Juniper."

Sophie heard him rub his hands together briskly. In her mind's eye she pictured him, tall, handsome, and elegant; the quintessential gentleman traveler, taking breakfast with his fellow passengers.

She didn't believe it for a second. She knew him to be a black-hearted scoundrel, even if Juniper couldn't be brought to recognize reality, because all men who looked like him and were charming and attractive were black-hearted scoundrels; they couldn't seem to help themselves. Sophie'd learned that lesson the hard way. And early. Very early. She did, however, wonder what Juniper perceived his future was intricately entangled with. The law, as like as not. The wrong side of it.

"Oh, yes! Yes, it's perfectly lovely out, isn't it, Mr. Caine?" Juniper sounded as happy as a child with a new toy.

"It certainly is, Miss Juniper."

Sophie could hear the smile in his voice. She'd bet anything he'd dressed in black again this morning. Black should be a sober, discreet color, yet on Gabriel Caine it looked positively dashing. He knew it, too, the bounder.

"Oh, Mr. Caine!" Aunt Juniper started to rise, sat down again, blushed, and fluttered her napkin at him. Sophie wanted to wring Juniper's neck. The man already thought he was God's gift to womankind; it irked her to have Juniper confirm his inflated opinion of himself.

"Oh, Mr. Caine," Juniper repeated. "Please join us for breakfast. The food on the train is so delicious, you know."

Sophie aimed a quick kick at Juniper's ankle. Juniper, anticipating such a warning from her niece based on past experiences, had already tucked her feet safely away under her chair.

"I'd be delighted to join you two ladies, if I wouldn't be interfering."

"Oh, no—"

"Actually, we were having a private conversation, Mr. Caine," Sophie said, drowning out Juniper's words.

"We weren't either," Juniper said, astonishing her niece.

She glared at her aunt. "No?" She gave Juniper one of her dangerous looks. For the first time since Sophie could remember, Juniper glanced away from her and defied that look. Sophie was dumbfounded.

"We had been chatting, Mr. Caine, but about nothing at all significant. It would be a pleasure to take breakfast with you."

"Thank you very much, Miss Juniper."

Deciding she had to look at him sometime, Sophie shifted her dangerous glare to Gabriel. He merely raised his left eyebrow in the most ironical expression she'd ever seen. Drat! The man was on to her. It didn't matter. Sophie could ignore the most practiced advances of the most practiced flirts. She'd learned how a long time ago.

She lifted her muffin again—and suddenly gave a thought to her weight. Although Sophie was not a slim girl, she hadn't troubled herself about her weight in ages.

Of course, after Joshua died, she'd virtually stopped eating. For eight or ten months, she'd been so devastated by the shattering grief of loss, she'd walked around in a fog of it. Her will to live crushed, she'd been unable to eat more than enough to sustain life. She didn't want to eat even that much, but eating was easier than listening to Juniper harp at her. She'd lost weight then. In fact, Juniper had despaired of her. Her clothes had hung on her like rags on a scarecrow.

So gradually that she wasn't even aware of it, the sharp edges of her anguish had blunted until the pain had become more of a constant, dull ache of sorrow, only flaring to sharp life occasionally. Then Juniper had given her the little pug puppy whom Sophie had named Tybalt, and she'd gradually dragged herself back among the living. At last she'd discovered herself able to eat without feeling sick.

And then the notion of exacting revenge had occurred to her, and her life had opened up. She had finally discovered a reason for continuing this wretched existence and, as a consequence, began to enjoy food again. Food was her only joy now. Food and Tybalt. And, since Tybalt shared her love of food, the pairing of the two had been an inspiration on Juniper's part.

After she'd fulfilled her plan, her life would be complete, and she wouldn't know what to do with herself anymore. But Sophie couldn't make herself care what happened after that. She'd have done her duty.

Generally, therefore, Sophie didn't give a thought to her weight. Only women who were trying to attract men worried about such nonsense. Sophie was definitely not one of those.

Yet today, this morning, she found herself wishing she weighed twenty or thirty pounds less than she did. On account of Gabriel Caine. She tried to lie to herself, couldn't do it, and hated herself for succumbing to such a nonsensical female anxiety. As if she should care about what he—or any other man—thought of her as a woman. Yet she did care. Damn him for upsetting her equilibrium.

"Where's your—er—little fellow in the overalls this morning, Miss Juniper?" Gabriel asked, serenely unaware of Sophie's inner turmoil.

Sophie would have laughed at herself if she were alone. Why should he be aware of it? Traditionally women pretended that their every living breath wasn't wasted on the impossible task of trying to make men care. Traditionally women lied to themselves.

"Dmitri never rides or takes his meals with us, Mr. Caine," Juniper said. "He prefers to guard our baggage."

"He's a midget, Mr. Caine," Sophie said bluntly. "It embarrasses him to be gaped at by rude people." She watched him and deliberately took a big bite of her jam-smeared muffin. Let him consider her fat; she didn't care. She wished she believed it.

"Is that so? I'm sorry to hear it."

His tone was so mild, Sophie was embarrassed by her own show of antipathy.

"He's a Russian, Mr. Caine," Juniper said in a confiding whisper. "I understand Russians always feel things deeply."

"Is that so?"

"Unlike the rest of us," muttered Sophie.

She had taken to frowning at Gabriel, and was unprepared for the grin that suddenly spread over his face. He turned it on her, full-bore, and she felt it in every inch of her body. "Oh, I suspect we all feel the slings and arrows of outrageous fortune, Miss Sophie. Some folks try to hide from them, some folks brazen their way through them, and some folks erect stone walls with spikes on them to try to keep 'em out."

Like me. She knew he was talking about her. "You seem to know a lot about your fellow men, Mr. Caine." She gave him a smile of her own, and hoped it was as cold and pointy as an icicle.

"A bit," he said, still grinning. "A bit. And you, Miss Sophie? Do you like to study your fellow men?"

She stared at him for a second or two, wondering why he was persevering in the face of her undisguised antagonism. She couldn't figure him out. At last she said, "I leave such nonsense to Aunt Juniper, Mr. Caine. Personally, I don't care."

He mouthed the word *liar*, and Sophie felt as though

he'd reached into her soul and squeezed her heart. *Damn him!*

The bitch. What the hell was the matter with her? Gabriel had never seen a woman like Sophie Madrigal before—and until this minute, he'd believed he'd seen them all. Maybe she was one of those man-hating females whose lack of prospects had made them bitter.

Eyeing her from across the table—overtly, since he saw no reason to be polite if she wasn't—he decided that wasn't the answer. No female with Sophie Madrigal's blond beauty and buxom charms could have been ignored by the other members of Gabriel's sex. There was too much of her, and it was too gorgeous and way too lush to ignore. No. There must be another reason for her hostility.

Perhaps the answer was as simple as that she'd been born mean. Perhaps there was a deeper reason. Perhaps she'd been seduced and abandoned. Abused in some way. For the life of him, he couldn't fathom why he cared. What the hell difference was it to him how this female had come to be such an unpleasant bit of goods?

Sophie lifted the lid on the wicker basket sitting on the chair next to her, gave her ugly dog a piece of breakfast sausage, and Gabriel realized there was his answer. Right there in that basket. That silly, squash-faced dog. Somewhere under Sophie Madrigal's prickles was a heart. Not, of course, that Gabriel had any desire to touch her heart, but it might be fun to figure her out. God knew, he had enough time in which to do it. If he worked at it, he might at least be able to touch the rest of her, which was an alluring prospect all on its own.

"So, Miss Juniper," he said, aiming one of his warmest smiles at Sophie's aunt, "did you consult the cards last night after you gave me my lesson?"

"Yes, I did, Mr. Caine."

And that was another thing: Miss Juniper Madrigal. Miss Sophie and Miss Juniper might have belonged to separate races of womankind altogether, for all the differences existing between them. Yet they had sprung from the same family of charming fortune-tellers. Also, no matter how much she tried to hide it, Sophie cared about her aunt.

Aunt Juniper's tiny hand covered his for a moment, a gesture that touched something deep in Gabriel's chest. "And, Mr. Caine, I did a reading on you, too!" She flushed and jerked her hand away.

"Did you now? And what did the cards tell you, ma'am? Or do I want to know?"

She giggled like a schoolgirl. He couldn't help but like Juniper. She was as different from her niece as a fluffy little kitten was from a Bengal tiger. He heated his grin up a degree just to see if her blush could get hotter. It could, it did, and he was enchanted.

"Oh, la, Mr. Caine! I'd never even have told you if the cards had said something awful. I don't believe in frightening people, you know."

"No?"

"Well, of course, I sometimes will give people a gentle warning," Juniper said seriously. "But, you know, the cards don't speak in absolutes. They might be able to hint a person away from a possible problem, but they aren't to be considered akin to the Oracle at Delphi."

"I see. And you'll tell a person if a problem is looming?" It tickled him that Juniper was so earnest about these cards of hers.

Juniper tucked in her chin. "If I can. I believe it to be my duty to help people in that way."

"That's very nice of you, ma'am. And exactly what I'd expect of a kind heart like yours."

Gabriel grinned when Juniper got flustered by his

praise and uttered several unrelated words, as if she were trying to begin a sentence but didn't know what she wanted to say or how to go about saying it.

"Of course, as I'm sure you're well aware, Mr. Caine, it's all bunkum."

"Oh!" Juniper looked stricken when Sophie's stark declaration smote her ears.

Gabriel, watching as Juniper seemed to wither under Sophie's caustic scorn, wished he could paddle the exasperating Sophie. He turned to find her glaring at him, her eyes flashing. She had wonderful eyes. They were hazel, he guessed. Today they looked green, probably picking the color up from the green velvet doodads trimming her collar.

"Your aunt doesn't seem to think so, Miss Sophie." He kept his voice soft, but pitched it at a level calculated to instill shame.

It didn't work on Sophie. She huffed and fed the dog a piece of buttered muffin.

"Oh, Mr. Caine, Sophie doesn't mean it. She only thinks she does."

Giving up on Sophie, who appeared as invincible as a mountain, Gabriel blinked at Juniper. "You mean there's a difference, ma'am?"

She nodded hard. "Oh, my, yes, Mr. Caine. Why, if Sophie's unpleasant experiences hadn't hurt her so badly, she'd know—*Ow!*"

Juniper turned the face of a chastened kitten on her niece. "There was no need to kick me, Sophie. You know I would never reveal anything you prefer to keep to yourself."

"It didn't sound like it to me, Aunt Juniper. I'd prefer it if Mr. Caine knew nothing at all about me, thank you very much."

She was as mad as a wet hen. Gabriel was nettled with her for hurting Juniper. "Miss Sophie," he said in

41

his sloppiest, honey-and-magnolia-blossom Virginia accent, "even though I'm just dyin' to learn every little thing there is to know about you, I reckon I can forego the pleasure if your auntie's silence will keep her safe from your sharp pointy toes."

Giving him a smile that would have stricken a lesser man dead on the spot, Sophie said, "Good. That's a wise course to follow, Mr. Caine. I'd hate to have to place the family curse on you."

"Sophie!" Juniper looked like she might burst into tears.

After several seconds, during which Gabriel attempted to decide between giving Sophie Madrigal the spanking she deserved and trying to make peace between her and her aunt, he said, "So, tell me, ladies: Why are y'all headed to Tucson? Do you plan to tell some fortunes there?"

It seemed an innocent-enough question to Gabriel, but from the look of terror Juniper shot at her niece, he guessed it wasn't. He repressed a heavy sigh. "I've got business there myself," he said, hoping to clear the air of whatever seethed in it.

Oddly enough, it was Sophie who spoke next. She sounded almost polite, too. Maybe she was feeling penitent because of her miserable behavior. Gabriel hoped so, because she should be.

"We have business in Tucson, as well, Mr. Caine."

"Yes, yes," Juniper said quickly. "Yes indeedy, we do. Dmitri will see to it that we have plenty of business, in fact. He's good at that, you know."

"Is he now?" Interesting. So Dmitri was going to have to drum up business for them, was he? In other words, they hadn't already been booked to perform at any of the venues in Tucson. Most interesting. Gabriel caught himself wondering why and frowned. What the hell did he care what these women planned to do in Tucson?

"What is your business in Tucson, Mr. Caine?"

He looked up to find Sophie watching him. She had an ironic expression on her lovely face, as if she expected him to admit he was traveling to Tucson in order to commit a felony. He decided to tell a portion of the truth because it might shock her.

"I'm after a man, Miss Sophie. A criminal. I'm going to bring him to justice."

He had the satisfaction of watching her sit up straight and open her eyes wide, giving her an almost-innocent appearance. He didn't buy it for a second, but he appreciated it. When she sat up that way, she displayed her considerable bosom in a manner of which Gabriel approved. Heartily. She was quite something, Miss Sophie Madrigal. Quite something indeed.

"A man?" Her voice was nearly shrill, and it rang with something Gabriel pegged as anxiety. Curious; although not so very curious as to trouble him.

"Yes, ma'am. I reckon the fellow's got himself a pretty black history. The man who hired me to find him indicated he's an unsavory individual who's perpetrated more petty crimes and outright felonies than most folks even know exist."

"Oh, my goodness, Mr. Caine," cried Aunt Juniper. "Are you one of those daring Pinkerton men we read so much about these days?"

He couldn't help but grin at the thrill in her voice, and wished he could tell her the truth. But he was on an undercover assignment with the Pinkerton Agency, and he wasn't about to give himself away. "No, ma'am. Sorry to disappoint you. The man who hired me—" He'd started to elaborate on his sorrow when Sophie broke in.

"What's his name?" Her voice was as sharp as the expression on her face. Indeed, her interest was apparently so avid that she forgot to glare at him or show him, by her expression, how much she loathed him.

Amused, wondering why people were so interested in criminals and the people who hired other people to find them, Gabriel said, "McAllister, Miss Sophie. Franklin McAllister. From Abilene, Texas."

Sophie seemed to deflate. She sagged in her chair, reached for her teacup, and downed a gulp of what must have been disgustingly cold tea. Gabriel cocked his head, curious again. "Do you know a criminal in Tucson, Miss Sophie? You seem mighty interested in my job."

"Your job?" She smiled slightly and looked him up and down as if he were a specimen in a scientist's laboratory. "I must admit to a certain fascination with bounty hunters and their ilk. I'd always heard they were a hard, rather disreputable lot. But no, I don't know any criminals in Tucson."

"Bounty hunters?" Although he knew his reaction was foolish, Gabriel was offended. "I'm not a bounty hunter, Miss Sophie. I was hired to bring a criminal back to face justice in Abilene. I'm not claiming a bounty on him. He killed one man and wounded the man who hired my firm in the perpetration of a robbery. The dead man's widow, the wounded man, and my employer want him to stand trial for it."

Actually, what McAllister—who was mad as hell about having been shot—wanted was to beat the living stuffing out of Ivo Hardwick before he tarred and feathered him, rode him into Abilene on a fence rail, and dumped him off in front of the sheriff's office. Whatever McAllister aimed to do with Gabriel's quarry was all right with Gabriel. McAllister was paying the Pinkerton Agency a king's ransom to bring Hardwick back, and Gabriel aimed to oblige. This was particularly true since Hardwick was reputed to be a cowardly individual and one not normally given to violence or devious thinking except in reaction to a perceived threat. Gabriel wasn't a fool, after all.

"I see." Delicately sipping her tea this time instead of gulping it, Sophie eyed Gabriel over the rim of her teacup. Her green eyes proclaimed a cynicism at stark odds with her tender years. Gabriel pegged her as a female of no more than twenty-two or twenty-three. A mere pup, actually, and much too young to harbor such bitterness in her heart.

Although he imagined it was useless to try to educate her in these matters, he said, "There's a big difference, Miss Sophie. Bounty hunters track down men for posted reward money. They're like hunters of game, and take in their prey dead or alive. They'll go after anyone for money. I'm looking for this fellow as a job of work, and my company was hired to do it by an individual who was hurt by the man. The aim of my mission is simple justice. That's all. There's a difference."

"Is there? I must confess I'm unable to perceive one." Her smile would have curdled cream if there'd been any on the table. It irked him a lot.

"Well, there is." Dammit, what was the matter with this woman, anyway? Gabriel had an urge to shake the nastiness out of her, she was so irritating.

"I see." She honored him with one last smirk before she resumed paying attention to her silly dog.

Seething inside, Gabriel wondered what in holy hell was the matter with him, to get upset over the derision of one frigid female. He took a deep breath to calm himself and turned his best smile upon Juniper. She appreciated him, even if her witchy niece didn't.

"I'd take it as a kindness if you were to show me some more about your cards today, Miss Juniper."

"I'd love to do that, Mr. Caine."

Juniper twittered and colored as if she were a princess and he a gallant knight. If he lived in a just world,

Gabriel knew Juniper's reaction to him would have been housed in Miss Sophie's body. Miss Sophie's coldness wouldn't have been out of place in a female of Miss Juniper's years, but it was unconscionably hard to take in a woman as young and glorious as Sophie Madrigal.

Because he figured it would annoy her, he eyed Sophie slantways and grinned at her. He had the satisfaction of watching her cheeks bloom with color, but couldn't tell if it was from anxiety or anger.

To hell with her. She was so damned mean, he'd take it as a challenge to break down her defenses—if they were defenses, and not merely the manifestation of a rotten personality. He'd met one or two people before in his life who were flat-out mean. Maybe she was one of them.

Suddenly Sophie sat up straight and looked at him strangely. "I'll tell you something, Mr. Caine."

"Yes?" He smiled sweetly.

"I shall offer you a prediction, actually." She gave him a glittering smile that made Gabriel a little nervous.

"Sophie!" wailed Juniper.

"I predict," Sophie Madrigal said, ignoring her aunt as usual, "that the end of your life—"

"So-phie!" Juniper's hands flew to press her cheeks in patent desperation.

"—will be actuated in this present endeavor of yours."

"Sophie!" Juniper stared at her niece, horrified.

Gabriel blinked, unsettled and faintly horrified himself. "Damn, Miss Sophie, that's right unkind of you."

She blinked back and shook her head once abruptly, as if she wasn't sure what she'd just said. "I—" She swallowed, lifted her chin, and regained her composure. "It's a mere prediction, Mr. Caine. You may disregard it if you wish." She waved a hand in the air as if the end of his life was nothing to her.

Which it probably wasn't. It took Gabriel a long time to soothe Miss Juniper's fidgets. His own, while less overt, took longer.

After Sophie, considerably rattled by her recent prediction—what in the world had propelled her to say such a thing?—took Tybalt to the newspaper-covered area in the baggage car which Dmitri had fixed up especially for him, she went back to the sleeping compartment she shared with her aunt. Since she held Tybalt on a leash and it wouldn't hurt him, she slammed his wicker carrier down on the floor. It made a less-than-satisfactory bang, and she wished she had something to hurl.

"Damn him!" she said to make up for the basket's refusal to cooperate. Tybalt paid no attention to her as he inspected the sleeper, searching for food, snuffling into all the corners and under the benches with dogged determination. He found nothing to eat, but appeared undiscouraged. Sophie had always admired Tybalt for his tenacity. It was a quality they shared.

She'd almost fainted when Mr. Slick-As-an-Oiled-Snake Gabriel Caine said he was after a criminal in Tucson. But the person he'd named had been a *Mac-something*. At least he wasn't after Ivo Hardwick, which spared her the problem of eliminating Gabriel.

Sophie would relish killing Ivo Hardwick. She didn't fancy having to kill Gabriel Caine first, no matter how much she didn't like him.

Chapter Three

By the time the train finally drew close to Tucson, Sophie was sick to death of desert scenery, saguaro cacti, barrel cacti, a million other kinds of cacti, bleached bones, dust, jackrabbits, and buzzards. For several days the train had chugged them through the driest, most desolate country she'd ever seen in her life, interspersed with long, breathless, stifling stops along the way, including a longer-than-normal stopover engendered by repairs needed to the train's engine. It had run into a cow somewhere in New Mexico Territory and damaged itself.

Sophie had felt sorry for the cow. She also figured Tucson would be a suitable place in which to dispatch her prey since it was already halfway to hell.

She and Juniper had made a bit of money telling fortunes for passengers, although business hadn't been what she'd call brisk. She didn't care much; she had other things to think about and telling fortunes bored her. People were so unbelievably stupid. And *they* had the gall to look down on *her*. Sophie would never understand so-called respectable society as long as she lived.

She was sick to death of train travel, too. Her legs felt cramped, her shoulders were stiff, and she needed a good long walk, preferably in some cool morning air. Which was a pity, since there didn't seem to be any available here.

Tybalt, too, appeared almost restless, although it was difficult to tell with Tybalt. His was not a nervous disposition. He did seem to be sighing more than usual, however, and his eyes looked sad. Of course, his eyes always looked sad, particularly when other people ate in his vicinity. Sophie imagined, however, that he wouldn't object to a long walk, especially if a juicy bone awaited him at the walk's end.

She'd also come to the reluctant conclusion—and then only when she couldn't ignore the truth another second longer—that no matter how much she resented him and knew him to be a bounder, and no matter how much her dire prediction about his fate still bothered her, Gabriel Caine was about the most charming, good-natured, pleasant traveling companion a body could have. As if it were nothing more nor less than what he'd been accustomed to doing all his life, he'd kept Aunt Juniper occupied and happy since the train left Laredo. He'd even made Sophie laugh a time or two, something she'd believed herself no longer capable of.

Of course, he didn't know that in occupying Juniper's time, he'd spared Sophie hours of frustration, since it would have been her task to entertain her aunt if he wasn't around. She didn't tell him, either. She'd been so unpleasant to him, she figured that if he knew he was helping her, he'd go away again.

He'd seduced Tybalt into adoring him, as well, drat

the man. Although she wouldn't trust Gabriel Caine to cross the street if he said he would, Sophie had to admit that he knew the secret of getting animate beings to like him. He was just like her father in that regard. He was also like another man she'd known once. Sophie decided, as long as she didn't forget that, she'd be safe from succumbing to his practiced charm.

At the moment, he and Juniper were studying his palm as if it were the most fascinating thing on the face of the earth.

"Now you see here, Mr. Caine. Your hand is a rare combination of the conical and the spatulate. This is very significant." Juniper was dead serious.

"Is it now?" Gabriel Caine, on the other hand, wasn't. His smile was as sweet as spun sugar, but Sophie saw how his eyes danced, blast the man.

He was kind to Juniper, though, and Sophie didn't hate him as much as she used to. She considered her changed attitude a serious flaw in her character, especially since she'd begun to experience very strong precognitive impulses and visions whilst in his company. This problem had never assailed her before, and she didn't like it. Perhaps she needed one of Juniper's restorative potions.

"Yes indeed," continued Juniper. "The significance, of course, lies not in the shape of your hand itself, but in its shape when read in conjunction with the lines."

"I see."

Juniper wiggled Gabriel's left pinkie. "You see how long this finger is, compared to the rest of them?"

"Yes." He drew the syllable out, and Sophie wondered if he was trying not to laugh. She'd hardly blame him if he did.

"Now, if it were only a little bit longer, it might indicate that you were an untrustworthy person, or one who possesses a devious nature."

Sophie uttered a small noise of disgust. Gabriel grinned at her. Juniper didn't notice. Sophie scowled at Gabriel and felt herself get hot. Drat.

"But," Juniper continued, "the counter-indications are so strong that the length of your little finger tends to indicate that, rather than deviousness, you possess a sensitive, intuitive nature. If one couples that with your other lines and the Mounts of Venus, Mercury, and Apollo which we discussed earlier, then we can clearly see that while you have yet to achieve your potential, you have the capacity for doing great good in the world and also for achieving devoted happiness in love."

"My, my. You see all that, do you?" Evidently, even Gabriel Caine himself wasn't so skillful an actor as to hear all those things said about himself and not succumb to irony. Sophie heard it in his voice.

Juniper did not. Naturally. "Oh, my, yes, Mr. Caine. Why, I do declare, yours is one of the most intriguing palms I've ever read. Yours and Sophie's."

"Mercy, ma'am, you almost frighten me."

Juniper giggled like a little girl. She'd been doing that for days now as she and Gabriel pored over the cards and various people's palms.

Sophie shook her head slightly, truly wondering for the first time if her aunt had both oars in the water. Except for her insistence on trusting in the cards, palms, and tea leaves, Juniper was a sensible enough woman. But this transcendentalist folderal . . . Well, Sophie could appreciate it for financial reasons, but she couldn't quite believe in any of it. Not any longer, she couldn't.

She shook her head as recent events flooded her mind. Bother. As soon as she dosed herself, she'd no longer be troubled by visions or predictions. She was sure of it. Almost.

As for herself, while Gabriel and Juniper discussed

51

the lines on Gabriel's palm, Sophie'd been pretending to reread *The Lady or the Tiger?* Her eyes kept blurring the words together as she listened to Gabriel twist her aunt more securely around his ever-so-slightly-longish pinkie finger.

Damn the man; he was a blasted expert. She wished she could manipulate people the way he could. Sophie, however, unlike Gabriel Caine, was not charming.

When Tybalt, sitting on the bench beside her and apparently starved for affection, nudged the volume out of her hand, she gave up even pretending to read. The book slipped from her fingers and fell to the floor. With a muffled sigh, she bent to pick it up—and discovered herself nose to nose with Mr. Gabriel Caine, who had stooped to perform the same task.

His grin was the most wicked she'd seen yet on his devilishly handsome face. Sophie felt heat flush across her shoulders, up the back of her neck, and creep into her cheeks. She jerked upright again and began petting Tybalt in a flurry of discomposure. Tybalt didn't care what emotion motivated her. He sank his head onto her lap with a rhapsodic snore of contentment.

Gabriel sat up more slowly, with the book clutched in his fingers. He undressed her with his eyes, and Sophie's blush deepened. She reached for the book, and he drew it away from her. She snatched her hand back and cursed herself for allowing him to play with her. He made a show of examining the book.

"The Lady or the Tiger?" He winked at her. "Now what could this be about, Miss Sophie? You gathering tips for your next big-game hunting trip into the heart of Africa?"

"Tigers live in India, Mr. Caine, not Africa."

His grin widened. "That so?"

Juniper giggled.

"Yes. It's so." Sophie reached out again. This time he

allowed her to yank the book from his fingers, and she felt as though it were she who was behaving childishly rather than he who was being cheeky.

"Actually," she said, thinking that maybe she didn't regret her prediction about him after all, "this volume tells the story of a young man who falls in love with a princess. He is imprisoned by her father for daring to set his sights higher than his station." She gave him a significant look which only provoked another sly wink. Sophie wished she'd not bothered to try to shame him into behaving with propriety. He wouldn't recognize propriety if it bit him on the butt.

"Poor fellow," said Gabriel with spurious sympathy. "What happened to him?"

It was Sophie's turn to bestow a catlike grin upon him. "That decision is left to the princess, actually, Mr. Caine. She is given the choice between two doors. She is to direct her lover to one of them. Behind one door is a man-eating tiger. Behind the other is a beautiful woman. She gets to decide whether to feed him to the tiger or give him to the lady."

She had the satisfaction of seeing his eyes open wide. She wasn't sure if his reaction was one of surprise or premonition but she supposed either would do, although his reaction wasn't anywhere near victory for her. His eyes were as dark as chocolate and meltingly beautiful, and Sophie could have stared at them forever if they'd been in the face of a decent human being. They were framed by lush black lashes, too, a circumstance Sophie deplored as obscenely wasteful of God, who should have given them to a woman. Not that God seemed to care much about waste, as she already knew to her everlasting sorrow.

"So—er—which door does she choose?"

Sophie wondered if her grin would split her cheeks. This was more fun than she'd had in years. "The author doesn't tell us, Mr. Caine. Each reader gets to choose his—or her—own ending to the story."

"My goodness," said Gabriel, swallowing. He recovered his composure almost immediately, drat him. "I wouldn't give the poor fellow odds, then. In my experience, most ladies would rather see a man die than go off with another woman."

"My thoughts exactly, Mr. Caine, although *I* was considering the poor woman upon whom the man was to have been inflicted. If the princess has a shred of mercy in her soul, she'll feed him to the tiger and spare both herself and that other poor woman from his villainies."

Gabriel looked astonished for perhaps three seconds. "My goodness, Miss Sophie. You are a bloodthirsty wench, aren't you? First you predict my death, and now you're killing off that poor fellow in the book."

Sophie only stared at him, pouring meaning after meaning into her look and trying not to feel guilty about her prediction.

Then he grinned again. "No offense, ma'am, but I can only be glad my life isn't in your hands."

"Ah, but perhaps it is." She showed her teeth in a glittering smile she'd practiced in front of a mirror. It generally sent men scurrying off, their tails between their legs—if that thing between their legs could be likened to a tail. This time it only succeeded in making Gabriel's own grin widen. She should have expected it but hadn't, and she found his reaction to her best evil smile very annoying. She didn't dare lower her gaze or stop smiling, however, because then he'd have won.

"Now Miss Juniper here—" Gabriel gave Juniper one of his brilliant, beaming smiles. "I'd trust my fate to Miss Juniper's hands any old day."

And he could, too, curse him. "Yes," said Sophie. "Aunt Juniper is ever so much more kindhearted than I."

He acknowledged the justice of her statement with a brief nod. "Yes, ma'am, I do believe you might be right there."

Juniper giggled again.

Sophie wanted to smack them both. "And she's always had a particular fondness for rapscallions," she added sweetly.

"Now Sophie, that's not true." Juniper turned to Gabriel. "She's talking about our family again, Mr. Caine, and they weren't rapscallions. They weren't." She looked at Sophie once more. "They weren't."

How her aunt Juniper could make her feel so guilty with just a look never ceased to amaze—and provoke—Sophie. It had something to do with Juniper's eyes, she decided. They were as blue as a robin's egg in spite of Juniper's more than sixty years, and they generally sparkled, albeit somewhat vaguely, with merriment and perfect innocence.

When Sophie said nasty things about the family, Juniper's eyes went as bleak as a frozen pond. Every time it happened Sophie felt ashamed of herself, no matter how wrong Juniper was about their family. They were carnival-show hacks, is what they were. Juniper was the only one in the whole lot of them who truly believed in what they did. She couldn't be made to admit it, though.

Sophie vowed she wouldn't apologize. At least not in front of Gabriel Caine.

He stroked his wicked black mustache; the one Sophie itched to feel to see if it was soft or wiry or prickly or—She couldn't stand it.

"Well, now, ma'am, you might be more right than you suspect about my relative rascality."

Sophie felt as if he'd punched her in the stomach. Her mouth fell open and stayed open for several moments before she found the wit to say, "You mean you admit to being a scoundrel, Mr. Caine?"

He inclined his head to one side as if modesty compelled him. Sophie pinched her lips together. He *was* a scoundrel, whether he planned to admit it or not.

"As to that, Miss Sophie, I don't believe I'm the best judge. However, while you might have been born into a family of occultists, I—" He splayed a hand over a portion of his anatomy which would have housed his heart if he'd been a person with a moral or two to rub together. Sophie hated it when she felt the urge to grab that hand and study its palm and see if Juniper's assessment of it had been correct. "Well, ma'am, I was born in a revivalist's tent."

She blinked, astonished. Then she had to fight a smile when she realized he considered revivalists in the same light as she considered clairvoyants. If, of course, he was telling the truth. She couldn't tell. And, since she still didn't trust him, she assumed his story to be unlikely. He'd probably just said it because he knew she'd be taken aback.

"Oh, Mr. Caine!"

Juniper's happy cry startled them both, and they turned to look at her. With her hands clasped to her bosom, Juniper smiled at Gabriel as if he'd just performed a holy miracle. He appeared confounded for a moment before he smiled a question at Juniper. "Yes, ma'am?"

"I just *knew* you weren't what Sophie called you. Why, you're as firmly rooted in the spiritual life as we are!"

Sophie felt her lips twitch as she endeavored to keep sardonic amusement from showing. Mr. Caine hadn't expected this; she'd bet money on it. He'd meant to scandalize them, and now Juniper was rewarding him with praise. Sophie hoped he'd choke on his embarrassment.

Fat chance. He recovered his composure at once. In fact, if Sophie hadn't been watching him like a hawk, she'd never have known he'd lost it. The blasted man really should have been born into her family; he'd have fit right in.

"Yes, ma'am," he said to Aunt Juniper, his face a masterpiece of piety. "Why, ma'am, I was saving souls by the time I was six years old."

Juniper beamed at him and sighed her pleasure. Sophie shook her head and took comfort in her dog. Dogs were infinitely superior to human beings; they were uncomplicated and sincere and never, ever lied.

Tybalt never once came to her for the pleasure of her caresses and called it love. He never claimed to cherish her when he only wanted food or the sensual pleasure of a good back-scratch. Yet Tybalt was the only being on earth in whose affection Sophie trusted. Tybalt and Aunt Juniper. She'd never considered the connection until today, and almost giggled like her aunt had been doing ever since she'd taken up association with Gabriel Caine.

Her near-lapse brought her up short, and she frowned to make up for it. Unfortunately, Gabriel saw the change in her demeanor.

"What's the matter, Miss Sophie? I'll wager you were hoping I'd been born the son of a black-hearted gambling man and a—lady of easy virtue."

"Oh, no. Not at all." She gave him a sugar-wouldn't-melt-in-her-mouth smile. "I'm sure being a tent-show revivalist suits you equally."

He acknowledged her hit with another grin. "You're right as rain, Miss Sophie. Right as rain. As usual."

"You know, Mr. Caine, although most people don't realize it, the study of the occult is deeply rooted in a belief in God's infinite mercy and love. I never begin the day or end it without prayers of gratitude to our dear Heavenly Father for honoring me with my humble gifts." Honesty oozed from every syllable that tumbled from Juniper's lips. Her cheeks were as red as ripe apples, and her hands clutched spasmodically at the cameo brooch pinned to her bosom.

Sophie sighed.

"Is that so, ma'am?" Gabriel looked at Juniper cordially.

"It's so," Sophie said. She hadn't meant to sound so tart, although her aunt didn't seem to notice. Juniper merely nodded and smiled, evidently happy that Sophie was agreeing with her for a change.

Gabriel stroked his black mustache again. Sophie tried to look away and couldn't. The man she'd been in love with all those years ago had worn a mustache. He hadn't been nearly as handsome as Gabriel Caine, although Sophie'd believed him to be the most handsome man in the universe at the time. Which just went to show how little she'd known him—and, more to the point, how much meaning good looks had if they were on the face of a rogue.

"I must admit, ladies, that I'd never connected religion and the occult before in my own mind."

Sophie had to hand it to him: He didn't even sound ironic.

"Oh, there's every connection, Mr. Caine. I belong to the Transcendentalist church myself, because I believe that God is the Universal Mind and can be found in all religions, but it's often difficult to find Transcendentalist churches unless one visits big cities."

"I can imagine."

"Aunt Juniper always makes do with what's available, though." Sophie smiled at her aunt and hoped Juniper wouldn't realize she was being sarcastic.

"Yes indeed," confirmed Juniper. "Why, as long as one is able to meditate upon God's great gifts—"

Sophie barely managed to stifle a rude comment.

"—and His love for us all, then I'm sure He doesn't care in what house of worship we choose to praise Him. That's why I like to think of God as the Universal Mind, don't you know. I find most churches very restful, Mr. Caine. Very restful indeed. Particularly when they use wax candles in their services. There's something so soothing about wax candles. Don't you think so?"

Juniper smiled brightly, and Gabriel gazed at her for a moment, apparently speechless. Sophie felt her lips twitch and had to fight another grin.

"Er, yes, ma'am. Yes, I certainly do. Wax candles. Sure."

Bestowing what looked to Sophie like an almost transcendental smile upon Gabriel, Juniper heaved a happy sigh and said, "Let's get back to your palm, shall we, Mr. Caine? We're discovering some excessively interesting features there."

"Er, yes. Yes, ma'am, we are indeed."

Sophie choked on her laughter, drawing his gaze. He gave her a grin and a wink, that left her weak in the knees and made her glad she was seated, before he turned his attention back to Aunt Juniper.

Against her will, Sophie raised her hand to the pulse at the base of her throat. It was hammering like a kettledrum.

The air was hot enough to cook an egg in its shell and as dry as an old maid's kiss. As soon as the porter opened the train door, heat hit Gabriel's face like a blast from hell.

He leaned out the door, glanced around, and shook his head. Great God Almighty, but Ivo Hardwick had chosen to go to ground in a mortally unpleasant place, if this was any indication.

He looked down the tracks and saw several people wilting under parasols and light-colored hats as they waited for passengers to disembark from the train. Men leaned against walls and sprawled on benches as if they were too enervated by the insufferable weather to move.

The level of noise in Tucson surprised him. It was so damned hot, he couldn't figure out how anything had energy enough to make noise. Yet dogs barked, people hollered, he heard the rumble of traffic some ways off, and even some gunshots in the distance.

Peering over the station's low-pitched roof, he saw what looked like a forest of windmills, and shook his head again. A booming little place, Tucson. And rough. It looked perniciously rough. He began to worry about the Madrigals.

Even though Sophie's prediction bothered him more than he'd ever admit to anyone, he still didn't want anything bad to happen to her. Dmitri, for all his undoubted loyalty, probably wouldn't be of much help to the ladies in a crisis, unless he was good with a gun. Thus far, Gabriel hadn't seen Dmitri with any weapon at all. In fact, he'd scarcely seen Dmitri at all, since the man preferred to hide out in the baggage car.

He hoped the weather cooled off at night here, or he might just have to buy one of those buff-colored hats to wear, and that would ruin his image. Hell, Miss Sophie might not even hate him any longer if he weren't clad all in black. He also hoped this job of his wouldn't take long.

The two Madrigal ladies had lined up behind him. He turned around and held out his hand to take Tybalt's wicker basket from Sophie's hands. After hesitating long enough to let him know she didn't trust him—as if he'd harbored any doubts on the matter—Sophie relinquished it. He gave her one of his best grins to disconcert her. Of course she didn't demonstrate her discomposure in any way. God, Gabriel admired the woman—he also wanted to paddle her luscious rump for being so damned difficult.

Refusing to give Sophie a chance to reject his offer of help, he held his arm out for Juniper, who took it gladly. He assisted Juniper down from the train, then aimed what he hoped like hell was a lady-slaying grin at Sophie, who eyed him back glacially.

"Where are you ladies staying, Miss Sophie? May I see you to your destination?"

"Thank you very much, Mr. Caine. Dmitri will seek lodgings for us. That's one of his functions."

She gave him a faint smile. It had never taken him this long to sunder a female's defenses in his life. Hell, he'd even gone so far as to tell the truth about his background, and it hadn't softened Sophie Madrigal's cold heart one iota. He'd never done such a thing before. It had shocked him damned near as much as her prediction.

"I'll just wait with you until he does it, then. I understand Tucson can be a pretty inhospitable place."

"Oh, thank you so much, Mr. Caine. It's so kind of you to offer." Juniper smiled at him as if he'd offered her a diamond necklace. The cynical side of his nature smirked; the side that had confessed to his embarrassing beginnings felt humbled. Damn, but Juniper Madrigal was a nice lady.

Sophie withdrew a handkerchief from her silly little beaded handbag and patted at her brow with it. Her skin glowed like a pearl in the blistering heat, and she was gorgeous. She looked like a rather large fairy-tale princess who'd been yanked out of her own lace-and-satin story and dumped into the middle of a rattlesnake-

and-leather dime novel. Gabriel had a mental vision of him and Sophie cooling off in a clear mountain spring in those mountains hovering around Tucson.

He shook his head, tickled by his own fanciful thoughts. As if. If they ever ended up in a clear mountain spring together, she'd more likely try to drown him.

"And I'd take it as a pure kindness if the two of you would be my guests at dinner tonight."

"Oh, Mr. Caine!"

Every time Miss Juniper fluttered like that, she reminded Gabriel of a pretty little bird. Miss Sophie, on the other hand, reminded him of an eagle about to swoop down and poke his eyes out. She retrieved Tybalt's basket from him with a jerk hard enough to interrupt one of the dog's more prodigious snores, and said, "Thank you."

"Oh, look, Sophie dear. There's Dmitri. I'll be right back."

Juniper tripped off as if it weren't a hundred and ten in the shade, leaving Gabriel and Sophie to stare after her. Dmitri appeared out of the heat ripples like an apparition, wearing the same overalls and cloth cap he'd had on when Gabriel first saw him. He noticed Sophie frowning after her aunt and knew she wanted to be the one talking to Dmitri. An itch to rib her, with which he had become familiar during their trip from Laredo, assailed him.

"Come on, Miss Sophie, taking a meal with me won't be so bad. I don't really bite, you know."

"Hmph."

He laughed. "It'll be fun, stepping out with me. You can tell me about your family, and I can tell you about mine. We can swap tales of knavery and vice and have ourselves a fine old time. Maybe you can offer me another prediction." His skin crawled even as the words left his lips, and he wished he hadn't brought that damned prediction up.

She eyed him slantwise and said, "There's no need for that, Mr. Caine. I'm sure the prediction is the same now as it was when you heard it. You have, after all, only one life." She smiled.

Suppressing a shudder, he slathered on the insolence and nudged her with his elbow, deciding to forget the prediction—if he could. "C'mon, Miss Sophie. You can see how much longer you can resist my charms, and I can see how much longer I can keep trying to seduce you without succeeding. And we can both see how much longer it takes Miss Juniper to figure out what we're doing."

Her lovely lips twitched, and he knew she was fighting a smile. Why in hell was she so determined to resist him? He really didn't want her to dislike him, and he realized with surprise that it had to do with more than his desire to get into her drawers. Not that he didn't want to do that; of course he did. Hell, any man would. But there was more to Miss Sophie than mere Amazonian beauty. She had within her something mysterious, something she kept locked tightly away, something that intrigued the daylights out of him.

Not only that, but he had discovered during the past several days that he actually liked the wench. She had character, did Sophie Madrigal. And heart, which she persisted in lavishing on her ugly dog. And that, damn it all, didn't seem right to Gabriel Caine, who wouldn't mind a little bit of her heart being lavished on him, God save him.

Juniper scuttled up to them, and he had to cease flirting. He was sorry about it, too, since Sophie seemed on the verge of an honest belly laugh. Gabriel had noticed more than once in his pursuit of women that they were more apt to be disarmed by humor than by melting looks—especially the smart ones, like Sophie.

"Dmitri said we should wait in the station until he returns, Sophie." She fluttered up to Gabriel, again reminding him of a little bird. "I'm sure we'll be fine, Mr. Caine. It was kind of you to offer to remain with us, but I'm sure Dmitri won't be long."

"Nonsense," he said with a smile guaranteed to make Miss Sophie scowl and Miss Juniper's heart go pitty-pat. "It will be my extreme pleasure to wait with you ladies. Then I'll escort you to your hotel."

"Oh, *thank* you, Mr. Caine. Although I know it's silly of me, I can't help but feel safer when a man is with us."

"My God," muttered Sophie.

He grinned his most wicked grin at her.

Aunt Juniper and Tybalt seemed sorry to bid him adieu at the door of their suite in the Cosmopolitan Hotel on Main Street. Gabriel thought the Cosmopolitan was a pretentious name for the dun-colored hotel in the dun-colored hellhole of Tucson, Arizona Territory, but he didn't say so. Miss Sophie merely gave him a superior frown as he tipped his hat and said he'd be by to fetch them for dinner at seven.

Gabriel didn't have the same exquisite requirements in temporary abodes as the Madrigal ladies. From what he'd gathered of their origins, he wondered where they'd acquired such refined tastes, but he couldn't help but appreciate them for having done so. After he'd deposited the Madrigals at the Cosmopolitan, he checked into his own hotel room on the second floor of the Oriental, a scrubby-looking building whose first floor was given over to a gambling hall. Gabriel felt right at home.

Once lodging was taken care of, he donned a clean white shirt and clean black trousers, brushed out his travel-stained black coat, and wiped his boots. Then he put on a fresh collar, straightened his tie, and pulled his white cuffs down to cover the derringer hidden up his sleeve. Then he stuffed a second derringer into his coat pocket, jammed his hunting knife into his boot scabbard, and stuck his Colt revolver into the back of his waistband.

After all that, he made sure his mustache was combed, his face was clean, and his hat settled at the appropriate damn-it-all-gambling-man angle. He checked to make sure his cocky, devil-may-care grin was in place and his teeth looked clean and bright.

Then Gabriel Caine went hunting.

Chapter Four

Sophie helped her aunt out of her gown and corset, and then Juniper lay down to take a nap.

"For you know, Sophie, I find this excessive heat dreadfully enervating."

Gratefully stepping out of her heavy bombazine frock, Sophie murmured, "It is, indeed." Then, as Juniper settled onto the bed, Sophie went about selecting a lighter-weight costume. She smiled at her aunt. Juniper reminded her of Tybalt as she fluffed her pillows, twisted this way and that, and finally settled into a comfortable position, curled up like a kitten, Tybalt snoring peacefully next to her. Sophie loved her aunt so much. She regretted having to hurt Juniper, but in this instance there was no way to avoid it.

After she'd loosened her own corset and donned a cooler dress, Sophie dug into her flowered carpetbag and withdrew her shiny Colt Lightning revolver. With an expert's care, she loaded, tested, and aimed it. For six months now, ever since she'd decided to rid the world of Ivo Hardwick, Sophie had taken every opportunity that presented itself to practice with her gun. By this time she could shoot the pips out of a playing card at twenty yards.

Putting a hole through Ivo Hardwick's black heart should be child's play. She could hardly wait to do it.

Then she thrust the gun into her handbag, donned her iciest expression in order to repel unwanted advances, picked up her parasol, and sailed out the door, making sure she locked it. She'd already told Aunt Juniper that she planned to take a walk and view the wonders of Tucson. Juniper, who always tried to avoid unpleasant truths until forced to do otherwise, had smiled and told her to have a good time.

Dmitri's room was down the hall from Sophie and Juniper's, and Dmitri answered Sophie's brisk knock immediately. She suspected he'd been waiting for it. Dmitri was the most loyal human being she'd ever met.

"All right, Dmitri, let us be off. I shall stop off at the front desk in order to ascertain the address of the boardinghouse at which Mr. Huffy is staying."

Dmitri nodded, not at all disconcerted by the prospect of aiding and abetting Sophie in the commission of a murder. No, thought Sophie savagely; what she had planned wasn't murder. What she had planned would be the execution of a murderer; there was a huge difference.

The front desk clerk eyed Sophie appreciatively and smiled.

She smiled back sweetly, willing even to be polite to something so foul as a man if it would promote her cause. "Can you tell me where I might find Miss Partridge's Boardinghouse, my good fellow? A friend of mine is stopping there, and I wish to pay a call upon her."

"Miss Partridge's, ma'am?" The clerk's smile faded. He looked troubled. "Miss Partridge's ain't in the best part of town, ma'am. I don't think you want to go there."

"Oh, but you're quite wrong." Sophie glittered at him, showing her perfect white teeth, and he swallowed and took a step backwards. *This* was the reaction she expected from that particular smile. *This* fellow was performing just as he was supposed to perform. Unlike some men she could mention. Or one man, at any rate.

"Yes, ma'am." Without further ado, the clerk gave her directions.

"Thank you very much." She bestowed one final glitter upon the desk clerk before she turned and marched away, Dmitri trotting at her side. She saw the clerk blink at her as if he wasn't sure what had hit him.

Damn all men to hell who believed a woman's place ought to be tucked away, out of sight, out of trouble, only appearing when and where men thought they should appear, and then only to perform the functions men approved of. Sophie wanted nothing to do with any of them. She wished more men could be like Dmitri: kindhearted, loyal, pleasant. On the other hand, if Dmitri weren't a midget, he probably wouldn't be as nice as he was, since he wouldn't have to be.

Bother. Sometimes Sophie wondered if she were becoming too cynical for her own good.

As for Miss Partridge's Boardinghouse, however, the desk clerk proved to be correct in that its location was not the best. Unflinching, ignoring the run-down condition of the neighborhood, Sophie trotted up the rickety steps and rapped on the door. Within minutes, she was face to face with Emerald Huffy, the man whose intelligence regarding the whereabouts of Ivo Hardwick had lured her to Tucson.

Huffy was a small, weathered man, who looked like somebody had left him out in the sun too long. He was a good four inches shorter than Sophie and as skinny as a fence post. He looked like he was about a hundred and ten, but Sophie knew for a fact that he was only thirty-eight years old. She guessed life in the Territories was hard on a man. Which was as it should be. After all, life everywhere was hard on a woman. Huffy led her and Dmitri to the shabby front parlor of Miss Partridge's.

"Is he still in Tucson?" Sophie asked without preamble.

Huffy, having worked with Sophie for several months now, was undismayed by her cut-and-dried manner. "Yes'm. I'll have to figger out where he's at, if'n you want to have a go at him right away."

"I should prefer to undertake my mission after dark, Mr. Huffy. My aunt and I are staying at the Cosmopolitan. We have a dinner engagement at seven, but I should be back in room two by nine o'clock." Her lips pursed when she contemplated how neatly Gabriel Caine had usurped her evening hours. "I can't imagine our meal taking any longer than that."

Huffy sighed as if he wasn't sure he should be doing what he was doing, even for money. Sophie, who had anticipated such a reaction, withdrew an envelope from her reticule. "I have a bonus for you, Mr. Huffy. You've done your job well."

Without a word, Huffy took the envelope, opened it, took out the banknotes, and counted them with fingers that looked like wrinkled brown twigs. Then he nodded and said, "Appreciate it, Miss Madrigal."

"You're quite welcome." Sophie took a deep breath. The next part was tricky. "In giving you that bonus, I expect a certain amount of discretion, Mr. Huffy. I trust the money will buy your silence."

Huffy looked up from the envelope, into which he'd returned the money. His nature was taciturn, which had been one of the reasons Sophie had chosen him in the first place. She'd looked long and hard for a man with Huffy's reputation for silence, sobriety, efficiency, and ruthlessness.

"I don't gen'ly blab much," he said.

"Good." Sophie inclined her head like a queen granting a favor to a subject. "Then I shall expect you to visit my hotel room shortly after nine o'clock this evening, bearing with you intelligence regarding Mr. Ivo Hardwick's whereabouts."

"Yes'm."

"That won't present a problem for you?"

"No, ma'am."

Nodding, Sophie rose. Dmitri pushed himself off of his seat, too. His feet didn't reach the floor, and he had to hop down from his chair. With another terse nod, Sophie turned and left Mr. Emerald Huffy to the questionable comforts of Miss Partridge's front parlor.

Gabriel ordered wine with dinner. If he hadn't, Sophie was sure she'd never have become involved in such an animated conversation with him. She was not, after all, an admirer of Mr. Gabriel Caine.

"I fail to see why you think women should be kept deprived of the vote, Mr. Caine," she said, girding herself to do battle. Not that she cared much about the vote. As much as she admired Elizabeth Cady Stanton for her spunk and valor, Sophie and politics didn't mix well. She'd as soon consign all politicians to the pit and be done with them.

She was, however, experiencing an odd sensation of delight with tonight's conversation. Of course, that was only because she seldom had anyone with whom to argue. Juniper would sooner die than disagree with anybody about anything. Sophie was also experiencing that odd sense of precognition that only seemed to as-sail her whilst she was in Gabriel Caine's company. Sophie found it rather invigorating.

"My opinion is based on experience, Miss Sophie."

"Of which I'm sure you have an abundance."

Although Sophie smiled sweetly, Aunt Juniper, mortified, whispered, "Sophie!" Sophie naturally paid her no mind.

Gabriel chuckled. "Enough," he said. "I reckon I do have enough experience to have formed a valid opinion."

"I doubt that the sort of experience to which you refer would have given you any indication at all of the intellectual capacity of women, Mr. Caine." Sophie sniffed and took another sip of the really quite delicious wine. She didn't understand how the proprietor of the hotel's restaurant could keep wine cool enough to maintain its integrity in this hellish place.

Juniper uttered a muffled moan.

Gabriel picked up his knife and fork, cut a small piece of his succulent steak, and popped it into his mouth. Sophie did likewise. She had a feeling he, like she, was recruiting his resources to continue their verbal sparring match. She couldn't offhand recall the last time she'd had so much fun, although she wouldn't admit it to a soul.

Juniper, watching them warily, evidently hoped to prevent bloodshed. Since both Sophie's and Gabriel's mouths were occupied in mastication, she hurried into the conversation. "I don't mean to disagree with you, certainly, Mr. Caine, but I tend to believe dear Sophie is in the right on this issue. I don't believe women are inherently inferior to men in intellect."

Sophie beamed benevolently upon her darling aunt. Juniper was such a dear to agree with her; she generally wasn't so obliging—mainly because she was usually too embarrassed to join in one of Sophie's arguments.

Gabriel smiled at Juniper as he might smile at a small child. Reaching for the saltcellar he said, "You may be right about intelligence, Miss Madrigal, but don't you believe women are a little more emotionally unstable than men?"

Sophie, recalling the prediction she'd had about him, pinched her lips together. "Nonsense," she said.

Juniper swallowed. "Well—I—perhaps—"

"Just the tiniest bit, perhaps?"

Gabriel Caine's seductive smile ought to be outlawed, Sophie thought bitterly. Perceiving that her aunt was fluttering in a sticky web, she spoke up for her. "Unstable? Not at all. Men believe women are emotionally unstable because most men—not all of them—can't be bothered to care about anything." Sophie knew it for a certified fact.

"Is that so?" It didn't look to her as if Gabriel believed a word of it. The rat.

Sophie went on, undeterred by his doubt. "Women pay attention to their emotions and those of others, unlike men, who like to pretend emotions don't exist. I believe such attention is to their credit, not their detriment."

"Is that so?"

"Yes." Sophie glared at him and took another sip of wine. She hated most of the men in the world with a passion at that moment. "Most men I've met are forever denying the obvious and professing it doesn't exist—or, worse, that it doesn't matter. Or," she added with the hurt and animosity that had been her companion for years, "they lie about it."

Gabriel's eyebrow lifted and he tilted his head to one side. "I believe I'll need an example if you expect me to swallow that one, Miss Sophie."

She wanted to smack his insolent face and show him exactly what she meant, but she figured he'd only chalk such a gesture up to emotional instability, so she didn't. And she'd be damned if she'd tell him her own story. It was precious to her, and he didn't deserve it. Instead, she chose a less personal topic and used an example from that.

"Women understand the emotional toll of, for example, war. Men are forever rushing about irritating each other so they can fight. Invariably, too, they attach noble motives to such basically infantile behavior.

"Women have more sense, because they understand beforehand what the costs of such reckless actions will be. Of course," she added acidly, "it's always the women who have to take care of the aftermath. They do the mopping up while their men are either dead or drinking away their victories or their losses in a saloon somewhere."

Aunt Juniper whispered a scandalized, "Sophie!" Sophie was sorry to see the bleak cast to her eyes. Juniper, unlike Gabriel, knew all about Sophie and her pathetic past.

Gabriel, however, actually tilted his wine glass at her. "Touché, Miss Sophie. I think you've made an excellent point."

His voice was as gentle as Juniper's, but Sophie reacted to it in a way she'd never reacted to Juniper. Ripples of chills chased hot charges through her veins. She could hardly believe she was actually responding to this beast's practiced lures. She'd understood herself to be crafted of sterner stuff. Or, if not so crafted originally, she'd assumed the fires of misery and disappointment had tempered her to a firmer steel than these chills and hot flashes indicated. She was angry with herself and stabbed a piece of steak as she wished she could stab Gabriel Caine.

His knowing grin told her he knew exactly what she wanted to do to his precious flesh. She glowered at him, which did as much good as it ever did. She wished she had Tybalt with her so she could pay attention to her own perfect dog and ignore the miserable, imperfect dog sitting at the table with her. But Tybalt was snoozing happily in her hotel room, and she had to contend with Gabriel Caine without any help at all.

She took heart from the knowledge that as soon as this interminable meal was over, she would, with luck and care, be able to consummate the purpose of her life. The realization calmed her, and her bad mood lifted. She even smiled at Gabriel, who looked almost as astonished as he had when she'd fed the young man to the tiger.

The meal ended at last, and Gabriel saw the Madrigal ladies to their hotel room. Sophie politely declined his offer of an after-dinner coffee with him in the hotel lounge, although Juniper was disappointed that she did so. Sophie tried to assuage her aunt's tender feelings by assuring her that a hotel lounge in Tucson, Arizona Territory, must be a shocking place and not at all refined enough for a delicate female.

"Oh, but I'm sure Mr. Caine would never take two ladies into a less than refined place, Sophie dear."

"And I'm sure you're wrong about that," said Sophie, who believed she knew Gabriel Caine better than did poor Juniper.

When at last she shut the door in Gabriel's face—rather more sharply than Juniper thought proper—Sophie breathed a deep sigh. The hour of reckoning had come. By the time the night was gone, she'd have fulfilled her dream.

She rushed across the room, wriggled out of her dinner frock, flung it on the bed, and stepped into the dark shirtwaist she'd laid out before dinner.

"What are you doing, Sophie?" Juniper's voice held an edge of worry.

Sophie gave her aunt her most serene smile. "I'm going to take the air with Dmitri. He feels more comfortable after the sun sets because of his stature, and he enjoys a little company since he's always hiding away from the world during the daytime. There's no reason for you to fret. I enjoy a little walk after dinner, you know."

Juniper knew no such thing, because Sophie had never been inclined to take walks after dinner. Sophie knew how much Juniper hated to face unpleasant truths, however, and she suspected her dear aunt wouldn't protest. She was almost right.

"Oh, Sophie, you mustn't!" Juniper cried. "You said yourself that Tucson is a crude town. I'm sure you shouldn't be walking out at night."

"Dmitri will be with me," Sophie reminded her gently as she tugged at the buttons on her skirt. Drat! She must have gained more weight. She'd have to let the buttons out again. She gave a thought to Gabriel Caine, and despised herself for it.

If any man disapproved of her because she was the least little bit plump, then Sophie wanted nothing to do with him. Not that she wanted anything to do with men anyway. And particularly not with Gabriel Caine.

Of course, no man would want her, even if her position on the subject of men were to soften enough to allow one to get close enough to realize she liked food a trifle too much.

She perceived her thoughts were tangling up in a knot, and swore softly.

Juniper whispered, "Sophie!"

"I beg your pardon, Juniper. I'm having trouble with these silly buttons."

"I'll fix them, dear. Why don't you take your skirt off and let me do it now." She bustled over hopefully.

Sophie grinned at Juniper, whose hands were

clasped in front of her and whose face held an angelic smile. The little minx. "Not tonight, Juniper. I'm going to take a walk."

Juniper let out a soulful sigh. "Oh, Sophie, your personality is so forceful. I wish it weren't so, dear. You're such a beautiful young woman. I fear no man will care to take up with a young woman of your strength of purpose and self-will."

Sophie felt herself gape at her aunt for a second before she found the wit to respond. "I should hope not! I want nothing to do with men, and you know it, Juniper Madrigal."

Sadly shaking her head, Juniper murmured, "Sophie, I do wish life hadn't treated you so harshly."

"It wasn't life," Sophie growled. "It was a man." Remembering Ivo Hardwick, she amended, "It was men."

Juniper's head continued to shake. "So sad. So unfortunate."

"Balls," muttered Sophie, although she generally refrained from using such words in front of Juniper, who abhorred unladylike behavior in her niece. Juniper blanched, and Sophie wished she'd controlled her tongue. It was probably the wine. Which had been ordered by Gabriel Caine. Who was a man. Which proved her point.

Without saying another word, she picked up her handbag, opened it, and pulled out her Colt Lightning revolver. Although she knew good and well she'd loaded it earlier in the day, she checked to make sure. Satisfaction flooded her. All was well. She grabbed her cloak and walked to the door.

"Sophie . . ."

Sophie turned. "Yes?" She smiled sweetly at Juniper, even though she knew full well that Juniper had seen her handling the gun.

"Please don't go out tonight, Sophie. I—I feel you

shouldn't. The cards are against it. Recall the Devil, Sophie. I'm sure of it."

The cards. Sophie restrained her mocking laugh. "Don't be silly, Juniper." She schooled her nerves. She was ready, and she sounded crisp and efficient. She felt crisp and efficient. She was going out to do an important job, and she aimed to do it right.

"But Sophie . . ."

On impulse, Sophie hurried to her aunt and gave her a kiss on the cheek. She had to lean way over to do it. "Please don't worry, Aunt Juniper. I'll be fine. Dmitri will be with me, and everything will be just perfect. I'll be back soon."

Or she wouldn't. At this point, Sophie didn't care if she died, too, as long as she took care of Ivo Hardwick first. Since she knew her own death or imprisonment would hurt her aunt deeply, she hoped neither of those things would transpire, but she didn't care a whit on her own account.

She heard Juniper moan pitifully right before she shut the door.

Sophie's heart was almost light when she walked down the hall and tapped on Dmitri's door. Emerald Huffy opened the door, and he and Dmitri joined her. They walked silently through the night. Mr. Huffy knew where they were going. Sophie knew what to do after they got there.

"He's in there," Emerald Huffy said, his phlegmatic voice emotionless. "I'll point him out and then I'll be off. I don't want no part in this."

"I understand." Sophie had hired him to find Ivo Hardwick and that was all he'd been hired to do. She was looking forward to finishing the monster off all by herself. Dmitri said nothing, but glanced around nervously.

Huffy pushed the batwing doors and, taking a huge breath, Sophie preceded her two companions into the place.

Saloons were appalling places. Sophie didn't understand how men could stand them, although entering this particular saloon and glancing around confirmed her already low opinion of the majority of the masculine gender.

Men were scattered everywhere, leaning against the bar and sitting at tables. They were drinking and gambling, and aping other typically manly behaviors. Sophie scorned them all. Here and there she spied painted women, some of whom looked much younger than she was, and she felt sorry for them. What an awful life they must live, at the mercy of the basest of men's basest urges. Sophie knew good and well no woman would sell herself like that unless she was desperate.

"Ugh," she muttered.

Dmitri nodded. He looked pretty gloomy. Sophie understood his distaste for mingling with full-sized men, because men were animals and often teased the little Dmitri, but she couldn't allow herself to become distracted by pity. She knew better than to rush this job, so she stood still and tried to adjust to the gloom and the poisonous atmosphere.

Tobacco smoke was as thick as a fog in the room, and it was intermingled with the stench of spilled alcohol and masculine sweat. Wrinkling her nose, Sophie pulled Dmitri over to a corner of the room where there weren't so many people. Huffy followed at a leisurely pace. She saw with misgiving that she had been spotted by several men who noticed her, appeared startled, and then began ogling her, some lasciviously, some suspiciously. She ignored them all.

"Is he here somewhere?" she asked Huffy under her breath.

Huffy nodded and jerked his head to the right. "Over there. At the table with the man in the straw hat. He's the one sitting and looking on." Huffy squinted through the haze. "Looks like he's laid down his hand."

Sophie squinted too. "Where? Oh, yes, I see him." Her heart gave a huge spasm and she almost forgot herself, reached into her handbag, and hauled out her Colt then and there. She controlled the impulse with difficulty. She wasn't going to risk making a mistake now. Not now that she'd run her quarry to earth. If she shot an innocent person by accident, she'd be no better than her prey.

"Hey, looky there," came a slurry voice from out of the smoky fog. "It's a li'l guy with a big girl." The voice laughed thickly.

Sophie muttered, "Ass."

Huffy said, "Reckon I'll be going, Miss Sophie."

"Fine." Sophie didn't care. Huffy had done his duty well.

"Hey, little guy!" the slurry voice said. "C'mere. Bring your friend. She's big, but she's purty."

Dmitri shifted his shoulders uncomfortably. Huffy strolled off toward the batwing doors.

Damn and blast, now everyone in the whole awful place was staring at them. Sophie frowned fiercely. "Dmitri, I'm going to approach Mr. Hardwick. Try to remain inconspicuous."

Which was already impossible. With a resolute squaring of her shoulders, Sophie told herself it didn't matter and, leaving poor Dmitri to fend for himself, walked firmly to the table at which Ivo Hardwick sat, staring stupidly at the poker game proceeding around him. Huffy was right, Sophie saw with some relief: He had already laid down his own hand. He'd undoubtedly be more difficult to dislodge from the game if he was still in the thick of it. The four men at the table, including Hardwick, glanced up at her and stared.

He didn't recognize her. Sophie could hardly believe it.

Steeling herself, she pasted on a smile she hoped was seductive and went straight up to Ivo Hardwick, whose Adam's apple bobbed up and down as he goggled up at her. Other men at the table sniggered and made rude comments—at least, Sophie presumed they were rude. She paid no attention.

"Hello," she said to Hardwick in a low, silky voice. "Want to come outside with me for a minute?"

Hardwick gulped audibly and pointed to his chest. "Me?"

She nodded and inclined her head toward the door.

"Sure thing, lady." With amazing alacrity, considering the circumstances, Hardwick popped from his chair and took Sophie's arm. He aimed a broad wink at his companions.

"When you're through, come back and give me a treat, lady," one of them said.

Sophie didn't respond, but guided Hardwick out the swishing batwing doors. Fresh air felt like heaven after the polluted atmosphere of the saloon. Sophie had already investigated the streets and alleyways surrounding the Oriental, so she knew exactly where the best place was to exact her retribution.

"Come with me," she whispered huskily into her enemy's ear.

"Sure thing." He was beginning to pant. Sophie was disgusted, although she wouldn't have expected anything better from this specimen.

The alley was dark as the pit itself. Which seemed fit and proper to Sophie. The faint sounds of rinky-tink piano music and men's voices accompanied them as she guided Hardwick to a spot in the very back, against another building. Faint lantern light from windows above them gave a ghostly aura to the scene, which was replete with trash cans, rubbish, and dirt. What an appropriate setting for Ivo Hardwick's last moments on earth. He belonged in the rubbish heap of life.

When they'd gone as far as they could, Hardwick reached for her. She anticipated him. She'd been fishing in her handbag for the past several seconds, had found the Colt, and now jammed it against his stomach and shoved him backwards. She was as tall as he, and weighed more—and he was in a state of drunkenness coupled with complete sexual befuddlement—so he stumbled and thumped against the building with an "Oomph."

"There now," Sophie said with satisfaction. "This is exactly the way I want it."

He blinked at her. "You got real strange taste, lady."

Chapter Five

Gabriel followed the sounds of strife with some irritation. Dammit, he'd wanted to sleep and pick up Ivo Hardwick in the morning when the villain would certainly be sleeping off a hangover. But the noise from the saloon below was keeping him awake. Not to mention the combined effects of Sophie Madrigal and that damned prediction of hers. Was it really a family curse? He wouldn't put it past her to lay a curse on him.

Not that he believed in such idiocy. Gabriel Caine knew full well that the nation's current love affair with occultism was silly, mainly because mysticism—Juniper Madrigal and her absolute honesty notwithstanding—was pure hogwash.

So why did he still feel itchy and uncomfortable every time he thought about that damned prediction? It was all trash, and he knew it. Somehow, however, knowing it didn't much help. Shoot, maybe he was just going crazy.

In the meantime, he was irked as hell at all the noise. He stopped dead on the stairs when he saw what the clamor was about. Then he pelted down the last of the staircase and strode with purpose over to the cluster of men harassing Dmitri in a corner. Gabriel hated bullies with a passion.

He positioned himself with his back to a wall so nobody could shoot him from behind. He didn't like violence, and he sure as the devil didn't aim to become a victim. "What the hell's going on here?" he asked in his deepest, loudest, and most dangerous voice.

One of the bullies, a big man with whiskers and a big belly, staggered a little, looked up with bleary eyes, and said, "Huh?" He held Dmitri's right arm in a hamlike hand. Poor Dmitri was struggling valiantly, to no avail, to get his arm back under his own control.

Gabriel rolled his eyes at this. Maybe Sophie was right about men. This crew sure seemed to be a worthless lot. "Step away from Dmitri, fellows." He smiled as he said it.

"Who's Dmitri?" asked the potbellied individual.

"Who says so?" another man, larger and darker than the first, asked in something of a growl.

Gabriel sighed, pulled his revolver, cocked it, and said, "I do."

Potbelly dropped Dmitri's arm immediately and took a step back, nearly falling over a chair in his haste. He lifted his hands, palms out. "Hey there, fella. I ain't doin' nothin'."

"Right," said Gabriel. He made a gesture to the large dark man. "Back up, friend."

"I ain't your friend," muttered the dark man.

"True," agreed Gabriel.

Another two men, who had been laughing and poking at Dmitri, backed away, evidently not relishing the prospect of gunfire. Thank God. Gabriel didn't relish it either.

"What right you got to inter'up our fun?" asked the dark man, and he hiccuped.

"The same right any man has to interrupt unfair play," Gabriel said reasonably. "Hell, man, what fun is it to pick on somebody that small? Find somebody your own size and make a fair fight out of it."

The dark man hitched up his trousers and leered evilly. "Like you?"

"I'd rather not," said Gabriel, hoping the idiot wouldn't charge.

His hopes came to naught. With what looked like it was supposed to be finesse, the large dark man lunged at him. Gabriel caught the man by the back of his shirt, hauled him upright, and tapped him behind the ear with his revolver. The man sank to the floor like a stone.

Gabriel, having never stepped away from the wall, asked obligingly, "Anyone else?"

Nobody answered him, but several of the men who had been harassing Dmitri held up their hands and backed away.

Gabriel kept his gun poised and ready. "You all right, Dmitri? Any damage that needs a doctor's attention?"

Dmitri was pulling himself together, tugging at his overalls and searching the floor for his cloth cap. He found it, whacked it against his trouser leg, and said, "No. I'm good."

"Glad to hear it. Want to get out of here? I'll walk you home." He kept his back against the wall and never once stopped scanning the saloon's occupants. Gabriel didn't fancy unpleasant surprises.

He was surprised when Dmitri shook his head. "*Nyet.* Miss Sophie. She go outside with a man."

"She *what*?" So startled was Gabriel by this news that he took his attention away from the men in the saloon for a second. It was just long enough for one of his adversaries—the dark one—to lunge at him. With a lift of his right leg, Gabriel foiled the attempt to throttle him, catching the lout in the stomach with the flat of a hard boot sole. The creature doubled over, clutched his midsection, and started retching.

Wrinkling his nose, Gabriel said to Dmitri, "Come with me. We'll see what she's up to." He wasn't altogether sure he wanted to know. If he discovered Sophie outside reading the man's palm, he'd be pleased. He anticipated nothing of the sort, however, and he felt a little sick at the thought of Sophie in another man's embrace.

But that was stupid. If she was engaged in amatory activities, why would she seek and find her lover in this squalid saloon? Gabriel didn't understand anything about Sophie, really, but he thought he knew her better than that.

Sidling against the wall and keeping his revolver trained on the company, he headed toward the door with Dmitri at his side, stolid and morose. Gabriel breathed a sigh of relief when they left the stale atmosphere of the Oriental. He didn't dare holster his revolver yet, but his nerves no longer shrieked.

"Do you know where she went?" he asked his small companion.

"Yah. In the alley."

In the alley? Good God. Gabriel could scarcely believe it of Sophie. If she was no more than a tart in magnificent disguise, he'd be terribly disappointed.

Gabriel heard her before he saw her. He also heard her companion, whoever he was, and what the two of them said made his nerves commence jumping again, worse even than before.

"I do believe I'll shoot you in the stomach," Gabriel

heard her say. "Then I'll have the pleasure of watching you die slowly and in great pain."

"Jesus," Gabriel whispered, appalled. What in the name of Glory was she talking about? Her voice sounded funny, an eerie blend of pain and exultation.

"You're crazy," the man with her said, his voice shaking as if a violent wind was blowing it.

"Perhaps," she said calmly, pleasantly. "But if I am, you made me so."

"But I didn't mean it!" the man cried. Gabriel clearly heard the panic in his voice. "Dammit, lady, it was a mistake! I didn't mean it! It was an accident!"

"Oh? I see. You murdered in error, so you should be forgiven? Is that so?" An uncanny, unearthly chuckle emanated from the darkness of the alleyway. "I don't think so, Mr. Hardwick."

Hardwick! Good God in a graveyard! Gabriel sped up. He barely heard Dmitri speed up, too, and commence trotting behind him. What in holy hell was Sophie Madrigal going to shoot Ivo Hardwick for?

"I didn't mean it. Shit, lady, I didn't mean it!" Hardwick started to sob.

"I don't care what you meant, Mr. Hardwick. You're an animal. A rabid animal. Rabid animals need to be exterminated so they can't infect the rest of humanity. And I'm very happy to be the executioner in this instance."

"No!" Hardwick wailed.

Gabriel was out of breath by the time he screeched around the last corner and saw Sophie, illuminated under the pallid light of an upper-story window, holding a small gun on Ivo Hardwick, who held his arms in the air and shook from head to foot with terror.

Both Sophie and Hardwick heard Gabriel arrive. Sophie swirled around, and Gabriel saw an expression of blind panic on her face the second before her gun discharged. The report sounded like a cannon blast in the confines of the alley. Dmitri hit the dirt behind Gabriel. Gabriel swore viciously.

Sophie screamed, "Damn you, Gabriel Caine!"

Nobody heard what Hardwick said, but when the dust cleared, he was scrambling over some fallen trash cans, making for a tiny space between buildings. Sophie, seeing this, tried to aim at him, but Gabriel caught her by the wrist and struggled to foil her aim. He had a hideous vision of Sophie killing Ivo Hardwick and hanging for it—and of him wiring the Pinkerton Agency and telling them he'd been thwarted by a female. The notion made him sick.

"Stop it!" she screamed. "Let me go!"

"What the hell do you think you're doing?" Gabriel hollered, too furious by this time to be the least bit nervous.

"I was trying to kill that man!" Sophie shrieked. "Until you spoiled it all!"

"Why the hell do you want to kill him?"

"*Damn* you!" Sophie cried again.

"To hell with damning me!" Gabriel hollered back. "What the hell do you think you're doing? I think you shot Dmitri!"

"What?" Wriggling like a maddened animal, Sophie glared over Gabriel's shoulder in an attempt, he presumed, to assess any damage to her faithful compadre. Her attention thus diverted for a second, he wrenched the gun out of her hand and stuffed it into his back pocket. It was a tight fit.

"*Nyet,*" Dmitri muttered. He picked himself up with some difficulty and tried to dust himself off. Given the state of the alley, Gabriel wouldn't give him odds.

"Thank God," whispered Sophie, and struggled harder.

"No thanks to you," Gabriel growled, gripping her

more tightly. "You might have shot him. Or me, for that matter."

"I wish I *had* shot you. Damn you!" Sophie shrieked again, renewing her struggle. "You were only trying to scare me when you said I'd shot Dmitri!"

"Christ," Gabriel said, enraged. "I think you're crazy."

"I'm not!" she bellowed. "You don't know what you're talking about!"

"Well, then, *tell* me, for God's sake!"

"Never!"

Gabriel figured he wasn't going to win this argument any time soon, so he elected to save his breath. He needed it to keep a clamp on Sophie, who wasn't giving up easily.

She fought like a wildcat for about a minute. For fully half of that time, Gabriel feared he wouldn't be able to contain her. For all her soft femininity, Sophie Madrigal was no China-doll miss. She was a large, full-bodied female, and she was strong.

He was still bigger and stronger than she, however, and she began to tire after about thirty seconds of furious fighting. He held her wrists and pulled her body to his in an effort to stifle her struggles. She was more than a handful, and Gabriel would have appreciated her succulent body pressed against his had the circumstances been different.

"Let me go!" Her voice was weakening. Gabriel thought he heard despair in it.

"No," he said flatly, still angry. "I'll be damned if I'll let you go until you quit fighting me."

She gave up all at once, and with a wretched groan collapsed into his arms. Confused for a second, Gabriel wondered if she was trying to trick him. He wouldn't put it past her. He was horrified when he realized she was crying. More than crying, really. Huge, wracking sobs shook her body.

"Here," he said softly, loosening his grip but not letting her go. In fact, he pulled her more closely to his body. Her patent misery hurt him, a fact he would have found astonishing had he taken time to think about it. "Here, Sophie, don't cry. It's all right."

"It's not," she moaned pitifully. "It will never be all right again."

Gabriel felt awful. Her emotional pain was so overtly evident that his heart—that part of his anatomy he'd successfully ignored for years—ached for her.

He searched over the sobbing Sophie's pretty blond head in an attempt to locate Dmitri. After a minute, he saw the little man, leaning against a building, trying without much success to pat the dust off of himself by smacking his clothes with his cloth cap. Dmitri looked up, took a gander at Sophie's condition, shook his head, and was about to return to his work when Gabriel caught his eye.

"What's wrong with her?" Gabriel mouthed, exaggerating the shape of the words for Dmitri's sake.

Dmitri shrugged, which didn't help much, and went back to whacking at his coat sleeve. Gabriel, realizing he wasn't going to get any help from that quarter, returned his attention to Sophie.

"Oh, Lord. Oh, God. Why?"

The words were broken into pieces by her anguish. Gabriel thought the word *heartbroken* would have been appropriate to her condition. It surprised him. Sophie Madrigal? Sophie, the great stone monument to womanhood? The impenetrable fortress against his most devious wiles? The beautiful ice maiden with the little ugly dog?

Shattered. That word fit too. Gabriel couldn't stand it much longer. If she carried on in this vein for another few minutes, his own fortifications would crumble, and he'd be groveling at her feet and begging her to let him

Emma Craig

take care of her. He'd sooner join a monastery and be celibate for life than let that happen.

Since he still felt sorry for her, though, he was gentle when he next spoke. "Sophie? Here, Sophie, let me take you back to your hotel. I'm sure Miss Juniper will be worried about you."

After sucking in a shuddering breath, Sophie seemed to make an attempt to get herself under control. She pulled away from Gabriel a little bit, but he didn't let her go, and not only because he remained worried about her state of mind. He also harbored a soupçon of doubt about the veracity of her emotions. Although, he had to admit to himself, if she was acting, she was doing the best job he'd ever seen in his entire life—and he'd been reared by actors, more or less.

At last she lifted her head from where it had been buried against his shoulder, leaving a wet patch that felt cool in the evening breeze. Gabriel gazed down at her in an attempt to assess her state, and his heart reeled.

Good God, the woman wasn't acting. Or if she was, she was another Bernhardt. "Here, Sophie. Here, take my handkerchief and wipe your eyes." He used the gentlest voice he'd ever heard issue from his lips, nearly startling himself into looking for a stranger in the alley.

She took the handkerchief with shaking hands and wiped her cheeks and eyes. No makeup was thus removed, Gabriel noticed, thereby proving his belief that Sophie's charms were natural.

She whispered, "Th-thank you."

Since she didn't add anything else, not even a disparaging comment about his morals, behavior, or person, Gabriel judged she was still pretty upset. "Are you—better?" He was going to ask if she was all right but, remembering her last response, he altered it.

She nodded and blew her nose.

90

That was all right with Gabriel. He'd gladly sacrifice a handkerchief to the cause. "Are you able to walk, Sophie? Do you need me to carry you?" It surprised him to realize he'd be happy to carry her—over hot coals, if necessary. He considered this a bad sign and endeavored to toughen his newly found heart.

"No!" she said with some force, from which Gabriel deduced that she was recovering her composure.

Rather than snap back at her, he repeated mildly, "Are you able to walk, Sophie?"

She sniffled, took a tentative step away from his embrace, which displeased him, and nodded again.

"You sure?" She was looking up at him so forlornly that Gabriel wished he could kiss her. Her lips were succulent in the dim light of the alleyway, and she looked so unhappy. Everything about her roused instincts within him that had never been roused before. This, too, was bad. How the prickly, unpleasant, self-sufficient Miss Sophie Madrigal could be stirring his protective instincts was beyond him—except that at the moment she wasn't prickly, she wasn't being unpleasant, and she was far from self-sufficient.

Struggling to get his own emotions to behave themselves, he said softly, "I'll walk you back to the hotel now, Sophie." He stopped himself from asking her if that scenario met with her approval, because he feared it wouldn't. And he wasn't going to let her go again tonight until he was absolutely sure she was safely tucked in and in the gentle, caring hands of Miss Juniper.

She nodded again, then said, "Where's my gun?"

Damn. She would remember the blasted gun, wouldn't she? He said, "Your gun is safe, and I'm not going to give it back to you now."

Her eyebrows dipped. Gabriel considered this the first real sign of her improved mental health. "Why not?"

91

"Because I don't trust you with it."

She sniffed, but didn't argue. Gabriel thought wryly that he'd been right not to trust her with it.

"Come on, Sophie. If you're well enough to walk, I'll see you and Dmitri back to the Cosmopolitan. I'm sure your aunt is wondering what's become of you."

"She knows." Sophie's voice sounded oddly dull. Gabriel chalked this phenomenon up to emotional exhaustion brought about by her recent outburst.

"I'm sure she doesn't know you tried to shoot a man."

Sophie shrugged, as if she didn't care if he believed her or not. She was acting very much like an individual who'd given up something precious; who'd fought hard and been defeated. Her attitude made Gabriel's insides hurt. He jerked a nod at Dmitri. "You all right, Dmitri?"

"Yah." The little Russian looked as morose as ever, but as he didn't limp or look bloody, Gabriel took him at his word.

"All right. Let me support you, Sophie."

"I don't need you to support me."

For the first time since he'd met her, Gabriel was pleased to hear the grouchiness in her voice. She'd be all right now; he was sure of it. At least, she'd recover from this particular fit. He had no idea what had propelled her to announce nothing would ever be all right again. Maybe he could get Miss Juniper to tell him. Never having experienced an itch to learn about another person, Gabriel mistrusted this one. Hell, maybe he was turning into a gossip in his old age.

He had his arm around her shoulder still, and Sophie's weight still pressed against him. He found himself wishing it would stay there all the way back to the Cosmopolitan. Her body was soft and supple and the parts he could feel through the fabric of her shirtwaist felt grand against him. He'd noticed her bosom with approval before; now he felt it with equal approval. He hoped one day he'd be able to see it, although he wasn't going to hold his breath.

Slowly and with great care, he led her down the alley, around the corner, and out into the street. There, lights from the buildings flooded the boardwalk and the motley assortment of men milling about. Several glanced at Sophie, Gabriel, Dmitri. One or two of them looked interested in Dmitri. Three or four of them looked interested in Sophie. One astute fellow, garbed as Gabriel imagined a dapper gambling man might be, winked at him as if to congratulate him on his conquest.

If he only knew. Still, Gabriel discovered himself pleased to know that he'd been taken for Sophie's lover.

Shoot, he was sinking fast. The notion terrified him and, at the same time, made him feel kind of good. Whatever was to come of his strange relationship with Sophie Madrigal, at the moment he was enjoying her lush flesh pressed against him.

Alas, she straightened after a few steps, and her pace picked up. After about two more minutes, she turned her head and looked up at him. "Thank you, Mr. Caine, I believe I am able to walk on my own now."

Gazing down into her watery eyes, Gabriel found himself loath to release her. "I think I'd better help you a little while longer."

He heard Dmitri make a disparaging, snorting noise, and frowned at the little man. Dmitri looked no different than he ever did.

"I'm perfectly able to walk on my own," Sophie said with a hint of the old grandeur back in her voice.

Gabriel sighed lustily. "I'm not going to let you walk home with only Dmitri to accompany you, Sophie Madrigal, so don't even think it." Something else occurred to him and he said grumpily, "And for God's sake, call me Gabriel. Hell, woman, I've stopped you from committing murder and held onto you through a sobbing fit. I think we should be on a first-name basis by this time."

"Do you?" The ice was back with a vengeance. Gabriel wished it wasn't. "Oh . . . very well."

That was something, he reckoned. At least he could call her Sophie and she could call him Gabriel.

Neither of them spoke, nor did Dmitri, as they finished tramping over the mean streets of Tucson. For a relatively small territorial town, the place was noisy. Gunshots rang out twice, dogs barked, and Gabriel was pretty sure he heard coyotes yipping in the distance. Not the kind of place he'd prefer to settle down in, if he were the settling-down type. Nor, he imagined, would it appeal to Sophie, even under more favorable circumstances and when she wasn't trying to kill someone.

And why, for God's sake, *was* she trying to kill someone? And why Ivo Hardwick? Gabriel knew full well that Hardwick had a criminal record as long as the Florida boot, but what was he to Sophie? Had Hardwick swindled her or her aunt? Had he done something beastly to Sophie?

Gabriel couldn't feature that possibility, since Sophie was probably stronger than the skinny Hardwick. Had he seduced and abandoned her?

That notion had no sooner entered Gabriel's head than he thrust it violently out again. There was no way on God's green earth that Sophie Madrigal could have become sexually entangled with Ivo Hardwick. Gabriel's every nerve ending rebelled at the thought.

No. It must be something else. Although he expected it would be a hopeless question, he asked, "Um, so why were you trying to kill that man, Sophie? What is he to you?"

"Nothing," she shot back immediately, and said no more.

Gabriel wished she weren't such a difficult female. He spent a moment or two trying to make his mind's eye picture an agreeable, obliging Sophie Madrigal, and he was singularly unsuccessful. The concept was so insane, in fact, that it startled a chuckle out of him.

"What are you laughing at?" Sophie asked in a hard, suspicious voice.

"Not you," Gabriel said.

She muttered an unintelligible syllable. Gabriel grinned into the semi-darkness. "Actually, I was trying to picture you as a sweet-tempered, mild-mannered lady."

"Don't be an ass."

"That's my Sophie."

"No, it isn't."

Gabriel gave up. He did, however, notice that Dmitri seemed to be smiling. Gabriel had never seen Dmitri smile before. It almost gave him heart.

He had no sooner knocked at the door to Sophie and Juniper's room than the door burst open and Juniper, looking frightened, stared up at him. Tybalt, with more animation than Gabriel had ever seen him display, yipped once and jumped up to paw Sophie's skirt. Juniper's eyes widened when she saw Sophie, and she pressed her hands to her cheeks for a second before she reached for her niece.

"Sophie! Oh, Sophie, what did you do?"

Interesting choice of words, Gabriel thought dryly. Juniper knew her niece well enough to know that it would have been Sophie who'd started any trouble that had transpired. Sophie wasn't so understanding.

"I didn't do anything," she said crossly. Releasing her aunt, Sophie stooped and picked Tybalt up. Immediately the dog began licking her chin, and Sophie made cooing noises at it. Gabriel's heart went all soft before he pulled himself together and spoke to Juniper.

"She tried to kill a man," he said with what he hoped looked like a genial smile for Juniper. Dmitri had gone back to his own room. "I stopped her."

"She *what?*" Juniper threw her arms around Sophie again, making Tybalt squeak and Gabriel smile at the sight of the tiny Juniper hugging her imposing niece. "Oh, Sophie, you found him." She sounded certain.

Gabriel ceased smiling. "If you're talking about Ivo Hardwick, she found him all right. Why was she looking for him, is what I want to know."

Sophie growled, "Juniper."

But Juniper evidently didn't need the warning. She let Sophie go and stepped away from her with a deep, soulful sigh. "I won't tell, Sophie. But really, dear, you know Mr. Caine can only help you. The cards say so."

"Do they really?" Gabriel found this intelligence quite interesting and not altogether unwelcome.

"Balderdash," Sophie announced, thereby soundly rejecting the cards, Juniper, and Gabriel with one word. She stalked over to the bed and laid Tybalt gently down on a quilt that looked as if it had been placed there specifically for him. He dug wildly at the quilt for a second, pushed his squashy nose into it, flipped it up a little, crawled under, and settled down to rest.

Gabriel was charmed. He also wasn't surprised that Sophie had thrown himself, the cards, and Juniper out as if they meant nothing to her.

Neither, apparently, was Juniper, although she appeared saddened by her niece's hard attitude. She rushed up to Gabriel and laid a placating hand on his sleeve. "Won't you stay and have a cup of tea with us, Mr. Caine? I'm sure Sophie should thank you for your part in saving her from shooting Mr. Hardwick, but she can't be made to be grateful for such things yet.

You must give her time, because she's been so grievously—"

"Juniper!"

Juniper jumped and squeaked at Sophie's violent roar. She glanced accusingly at her niece. "I shan't say anything you don't want me to, Sophie."

"Mr. Caine doesn't need to know anything—not one, single, solitary thing—about me, Aunt Juniper. Thank you." She yanked off her hat and, with a violent gesture, flung it on her bed. "He can stay for tea if he wants to," she added grudgingly.

"Why, thank you, Sophie. What a pleasant invitation." Although Gabriel was sorry, because Juniper obviously didn't care to listen to dissension, he couldn't keep from sounding sarcastic.

Sophie whirled and pinned him with a glare. "It's not an invitation. Juniper already issued the invitation. It's merely resignation. I know blasted well you don't want to leave yet. You want to stay and try to figure out what's going on with me."

"I'd say you're on the money there," Gabriel acknowledged mildly.

"Well, you can't do it. However, since you're a man and as obtuse and disobliging as most other men in the world, I expect you'll have to find it out on your own."

And with that, she sailed out of the room once more. Gabriel started after her, worried that she'd try to find Hardwick and tackle him with her bare hands since Gabriel still held her gun, but Juniper forestalled him.

"Please don't chase after her, Mr. Caine." Her voice was small and sad. "I believe she's only going to the washroom. She—she needs a little time to herself, I believe." She gave him a ghost of her usually perky smile. "I'll fix the tea."

And, over a small portable burner that looked as if it had been traveling with the Madrigal entourage for fifty years or more, she did. She was right about Sophie, who returned in a few minutes, with her face looking pink and scrubbed.

Sophie was also right. Gabriel had thus far learned not one tiny thing that might give him a clue as to why she seemed determined to kill Ivo Hardwick, not even when she'd been in the throes of hysteria.

He perceived this job of his wasn't going to be as easy as he'd first imagined. As he settled himself in a chair at Miss Juniper's insistence, he mulled over this last point in his brain—and grinned.

Chapter Six

Gabriel and Juniper were sipping tea like two old cronies when Sophie slipped quietly into the hotel room. Damn and blast. She'd been hoping he'd have had the grace to leave before she got back. She ought to have known better. Gabriel Caine would never be so obliging.

Juniper jumped up. "Oh, Sophie, you're back!"

Inane, but absolutely Juniperesque. Sophie quelled the urge to shout at her sweet, addled aunt. Her smile felt tight and strained, but she managed it and said, "Yes, Aunt Juniper. I'm back."

"Here's a cup of tea for you, dear."

"Thank you very much." She took the cup and saucer and was touched to see that Juniper had put a lump of sugar in it and placed a little teaspoon on the saucer. Normally, Sophie would take milk in her tea as well, but there wasn't any in the hotel room. She gave Juniper what she hoped was a warm, thankful glance, knowing in her heart that Juniper didn't deserve the agony Sophie was putting her through.

Since, however, Sophie would never, ever, for any reason, give up her quest for vengeance, she could only pray that Juniper wouldn't be too badly bruised in the process. If she was, Sophie would leap that hurdle after she'd fulfilled her goal.

Gabriel, Sophie noticed, had risen from his chair like the gentleman he wasn't, and was staring at her with overt curiosity. Damn him, the rude beast. She waved him back into his chair and avoided meeting his gaze as she walked with her cup of tea to the window. There she pulled the curtain aside and stared out into the dark night. What a miserable place Tucson was, to be sure.

In the light cast by what seemed at least a thousand kerosene lamps, she saw ghostly windmill blades whirring lazily in the almost-still night air. The scene was eerily akin to something out of one of her nastier nightmares: barren, dusty, deserted, and ugly, as if all life had abandoned it and left it bereft.

No, Sophie amended. The street wasn't quite deserted. Someone stumbled down the boardwalk, drunk, she presumed, and trying to get back home before he fell over and passed out. How disgusting some men could be without half trying. She hated them all.

She heard Gabriel clear his throat and anticipated a number of the things he might say. What he did say when he got around to it, therefore, came as no surprise to her.

"So, Sophie, why don't you tell me why you were in such an all-fired rage to kill that poor man."

"That poor man," Sophie mocked, "is a murderer."

"Yeah. I told you that myself. But I didn't know you were after Ivo Hardwick, too."

Shocked to hear the name of her mortal enemy on

Gabriel's lips, she whirled around, slopping tea out of her cup and into her saucer. Her teaspoon rattled against the china and sounded like a little bell. "How do you know his name?"

"Beg pardon?" He blinked at her.

"Did Dmitri tell you?"

He had sat at her gesture and now eyed her oddly, as if he were wondering if she'd gone loony. "I don't rightly recall what Dmitri said. From what I gather, you left him alone in that saloon. When I encountered him, he was being harassed by three or four big bullies."

Consternation piled itself on top of her surprise, and Sophie gasped. "He what?"

With a nod, and looking mighty self-righteous about it, Gabriel said, "Yes, ma'am. I think you'd better arm the poor little guy if you expect to be abandoning him in very many more Wild Western saloons. This part of the country isn't as meek and mild as where you're from, I reckon."

Ignoring his criticism, Sophie asked frantically, "Was he hurt?" She rushed over to Gabriel and would have grabbed him by the arm if she wasn't holding onto her teacup. "He didn't look hurt. Did any of those beastly men hurt him?"

Somewhat irritably, Gabriel said, "No, he wasn't hurt. But that wasn't his fault. Or yours."

Again ignoring his implications, Sophie pressed a hand to her galloping heart and realized the hand holding her cup and saucer shook like a leaf. Her teaspoon had dropped to the floor. There was now more tea in her saucer than in her cup. She set the cup on the dressing table with a clink and stooped to retrieve the spoon. "Oh, my goodness. I didn't even think about any of those horrid men attacking Dmitri. You're right. I should have given him a weapon."

101

Gabriel snorted. "And did you think about them attacking you, pray tell?"

Taken aback, she stood, turned, and said, "Of course not!"

Looking peeved now, Gabriel snapped, "Well, you should have. I don't care how big and strong you think you are, or how much you think you can take care of yourself, if you ever have to face being attacked by several rowdy drunks, you'll discover your mistake in a hurry."

"Oh, dear," Juniper murmured, pressing a hand to her cheek.

Sophie was furious. "Stop worrying my aunt, Gabriel Caine!"

"I'm not the one who's worrying her. You're doing that all on your own, with your harebrained schemes to kill that man."

"Oh, dear, dear, dear." Juniper lifted a cup to her lips with a trembling hand. Her face had drained of color, and she truly did look frightfully worried.

Sophie felt terrible. Turning again abruptly, she huffed, "Oh, for heaven's sake. I made a mistake tonight. I should have armed Dmitri." Eyeing Gabriel glacially from over her shoulder, she added, "*I* was well armed, and I know very well how to use my weapon."

She was gratified to see Juniper nod slowly, as if acknowledging the justice of Sophie's declaration. She was even more gratified when Juniper said in a quavering voice, "She's been practicing for months with that awful little gun of hers, Mr. Caine."

Gabriel didn't seem the least bit mollified. "Hogwash." He sucked in a breath and smiled apologetically at Juniper. "That is to say, I'm sure you're correct about her practicing, Miss Juniper, but I still say Miss Sophie isn't fit to be going head to head with drunken Westerners."

"Fiddlesticks. You're just angry because I was able to defend myself without your help."

Gabriel stood and Sophie was alarmed to see the angry look in his eyes. "That's stupid. You may be able to aim and shoot a gun, Miss Sophie, but you're nowhere near as tough as most of the men who live out here. Most of them are flat uncivilized, and very few of them have any scruples."

That, Sophie reluctantly admitted to herself, was probably true. She wouldn't say so for worlds. "Fiddlesticks," she said again. Perceiving it as a weak response, she went on, "That may be true, but even the most immoral lout couldn't withstand a bullet in the stomach. Even you have to acknowledge that much, Gabriel Caine."

"You're being deliberately obtuse," he said in a flat, hard voice. "What's more, I want to know why you're after Ivo Hardwick."

A pain with which she was all too familiar stabbed Sophie in the heart. She glared at Gabriel. "That's my business."

Juniper tutted from her chair, and Sophie gave her a good hot scowl in case she might be tempted to tell Gabriel the truth. Juniper held up a placating hand and let it drop into her lap. She looked very forlorn. Sophie regretted her aunt's unhappiness, but she couldn't fix it.

"It's my business too, dammit. I want to know what the hell you were doing, trying to kill Ivo Hardwick. I'm supposed to be taking him back to Abilene. I'll be damned if I'll let anybody kill him first." He turned a guilty glance upon Juniper. "Sorry, Miss Juniper. Your niece is driving me crazy, and I reckon my language suffered there for a minute."

Sophie barely heard him apologize to her aunt. She was benumbed by his admission. After a stunned moment, she spoke. "You *what?*"

He turned back to glare at her. "I've been hired to bring Ivo Hardwick back to Abilene, and that's what I aim to do. I'm not going to let you kill him before I get at him."

"You said you were after a man named Mac-something or other! You lied to us!"

Gabriel looked puzzled. Sophie thought for a moment he was pretending befuddlement, but the expression seemed so genuine, she gave up that reason for hating him—for the moment, at least. Less sure of herself, she said, "Well, you did."

He shook his head. "Couldn't have, because it isn't so. The man who hired me is McAllister." He snapped his fingers as, apparently, the old conversation returned to him. "That's what it was. You asked who'd hired me."

Absolutely positive again, Sophie snapped, "I did not. I asked whom you were after."

"That's not the way I remember it."

"Then you remember it incorrectly. Anyhow, I don't believe you."

"Oh, but Sophie, I remember it, too. I believe you did ask who had hired him, dear."

Sophie and Gabriel both turned to stare at Juniper, who tucked in her chin and appeared flustered at the attention. For a second, Sophie wanted to holler at her aunt, then gave it up. Juniper never lied, so she and Gabriel both must have misunderstood her question way back there on the train. Drat. Sophie hated giving up a good outrage for the sake of the truth. Especially if it meant apologizing to someone like Gabriel. To the devil with apologies. She'd apologize to Juniper later.

Turning back to Gabriel, she said, "Well, I meant to ask whom you were after."

Gabriel shrugged, and Sophie wished she could pummel him with her fists. He was stronger than she, though—much to her regret—so she didn't.

"Whatever you thought you asked, I've been hired to bring Ivo Hardwick back to stand trial in Abilene," Gabriel said with a touch of asperity. "And I'd appreciate it if you'd leave him alive so I can do my job."

Sophie sniffed. "That's too bad, because if I can find him again, I'll kill him." She frowned ferociously. "And I'll kill you, too, if you ever try to stop me again."

"Sophie!" Juniper wailed.

"I will," Sophie repeated stubbornly.

"Good God," muttered Gabriel. "I think you really are crazy."

"You may think what you like."

"Oh, but Sophie, please, dear, reconsider this awful thing you want to do," Juniper cried from her seat. "It's wrong to murder that man."

"It's not murder!" Sophie yelled, outraged. "It's retribution. It's exactly what the law should have done to him and didn't!"

Juniper shook her head disconsolately. Gabriel stared at her, confounded.

Juniper said, "But it's wrong, dear. It's wrong for you to seek another's death, no matter how much you feel you're justified. Leave justice to God, Sophie. Please."

"Fiddlesticks!" Sophie spat the word out as if it tasted bad.

Sadly, Juniper went on, "I know your faith has suffered because of—of everything."

Sophie uttered a strangled noise and turned away from her aunt. Because of everything. Yes. Because Ivo Hardwick murdered Joshua, Sophie's life had been shattered.

105

"I know your grief, Sophie," Juniper said. "And I know this course you're following will lead to terrible sorrow for everyone if you succeed."

Recovering her composure, Sophie asked sarcastically, "Did the cards tell you so?" Instantly she regretted it when her aunt flinched. Blast! She was always hurting Juniper's feelings, and Juniper didn't deserve to be treated so poorly.

Sophie wished she could pick Tybalt up and cuddle him, but she wouldn't give Gabriel Caine the satisfaction of knowing she needed cuddling. In a flash, a vision of Gabriel cuddling her entered her mind's eye. She rejected it at once, but it left an odd, lonely, icy patch in her heart. Blast again.

Juniper sighed deeply. "I don't need the cards to tell me that much, Sophie. It's wrong, what you're doing, and you know it as well as I do. And so does Mr. Caine."

"It's not wrong," she said stuffily.

Juniper sighed again and gave up. Thank God, her aunt wasn't a tenacious woman.

"I still want to know what you know about Hardwick, Sophie. He's got a past as black as ink, and he's wanted for manslaughter in the Indian Territory."

Sophie felt her eyebrows arch. "Really? That hardly surprises me. He's an evil man."

"He is that," concurred Gabriel. "And he's also wanted for theft and worse in Texas. He shot Franklin McAllister, the man who hired me, and killed one of McAllister's cowboys. McAllister wants him to stand trial for it."

"He's done worse than that to me," muttered Sophie, and she shot Juniper another warning glance just in case she got any smart ideas. But Juniper knew better, and only looked sad and dejected as she sipped her tea.

"What was it?" Gabriel asked, almost shouting in his

frustration. "*What* has he done to you? If you'll tell me, maybe I can help you."

Her heart went cold at the thought. Sophie would roast in hell before she'd allow anyone else to exact retribution for her. She had to do this herself. Ivo Hardwick had, in a moment of sublime indifference to everything that makes animals men, opened a huge, bloody, wound in Sophie's heart and ruined her life forever. She'd not allow any state, territory, Gabriel Caine, or anyone else to kill him for her. "I don't want your help." Her voice, she noticed, quivered with ice-cold passion.

"Oh, Sophie!" Juniper whispered pitifully. "Please don't, dear."

Sophie ignored her.

"But why?" Gabriel held his hands out in a gesture of despair. "Why, for God's sake is killing him so important to you?"

"That's my business."

Another vision whacked her mind's eye, this one of Gabriel holding her as she wept in that wretched, dirty alleyway. She had to stiffen her nerves against the thought. She'd felt so good in Gabriel's arms. Protected. Cared for.

Which was probably the stupidest thing she'd felt since she was an innocent child of sixteen and learned to her everlasting regret that the emotion of being protected and cared for by a man as handsome and appealing as Gabriel was an illusion. Such men were reared to torment women. It was a *cruel* illusion, what's more, fostered by idiots and rammed down little girls' throats before they were old or wise enough to know a lie when it stood before them in the all-too seductive flesh. Such a man could never be anything but a curse to Sophie Madrigal.

She was being an ass even thinking about being protected and cared for, and she despised herself for it. Staring Gabriel straight in his gorgeous brown eyes, she said, "I shan't tell you why I plan to kill Ivo Hardwick, but you may rest assured that I *will* kill him, if it's the last thing I do."

Juniper moaned piteously.

Gabriel stared back at her for about ten seconds, shook his head, put his teacup down, and bade Juniper farewell for the night. He didn't say another word to Sophie.

That was fine with her.

The first thing Sophie did the following morning, even before she took Tybalt outside for his morning exercise, was ascertain the exact state of Dmitri's health. She wished she'd done it the night before, but Juniper had dissuaded her, citing the time, which by then was well past midnight. Sophie had obliged her aunt, and had suffered a bad night in consequence. She considered insomnia a just punishment for having put Dmitri in peril.

Now, as Tybalt snuffled at her feet, eager to go outside and piddle, she stood in Dmitri's hotel room doorway and asked, "Are you sure you weren't hurt?" She eyed the little man closely, trying to determine if there were bruises or breaks he was trying to hide.

He shook his head, gloomy as usual. "*Nyet*. That Mr. Caine, he help me."

Sophie felt her lips pinch and endeavored to smooth them out. She didn't like knowing that Gabriel had saved Dmitri from a situation brought about by her own single-minded pursuit of vengeance. Her goal sounded bad when looked at in that light. But it wasn't bad. Not at all. It was just and proper.

Sniffing, she said, "I'm glad he came to your assistance. I must say I'm rather surprised that he'd do such a thing. I didn't think he possessed the compassion."

She was also surprised when Dmitri shook his stubborn Russian head and growled, "Mr. Caine good man. He help me. Besides, Miss Juniper say so."

Sophie couldn't keep from rolling her eyes. Good heavens, Gabriel Caine had not only succeeded in worming himself into Juniper and Tybalt's hearts, but he'd even conquered Dmitri, who barely tolerated the majority of people cluttering up the earth. She could hardly stand it.

"At any rate," she said stiffly, "I'm sorry if my brazen actions last night put you in jeopardy. I shan't do anything so foolhardy again." Not if she had to walk into saloons all by herself.

Dmitri frowned up at her, as if he'd read her unspoken vow. "Not a problem. I help you. I don't mind."

"Nonsense. I shan't drag you into my troubles."

"Not trouble. I help."

Well, Sophie thought, there it was. She was stuck. Now she'd not only have to find Ivo Hardwick—again—and kill him, but she'd also have to protect Dmitri, who would insist upon accompanying her, as well. Lord, life could get complicated at the worst times.

However, there was nothing she could do to dissuade the tiny Russian at the moment. Resigned, she said, "I'm going to walk to Mr. Huffy's boardinghouse and ask him to track down Hardwick again. I'm sure the lout has left Tucson by this time." Shaking her head in anger, she added, "Thanks to Gabriel Caine, Hardwick knows I'm after him now, so he'll probably be harder to track."

Without a word, Dmitri went into his room, retrieved his cloth cap, pulled it down on his head, walked into the hallway, and shut the door behind him, ready to accompany Sophie and Tybalt into hell itself if Sophie wanted him to. Or even, Sophie reflected unhappily, if

109

she didn't want him to. With a sigh, she set out in the direction of Miss Partridge's Boardinghouse.

"You didn't get him?" Emerald Huffy was incapable of looking incredulous, but his bland features did crinkle a bit as he stared at Sophie. "I brung you right smack to him."

Sophie didn't appreciate the accusation she heard in her hireling's voice. "Indeed, you did. And I got him out in the alley and had the gun trained on his evil heart. Unfortunately, before I could finish the job, somebody interfered." If she ever got Gabriel Caine alone, she'd teach him a lesson about interference he'd never forget. Preferably with a knife or a gun.

Good Lord, she never used to have violent thoughts about anyone but Ivo Hardwick. For the briefest of moments, Sophie wondered if her pursuit of retribution was maiming her essential and basic nature, which used to be rather kindly—at least toward those she loved.

But she couldn't afford to think like that.

Huffy pulled at his lower lip. "Well," he said slowly, "I reckon I can trace him. He ain't too hard to follow, but it's going to take more time. You got the money?"

Cold old chap, wasn't he? Since she'd hired him, in part, for that very characteristic, Sophie knew she was being foolish to resent it now. "Oh, yes, I have enough money. Nothing is going to stand in my way this time."

Huffy nodded. "All right. I'll get on it. You still at the Cosmopolitan?"

"Yes, we'll stay there until we get word from you." With Dmitri to drum up business, Sophie expected to be reading palms and telling fortunes for the rest of the next day or two. People were such idiots. They'd believe anything if Juniper saw it in the cards. Yet most, if not all, of them would swear they were sane, balanced individuals who weren't easily duped.

Sophie knew from experience that the sanest, best balanced person could be duped by a scoundrel without the slightest trouble. She needed look no farther than the nearest mirror if she ever began to doubt it.

On that dismal note, she, Dmitri, and Tybalt took their leave of Emerald Huffy. He was counting the bills Sophie had handed him when the door closed.

Furious with himself for oversleeping, Gabriel bounded down the Oriental's staircase, aiming to race to the Cosmopolitan before Sophie and Juniper could slip through his fingers. He'd be fried if he'd let them loose on the world without his supervision. With any kind of luck at all, Sophie would find Hardwick again, and if she had her way, she'd kill him, and then Gabriel's job would be ruined.

"Damn her," he muttered as he slammed through the batwing doors.

And that was another thing. Everything had worked out all right last night, because his sleeping quarters were directly above the saloon where Sophie had tried to do her dirty work. But he was getting too damned old to sleep through the noise that emanated from even the tamest saloon—and the Oriental was far from tame.

As much as Gabriel hated to give in to age, still more did he cherish sleeping a full night through. From now on, he'd stop wherever the Madrigals were stopping— if they intended to follow Hardwick. Since he'd as yet no reason to doubt Sophie's dedication to her pursuit of the villain, he assumed they did.

He hoped like hell they hadn't already skedaddled this morning. If they had, he'd have to figure out where they'd gone. Dammit. But he wouldn't allow her to tackle Hardwick alone again. For the love of Mike, Hardwick was a grade-A bastard who'd as soon kill Sophie as look at her. The notion made Gabriel's blood run cold.

Muttering soft curses as his long strides ate up the boardwalk, Gabriel screeched to a halt when he turned the corner. By damn, there she was. With her ugly dog and the little Russian tagging along as usual. Relief flooded him so fast, he clapped a hand to his chest, alarmed. Criminy, that had never happened before. Maybe he really *was* getting old.

Stifling his odd reaction to finding Sophie in Tucson—and evidently alive and well—Gabriel trotted over to the odd-looking trio.

Sophie didn't see him until Tybalt whuffled excitedly and tugged at his leash. Then, looking up to see where her dog wanted to go, she spied Gabriel—and frowned.

Gabriel had expected it, so her frown didn't much diminish his delight in finding her. Oh, sure, he was accustomed to pretty women smiling at him, generally in a come-hither manner, but this wasn't merely a pretty woman. This was Sophie Madrigal, blight of his life, and the only woman he could ever remember actually fascinating him.

Hoping to disconcert her, he swept his black hat from his black hair and bowed formally. "Top of the morning to you, Miss Sophie. I hope the new day finds you well." He winked at Dmitri. "You all right this morning? No lasting damage?"

Dmitri grinned and nodded. Sophie, Gabriel noted, didn't approve of the little guy grinning at interfering old him. Too bad. Dmitri might be dead now but for Gabriel's interference. His heart stammered when he thought about what might have happened to Sophie if she'd succeeded in shooting Ivo Hardwick. Or in merely wounding him.

All at once, he wanted to holler at her, to rage and stomp and demand to know if she had any idea what the authorities would do to her if she fulfilled her bloodthirsty scheme. Or what Hardwick might do if he only maimed him. He knew that if he succumbed to the impulse to holler, she'd only sneer at him and say she didn't care. Gabriel cared, however, and he had a momentary, mad impulse to pull his hair out—or hers.

Subduing all of his violent urges with some difficulty, he pasted on his suavest smile and cocked his head at Sophie, trying to convey his interest in her answer to his query about her health. His suavity didn't last long because Tybalt was leaping on his trouser leg and digging his sharp little claws into the fabric. Gabriel bent over to forestall damage from his affectionate greeting. "You're in fine fettle this morning, Tybalt." Because he couldn't help himself, he added, "And your mistress is still alive to tend to you, too, through no fault of her own."

Sophie uttered a strangled noise. Gabriel glanced up blandly. "It's true, you know." Dmitri, he saw, nodded. If that didn't set her off, he expected nothing would.

"You," she said, her voice shaking with wrath, "have no idea what you're talking about."

"Right." Leaving Tybalt to snuffle at his feet, Gabriel stood up again. "I don't suppose we'll ever find common ground regarding that particular subject."

"For once, I believe you're correct." She gave him one of her more imperious sniffs.

Gabriel smiled. "So, will you be staying in Tucson for a few days, or will you and Miss Juniper be shoving off to parts unknown in pursuit of your prey?"

She started walking away from him, dragging Tybalt, who wanted to remain with Gabriel. Gabriel, who wasn't going to let her get away, and who harbored in his heart a good deal of compassion for dumb animals, ambled along with her. She speared him with a fierce glance from out of the corner of her eye, huffed, and walked faster. He kept up easily, although Dmitri, he saw, was puffing while trying to keep pace.

"You're wearing out your faithful servant," Gabriel said. "You didn't succeed in killing him last night. Are you trying to exhaust him to death?"

She stopped short and turned around, almost stepping on poor Tybalt, who gave a sharp, high-pitched yip of fright.

Amused, Gabriel said softly, "Just thought I'd mention it. I know you don't much care about the folks in your employ, but—"

She whirled again, this time stopping with her face directly aimed at Gabriel. He kind of liked the fact that they were almost nose to nose. Most women were a lot shorter than the queenly Sophie Madrigal. "How dare you!"

She stamped her foot, something Gabriel hadn't expected. That amused him, too. With a shrug, he said, "It's the conclusion I've drawn from observing the way you treat poor old Dmitri here."

Dmitri caught up with them then, and stood with his chest heaving. While Gabriel felt kind of sorry for the poor little guy, Dmitri was at least proving Gabriel's point. He deliberately stared at the panting Dmitri—in case Sophie hadn't caught his meaning.

"It's his own choice!" Sophie declared hotly, pointing at Dmitri, who pressed a hand over his heart as if trying to get the organ to slow to a more sedate pace. "I didn't tell him to come with me!"

Gabriel shook his head. "That won't wash, Sophie sweetheart. You know good and well that Dmitri's between a rock and a hard place. If he let you go roaming off on your own and you got yourself killed—or arrested, say, for murder—Miss Juniper would be crushed, and Dmitri would think it was his fault for not going with you and trying to stop you."

He saw Sophie take in a breath through gritted teeth. She was peeved with him, and no mistake. Gabriel didn't care. He was peeved with her, too, so they were even.

Chapter Seven

This was the limit. Sophie couldn't take much more. Not only was Gabriel Caine evidently determined to butt into her personal business and make her life miserable, but she could no longer avoid the one certain, absolute fact that made his presence intolerable to her.

Somehow or other, he, Gabriel Caine, this worthless piece of human flesh, this mere man, this person who had been the scourge of her life since the moment she'd met him, worked as a conduit between herself, Sophie Madrigal, of all people, and the "Other Side," as Juniper was so fond of calling the mystical aspects of life. How else could she account for what happened to her whenever she was in his presence?

Besides that, the visions she kept having involved not merely Sophie herself, but the both of them. This was very bad. Very, very bad.

She wanted to stamp her foot again, and then screech and scream and throw a full-fledged temper tantrum right here on this filthy Tucson boardwalk. Even when Sophie was a child, she'd never thrown tantrums; she'd had too much pride. But pride be hanged. This was by far the worst thing that had ever happened to her—barring one or two other events that she couldn't bear thinking about.

She took three furious steps away from him, then stopped suddenly and turned, making Gabriel bump into her, Dmitri bump into Gabriel, and Tybalt bark. She apologized to her dog.

"There's no getting rid of you, is there, Gabriel Caine?" she said bluntly. Might as well face the truth straight on and quit shilly-shallying.

He backed up as soon as Dmitri did. He, too, apologized to Tybalt, because he stepped on the poor thing's toe. Tybalt yipped pitifully, and Sophie swooped him up and glared daggers at Gabriel. He was probably getting used to her glare by this time.

"Nope," he said, petting Tybalt, who licked his hand.

That was the only thing about dogs Sophie didn't fully appreciate: They couldn't hold grudges worth a tinker's dam. "I didn't think so." She turned again, as abruptly as she had the first time, and set off for the Cosmopolitan at a furious clip. She heard Gabriel and Dmitri behind her, the one stomping hugely and keeping pace with ease, the other pattering, trying to keep up.

Even mad as fire, Sophie couldn't justify beleaguering Dmitri more than she had to, so she slowed her steps and put Tybalt back down on the boardwalk. He loved to walk, and she didn't feel justified in depriving him just because she wanted Gabriel Caine to drop dead.

She didn't want to slow down. Rather, she wanted to walk the length of Tucson, and then walk back again. And then repeat the process until she was so worn out, she wouldn't be able to do anything but collapse from sheer fatigue. With luck, she might even have worn Gabriel down. She couldn't do that to her precious Tybalt, though, or to Dmitri, so she spent the time it took to walk to the Cosmopolitan in thinking.

This leech-like quality of Gabriel's was going to make her job more difficult; there was no getting away from it. She was still angry about his fibbing to her regarding the name of his prey. Oh, she knew he *said* she'd asked who'd hired him, but she didn't believe it.

Of course, Juniper had said the same thing. Blast. Well, Sophie was sure the misunderstanding was all Gabriel's fault, however it had happened.

He caught up with her and took her arm. She tried to wrench it away from him, but he was stronger than she. Damn and blast. The one person on earth whom she could use as a real, legitimate conduit to the Other Side, and he had to be bigger than she. Why couldn't it have been Dmitri who served as her conduit?

What was she thinking of? The "Other Side," her hind leg. She didn't even *believe* in such nonsense. Did she? How could Gabriel be a conduit to something that didn't exist? And why would she need a conduit to it, even if it *did* exist and she believed in it?

Stopping, again so abruptly that she created a pile-up on the boardwalk, she pressed a hand over her eyes. Since it was the hand at the end of the arm Gabriel had taken, she lifted his hand, too, and the back of it, and a good deal more of him besides, pressed against her bosom.

Good God! She pulled away instantly, and felt her entire body get hot. He, the fiend, grinned at her as if he knew exactly how embarrassed she was. She heard Dmitri puffing beside her, but she couldn't look away from Gabriel. Tybalt, ever happy to be anywhere with his humans, commenced sniffing the delicious odors emanating from the boardwalk.

Endeavoring with every fiber of her being to ignore her blush, Gabriel's knowing look, Dmitri's exhaustion, Tybalt's snuffling, and her own humiliation, she spoke coldly to Gabriel. "Very well, if there's no way to shake you off, I suppose I shall have to put up with you."

"Good idea." His smile broadened. "I think that's a right sensible course of action. In fact, I think we ought to go upstairs to your room right now, and discuss this matter of Ivo Hardwick."

"I will never, ever, tell you one single thing about Ivo Hardwick, Gabriel Caine, and don't you even think it."

His smile faded. "That's stupid, Sophie."

"It is not! And don't you dare call me stupid!"

"I'm not calling *you* stupid, dammit. And keep your voice down, for God's sake. Do you want some chivalrous frontier knight to shoot me right here in front of the Cosmopolitan?"

"Yes!"

He looked around, as if he expected the whole town to have heard her holler and to gather around.

Damn him. He was right. Sophie glared around, too, and saw several men who had stopped whatever they'd been doing to stare at her. Interfering beasts. She scowled at them, and they only grinned back. That was another problem with these foul western territories: Nobody had any manners.

"Come inside," she growled at Gabriel, and yanked Tybalt's leash more strongly than she'd intended. Good heavens, she had to calm down. Gabriel was affecting the way she treated her dog—and since Joshua's death, Tybalt was the only thing on earth that gave her any sort of comfort at all.

She tried to take deep, calming breaths, but she'd laced her corset too tightly this morning, and was thus impaired from doing so. Corsets. She hated them with a passion. She'd only laced it tightly because of *him*. She knew it in her heart, even though she wished it wasn't true. She wanted *him*, the second most despicable human being in her life—perhaps the third—to consider her attractive. She, Sophie Madrigal, whose life had been ruined practically before it had started, and by a man who reminded her a good deal of Gabriel Caine, was now trying to impress another one.

Sophie *really* didn't like men. Except Dmitri. And Tybalt. And her father and uncle, she supposed, although the former was a stretch. Oh, very well, perhaps she didn't dislike *all* men; only the horrid ones. Unfortunately, there seemed to be an awfully lot of horrid men extant in Sophie's universe.

She caught her breath on a sob, and told herself to get a grip on her emotions. She had learned about her father and mother the hard way, but she had learned—and they had loved her with all the love they had to give. And she'd loved them back. It was evil of her to be thinking unkind thoughts about them now, just because she was upset.

Still raging, she swept past the registration desk, where she saw out of the corner of her eye that the clerk was watching her warily, lifted Tybalt in her arms, and strode up the stairs to the second floor of the hotel, defying her corset and the laws of human anatomy. She was suffering from lack of oxygen when she finally stormed to the door of her room, set her dog down, and began fumbling in her reticule for the room key. By this time, she was near to passing out, but she wouldn't give Gabriel Caine the satisfaction of watching her fail. Before she had found the key, the door opened. Sophie looked down at her mild-mannered aunt and growled, "We have company, Aunt Juniper."

Juniper was holding the cards in her hand. Sophie

wasn't surprised. Her aunt lived by those foolish cards. Also, far from looking angry, as Sophie deemed appropriate, Juniper took one glance around Sophie's large form blocking her view, saw Gabriel standing in the hall, and smiled as if she'd never been so happy to see anyone in her life.

Exasperated and about to faint from lack of breath, Sophie huffed angrily and went into the room, where she stepped behind the Chinese screen in the corner, ripped the buttons of her shirtwaist open, and loosened her corset. What a relief. She would never, ever, for as long as she lived, lace it tightly again, Gabriel Caine or no Gabriel Caine. Let him think her fat. What did she care, damn him?

And Gabriel, of course, had no earthly idea she'd tormented herself on his behalf, the rat. And, if he ever learned of it, her foolishness would probably merely amuse him. Sophie wished she could heave something heavy at him.

Instead, she rudely interrupted the friendly conversational greetings he and Juniper were exchanging. Dmitri, she noticed, had removed his cloth cap and now stood in a corner, looking morose, and observing the scene as if he expected it to be broken up by a herd of rampaging Cossacks any second. Maybe Juniper was right about the Russians, Sophie thought.

"Mr. Caine refuses to leave me alone about Mr. Hardwick, Aunt Juniper, and he threatens to dog our footsteps as we try to find him, so I suppose we'll have to put up with him."

Chat ceased immediately, and Gabriel and Juniper turned to look at her. Juniper said, "Oh?" She glanced back at Gabriel. "How nice, Mr. Caine."

Sophie chuffed.

Gabriel, smiling wolfishly, said, "Need any help, Miss Sophie?" in a voice so perfectly innocent, Sophie's desire to heave heavy things at him rushed back. She grabbed her shirtwaist so precipitately, she nearly upset the screen.

"No. Thank you," she said in the most frigid tone in her repertoire. "But we're going to have to talk about this. I most certainly don't like the notion of you following us about all over the country in pursuit of this demon, Hardwick. Since, however, there seems to be no way to stop you—"

"Right," Gabriel said obligingly, and sat on the small love seat against the wall at Juniper's gestured suggestion.

"—then at least we can formulate some ground rules."

"Ground rules?" He lifted one of his gorgeous black eyebrows over one of his gorgeous brown eyes, and Sophie's heart squeezed painfully.

None of this was fair. After months of existing in a pit of hellish pain, she'd finally discovered some motivation to life—had even begun to take some meager interest in living the rest of it—and here was a man; a big, handsome man; the kind of man Sophie could have loved madly if she didn't know better, ruining the only thing that gave her life meaning. She felt a sudden, severe compulsion to cry, which she throttled ruthlessly.

"Yes," she said coldly. "Ground rules."

Much more comfortable in her loosened garb, she stepped out from behind the screen and stood before Gabriel, who looked her over with what appeared to be great pleasure. The bounder. She wished she could ignore the spurt of pride and gratification that shot through her when she realized he found her desirable.

A man's desire, and her responsiveness to it, was what had started this whole miserable journey of hers. She'd spent her life ever since trying to rid herself of any remaining hint of carnality. If she hadn't done so yet, it wasn't for want of trying, but her lack of success rankled and made her spirits droop considerably.

Juniper, her cards laid sedately aside, her hands folded in her lap as she sat in a straight-backed chair, smiled up at Sophie with her customary vague pleasantness and said, "What kinds of rules are those, Sophie, dear?"

Sophie turned on Juniper, who was startled by her vehemence. Drat. Poor Juniper always seemed to suffer from Sophie's strong-mindedness, and Sophie always felt sorry about it—but not sorry enough to desist, or to reign in her energy beforehand. "Those are the kinds of rules that will assure us Mr. Caine won't be forever poking his nose into business that doesn't concern him."

Juniper blinked up at her, plainly puzzled. "I don't think I understand, dear."

"Neither do I," said Gabriel.

Sophie shot him a glare. "What I mean is that when Juniper and I are conducting business—business unrelated to Ivo Hardwick—you can jolly well keep your distance. That's what I mean."

Gabriel rubbed his chin. Sophie noticed Dmitri still standing in a corner and told him to sit down if he wanted to. He thought for a moment, looked from her to Gabriel to Juniper, then said, "*Nyet*. I go to room."

Giving a thought to Emerald Huffy, Sophie said, "Fine. Thank you for helping me this morning, Dmitri. If Mr. Huffy should get in touch with you, please let me know as soon as possible. Did you hire a parlor downstairs for this evening's work?"

He nodded, and Sophie relaxed enough to give him a genuine smile. She appreciated Dmitri a lot, even though she didn't often say so. She did so now. "Thank you very much, Dmitri. I don't know what we'd do without you. You're so very efficient."

"My goodness, yes, you are!" Juniper agreed happily. She beamed upon Dmitri.

Sophie thought how nice her own life would be if she were more like her aunt. If she were able to believe in the cards and crystal balls and so forth without doubting—or in anything at all, for that matter. But, no. Her fate couldn't be that simple, could it? The only time she felt an otherworldly connection was when she was in the presence of Gabriel Caine, the man who, although he didn't know it, was set to defeat her life's one ambition. It simply wasn't fair.

Without smiling or showing his pleasure at being appreciated in any way, Dmitri clicked his heels together, bowed sharply, and departed. Sophie almost laughed when she saw Gabriel gape after him. "He always does that, Gabriel. He used to be a footman in some Russian prince's palace or something."

"A footman? A midget?"

Sophie sniffed. "Evidently, the prince found it amusing to have little people waiting on him."

From the expression on his face, Sophie gathered he felt the same disgust at the prince's callous enjoyment as she did. Which was moderately distressing, as she didn't want them to be alike in any way. However, that was nothing to the point. She sat next to Juniper in the room's other straight-backed chair. "Now, do you agree that when my aunt and I are working, you should stay away from us?"

He seemed to have to drag his attention away from the door and lingering thoughts of Dmitri. When he spoke, however, it was in answer to Sophie's question. "As to that, I'm not sure I can trust you, Sophie, if you'll forgive me for saying so."

Juniper giggled. Sophie scowled at her, then looked

at Gabriel. "I don't know why I should. What reason do you have for not trusting me?"

A lopsided grin visited Gabriel's gorgeous mouth. Sophie wished like thunder she didn't find him so blasted attractive. "Well, now, ma'am, it might have something to do with the fact that you seem to hate my heart and liver. And gizzard, too, unless I miss my guess."

"Human beings don't have gizzards," Sophie ground out through clenched teeth. "And I don't hate you." She hated lots of things about him, the good Lord knew, but she couldn't honestly say she hated him.

"Could have fooled me, ma'am."

She wasn't sure about that, actually, since she'd tried to fool him a couple of times and he hadn't bitten, but she didn't point that out. "I hate the fact that you foiled my purpose in that alleyway," she said. "And I hate the fact that you seem determined to follow my footsteps wherever I go."

He held up a hand. "Only if you go in the direction of Ivo Hardwick. I've been hired to bring him back to Abilene to stand trial. That's the only reason I care about Hardwick."

"Yes, so you've said." Sophie wished that were the only reason for her own interest in Hardwick. She tapped her chin with a fingernail that needed attention. Blast. She had to fix herself up if she was going to make a good impression on the customers this evening. There were lots of things besides the gullibility of the public and their scorn for her that she disliked about the family business.

"However, I *do* think I can trust Miss Juniper," Gabriel continued. "I get the feeling she and I are on the same side in this instance." He gave Juniper one of his beautiful smiles.

Juniper smiled back and began gushing. "Oh, my, yes, Mr. Caine! I've told Sophie over and over that I

125

know this pursuit of hers is going to end badly. It's wrong to seek vengeance, and—"

"Juniper!"

Sophie hadn't meant to roar quite so loudly, and when Juniper jumped in her chair and slammed a hand to her chest, she regretted it. She would not, however, allow her chatty aunt to tell Gabriel Caine her story.

Her feelings hurt, Juniper said in a shaky voice, "You know I would never say anything you don't want me to say, Sophie."

Sophie felt awful. She didn't trust sweet Juniper, though, not in the way Gabriel didn't trust Sophie— Juniper would never, ever tell a lie, for instance—but because Juniper wasn't strong like Sophie. Juniper might one day be compelled by some feeling of guilt or compassion or even love to tell Gabriel that which Sophie chose to keep to herself. She wasn't sure she could survive if her story became known by him. Some things were too precious to be shared with just anyone, and Sophie's memories of Joshua were golden to her.

She took a deep breath and let it out slowly. "I'm sure you would never do so on purpose. I don't think we need to go into how much you don't approve of what I'm doing. I know you disapprove, Mr. Caine knows you disapprove. Even Dmitri knows it. I'm doing it anyway."

Juniper shook her head. "It's not disapproval, Sophie. It goes far deeper than that. What you're doing is wrong. It's close to evil."

"Evil!" Sophie spat the word out with scorn. "And what is Mr. Hardwick, pray, if he isn't evil?"

"But that doesn't make what you're doing right, Sophie." Juniper gestured at her deck of cards, the stand-ins for her special Tarot deck. "The cards have been telling us so ever since you started, dear. You know that."

"The cards," said Sophie, "are fiddlesticks."

Juniper sighed deeply and shook her head some more. She glanced at Gabriel, a pleading expression on her sweet face. "I wish you could convince her, Mr. Caine. She won't listen to me."

When Sophie turned her head to see what Gabriel thought he could accomplish in the face of her determination, she got a shock. He didn't look scornful, and he didn't look amused. In fact, he looked as if he felt sorry for her.

She stood abruptly. "This is nonsensical." She might have to put up with him, and she might have to put up with Juniper's constant carping, but she'd never allow this man to offer her sympathy. Never. "Just know this, Gabriel Caine. Juniper and I are working women. We have to earn our ways in the world, and in order to do so, we have to perform the family business. Stay out of our way when we're working. Will you do that?"

Gabriel stood, too. "Yes, ma'am. Wouldn't dream of interfering."

"A likely story."

Yet that night, when Sophie and Juniper went downstairs and entered the private parlor Dmitri had hired for them, Sophie noticed Gabriel sitting in a far corner of the lobby, discreetly reading a newspaper. She didn't much appreciate his way of not interfering and eyed him coldly, but he didn't even glance up.

Good. Perhaps he'd keep his distance after all. She'd as soon he'd keep a farther distance, but supposed she could understand—a tiny bit—why he might not want to let her out of his sight. Especially if he thought she had methods of tracking Ivo Hardwick that he didn't possess. Which she did, damn him. She prayed that Gabriel would never discover the existence of Emerald Huffy.

* * *

Gabriel watched with interest as Sophie and Juniper entered their rented parlor. Sophie, he noticed, had left her wicker basket upstairs, so he assumed Tybalt was sleeping off any gastronomic overindulgences in her room. She sure did love that ugly dog; whenever Gabriel felt like whapping her upside the head, he remembered Tybalt and his heart melted. It was a definite flaw in his character.

He'd helped Dmitri set the room up for the evening's occult occurrences, and it looked really quite splendid, draped as it was with black and scarlet hangings, mystical symbols, and Christian emblems. The combination appeared strange to Gabriel, but obviously Juniper believed with her whole heart in all of it. At any rate, the simple hotel parlor now looked mysterious, otherworldly, serene, and inviting, a concoction that impressed him a great deal.

The Madrigal ladies knew how to set an atmosphere. His father had been good at that aspect of his business, too. Gabriel recalled with a certain fondness the crosses and Bibles and white cloths he'd thought of as the "Jesus trappings" of his father's trade, and which his father had carried with him around the country. His father had been every bit as convinced of his calling as Juniper was convinced of hers. Gabriel had been more like Sophie, which didn't surprise him a lot when the thought occurred to him.

He shook his head and wondered what propelled people to travel the roads they took in life. What had called his father to become an itinerant revivalist? His old man, George G. Caine, claimed to have honestly felt the call of the Lord to preach and save men's and women's souls. Had he been telling the truth? After pondering the question for years; Gabriel guessed he had been.

He'd told a very affecting story about his conversion.

He'd told about how, when he'd been a lad on the moors of Scotland, and had been forced to make his way home one night whilst afflicted with drunkenness, he'd asked the good Lord to protect him. He'd made a promise to God that he'd never drink again if the good Lord answered his prayer. And, according to Mr. Caine, the good Lord had done exactly that, and so had he.

In all the years he'd spent living with his parents, Gabriel had discovered no reason to doubt his father's story, although it made no sense to him. As yet in his own life, he'd seen no personal evidence of any Lord at all, good or otherwise.

Gabriel had loved both his father's story and the revivalist's life when he was young. He'd been a handsome lad, and had first discovered the joy of performing in that revival tent. He could still remember the almost orgasmic thrill of holding an audience—his father had called it a congregation—in thrall with his young voice. He'd wowed 'em in the sticks down South. He grinned, remembering.

And now here he was, watching over two ladies who were wowing 'em in the sticks out West. He laid his newspaper down as folks began showing up for prearranged appointments with the Madrigals. Dmitri was minding the gate so that no one would enter who didn't already have an appointment.

It had taken some sweet-talking on Gabriel's part to convince Dmitri to let him have an appointment with Sophie. He could hardly wait to see what she said about his palm. Or his head, if she was an advocate of phrenology. Or his cards. Whatever method she used to discern his future, he was eager to hear it.

The prediction she'd already made about his future smote him, and he frowned. That hadn't been nice of her, and Gabriel intended to ask her about it tonight.

Dammit, he knew occultism was so much hogwash;

129

he couldn't understand why that blasted prediction bothered him so much. He had a sneaking hunch it was because Sophie had made it, and his hunch bothered him almost as much as the fact that the prediction bothered him at all. He didn't want to care what Sophie Madrigal, the most difficult woman he'd ever encountered, thought about him.

The variety of folks who consulted mystics was entertaining to behold. Gabriel watched as sober businessmen—a type that seemed out of place here, in Tucson—respectable women, giggling schoolgirls, and women who were obviously ladies of the night, entered and left the parlor. None of them looked particularly distressed when they departed from their appointments, from which Gabriel gathered that Juniper's policy of not revealing distressing news still prevailed.

One young man left his appointment beaming. Gabriel experienced a sudden intuitive notion that the boy had sought advice on matters of the heart, and that he liked the news revealed by the cards. Or the crystal ball. Or the palm of his hand. He gazed at his own palm and chuckled out loud.

When Juniper had first explained all the lines and lumps to him, he'd been unable to find one of the mounts. He thought it was the Mount of Apollo, but he couldn't really remember. Whatever it was—or wasn't—he couldn't find it, and had wondered what Juniper would make of its lack. He was sort of hoping for something momentous, perhaps that the absence of the Mount of Apollo signified a cursed nature or something.

But Juniper had pointed out to him that his own personal Mount of Apollo had merely slid a little sideways and was there, only smack up against its next-door-neighbor mount. He couldn't remember which one that was, either.

This fortune-telling nonsense took a good deal of research and memory. Gabriel didn't have the interest in it. Or perhaps it was the calling he lacked. He'd never been terribly fascinated by saving people's souls, either, although he'd learned how to do that from the cradle, so he'd done it well when he was young. It was the glamor he'd been drawn to. The overwhelming emotional impact of the experience. He'd quit doing it when he'd begun to feel like a confidence trickster, much to his father's remorse.

Since he didn't want to think about his father's remorse, Gabriel wandered over to talk to Dmitri when he got bored. The ladies had been at it for an hour or so, and there was still an hour to go before Gabriel's own appointed time to meet with Sophie.

"How's it going, Dmitri?"

The little Russian looked up and nodded solemnly. "Good. Good. Miss Juniper and Miss Sophie, they do good."

Gabriel hauled up a chair and sat beside the small man. "So, what do you think of all this, Dmitri? Do you think spiritualism is bunkum, or do you believe the Madrigal ladies can really tell the future?"

Dmitri drew slightly away from Gabriel and looked at him as if he'd uttered an iniquitous blasphemy. Gabriel held up a palm in a calming gesture. "Guess that answers my question. I'm sorry, Dmitri. Didn't mean to cast aspersions on the ladies. I think they're both swell myself. I just wondered what you thought about their mystical powers."

To Gabriel's astonishment, Dmitri reached inside his shirt and dug out a carved wooden cross hanging from a leather thong, kissed it, and made the sign of the cross with his hand. "They are blessed by God and Saints Anthony and Agnes and—and—Jerome Emiliani."

Now who, Gabriel wondered, were those guys? His father never had much truck with the saints, being the

131

sort who believed in going directly to the source and bypassing the middleman. Nobody was going to intercede with George G. Caine when it came to communing with his Savior. Mr. Caine even believed in the laying on of hands to cure a variety of ills. The personal touch was what Mr. Caine excelled in.

But poor Dmitri fairly vibrated with passion, and Gabriel was sorry to have riled him. He laid a hand on Dmitri's shoulder, hoping to soothe him. Dmitri jerked away from him as if he were hexed, and Gabriel guessed he'd better do some fence-mending quickly. He didn't want to lose Dmitri as an ally.

"I'm sorry, Dmitri. I really didn't mean any disrespect. I think the Madrigals are very special ladies. And they're obviously good at their work. And—well, if they're blessed by all of those saints, I reckon they're in the right profession."

Dmitri gave him a hard stare that lasted several seconds and made him uncomfortable. At last, though, the little man relaxed and nodded. A patron walked up and presented a ticket at that moment, and Gabriel wondered if some saint was hovering over his own paltry soul at the moment, to have distracted the Madrigals' factotum so well in this particular instance.

But no. From what Gabriel had seen of it, life seemed to be a bundle of chances, in which things happened by accident, and for which there was no rhyme or reason. If God had created it in the first place, He'd evidently abdicated any responsibility for running it afterwards.

He remained with Dmitri, chatting, hoping to spread more balm on the small fellow's wounded spirits—and rebuild his own image in Dmitri's eyes—until midnight rolled around—his appointed time.

His heart gave a quick kick as he rose, fished his appointment card out of his vest pocket, and showed it to Dmitri. He winked down at the Russian. "Wish me luck."

Without a flicker of frivolity, Dmitri nodded. "Good luck to you."

And, on that solemn note, Gabriel entered the parlor.

Chapter Eight

Sophie pressed a hand over her eyes, and wished it were time for them to quit. She knew she ought to be grateful to Dmitri for drumming up so much business, but she was feeling mighty tired at the moment.

As much as she hated to admit it, reading palms and cards and the crystal ball took a good deal of psychic energy, if only because she tried to read the personalities of the people she met with so as not to make unfortunate mistakes. Once, she'd predicted a child for a respectable spinster lady who'd taken exception. Ever since, Sophie had tried her best to concentrate, but it was exhausting work. Occasionally, too, she wondered if the respectable spinster lady had ended up with a child somehow, but she didn't dwell on it; there was no way to find out.

They'd done a good job on the room, she had to grant, even if Gabriel had helped. The cranberry globes on the oil lamps cast a soft pinkish gleam over everything, and she and Juniper always used a lot of crimson and black velvet to create a mood. The mob gobbled up such trash like candy. Sophie sighed and wished the night were over.

A screen separated her from Juniper, so she didn't even have the solace of conversation with her sweet aunt in between customers. Not that there was much time to converse. If she'd brought Tybalt's basket, she'd at least have had him to pet. But, as much as she loved Tybalt, he distracted the customers and was so adorable and ugly that Juniper feared he'd detract from the aura of mystery and intrigue they tried so hard to convey. So Sophie hadn't brought him, and now she was stuck with nobody but herself for companionship as the gullible flock poured in to hear their futures.

Sophie gave an internal snort. As if it made any difference. Whatever was going to happen was going to happen. Nobody in her entire family had foreseen Joshua's death, and if there was anything to fortune-telling, it should have been obvious to any of them. *All* of them. Frauds. They were all frauds. Except Juniper.

The door opened, she looked up, and there stood Gabriel Caine, hat in hand, grinning at her. She sighed. She might have guessed he'd do something like this. With one of her better scowls, she asked bluntly, "What do *you* want?"

Gabriel held up his appointment card. "I'm legitimate, Sophie. I've paid my way in, and I expect to get the business. You do aim to service me, don't you?"

The lecherous rogue. "You're not being particularly subtle, Gabriel. I hope you know that." She wished she didn't experience that silly spurt of gratification every time he made a suggestive remark. He'd probably act exactly the same if she were a two-headed ape. Maybe not.

"Yup. I sure do." He strode over as if he owned the

world and everything in it, tossed his hat aside, and sat in the chair across from her. A crystal ball was perched on an ebony stand between them on a table spread with a crimson cloth. It was a lovely ball and a lovely cloth, but at the moment, both seemed ludicrous props to Sophie.

Still scowling, she said, "Do you want the cards read, your palm read, or would you prefer that I consult the crystal ball?" Now there, she thought, was something heavy to heave at him. It would be like playing tenpins. She shook her head, trying to banish the sudden gruesome vision that had sprung up in it.

Gabriel pretended—at least, it looked like pretending to Sophie—to think for a moment. "Do you know something, Sophie? I've had a terrible longing for you to hold my hand for the longest time now. Why don't you read my palm?"

"My aunt read your palm the first day we met you, Gabriel. Why don't I read the crystal ball?"

"I want you to read my hand. It'll give me an idea whether or not to believe this stuff, if you both tell me the same thing."

"That's silly. I was there. I might remember what she said."

"Not you. You were so damned mad, you were deliberately not listening to anything she said." He grinned his devil's grin.

She cast an exasperated glance at the ceiling and hoped he'd choke on it. "Very well. Hand it over."

Gabriel's grin broadened. "So to speak." He held his hand out to her.

For the briefest moment, Sophie hesitated. She didn't want to touch him. For that one tiny moment, she was almost blinded by the knowledge that if she allowed herself to get any closer to Gabriel Caine, she'd never be able to disentangle herself.

136

Lord, Lord, this was terrible.

However, there was no point in hesitating further. If their lives were destined to be snarled up with each other, she supposed there was no stopping it. As little as Sophie believed in foretelling the future, still less did she believe that one could buck the fates. They'd get you if you were in their sights, and there was no escaping them. Psychic bonds decreed by fate had nothing to do with crystal balls or palm-reading, blast it.

She took his hand. Instantly, her head filled with light, and vision upon vision sped through her mind's eye. She and Gabriel. She and Joshua. She and Juniper and Gabriel. She and Juniper and Gabriel and Joshua. Ivo Hardwick. Herself. Gabriel. Joshua in that tiny little casket they'd crafted for him before they lowered him into the cold earth and shoveled dirt on top of him. Sophie crying. And crying. And crying. She shut her eyes because she didn't want Gabriel to know how much his touch this evening, in her mystical milieu, was affecting her.

Good heavens, she really did have a connection with this man; this man who had vowed to keep her from achieving her life's one goal.

She didn't know how long she'd been sitting there, holding Gabriel's hand and not speaking, when his voice filtered through her tangled thoughts, pushing the brilliant visions aside. They twinkled on the sidelines like multi-colored exclamation points as he spoke.

"Um, Sophie, I like having you hold my hand, but you can't read it if you don't look at it, can you?"

Ruthlessly suppressing her visions, Sophie opened her eyes. She even managed a frigid smile. "Indeed. I was acclimating myself to your body."

His eyebrows rose, making him look almost boyishly eager. Oh, this wasn't fair! It wasn't fair that he should be so absolutely perfect in all aspects of masculine beauty.

"I can think of better ways to do that, sweetheart. And if you're interested, I'll be more than happy to oblige."

"Don't be disgusting." She kept her voice as cold as ice, even as her body heated alarmingly.

He sighed. "It was worth a try."

"Be quiet. I have to concentrate."

"I thought you didn't believe in this stuff."

"Hush!" She believed in some of her family's gifts, all right, even when she didn't want to. The truth was unavoidable, as she'd discovered long ago.

"Yes, ma'am."

Drawing Gabriel's hand closer to the oil lamp burning low on the table beside her, Sophie bent her head to peer more closely into it. She smoothed her finger lightly over the warm skin of his palm, noting with interest that his hand was a combination of the spatulate and the conical, just as Juniper had told him that day on the train.

Hmmm. Perhaps Juniper was right about him and what she perceived as a spiritual bent to his psyche, although it seemed seemed unlikely to Sophie. She still wouldn't trust him if her life depended on it. Nevertheless, she supposed it was possible that under his brash and overbearing exterior, there did actually lurk a hint of spirituality.

Curious, she said, "Didn't you once say you were involved in the revivalist movement when you were young?"

"What does that have to do with my palm?"

Startled by the rough quality that had invaded his voice, Sophie glanced at him. "I only asked because I noticed a certain inward tendency in the shape of your hand that seems at variance both with your professed business and the personality you show to the world."

"Yeah? Like how?"

She shrugged slightly. "Oh, well, the shape is indicative of one who does a good deal of introspection, who is interested in something besides the physicality of life." She expected him to snicker, but he didn't, so she went on. "One generally finds hands shaped like yours attached to the arms of scholars or philosophers. Or ministers, I suppose." Bowing her head over his hand again, she wondered if he'd say anything now.

He did. "My father was a minister."

"I see." She left it at that, sensing he wasn't eager to speak about his past. Which, all things considered, made his interest in her own past more than a trifle hypocritical.

"Maybe I inherited the shape from him."

"Mmmm." She peered more closely and gently manipulated the fingers. Flexible. But not too flexible. Still, they were more flexible than Sophie had anticipated. He was such a pigheaded man, she'd expected to find them crafted of stone. She gently pulled his thumb back and felt resistance. So, she was right in part. He was a strong-willed son of a gun. "What about your mother?"

"What about my mother?" Again, his voice grated harshly.

"Was she also called to the ministry? Believe me, I understand how conflicts can arise when one person feels called by the Almighty to something and his or her partner doesn't." Her own parents had showed her that, to everyone's unhappiness.

This time he shrugged. "I think they were both drawn by the same glorious vision of saving the world and its inhabitants from eternal damnation." His voice had gone from wryly grating to as dry as old bones.

"They didn't quarrel over your father's ministry?"

"What the hell does that have to do with my palm?"

She looked up quickly. "My, my, aren't we touchy this evening?"

"My parents don't have squat to do with my palm, Sophie, and you know it. You're only trying to avoid reading it."

"I am not, and I do not know it. You inherited everything you are from your parents, including your palm. And your attitudes, one presumes."

"That's a load of horse poop. My father would roll over in his grave if he saw me now."

Gazing into his deep, dark eyes, she sensed he wished he hadn't said that. She let it go without a word and leaned over to gaze at his palm some more. "The lines are deeply etched and clearly defined. You're not a vacillating type of man, Gabriel Caine, and you're definitely a worldly one, whatever meager spiritual tendencies you might possess."

"Hmph. I could have told you that without your having to look at my palm."

"Ah, but you paid me to do this." She smiled. All at once, she felt not half bad about having to read this particular palm. If they really and truly did have some sort of preordained connection with each other, the more she knew about him, the better. Besides, this was giving her a sense of power over him that she'd never experienced before. She liked it.

He had calluses on his palms. "You do whatever it takes to get a job done, don't you?" This was an aspect of her own personality, as well, and Sophie considered it small wonder that she and Gabriel should clash, since they wanted wholly different things from the same source.

"I expect I do." He sounded noncommittal.

She didn't press the issue. "The temperature of your palms is warm."

"Getting warmer every second."

She glanced up at him, her lips pinching. She decided to ignore his implication. "Your health appears to be good." *That's* what a fine, warm palm meant, blast him.

"Glad to hear it."

She spent a good deal of time on his thumbs. Thumbs were good indicators of a person's overall personality—if, of course, one believed in this sort of rubbish. Unfortunately, this evening Sophie discovered she was fascinated by it. "You have a definite stubborn streak," she said easily, unsurprised.

"Hmph."

"But you're fairly generous."

"Only fairly?"

She heard a laugh in his voice and decided to ignore it. She wiggled his thumb, then drew it down and away from his forefinger. "Hmmm," she murmured. "Compassion. How strange."

"You're only irked to find any good qualities in me, Sophie. Admit it."

In spite of herself, she smiled. "Perhaps." She spread his hand on the table in front of her. Their heads almost touched as they both bent over to study his fingers. "I should say your fingers are predominantly spatulate," she said musingly.

"That sounds bad."

"It's not bad, really. It merely indicates generosity, practicality, and maybe a touch of inventiveness."

"That sounds good."

She glanced up, and found herself staring into his magnificent eyes. "Yes, I should say those were good qualities for a person to possess." She had to lick her lips to get them to move far enough apart for the words to come out. She glanced down again quickly. Mercy, but he was a handsome man. "Um, and now let's take a look at the mounts."

141

"Let's."

His voice had gone soft and husky. Sophie had to close her eyes for a moment to gather her wits. She had a mad urge to fling his hand aside, grab him, kiss him, and beg him to make mad, passionate love to her. This was awful. She hadn't found it so difficult to suppress her carnal urges for years. Decades.

"I notice that your Mount of Apollo—"

"I think that's the one I couldn't find when Miss Juniper tried to teach me this stuff."

Grateful for a reprieve in humor, Sophie chuckled. "Yes, I can understand why you might have believed it to be missing. But you see here? It's only a little closer to the pinkie finger than some are. That means you're more interested in the practical side of artistic pursuits than in pure art." Taking a chance, she glanced up again, and was wildly relieved to see that he was frowning down at his palm.

"Oh, is that what that means?"

"Indeed. Personally, I'm not surprised." She wondered if he'd make anything of that, and realized she was once again enjoying herself. Hugely. This was probably a very bad thing, but she couldn't seem to care much at the moment.

He made a funny face, as if he were thinking about his cockeyed Mount of Apollo and its implications. "Yeah, I guess I'm not surprised, either. In fact, I reckon it makes sense. I could be a business manager without much trouble at all. I've even thought about it."

Wouldn't that be nice? Sophie thought at once. To have the capable, levelheaded Gabriel Caine overseeing their business?

Good God, what was she thinking?

Snatching her wandering brain back from the pit over which it teetered, Sophie said, "Yes, it shows here." She tapped his palm. "Now here," she said pressing the fleshy spot beneath his pinkie, "we see your Mount of Mercury. Yours is developed quite fully, I notice."

"Is that good?" He sounded doubtful.

"It's not bad. It means you're quick-witted and express yourself well."

"Is that so?"

"Mmmm. You needn't sound so proud of yourself. I'm sure you inherited both qualities from your father. If he went around saving the world and its occupants from eternal damnation, he must have had a glib tongue."

"And *you* needn't sound so sarcastic. My father was a good man, even if he did believe in a few ideas that I consider hogwash."

Which pretty much expressed Sophie's attitude about her own father. Interesting. "Yes, well, let's move along here."

"Let's get to the interesting part. Isn't there something about passion and lust in there somewhere?"

Sophie found herself suddenly reluctant to look at him again. She also discovered herself getting warm and squirmy. Her own passionate, lusty nature had been her downfall, and she could barely contain her eagerness to see what Gabriel's palm said about his. If they were each as passionate as the other, the rest of her quest to find and kill Ivo Hardwick might at least be interesting.

Mercy, she wished she could fan herself. She wouldn't give Gabriel the satisfaction of knowing he'd flustered her, however, and merely said, "We're getting there. There are many aspects to a person's life other than lust and passion. Aspects that endure longer and are more important." She added that last part with a smug bite to her voice that she didn't necessarily feel.

"Maybe. But I figure you might as well enjoy the fun

stuff while you can. After all, a person's body is only young once."

"Yes." She felt sad all at once, thinking of Joshua, who would be young forever. "Yes, I suppose that's true."

"All right. Go on. What else does my palm tell you about me? So far, you know, you haven't predicted anything. All you've done is tell me about myself, which I could have done."

She tutted, trying to get her sense of humor back. Joshua clung to her mental processes, as he'd clung to her in life, and the task was a hard one. She concentrated on Gabriel's hand, and began to feel a little better. She poked the space below Gabriel's middle finger. "Now here," she said, "your Mount of Saturn lies fallow. You see? There's no mound there."

He leaned over and stared at his palm. "Holy God, what does that mean?"

She laughed, genuinely diverted and glad for the easing of her own spirits. "You needn't be worried, Gabriel. That only means that you're neither a drunken sot nor a disagreeable sobersides."

"Whew." He glanced up at her and grinned. "You had me worried there for a minute."

"Indeed. As well you should be, I'm sure." She poked the spot again. "However, if you had a large and fleshy mound here, you would probably be a morbid, reclusive individual. Obviously, you aren't."

"True, true."

"And if it were large and hard to the touch, you'd probably be a disagreeable, hard-headed person. Now *that*, I must say, wouldn't have surprised me."

"I'm not disagreeable. I'm charming. You're the disagreeable one."

Oh, Lord, he was right. She smiled sweetly. "I do try to be." With a flutter of her eyelashes, she went back to studying his palm. She was gratified by his laugh.

Now came the tricky part. "All right." She feigned aggravated forbearance. "I suppose we must move on to the Mount of Venus."

"Is this the good part?"

"They're all good parts," she said severely.

"I don't know. When I'm alone with you, I think this one is apt to be the most interesting."

She glanced at him sharply. "None of that, Gabriel Caine. This is serious business."

"Balderdash."

"Hmmm. Well, you paid, so you're going to get it."

"I wish that were true."

She smacked his wrist. "Will you stop that? I have to concentrate."

He grinned evilly. "I'm just too much of a man for you, aren't I, Sophie? You want me. Admit it."

Never. No matter how right she feared he was. "We're getting down to business now, so I ask that you be serious." She spoke in her most aloof tone. "Let's look at your Mount of Venus."

"Let's."

She wanted to sigh, but didn't dare. She wished he'd just let her speak and be done with it. But no. He was going to make it difficult for her. Of course. No surprise there. She bent to her task and pretended she wasn't more interested than she wanted to be. His Mount of Venus was as well-developed as she'd expected it to be. She waited a few seconds while she tried to think of unprovocative words with which to express her findings.

She pressed the base of his thumb. "All right. You obviously have a zest for life and appreciate its infinite variety."

"You've got that right."

"But," she added with some amazement, "you're not

145

a blatant sensualist. You live within limits."

"You sound shocked."

She gave him a short glare. "I am."

"I'm not as bad as you think I am, Sophie."

"I already know that's not true."

"What does your Mount of Venus show?"

"We aren't talking about me." She was getting testy. This wasn't going well anymore, and she wanted it to end.

"Hogwash. I want to see your palm."

She snatched her hand away and put it behind her back. "You leave me alone, Gabriel Caine."

He watched her, those brilliant eyes of his twinkling like stars, for what seemed like an eternity. Then he shrugged and sat back, leaving his hand, palm up, on the table. "Never mind. I'll find out all about you one of these days."

She sniffed.

"Oh, I will, Sophie. I promise you that. I'm a determined fellow, remember?"

"I'm determined, too."

"Yeah, but I'm bigger than you are."

"You'd never force a woman." She said it scornfully, because she knew it to be true. Then she wished she hadn't said it at all.

"I won't have to force you."

"This is preposterous." She started to rise, but he forestalled her with a snake-quick extension of his arm, grabbing her wrist.

"No, you don't. I've got—let me see here." Still holding onto her wrist, he withdrew a silver pocket watch from his vest pocket and squinted at it. "Twenty minutes left."

"Twenty minutes? But that's longer than—"

"I paid for two appointments. I get a whole hour."

She sank back into the chair. "You would have."

He only grinned.

"All right, but you have to sit still and promise to stop being so—so—"

"Tantalizing?" he suggested.

"Ludicrous, was more what I was thinking."

"I don't believe you."

She huffed and tipped her head so that she was again leaning over his palm. He lowered his head, too, and soon the tops of their heads were almost touching. Smoothing her fingers over his palm, she said, "We really ought to compare your two hands. You're right-handed."

"Ah, you noticed."

She clucked. "Of course I noticed. This is my business."

"Hmmm." He sounded as if he knew very well she hadn't noticed because it was her business, but because she was interested. And he was probably right, damn him.

Nevertheless, he placed his left hand on the table, palm up, for her to compare with his right. Goodness, he had interesting hands. Sophie thought it was most unfair of him to be utterly fascinating in every detail. With an inward sigh, she lifted both of his hands and gazed into them, comparing the lines of each. "You don't need anyone to prod you into doing what needs to be done."

He didn't speak.

"Your life's achievements thus far don't match your life's potential, but there are clear indications that this will change."

"What was it that poet said? The saddest words are *it might have been*?"

She gave him a sharp glance, but could read nothing in his expression. "Yes, well, it doesn't appear from here that you'll experience that particular sadness, although so far, you haven't achieved anywhere near your potential."

"Potential," repeated Gabriel, as if the word tasted bad.

She laid his left hand back on the tabletop and stared closely at his right. He had a pronounced Girdle of Venus, but she was reluctant to point it out since he'd undoubtedly make some kind of suggestive comment. Her hand began to tingle where it touched his, but she didn't release it.

His Line of Destiny tantalized her. It was so distinct and clear. Not like hers, which was broken in two—just like her. Of course, hers picked up again, but it was linked with something else she hadn't been able to put a finger on yet. A faint alarm stirred within her. Perhaps she was linked with Gabriel Caine? Is that what her Line of Destiny foretold?

No. That was too absurd.

Yet she couldn't stop staring at Gabriel's palm and thinking—and wondering.

Almost against her will, she looked at the line indicating the possibility of marriage and children. She was again surprised. Indeed, she was almost shocked. There, as if the Almighty had carved it out of granite, was the deepest, firmest marriage line she'd ever seen. And children. Good heavens, Sophie could hardly feature Gabriel Caine as a father. Yet his palm indicated great and abiding happiness in family and love.

Which again showed how futile all of this palm-reading and card-reading was. Her own marriage and family line showed the same things, and look what had happened to her.

Without her being aware of it, silence had filled the room during the past several minutes. Silence and a sweet fragrance, almost like the incense her aunt Juniper loved so well. Sophie lifted Gabriel's palm closer to the lamp, which glowed a soft rose under its cranberry globe and made his hand look perfect, as if it had been sculpted by Michelangelo centuries earlier.

"What do you see there?" he asked, his voice not breaking the spell so much as blending into it.

"Interesting," she murmured.

She was neither alarmed nor surprised when Gabriel's hand kept lifting, without her prompting, and cupped her cheek. Her own hand covered his, and she responded to the faint pressure of his fingers and lifted her head to look into his eyes. Oh, his eyes. They were the most wonderful eyes she'd ever seen.

"You're a very beautiful woman, Sophie," Gabriel said, his voice a whisper that brushed the back of her hand and made gooseflesh rise on her arms.

She couldn't speak. The room had become thick with something deliciously seductive.

"What's your story, I wonder," he went on. "I know you won't tell me."

She shook her head the tiniest bit, and very slowly.

"But I want to know, and I will know. Some day."

Again, she shook her head. Oh, those eyes of his were wicked. They drew her like a siren's song or an angel's harp, made her feel as if all she had to do to achieve lifelong peace was succumb to their lure.

She knew better.

Knowing better didn't seem to be helping at the moment. Doing so without her compliance, her face drew closer to his as if compelled by a force stronger than her. Or him. Or the both of them together.

"Sophie," he whispered.

When his lips covered hers, Sophie felt as if the one thing she'd been missing all her life had just been given to her. She felt complete. A sensation of fullness engulfed her, of happiness all at odds with her situation and her life until now. This was one perfect instant in time, and she wished she could die now because she knew, even though her thought processes had ceased functioning, that life would never be this sweet again.

He deepened the kiss, his warm tongue moistening her lips before it gently pressed between them and entered her mouth. Sophie writhed slightly in her chair. The sweet fragrance she'd barely noticed a few minutes earlier seemed to have filled the room. It wasn't cloying or sickly, but beautiful. Perfect. Alluring. She didn't know what the fragrance was—sandalwood and jasmine and gardenias and orange blossoms and all the sweet things in the world combined.

"Sweet Jesus," Gabriel murmured, and he stood up, breaking the kiss.

Sophie blinked up at him, fuddled. He didn't give her time to recover or become embarrassed, but with two great strides, came around the table, pulled her out of her chair, and clasped her in his arms.

Never in her life had she experienced anything like this.

"I want you, Sophie. I want you."

His voice grated in the air, displacing a little of the fragrance and adding something smoky and dark to the atmosphere. Whatever it was he added, it fit somehow. Absolutely. Sophie didn't say a word. There was nothing to say. The moment was immaculate all by itself. She felt the hardness of his masculinity pressing against her thigh, and relished the knowledge that he did want her. Badly. As she wanted him.

"Sophie, dear, do you—Oh!"

Sophie felt drugged when Gabriel released her. She staggered back a step, and was only prevented from falling over by Gabriel's strong arm, which held her upright. Aunt Juniper stood at the curtain separating the two halves of the parlor, her hand clutching the drape, her eyes wide and staring.

"Oh, my goodness, I didn't mean to interrupt," Juniper twittered. "Only I began to smell that odd, sweet smell, Sophie. The one that means there's true magic in the . . ."

Sophie glanced up at Gabriel, who looked as if he'd been caught poaching on the king's preserves. He licked his lips, shook himself slightly, and recovered. Damn him. He would.

"I beg your pardon, Miss Juniper. I reckon Miss Sophie and I got a little carried away in here. It was my fault," he added chivalrously. If Sophie had been in a less muddled condition, she'd have snorted.

Juniper shook her head. "I do wish I hadn't interrupted. You two were meant for each other, you know."

Gabriel gazed blankly at her.

Sophie, trying with all her fuzzed strength to compose herself, spat out, "Tripe!"

Chapter Nine

"But Sophie, I mean it."

"I know you do, Aunt Juniper." Sophie stuffed her crystal ball into its red velvet sleeve and yanked the drawstrings up violently.

"You *are* meant for each other. I knew it the moment I saw Mr. Caine on the train."

"Tripe," Sophie said for the fourth or fifth time.

Juniper sighed and tidied her deck of Tarot cards. She was using her specially painted deck this evening. Anything to give the natives a thrill, Sophie thought cynically.

Oh, that kiss! She paused in her stuffing and yanking and tidying and shut her eyes for a moment as remembered sensations washed over her.

It wasn't fair. Nothing about this whole situation was fair. Why had Gabriel Caine come into her life? And why now, of all times, if he had to come into it at all?

Juniper stamped her little foot, startling Sophie into

opening her eyes. She picked up her own Tarot deck, one bought from an occultist in St. Louis. It was nowhere near as fine as Juniper's, and Sophie didn't care as she jammed it into her traveling kit. Juniper had embroidered the kit with occult symbols and signs of the Zodiac. Sophie considered it merely another trapping of her trade.

"You know as well as I do that the mystical incense doesn't show up for just any old reason, Sophie Madrigal! There was real magic in the air tonight, and it was generated by you and Mr. Caine. Together."

Perceiving there would be no arguing with Juniper on this subject—or, rather, that if she argued, she'd be doing so all night—Sophie said, "Very well. Mr. Caine and I make magic together. Let's go to bed."

Unfortunately, what Juniper said was the truth. Sophie wished it weren't, and had no idea how she was going to fight it until she'd achieved her goal. Fight it she must, however, and she'd figure out some way to do it.

"Oh, Sophie." Juniper sounded close to despair. "I wish life hadn't damaged you so badly."

"It wasn't life," Sophie ground out. "It was Ivo Hardwick. And I'll soon take care of him."

Juniper moaned and fluttered through the door of the parlor behind Sophie. Sophie was neither happy nor unhappy to see Gabriel there, sitting next to Dmitri, chatting as if the kiss they'd shared hadn't been the most shattering event of his life. Which, she thought sourly, it unquestionably hadn't been. She and Gabriel might make magic together—according to Juniper— but apparently Sophie was the only one who felt it.

Which figured. Sometimes Sophie thought life had been out to get her from the moment of her birth.

Gabriel rose, as did Dmitri, but before anyone could speak, a tall man strode toward Sophie. He had a fatuous smile on his face, although he was a fairly hand-some specimen of the gender. He looked vaguely familiar.

Ah, yes. Sophie remembered him. He'd come in earlier in the evening, accompanied by his wife, a plain, mousy woman, who had obviously worshiped her husband. Sophie'd told them a lot of bilge about their happy future together and how strong and smart their children would be.

It pained her, but she smiled at him, trying as she did so to recall his name. Oh, yes. She remembered now. Patterson.

"Miss Madrigal," Patterson said, sweeping a low bow.

Sophie's nose wrinkled at this show of bravado, and she made an effort to smooth it out. "Mr. Patterson, is it?"

He rose from his bow like a courtier, and gave another, smaller bow, to Aunt Juniper. "It is indeed, ma'am."

Silence. Sophie glanced at Gabriel, who was frowning at the newcomer. Juniper smiled at Mr. Patterson, her innocent heart seeing nothing but a friendly Tucson resident come to pay his respects at this odd hour of the night. Sophie had a feeling she knew why Patterson was here, but she hoped she was wrong. She waited.

"Er," Patterson said into the silence, "I knew you were going to be finished around this time, and I—well, I thought you might consider spending part of the evening with me, Miss Madrigal."

Taken slightly aback by this bold approach—as a rule, these unprincipled brutes sidled up to a proposition, taking their time about it, trying to pretend they weren't after one thing. Sophie said, "I—beg your pardon?"

"Oh," said Juniper, with one of her ingenuous smiles, "do you know each other, Sophie? I didn't realize. Well, do have a good time." She tripped lightly off, serenely oblivious to what seemed obvious to Sophie were Patterson's sinister motives. Well, she could pretend oblivion, too.

She tilted her head slightly to one side. "I don't believe I understand, Mr. Patterson. Do you and your wife—" She emphasized that word. "—wish to consult with me some more? I believe I gave you a rather thorough reading earlier in the evening, and I'm a little tired now."

"Consult with you?" Patterson gave a hearty laugh that sounded a bit strained to Sophie's keen ears. "Don't be silly, my dear Miss Madrigal."

Silly, was she? Irritated, she stiffened. "What, exactly, do you want from me, then, Mr. Patterson?" She wanted him to say it. Right here. In front of Gabriel Caine and God Almighty. She wanted Gabriel to know what she had to endure in her life. And this was nothing compared to what she'd already endured.

"Come, come, my dear. You're a lovely woman. I'm sure you do more than merely tell fortunes for your keep." He winked at her.

Before Sophie could concoct a suitably cutting response to this salacious piece of nonsense, Mr. Patterson was suddenly jerked around, rattling Sophie into a start of surprise. Then a fist struck him, square on the chin, and sent him toppling over. Sophie had to jump aside or be flattened by his falling body.

"Get up," Gabriel growled, standing over Patterson like an avenging angel, his hands bunched into fists the size and general shape of hams. "Get up, you bastard, so I can finish killing you."

Pressing a hand to her thumping heart, Sophie said, "Good Lord, you hit him."

"I'm going to hit him again."

"No, please don't. Just come away."

155

"Dammit, Sophie, that man can't say things like that to you. I won't let him."

From the floor of the hotel lobby, Mr. Patterson groaned. Sophie glanced at Dmitri, who shrugged philosophically, then returned his attention to the prostrate Patterson.

Sophie took Gabriel's arm. It felt like iron under her hand. "Please, Gabriel, come away. Don't make any more of a scene."

"Me?" Gabriel whirled and stared furiously at Sophie. "Did you hear what that man said to you?"

"Of course I heard him!" She was getting peeved. "I've heard it before, and I'll most assuredly hear it again. You don't seem to realize that people in my line of work are fair game to predatory fiends like this man." In case Gabriel wondered which man she was talking about, she nudged Patterson with the toe of her boot. Hard. He groaned again.

"But that's not fair!" Gabriel looked appalled.

A bitter sense of gratification twisted in Sophie's heart. "You finally figured that out for yourself, did you?"

"Here, what's going on here?"

Apparently drawn by the loud voices, the night clerk rushed up to Gabriel, Dmitri, and Sophie. He gaped at Mr. Patterson, then leaned over and tried to help him rise, patting his coat sleeves and front as he did so, as if attempting to remove a film of dust. "Here, sir, please, what happened?"

"Don't waste your time on him," Gabriel said roughly. "He made an improper suggestion to Miss Madrigal, and I hit him. And I'll do it again, too."

A bit curious as to how the night clerk would respond to this—Sophie had seen him eyeing her lasciviously more than once—she shifted her red velvet bag and traveling kit so that their weight was distributed more evenly, and waited. She wasn't surprised at what she heard.

"You mean Mr. Patterson here—uh—he—"

"Dammit, he made an improper advance toward Miss Madrigal," Gabriel shouted.

Mercy sakes. A man had never stood as Sophie's champion before. She wasn't sure what to make of it. Especially as the champion in this instance was Gabriel Caine. It was all vaguely interesting. Even flattering, she guessed.

"She's a little tart." Patterson now stood, albeit unsteadily, and he leaned heavily on the night clerk's shoulder. "I figured she wouldn't mind." He uttered a small shriek when Gabriel drew his fist back to punch him again.

The night clerk forestalled more violence by jerking Patterson aside. Gabriel's swing clipped the suited man on the shoulder and staggered him, but he didn't go down again.

"Please, sir, desist," the night clerk said sternly. "This is no way to behave in a respectable hotel."

"There was nothing," Gabriel said in measured, dangerous tones, "respectable about what that man said to Miss Madrigal."

"Well, now," the clerk said, equivocating for all he was worth, "I reckon he got the wrong idea or something." He gave Sophie a look that spoke clearly of his own idea about her morals. "She's a—well, she reads palms and such, sir. You can't blame a gent for—"

"You stupid son of a bitch." Gabriel took a step toward the night clerk, who drew back instantly and looked scared to death. "After I kill him, I'll kill you. You bastard son of a two-headed cow, this woman is a lady, and you will treat her as one, or I'll teach you a lesson in manners you'll never forget. Do you understand me?"

By this time, Gabriel was nose to nose with the night clerk, who was trying to use Patterson's body as a shield. Patterson muttered sourly, "I think my jaw's broken."

Gabriel turned to him. "Glad to hear it. Let me take you home and tell your wife how you managed to have such a terrible accident. I think she deserves to know what kind of a bastard she's married to."

"What? What?" Now it was Patterson who looked terrified.

Sophie could hardly believe it, but she was actually enjoying this show. She walked over to Gabriel and tapped him lightly on the shoulder. "I think you've made your point, Mr. Caine. These fellows are clearly stupid, ungentlemanly specimens, and I don't believe you need waste any more time on them." In her most lordly manner, she spoke to Dmitri. "Will you please carry my things up to my room, Dmitri?"

The little Russian gave a majestic bow, retrieved the velvet bag and traveling kit from Sophie, saluted Gabriel as if Gabriel were a general—at least—and did as Sophie had bade him. Sophie watched him for a moment, then turned to the tableau of men that seemed to be frozen in place in the hotel lobby.

She eyed Patterson with distaste. "You," she said, "are contemptible. You have a fine wife who thinks far more of you than you deserve. *You* deserve that Mr. Caine take you home in your present condition and tell your wife exactly what you did."

"But—but—but—"

Gabriel reached out a hand, grabbed Patterson by the front of his coat, and shook him. "Shut up."

Patterson shut up.

"However," Sophie went on, thinking what a perfectly timed pair she and Gabriel were tonight, "your wife would be hurt if he did that, so I recommend against it. Your wife unquestionably has enough to put up with, without having your infamous misdeeds thrown in her face."

"I guess that makes sense." Gabriel spoke reluctantly, as if he'd relished the opportunity to show Patterson up for the snake he was.

"And as for you . . ." Sophie turned abruptly to the hotel clerk, who seemed to shrink. "I have put up with your waggling eyebrows and offensive leers for entirely too long."

"What did he do?" Gabriel's roar rattled the globes on the oil lamps in the lobby.

"He has treated me with the utmost disrespect, actually."

"Why, you scrawny son of a bitch, I'll kill you." Releasing Patterson's coat front, Gabriel grabbed the night clerk, who really was scrawny, by the front of his shirt and lifted him right up from the floor. Sophie was impressed. She'd like to see Gabriel's muscles for herself but, unfortunately, they were covered by his clothes at the moment.

The night clerk's feet pumped wildly in the air, and he gurgled as he fought for air. Gabriel drew his face right smack up to his own. "If I ever hear of you doing such a thing again, you won't have to worry about making any plans for your worthless future." He shook the clerk, whose limbs reminded Sophie of those of a puppet that had been left to dangle helplessly in a high wind.

"Guhgh," the night clerk said. He'd begun to turn purple. Sophie didn't intervene. The no-good reptile deserved at least this.

"Do you understand me?"

Frantically, the clerk nodded. His eyes began to bulge.

"Good." Gabriel dropped him and he fell to the carpeted floor like a sack of sand.

Patterson had backed up a way. His nose was bleeding, and his jaw had begun to swell enormously. Sophie was pleased. He'd have some quick explaining to do to his wife when he went home this evening. The stinking rat.

"Get out of here," Gabriel said, his voice like steel. "Both of you."

Patterson glanced wildly around, searching, Sophie presumed, for the hat that had fallen off of his head when Gabriel hit him. She walked over to where she saw it lying crown up on the carpet next to a chair, and deliberately stepped on it. Right smack in the middle. "Oh, dear," she said, and stooped to pick it up. "I do believe I crushed your hat, Mr. Patterson. Perhaps your wife can fix it." Smiling sweetly, she took it over to him, noticing as she did so that he backed up as she walked forward. He was afraid of her. How satisfying. She held out the crumpled article, and he snatched it out of her hand.

Then he turned and headed for the door, saying as he went, "You're both crazy. You're a couple of lunatics."

Sophie sighed, feeling more satisfaction after a night's work than she generally felt. She turned to see the end of the hotel clerk.

"Your turn," Gabriel was telling him.

The skinny man looked petrified. "But—but—I got a job here. I can't leave."

Gabriel took a step toward him. "Oh, yes, you can."

Sophie decided intervention in this instance would be to her advantage. After all, she didn't want the hotel to be robbed or anything because two men had mistaken her for a trollop. She walked up to Gabriel and laid a hand on his arm. Tingling warmth ran up her arm from her fingertips where she touched him to her head. This took her slightly aback, but she continued. She already knew that they were psychically linked somehow. The problem was not to show it. Therefore, she said calmly, "The idiot is right, Mr. Caine. He does have a job to perform. And, if he doesn't do it very well, I don't suppose it's up to us to send him packing. I'm sure the owner of this establishment will discover one day that this fellow is a fool."

Gabriel had been glowering ferociously at the night clerk. He turned his glower on Sophie. "But you said—"

"I know what I said. I said he leered at me. He did. That, however, is an aspect of my profession that I have become accustomed to. Men often behave as base creatures. He's merely more base than most."

The night clerk stammered, "I—I—didn't mean—I mean—"

"Oh, do be quiet," Sophie said, her voice dripping disgust. "I know exactly what you meant, and so does Mr. Caine. You're a contemptible animal, and I don't want to listen to you any more."

"Well," said Gabriel, and Sophie noticed that the muscles in his arms relaxed slightly. "If you really think it's better to let the ass go . . ."

"I do." She nodded.

"It goes against the grain." Gabriel released him.

The night clerk clambered to his feet and scampered to the registration desk, where he proceeded to try to hide.

Sophie was left with Gabriel, alone, in the hotel lobby. She looked up at him and smiled. He looked down at her and smiled.

"Thank you, Gabriel. That was very dashing and noble of you."

He shrugged. "They made me mad, is all." A frown

161

creased his brow. "Do you have to put up with that sort of thing very often?"

"All the time, I fear."

He shook his head. "You need a business manager."

"Nonsense. I can take care of us." Because she didn't want him to think his offices went unappreciated, she added, "Although, I truly do appreciate your stepping in tonight. It's rather nice to have a champion."

His breathing was heavy, and he still looked angry. Sophie had to admit—to herself—that she'd been genuinely impressed, both by his quickness to act and by his boldness. She'd often felt like belting rude men, but she'd never done it. She felt more charitable toward Gabriel Caine than she had since she'd met him—even more than when they'd shared that incredible kiss. After all, she was only human; she knew she had needs that she tried to suppress most of the time.

But his stepping in to prevent the odious Mr. Patterson's advances had touched her heart.

She was sure this wasn't a good thing, but she had a hard time caring at the moment. She held her hand out to him. "Thank you very much, Gabriel. I never would have expected such a thing from you."

He grimaced. "I'm sure *that's* true. That's because you don't know me."

Oh, yes, she did. She considered it prudent not to say so. He finally took her hand so that she could shake it with proper gratitude. Then he didn't let it go. Sophie frowned up at him. She was about to say something cutting, about him being cut of the same cloth as Patterson and the nonsensical hotel clerk, when he spoke first.

"You really don't know me, Sophie. Not really. But you will one of these days. I promise."

Since she'd already decided on a prudent course of action—which definitely didn't include getting to know

Gabriel Caine any better—Sophie decided to stick to it. She only murmured, "We'll see. But I truly do appreciate what you did tonight."

"Let me see you to your room."

"Thank you, but it's only at the top of the staircase. I'm sure I shan't be molested on the way." She gave him her most superior glare to put him off, knowing as she did so that it probably wouldn't work.

It worked to a degree. He grinned as if he didn't care how superior she pretended to be and said, "Maybe not, but I'm going to wait here until I know you're safe."

The excitement of the past several minutes had disguised her fatigue, but it hit her now, full-force. So she didn't protest, but only bowed her head, giving him leave, and said, "Very well." She added, "Thank you," again to be polite. Lord, she wanted her bed.

She felt his gaze drilling into her back as she walked up the stairs. It felt like infinitesimal pinpricks of light or, perhaps, fire, penetrating her clothes, whalebone and all, and dancing with tiny burning feet against her skin. How heavenly it would be to undress, climb into a soft, warm bed, and be engulfed by those strong arms of his. To feel them all over her body.

But that sort of thing wasn't in the cards—Tarot or otherwise—for Sophie Madrigal, and she knew it. With a soft humph of derision for herself, she turned at the top of the staircase and gave a little wave in Gabriel's direction. He stood directly at the foot of the stairs, looking up at her, his beautiful eyes hot and powerful and compelling. As she turned, Sophie put the hand she'd waved at him with against her cheek, and felt hot moisture.

Good God, she was crying. She must be more tired than she knew. Noiselessly, she walked down the hallway to the room she shared with Juniper. As she passed Dmitri's room she heard a soft "Psst."

Turning, she saw Dmitri's door about an inch ajar. When she glanced down, she saw the small Russian's nose protruding from the crack at the level of his face. Glancing back to make sure Gabriel hadn't followed her up the stairs, motivated by some misguided knightly impulse—she'd acquitted him of vile motives this evening, although she reserved the right to think ill of him later—she stooped so that she could hear what Dmitri wanted to say.

He didn't say much, but handed her a slip of paper. Then he whispered, "Mr. Huffy, he come by."

"Oh." Her heart stumbled once, then raced. "Did you speak to him?"

She saw the little man nod. "I go and make tickets for train tomorrow morning."

"My goodness." Lord, she appreciated Dmitri. He was so efficient. "Thank you so much, Dmitri."

Dmitri opened the door a fraction of an inch wider. "Tomorrow. Noon. Train go."

She thought about asking where the tickets were going to take them, but imagined the information would be printed on the note he'd handed her. She whispered, "Thank you, Dmitri. You're a wonder."

He nodded once, backed up a step, and closed his door. She almost ran the last few steps to her own room. As soon as she set foot inside it, she unfolded the note. Blast, it was too dark to read the bloody thing.

In her excitement about the note, she'd forgotten all about Tybalt, but he hadn't forgotten her. She'd no sooner taken a step away from the door than he whined at her, and she realized her single-mindedness had led her to ignore him. And he didn't deserve to be ignored. He was like Joshua—naive and perfect and precious and unschooled in the arts of deception or fraud.

So she spent a good minute or two greeting her happy pug, who licked and slurped her and made her smile. How wonderful dogs were. They were always so happy to see you, no matter how horrid a human being you were. At last Tybalt waddled back over to his own fuzzy rug on the floor at the foot of her bed, turned around twice, dug furiously for a second, and sank down with a deep, puggy sigh.

Immediately, Sophie returned her attention to the note. Juniper was sleeping the sleep of the innocent—which was as it should be—but she'd kept a lamp burning low on the dresser for Sophie. Bless Juniper's kind heart. Sophie tiptoed to the lamp and held the paper up to it.

"Los Angeles?" The two words hissed through the room, and Sophie turned quickly to see if she'd disturbed Juniper. She hadn't.

But—Los Angeles? That was at the end of the earth, for heaven's sake. Sophie and Juniper had been to San Francisco several times, but—Los Angeles? Didn't they grow oranges there or something? Good God.

As she removed her clothes, every inch of her body ached with fatigue. She couldn't recall being this tired in a long, long time. And now she had to go to Los Angeles. To chase down and kill Ivo Hardwick.

When she'd set out on this trek, she never realized she'd be seeing so much of the country. It was certainly a vast one. The states and its territories covered the span of an entire continent. And she'd soon have traveled it from one end to the other. That should probably afford her some satisfaction, but it didn't. She'd rather have Joshua back.

Lord in heaven, she didn't need to start thinking things like that now, of all times.

She eased herself into bed with a tremendous sigh, rolled over, and sank into the soft feather mattress. Her last thought before sleep claimed her was of Gabriel

Caine, and of how much she wished he were here with her in this bed.

Her dreams were filled with violent men chasing her and Gabriel Caine protecting her. She woke once, around three o'clock, with her heart trying to rip itself out of her chest in panic. She pressed a hand to her bosom and stared into the blackness of the room. In her dream, Gabriel had turned against her, and at the end, she'd been trying to escape him.

How typical.

Sophie cried herself back to sleep.

Chapter Ten

"Tarnation, Miss Juniper, I do believe the world's gone mad."

"Really, Mr. Caine? I must say I'm not surprised. It's always seemed a little off kilter to me. Why is it mad this time?"

Gabriel glanced at Juniper from behind his newspaper and grinned. She'd laid her mystical trappings aside in favor of knitting this morning. It looked to him as if she was working on a sweater crafted from bright red yarn. Pretty, that. Gabriel liked red. If he didn't wear black as a matter of principle, he'd probably wear more red.

Actually, what he'd like to do is dress Sophie all in red, himself all in black, and take her out to paint the town. Which town didn't much matter to him, although a highfalutin one would be the most fun. San Francisco, maybe.

He almost laughed at his too-vivid imagination. If he

Emma Craig

didn't watch out, he'd find himself entangled in a full-blown infatuation, and that would never do. What would happen to his image then?

The train was chugging its way across Arizona Territory, on its way to California, and he felt pretty damned good today. He'd taken a room at the Cosmopolitan last night, because he'd wanted to be close enough to the Madrigals to waylay Sophie if she got any murderous ideas, or if Patterson or the desk clerk decided to pay her a visit for illicit or immoral purposes. He didn't have any faith whatever in Sophie's claim to be able to take care of herself. Why, the whole of Tucson might be chock-full of slime like Patterson. Sophie might be tough, but she wasn't tough enough to take on an entire town.

The hotel clerk hadn't protested when Gabriel had demanded a room—indeed, he'd gone out of his way to be pleasant to him. Gabriel recalled the incident with a spurt of cynical satisfaction.

Of course, it had been pure-D luck that he'd run into Dmitri first thing this morning. Dmitri had told him right off that the Madrigal ladies aimed to set out for Los Angeles at noon today. Gabriel had hied himself to the train station directly, bought a ticket, and here he was.

Thus far, Sophie had been keeping to the Madrigals' sleeping compartment. Juniper said she'd passed a restless night, poor dear. It had been Juniper who'd added the *poor dear*, although Gabriel agreed with her. Poor Sophie. He'd had no idea her life was fraught with so much pure crap. No wonder she seemed to hate men, if they were all like that Patterson oaf and that pipsqueak of a hotel clerk.

But Juniper had asked him a question, and he guessed he might as well answer it. "Well, the world's gone mad this time because there are riots in Chicago, and the police are shooting at striking workers—it says here they killed a couple of them—and the anarchists are throwing bombs in New York City, and the peasants are revolting in Russia."

Juniper smiled almost gaily. Gabriel wondered why she thought all these terrible events merited a smile. She said, "If Sophie were here, she'd say in that dry, witty way of hers that peasants are always revolting. Then she'd probably say something about the benefits of using sufficient soap and water. I don't know what she'd say about the riots and the bombings, but she'd come up with something, I'm sure." Juniper began humming a tune that sounded familiar to Gabriel, although he couldn't place it. He thought it was a hymn.

He chuckled. "I'm sure you're right." He continued his perusal of the newspaper and didn't know that Sophie had joined them until he heard her say, in an unhappy voice, "You!"

Gabriel lowered the paper to his lap. Sophie stared at him with overt disapproval. Naturally, he grinned broadly in reaction to her hostility. "And a bright good morning to you, too, Miss Sophie. You're looking healthy and chipper this fine day." He took in a deep breath, as if of fresh air, and beamed at her. "Lovely day for a trip, isn't it?"

Sophie, who had Tybalt's wicker basket over arm and was wearing the same gown she'd had on when he'd first seen her, glared at him for a moment, then said, "I do wish you'd leave us alone, Gabriel." He wanted to eat her up. Right here and now. Pity she was being so damned prickly.

Juniper protested, "Sophie!"

Gabriel said, "Too bad, Sophie sweet. I'm going to get to Hardwick before you do, and I'm going to do everything in my power to keep you from killing him."

"I wish you'd just leave him to me. I'm sure that man

169

who hired you would be just as happy to know Hardwick is dead."

Gabriel shook his head. "Nope. I'm taking him back to stand trial."

"Waste of the taxpayers' money, if you ask me," Sophie huffed. She set the basket on a seat and positioned her lovely bottom next to it. Gabriel would like to see Sophie's bottom. He sighed.

Ignoring him, Sophie turned to her aunt. "That's a nice color, Juniper. It looks like you're knitting a sweater."

"I am, dear. Isn't this a pretty red?"

Sophie picked up a sleeve. "Yes. It's very bright. Eye-catching. It's awfully big. Are you making it for Uncle Jerome?"

"I don't think so," Juniper said placidly, and resumed humming.

That was it! Gabriel recognized the tune now. It had been one of his father's favorite hymns. His dad had always favored hymns of praise and jubilation, often with bouncy melodies, which Gabriel thought was kind of sweet.

Because he felt good this morning, and because he had managed to hang on to Sophie Madrigal through another extended train trip, and because he suddenly remembered how much he used to love to sing, he began singing now. Very softly, he sang the words along with Juniper's humming. "Praise to the Lord, the Almighty, the King of creation." It really was a pretty tune. "O my soul, praise him, for he is thy health and salvation!"

Juniper's knitting needles, which had been clicking along at a steady clip, stilled, and she turned to look at Gabriel, who smiled at her and nodded, encouraging her to keep humming. She did better than that. In a clear, somewhat thready soprano voice, she joined in.

"All ye who hear, now to his temple draw near; join me in glad adoration!"

When Gabriel glanced over to see how Sophie was taking this new musical twist, he found her gaping in patent astonishment, not untainted with horror. He felt like laughing. Instead, he sang louder. He knew he had a superior bass-baritone voice. Gabriel's voice had been a real boon to his father's revivalist efforts. The ladies had all but swooned when he sang.

"Praise to the Lord, who o'er all things so wondrously reigneth, shieldeth thee under his wings, yea, so gently sustaineth! Hast thou not seen how thy desires e'er have been granted in what he ordaineth?"

Tybalt peeped out of his basket, propping his fat little feet on its edge and sniffing, as if he smelled something tasty in the air. Sophie petted him absently as Gabriel and Juniper sailed on into the third verse. By God, he hadn't thought about his hymn-singing days for donkeys' years. This was fun.

"Praise to the Lord, who doth prosper thy work and defend thee; surely His goodness and mercy here daily attend thee. Ponder anew what the Almighty can do, if with his love he befriend thee."

Gabriel put an arm on Juniper to stay her voice from commencing the last verse. "Come on, Sophie, join in with us. It's fun."

"Oh, yes, do, dear. You know it's your favorite hymn."

Sophie frowned at her aunt. Undaunted—or only faintly daunted—Gabriel began the last verse. "Praise to the Lord! O let all that is in me adore him!"

To his astonishment, another voice had joined them by the end of the second sentence. He glanced from Juniper to Sophie, who scowled, but didn't stop singing. She was an alto or tenor, he noticed. He would have predicted such, if he'd been in the predicting instead of the soul-saving profession. Again, he felt like laughing.

"All that hath life and breath, come now with praises before him! Let the amen sound from his people again; gladly for ever adore him."

And, in one final crescendo, the trio sang a long, tuneful, harmonic, "A-men!"

They sat in the smoking car, although this early in the day, they had it practically to themselves. The only other passengers were two gentlemen who looked to Gabriel like drummers on a sales trip. When their "Amen" ended, the two men, who had turned to stare at the trio, applauded. Gabriel grinned and bowed from his seat. Juniper smiled shyly at the pair. Sophie didn't even bother to turn around. Gabriel presumed she was embarrassed, the silly wench.

Her cheeks were as pink as roses. So were Juniper's. Even Tybalt was wagging his tail. Gabriel didn't know what he looked like, but he couldn't offhand recall the last time he'd felt so lighthearted. Maybe there was something in this religion stuff. Maybe not. It was probably the admitted beauty of the hymn and the glorious blending of voices that had stirred him.

Juniper clapped her hands, knitting needles and all. "Oh, what fun! Let's sing another one!"

"Really, Aunt Juniper," Sophie muttered repressively. "There are other people on the train, you know. They might not appreciate a concert."

"Feel free, little lady," said one of the drummers, gesturing with his cigar. "I ain't heard nothing so pretty for a long time."

Sophie said, "Really."

Gabriel nudged her knee with his hand. "Come on, Sophie. Don't be such a spoilsport. Even Tybalt likes it." He reached over to scratch Tybalt behind his small ears, and got his hand licked. "See?" he said to Sophie.

"You don't want to disappoint Tybalt, do you?"

She rolled her eyes. Not very ladylike. Then she said, "Oh, very well, if it will keep you from fussing at me."

"Come on now, Sophie. You know you like me underneath."

She frowned at him. "Underneath what?"

He shrugged. "Everything." Then he winked at her, and had the pleasure of watching her cheeks get pink again. Lord, she was fun to rile.

"What shall we sing next?" Juniper asked brightly. Her knitting needles had recommenced their clicking, and she looked happier than Gabriel had seen her for a while.

"Let me think. My father used to like the happy ones."

"Oh, so do I, Mr. Caine," exclaimed Juniper. "I always think that if one is going to sing to or about God, one owes it to His goodness to offer up joy." Juniper, as if realizing she'd said something wrong, glanced sideways at her niece.

"If one can find any," mumbled Sophie. She stared out the train's window at the uninspiring scenery flitting past.

"You're just being a grump," Gabriel told her. "Come on, help me think of a good hymn."

"I'm sure you can do quite well on your own."

Since Sophie was obviously not going to enjoy herself if she could help it, Gabriel decided to leave her alone. It was enough for him if she'd keep singing with them. It was a start and, by God, he'd wear her down the rest of the way eventually.

"I have a good one," he said suddenly, having thought of his father's all-time favorite hymn. His father had loved it because it had been written by a man who'd been saved from sin and degradation, one deduced, by God's grace, and Gabriel's dad had experienced the same sort of salvation. He cleared his throat and began the hymn as a solo. Considering how long it had been since he'd sung anything, he was pleased that his voice still sounded good. Maybe he could seduce Sophie with sweet song, like the troubadours of old.

"Amazing grace, how sweet the sound that saved a wretch like me." He peered at his companions to see how they liked his selection. To his surprise, he found that Juniper had dropped her knitting into her lap, and was staring at Sophie with worried eyes.

"I once was lost, but now am found, was blind but now I see." He turned to look at Sophie and stopped singing at once.

Her pink cheeks had bleached of color until her green eyes stood out like jade against white marble. She'd lifted a hand to her lips, and to his horror, Gabriel saw huge tears welling up in her eyes. He jumped to his feet.

"Sophie! For God's sake, I'm sorry. I didn't mean—"

"It's nothing!" she cried, and lurched out of her seat. Without even waiting for Tybalt, who stared after her and yipped in bewilderment, she all but ran the length of the smoking car, past the two gentlemen who'd comprised their audience. She bolted through the door at the end of the carriage as if demons were after her.

Gabriel turned to stare down at Juniper. He held his hands out helplessly. "What did I do?"

"Oh, dear." Juniper's hand lifted to press her cheek. "Oh, dear. They played that at his funeral. Sophie hasn't been able to listen to it since."

"Whose funeral?"

"Joshua's."

"Who's Joshua?"

But Juniper only stared up at him, with gigantic, sad eyes, her face as pale as death, and shook her head. "I'm sorry, Mr. Caine. Sophie won't let me."

174

Crap. Sophie and her damned secrets were about to drive him loony. Pausing only to lift Tybalt back into his basket so the poor little fellow wouldn't try to jump from the seat and break a pudgy leg in pursuit of his mistress, Gabriel ran down the car after Sophie. He wanted to get to her before she could lock him out. He was heartily sick of being locked out by Miss Sophie Madrigal.

He made it to her sleeping compartment a bare second before she could shut the door on him. His flat palms slammed into it, and try as she might, she couldn't outpush him.

"Give it up, Sophie. I'm going to get some answers, and I'm going to get them now."

"Go away."

"No."

"*Damn* you!"

She let go of the door all at once, and Gabriel damned near fell on his face as he stumbled into the room. Sophie had flung herself on the cushioned bench that, at night, served as a bed, and beat her fist against the cushioned back. Gabriel's heart pitched as he watched her. Immediately, he felt inadequate to soothe her monumental grief.

It was grief, too; he could tell. It wasn't a transitory temper tantrum. This was honest-to-God anguish, and it almost broke his heart.

He sat next to her and put his hands on her shoulders. They were shaking as if an earthquake were happening inside her. "Sophie, Sophie, what am I going to do with you?"

"Nothing!" she choked out furiously. "Leave me alone."

"Not a chance." Gabriel rubbed his hands lightly over her arms and back. He massaged her neck, feeling steel-like tension in the muscles there. "I'm truly sorry,

Sophie. I had no idea that hymn would have such a sad connection for you."

"I know."

Her voice was so muffled, he scarcely heard her. But he appreciated the words. At least she didn't think he'd done it on purpose. As if he could, since he didn't know anything about her. Which galled him, as he wanted to know everything there was to know about her.

"Listen, Sophie," he said gently. "Maybe you ought to talk about—"

"No!"

He sighed. "Sometimes it helps to talk about things."

"No."

For a few moments, Gabriel remained silent. For the first time in years, he tried to think about what his father used to do when confronted by another person's unrelenting sadness. His father had never given up, no matter how troublesome the person with whom he dealt. Gabriel had admired that quality in his father. No matter how many insults, denials, or fits of temper a body threw, Gabriel's father had hung in there because—well, because it had been his calling.

While Gabriel had never felt any kind of calling, he knew good and well his father would have counseled revelation in this instance. He'd been a great gun for confession, the reverend Mr. George Caine, contending that the bitter things a body kept inside himself eventually festered and began poisoning the whole person. And, while the word *confession* might mean a host of different things to a host of different people, Mr. Caine had held that it wasn't merely one's sins one needed to confess. In order to cleanse oneself inside and out, it was best to get rid of one's secrets, which could infect one's soul as easily as a hidden crime.

Gabriel sensed Sophie didn't need to confess to anything underhanded or criminal. He had a feeling that whatever she held inside wasn't to her own detriment.

He wondered if this had something to do with Ivo Hardwick, and his eyes narrowed. Interesting possibility.

And who the hell was Joshua?

Because he felt the need to be of use to her whether she wanted him to be or not, he gently drew her away from the cushioned backrest and into his arm. He pressed her head onto his shoulder and held her closely. As he gently rocked her, he whispered sweet nothings into her ear.

"It's all right, Sophie. We all have sorrows. Time generally heals them, at least on the surface. If the wounds cut deep, then we'll always ache from them, but it won't be this bad forever."

"How would *you* know?" she asked with a hint of the old, fighting-spirited Sophie.

She couldn't see his wry grimace because her eyes were shut. "Oh, I've endured my share of life's slings and arrows, believe me."

Returning no answer, Sophie continued to cry, in big, hiccuping sobs.

Gabriel took a big chance. "Um, who's Joshua, Sophie?"

She jerked back as if he'd struck her a mortal blow. With her face blotchy and streaming with tears, she gaped at him, her eyes reminding Gabriel of emeralds under water. "Who—" She took a swipe at her eyes. "Who told you about Joshua? If Juniper told you anything, I'm going to—"

He tried to draw her to his chest again, but she resisted. "Cool down, Sophie. Juniper didn't tell me anything except that they played 'Amazing Grace' at Joshua's funeral. She didn't tell me who Joshua was."

Sophie glared at him with undisguised suspicion.

With a flash of intuition, Gabriel asked softly, "Was he a lover, Sophie? Your husband?"

Her lips, which she'd been pressing into a thin, tight line, quivered. She didn't try to speak, but only shook her head.

Oh. Well, crap, what did that leave? A brother? A favorite cousin? An earlier edition of Tybalt, the Pug? Gabriel didn't feel like playing a guessing game with her, even though he was perishingly impatient to learn who this Joshua character had been and why his passing had wounded Sophie so deeply.

Her strength gave out all of a sudden, and he was able to pull her close again. "It's all right, Sophie," he said, even though his curiosity had not abated an iota. "Just cry it out. You'll feel better."

"No, I won't." Her voice sounded as if it came to him through an ocean of salt water.

Not being his father, who'd had the knack of saying the one perfect thing in any situation, Gabriel could only cluck softly and rub her back with his big hand and wish he could help her.

He didn't know how long they sat there, Sophie crying, he holding her and wishing, but after what seemed an eternity, Sophie spoke again. Her mouth was pressed against his shirt, and the words were muffled, but he heard her say, "Joshua was a little boy."

"A little boy?"

She nodded.

A little boy. Shoot. That opened up a whole new line of questions Gabriel wished he could ask. He knew better. It had taken a major emotional catastrophe on Sophie's part to get her to admit this much. If he pressed the issue, she'd probably only get mad at him and never say another word.

Because he felt the need to say something, he said, "I'm sorry."

A miserable sniffle answered him.

Damn, he wished he could ask. Maybe he should talk to Juniper. She was nowhere near as tight-lipped as Sophie.

But no. That would be sneaky and devious, and Gabriel's integrity, which could on occasion be a flexible asset, rebelled. He wanted to know every single thing there was to know about Sophie Madrigal—but he wanted her to be the one to divulge it. It wouldn't be fair to get it from Juniper. Dammit. He always hated it when his conscience decided to emulate his father's. An uncomfortable commodity, his father's conscience. His own was seldom so picky, and Gabriel much preferred to take life the easy way.

In the case of Sophie Madrigal, though, he sensed that if he was ever to conquer her, it would have to be *mano a mano*, so to speak. Using intermediaries would be cheating.

After another eternity or two, Sophie's tears began to subside. She pulled away from him—an unfortunate circumstance in Gabriel's opinion—and said in a shaky voice, "I beg your pardon, Gabriel. You probably think I'm out of my mind."

Her head was bowed, her fair hair had become undone, and he looked down upon a sea of tumbling blond curls. Because he couldn't seem to help himself, he began smoothing them back from her face. "I know you're not out of your mind, Sophie. You're the sanest female I've ever met."

"Ha."

Gabriel wasn't accustomed to pretty young women doubting his flirtatious words. As a rule, women liked to believe good things about themselves. Sophie's doubt rankled. "You can disbelieve me if you want, but it's the truth."

She didn't speak, but fumbled in her reticule, which

still dangled from her wrist or she'd have lost it in her pell-mell flight through the train. After a moment, she drew out a handkerchief with which she began mopping her cheeks.

"Is there anything I can do, Sophie? Do you want to go back to the smoking carriage?"

She shook her head. "Thank you."

Dammit, he wanted to do something for her. Anything. He didn't want to leave her, stewing in her grief. "May I bring you a cup of tea?"

"No, thank you."

"A drink? They say brandy is good for whatever ails a person."

"No, thank you." This was accompanied by a shudder, from which Gabriel deduced Miss Sophie didn't care for spirits.

"Coffee?"

"No!" Another shudder rattled her, and she drew in a deep breath. "I beg your pardon, Gabriel. I didn't mean to snap at you. I'm upset."

He grinned. "You must be. You've never apologized for being snappish before."

She said, "Hmph," rather thickly, and blew her nose.

"Let me at least bring you something, Sophie. Please? I—I feel like doing something for you." *Even if you won't tell me what's wrong*. Not having experienced altruistic urges—at least not since he was old enough to know a con when he met one—this one took him aback.

Evidently, Sophie didn't think as ill of him as he did of himself, because she said merely, "Thank you, but—Oh!"

Lifting her chin, she gave Gabriel a perfect view of her face, ravaged by misery and tears. His heart turned over and started aching for all it was worth. "Yes?" he said, amazed at the mildness of his tone. He experienced a violent impulse to leap upon a white charger and go forth to slay dragons for her. As if she, of all women, needed a knight in shining armor. Hell, her sharp tongue could bring down a dragon at fifty paces.

"Would you bring me Tybalt, please? I'm sorry to be such trouble."

"You're no trouble at all, sweetheart." And she wasn't.

Good God, when had this happened to him? He also discovered an almost insurmountable reluctance to leave her, even for so brief an errand. When had this happened to him? He was beginning to feel a little ill-used—and by his own treacherous emotions. He hadn't believed himself capable of such urges, passions, and longings as those he was experiencing right this very minute.

It was probably nothing and would pass soon. "I'll be right back." It had better pass soon, or Gabriel had a sinking notion he was a goner.

Juniper had put her knitting away and was feverishly dealing out the cards when Gabriel rejoined her. She looked up, and he read worry and fear in her expression.

"Oh, Mr. Caine, is Sophie all right?"

Was she all right? Gabriel didn't know. He opted to tell the truth. "Well, Miss Juniper, she's still pretty upset, but I think she's getting better. She asked me to bring Tybalt to her."

Juniper gnawed on her lower lip. "Oh, dear, I'm so sorry this happened. It wasn't your fault, you know. You couldn't possibly understand what that hymn means to Sophie."

He nodded and almost asked her to tell him. That would be cheating, though, and his internal barometer of self-interest held him back. If Sophie ever found out he'd questioned Juniper about her past, she'd never forgive him. And if Juniper slipped and told him, Sophie would never forgive Juniper, and that would be a flat tragedy. It seemed to Gabriel that these two had only each other in the big, ugly world, and if they ever became estranged, neither of them would ever be happy again.

Offhand, it didn't appear to him as if Sophie aimed ever to be happy again anyway, but he didn't dwell on it. He smiled at Juniper. "What do the cards say today?"

She heaved a sigh so big it nearly lifted her off of her seat. "They're predicting rocky times ahead, I fear." Her eyes crinkled at the corners and her lips pinched. "I do wish Sophie would drop this quest of hers. It's sure to lead to grief."

Hmmm. Gabriel didn't think it would be prying to ask, "You mean her quest to rid the world of Ivo Hardwick?"

She nodded sadly. "I hardly blame her, but it's not good to seek vengeance. The Lord will take care of all of us eventually."

Right. Gabriel felt guilty about the cynical twist his innards gave. "Eventually isn't quick enough for some of us, I reckon."

"I suppose not."

He picked up Tybalt's wicker basket and stood before Juniper with it slung over his arm for a moment. "You know," he said, after clearing his throat, "I might be able to help, since I've been commissioned to bring Hardwick to justice in Abilene. If Sophie would leave the business to me, Hardwick would be punished, and she wouldn't have to go to so much trouble. I mean, the authorities in Abilene are probably going to hang him for murder. It's not as if he's going to escape justice."

Juniper's smile was enchanting in its sadness and innocence. "Dear Mr. Caine. You're so good to us. But it won't work, you know. Sophie believes she needs to do this on her own." She glanced down at the cards she'd just laid down and sighed again. "Oh, dear. There's that pesky Ten of Swords again. And the Devil. My dear heaven, I pray so hard for her." When she lifted her face to him again, Gabriel saw tears in her pretty blue eyes.

"That's bad, is it?" The prediction Sophie had laid on him galloped back into his mind, and he sighed a sigh as deep as Juniper's. "How can you get them to change?"

She lifted her hands in a gesture of helplessness. "The cards only reflect one's life, Mr. Caine. They can't affect its outcome. If Sophie persists in this course of action, they predict nothing but more pain and heartache for her."

"I see," said he, although he didn't. What the deuce good were the cards if they only told you what you already knew? He didn't ask.

Juniper brightened a little. "But you, Mr. Caine, are on the road to clearing up a goodly number of uncertainties in your own life."

"I am?" Gabriel blinked down at her.

"Oh, my, yes. Why, I did a reading on you right after you ran after Sophie. Your life is changing even as we speak." She looked mighty happy about it.

"Oh," he said. Then he said, "I see," again.

Juniper lifted a hand and placed it on Gabriel's wrist. The gesture touched something way down deep in him, although he couldn't have said why.

"And, Mr. Caine, please don't despair about Sophie and that silly prediction she made for you. Don't forget, ever, that there are many, many ways in which one's life can end. Often, it will begin again on a much happier note."

Was that so? Gabriel didn't think he'd better ask, or

he might be in for a lecture on reincarnation or something. Juniper had never mentioned past lives before, but he wouldn't put much of anything in the nature of the occult beyond her. Since, however, he couldn't think of anything else to say, he lifted the basket, as if to show it to Juniper. "Guess I'd better get this back to Miss Sophie now. I reckon old Tybalt is a comfort to her."

"Oh, yes. Tybalt is the only living being on earth that can give her comfort. At the moment." She gave him such a significant look that Gabriel almost blushed. Devil take it, was Juniper playing matchmaker here?

The thought was too much to contemplate under the circumstances. He gave her a friendly smile, and took Tybalt back to Sophie, where she greeted him—Tybalt, not Gabriel—with open arms. Then she shut the door in his face—Gabriel's, not Tybalt's.

With a shrug and a sigh, Gabriel went back to the smoking car. He admired Sophie Madrigal more than he'd ever be likely to admit to a soul, but he *really* appreciated the uncomplicated Juniper, who liked him in spite of himself.

Chapter Eleven

Sophie hugged Tybalt to her bosom, stroking him into a state of abject bliss, and contemplated the nature of fate. Whatever constituted fate, it hadn't been on her side up until now, and she thought it was about time for things to change.

For instance, she'd never in her life experienced precognitive impulses until she'd met Gabriel Caine. But she was experiencing them now, in his presence. This was, perhaps, the unkindest cut of all, barring Joshua's death, because it meant that the man who stood as her mortal enemy—oh, very well, perhaps not *mortal*, but an important enemy nonetheless—seemed to be her first and only conduit to the Other Side.

Disturbed and still reeling from her recent attack of the vapors, a condition she despised in other women, Sophie muttered to Tybalt, "Why couldn't it be Juniper in whom resided the other half of myself?"

Tybalt returned no answer, but he did sigh soulfully, and Sophie appreciated him for it.

"It's obvious that my life and Gabriel's are entwined somehow," she said glumly. "Even Dmitri would be better than Gabriel. Although," she admitted with innate honesty, "I don't think I'd like to have to work through a Russian dwarf. I'm beginning to agree with Juniper about Russians. They're such a grim and oppressed lot."

As Tybalt snuggled more closely to her, sticking his nose between her arm and her side to secure the most warmth from her body, Sophie stroked his chubby belly. "Or even you, Tybalt. I wouldn't mind having you as a medium." Tybalt never had and never would hurt her, and she knew it. She was nowhere near as sure of Gabriel Caine. In fact, she was pretty sure that if she gave in to his lures, she'd be thoroughly wretched. She'd been wretched too much already in her life.

Tybalt wagged his tail, a gesture Sophie interpreted as one of agreement. Perhaps even pleasure at the thought of serving his mistress thus.

She said, "I feel too close to him already, Tybalt. This is a very bad thing. I ought to have guarded myself better."

Sophie frowned at her pug, who was still wagging his curly tail happily. "Yes, I know, Tybalt. You like Gabriel Caine, don't you?" Another wag greeted this question, and Sophie sighed. "It's probably only because he gave you food."

Sometimes Sophie wished she'd been born a domestic animal instead of a human being. Not the kind of abandoned cat or dog that lived in the streets of big cities, because their lives seemed even more uncertain and perilous than her own. No, what she wanted to be was a pampered house cat. Perhaps she could belong to some fantastically rich matron in New York City, who only fed her pets the best of foods and gave them beds of velvet upon which to sleep. How pleasant it must be to be free of responsibility and to be waited on hand and foot.

"But, no," she said grimly. "I had to be born a female human being, cast into a family of tricksters, despised by the general populace, and responsible for all sorts of things I don't want to be responsible for."

She hadn't minded being responsible for Joshua. Pain struck her so sharply and unexpectedly that she gasped and had to squeeze her eyes shut against it. "Oh, Tybalt, I don't know how I can live much longer with this burden in my heart."

Distressed by the tone of her voice, Tybalt withdrew his head from her armpit and nudged her hand with his squashy nose. To show how much he cared, he whined softly.

"Thank you, Tybalt. I love you very much, and I truly do appreciate your condolences. I wish you could have known Joshua. You'd have loved him, and he'd have adored you."

Wishing she hadn't said that, because it engendered so many thoughts of things that could now never be, she stared through the dirty window at the scenery flying past. There didn't seem to be much of it; mainly lumps of scrub brush, creosote bushes, and those huge saguaro cacti that reached for the sky as if they were praying or begging a boon from God.

Which motions didn't solve anything. She still had to figure out what role Gabriel Caine was to play in her life. She couldn't imagine allowing another man to become close to her; not after her experiences. In truth, she was surprised that she'd felt such intense passion when he'd held her in Tucson.

Desire hadn't been present when he'd comforted her in her sleeping compartment, but as much as she hated to admit it, it had felt right when he'd held her and tried

187

to soothe her wounded spirits. Still, she didn't want him in her life. She absolutely didn't want to have to depend on him for anything. She knew from unfortunate experience that the men to whom she was attracted were unreliable and not to be depended upon. For anything. Ever.

Yet Gabriel belonged in her future somewhere, and there was no getting away from it. Blast it, if his only fate in regard to her was to stop her from killing Ivo Hardwick, she wouldn't stand for it. To be sure, she didn't know what she could do to prevent his interference, but she aimed to try.

"He certainly has a beautiful voice, doesn't he, Tybalt?" The tune of "Amazing Grace" had been sliding around in her head ever since Gabriel had started singing it.

Oh, but that had hurt! To have been thrust unexpectedly back to that horrible, rainy day when those men had lowered the little coffin into the ground, had been a dreadful wrench. Every time she considered Joshua lying in the cold, dead earth, she wanted to scream. Or die.

The only aspect of the whole thing that in any way softened Sophie's anguish was that Joshua now shared an eternal resting place with her mother and father and a whole host of Madrigals past. It was idiotic of her, but she liked knowing he was with family. Her family. "What an ass I am sometimes, Tybalt."

Tybalt's curly tail wagged.

She didn't speak for a minute, but let her mind drift here and there. After only a few seconds, it drifted to Gabriel. She could still hear his voice combined with Juniper's as they sang "Praise to the Lord." He must have practiced his singing a lot, because even a fine voice couldn't achieve that timbre without lots of practice. Sophie had always admired deep voices in men. Gabriel's had sounded like black velvet.

"He probably sang during his father's religious services. Helped the old man save souls by touching them with music. Oh, dear, I'm being cynical again, aren't I?" She knew cynicism was unladylike. She didn't care.

Tybalt yawned. Sophie grinned, and decided coming into this world as a pampered pug wouldn't be half bad, if all the positions for lazy house cats were already filled.

It took her almost an hour to get her nerves under control so that she could rejoin Juniper in the smoking car. She didn't like leaving Juniper by herself for very long at a time, because Juniper attracted people, and she was indiscriminate. She was prone to allowing all sorts of human beings into her orbit, from princes to bums. Juniper loved them all. She was as unlike Sophie in that regard as she was in almost every other regard.

Answering the ring of her bell, the porter brought her warm water. She washed her face, squinting into a mirror. "I'll never get my eyes to unpuff." She looked as if she'd just endured a prolonged crying fit, actually, which she had.

She tried, however, to repair the damage. She even went so far as to use a little powder and rouge, hoping by those artificial means to get people to focus on her cheeks rather than on her eyes, which were still swollen and bloodshot.

Lord, the things women did so that men wouldn't despise them. *Men*, of all the insignificant creatures on this unhappy earth. She knew she was going to all this trouble for Gabriel Caine's sake, so he would think she was pretty, and she reviled herself for it even as she brushed out her curly blond hair and wound it up in a new knot which she pinned at the back of her neck.

Sometimes, Sophie wished she were more like her

aunt. She'd love to be able to accept the world as Juniper did, unconditionally and liberally, unfettered by resentments or expectations. She'd also love to be able to take all the hog slop attaching itself to the family business with grace and faith, as Juniper did. Sophie no longer believed in faith. Or grace. If she'd ever had any of the former, she'd lost it when she'd lost Joshua. And if grace were being bestowed upon anyone, anywhere, it wasn't her. She'd been in the other room when grace had been handed out. She sighed, wondering if that made her a heathen.

When she reached the smoking car, a wave of trepidation assaulted her. Both Gabriel and Juniper had been worried about her. Had Juniper been so upset, she'd divulged Sophie's secret to Gabriel? If she had, Sophie didn't think she'd ever be able to forgive her for it. Joshua had been Sophie's, and Sophie's alone, and it was up to her to decide who deserved to be told about him. It would hurt Sophie greatly to have to turn against her aunt, but Joshua was more important than Juniper, Sophie, and Gabriel Caine combined. And even Tybalt.

She was more than surprised when she entered the car and beheld Juniper, Gabriel, and Dmitri, of all poor lost Russian souls, laughing up a storm. The scene was so unusual that she had to stop and rub her eyes. She remembered she'd put blacking on her eyelashes and hoped she hadn't smudged it. But Dmitri was laughing. She'd never seen him laugh.

Loath to intrude, she hesitated at the door to the carriage. Several men who had graced the smoking car with their presences after she'd left it eyed her with appreciation. She scowled at them and saw them shrink back and turn their heads away, and she felt a little better about life.

But should she join that jolly group? Was it fair of her

to do so? She knew good and well that she could dampen any frivolous gathering without half trying, and she didn't want to do it now. They were having fun. Sophie had forgotten how to have fun about a year or so ago.

All at once, she felt completely alone and left out. She had just made up her mind to turn around and go back to her sleeper, when Gabriel spotted her. Blast.

He charged out of his seat and headed straight at her. Because she'd been disconcerted to see those three people acting in so chummy a manner—without her— she frowned as he approached. This wasn't the same warding-off scowl she'd used on the strangers, but one of the ones Gabriel was probably accustomed to receiving from her by this time.

"I don't want to interrupt you," she said before he had a chance to talk.

"Don't be more of a twit than you can help being, Sophie."

She drew herself up straight and her frown turned into a glower. Unfortunately, he was used to receiving her glower, too, as his next words showed.

"And don't look at me like that, either." He laughed.

Sophie was offended. "Thank you very much. I don't believe I care to socialize at the moment."

"Well, now, isn't that too damned bad?" Gabriel still sounded cheerful, but he got a grip on Sophie's arm that was going to leave bruises unless she was much mistaken. "We've been waiting for you. Dmitri's found something you'll enjoy."

"Dmitri?" This was a new twist.

"Yes, indeed. He's got something really keen. I know you'll love it."

Sophie doubted it, but she respected Dmitri and would not hurt his feelings if she could help it. She huffed irritably, but said, "Oh, very well. Here, make yourself useful and carry Tybalt's basket."

"Sure thing." He took the big wicker basket and, still maintaining his firm grip on her arm, propelled her and the basket back to where the Madrigal company had assembled.

Aunt Juniper, her eyes as bright as stars, beamed at her expansively. "Oh, Sophie, you must see this! Dmitri bought it from a Gypsy in Tucson."

"I didn't know there were Gypsies in Tucson." Although she tried not to sound grumpy for Juniper and Dmitri's sake, her words were a trifle sullen.

Juniper, as might have been expected, didn't notice. *Thank God for thickheaded aunts*, Sophie thought with a marked lack of charity.

When she looked at Dmitri, shock replaced spite. Dmitri was smiling at her, too. Dmitri! Smiling and laughing. Dmitri, the morose and cranky Russian dwarf who, in Sophie's mind, had every reason in the world to be morose and cranky. Would wonders never cease? With an effort that nearly made her faint because she'd again laced her stays tightly, Sophie returned his smile. She liked Dmitri. She wouldn't be mean to him under any circumstances.

Fortunately, she felt no such constraints regarding Gabriel Caine, so she took her shortness of temper out on him. Snatching her arm away from him, she growled, "You may unhand me now, Gabriel."

"Gladly," he said.

Sophie heard some asperity in the one word, and was pleased. Why should she be the only one to suffer, after all? Even as the unworthy thought manifested itself, she knew she was being unreasonable—it wasn't Gabriel's fault that Joshua had died, or that "Amazing Grace" had been played at his funeral. Ah, well, that's the way the world turns. None of that was her fault either, but she'd been made to suffer unconscionably for the idiosyncrasies of a capricious fate.

It seemed that Gabriel wasn't one to hold a grudge, because his tone was quite pleasant when he said, "This thing is all the crack, Sophie. You'll love it."

"Will I?"

He laughed as he set Tybalt's basket on the bench and helped her to sit. "Of course you will. It's right up your alley. According to Miss Juniper, people have been consulting them for ages, but they've only recently gained widespread popularity in the States."

Because she felt mean and surly, Sophie muttered, "We're no longer in the States. We're in one of the States's more despicable territories."

"Stuff and nonsense. You're just being a pain in the neck for its own sake." With undiminished cheer, Gabriel took a spot on the bench next to her.

Sophie tried to wriggle farther away from him, but the basket was in the way. She felt defeated. He was right about her, blast it. Her insides hurt, and she wanted to inflict pain on others. Not a very noble ambition. In fact, Sophie felt a bit guilty about it. Neither Juniper nor Dmitri deserved her bad temper. For that matter, although she hated to admit it, neither did Gabriel. Despite the fact that it went against the grain, she silently swore that she would at least try to be civil to everyone—or, if that proved too much of a hurdle to leap—she would be civil to Juniper and Dmitri.

Her task became easier when she realized the plaything in question was a board and planchette. The board had the alphabet printed in an arc in its upper reaches and numbers below. Also printed on the board were the words *Yes* and *No*, one on each side.

"A spirit board!" she exclaimed, genuinely intrigued. She'd heard people call this type of device by different names, but she'd always preferred *spirit board*.

"Isn't it wonderful, Sophie?" Juniper had her fingers resting with eiderdown gentleness on the planchette. Dmitri, seated across from Juniper, had his hands positioned likewise. "Ask it something, Sophie. Do, dear." Juniper, her face a perfect picture of ecstatic whimsy, gleamed up at her.

Since the only questions Sophie felt like asking the board at the moment were questions she didn't want anyone else to hear, she asked a question of her aunt instead. "I'm surprised the thing works here—assuming, of course, that it works at all. I mean, doesn't the planchette need some kind of spirit to guide it? There must have been hundreds—even thousands—of passengers on this train since it started running."

"You're such a skeptic," Gabriel said with a laugh. "Miss Juniper explained it all to me. One need never worry about finding a spirit to assist one, because there are the spirits of generations of our ancestors floating around everywhere."

Sophie eyed him, and he winked at her. For some inexplicable reason, his wink reassured her. For a moment there, she'd almost thought he actually believed in this folderol. It came as an unpleasant shock to her when she realized she'd begun to look upon Gabriel Caine as her ally in an insane world. This would never do.

Because she didn't have the time or privacy to contemplate this current disaster with any kind of detachment, she decided to shelve it for the nonce. "I beg your pardon, Juniper. Did you connect with a spirit?"

"Oh, my, yes!" Juniper cried delightedly. "And it's a perfectly fascinating one, too."

"Really."

She must have sounded dryer than Gabriel thought appropriate, because he nudged her with an elbow. She turned to frown at him. He grinned back. "Don't

194

be such an old stick, Sophie. Ask the thing a question."

"Please do, Sophie. This is so fascinating. Why, it's already told Dmitri that he won't ever have to return to Russia. He'd been afraid of having to go back, you know, for some time."

"Why would he be afraid about having to return to Russia?" Turning to Dmitri, Sophie asked, "Were you fearful of some mad Russians kidnapping you and tossing you onto a boat or something? Like the British Navy used to impress sailors or something?" The scenario sounded mighty fanciful to Sophie.

"*Nyet.*" Dmitri shrugged. "Bolsheviks, Mensheviks, anarchists, revolutionaries. They're all over the world."

"And they want you?" She didn't understand.

Dmitri shrugged again, as if to say he didn't know, but he wouldn't put anything past the political radicals rampaging through Eastern Europe at the moment. Gabriel nudged her again, harder this time.

Turning and giving him a ferocious scowl, she snapped, "Will you please stop that?"

"Not until you quit being crabby."

"I'm not being crabby!"

"You are, too."

She huffed indignantly. "Oh, you're impossible."

"Probably, but why don't you quit stalling and ask the board a question?"

Juniper said doubtfully, "I'm not sure it will answer a question from you unless you're handling the planchette, dear. Would you like to take my place?"

"No." Perceiving the answer was too crisp and might be interpreted by the sensitive Juniper as a snub, Sophie enlarged on her answer. "That is, why don't I ask it something and we can see if it works this way."

"All right, dear."

Sophie shook her head, amazed as always by her

aunt's sunny disposition. Why couldn't Sophie have been born with a bright nature?

It occurred to her that, perhaps, she had been. Indeed, until her sixteenth year, she had been relatively good-natured and even-tempered, if not exactly happy. Then a man had come into her life, ruined it, and she'd been a grump ever since. Which meant, now that she thought about it, that she'd given that traitorous, conniving, sneaking coward of a man an awful lot of power over herself.

She didn't like thinking these things, so she scrambled for a question to ask the board. "Um, will we enjoy our stay in Los Angeles?"

The planchette seemed to vibrate under the fingers of its human controls, then zipped over to the "Yes." Before Sophie could exclaim in pretended enthusiasm about the answer, it made a sudden dash to the other side of the board and landed on the "No." From there, it proceeded to slide back and forth between the two words. Sophie, Juniper, Gabriel, and Dmitri watched its antics with varying degrees of interest, suspicion, and doubt.

"Are you sure you're not moving it yourself?" Sophie asked Juniper after several seconds of that.

"Good heavens, no. This is very unsettling." Juniper's happy smile tipped upside down.

The quartet continued to observe the planchette's capers for another moment or two.

"Can't it make up its mind?" Sophie asked presently.

"I don't know." Juniper was frowning in concentration as the planchette zigged and zagged.

"Hmmm," said Gabriel. "Maybe it's trying to tell us that your stay in Los Angeles will be a mixture of success and failure."

He glanced at his fellow spirit-board watchers as if seeking assent or denial. He looked sheepish to Sophie, who gathered he felt silly saying such things about a piece of painted board and a triangular-shaped wooden disk glued to little wooden feet. As if a couple of pieces of wood could tell the future. It was laughable.

The planchette made one last dash across the board and landed on the "Yes." They all stared at it.

Gabriel cleared his throat. "Does that mean our stay in Los Angeles will offer both success and failure?"

The planchette quivered and remained on the "Yes."

"Hmmm." Gabriel, evidently nonplused by this communication from beyond, sat back, as if he couldn't think of anything else to say.

Sophie could. To the devil with questioning that nonsensical board. She concentrated on her aunt. "You didn't finish telling me about the spirit, Aunt Juniper. Does it have a name?" Perhaps she shouldn't have called it an it.

Dear Lord, she was acting as though she believed in this tripe.

"My, yes, dear. In fact, he's one of the more fascinating communicants I've been in touch with over the years."

"Really?" Sophie made an effort to sound less skeptical and succeeded to a degree.

Juniper nodded. "Yes. He's an Indian."

"Mercy." And, what's more, he was an Indian who could understand English and read well enough to spell out answers. "Any particular tribe?" She decided not to ask about how he became conversant in a foreign tongue.

Juniper's brow wrinkled, giving her the appearance of an elderly, sweet-natured sprite. Watching her, Sophie was reminded how much she loved her. Juniper Madrigal never had and never would hurt another living being, and Sophie admired her for it. For perhaps the thousandth time, she wished she were more like her aunt.

"Well," Juniper said dubiously, "he claims to be from a tribe I've never heard of. Not that I know much about our native Indians, you understand, but one does read things. I've heard of the Navajos, and the Hopis, and the Apaches and Comanches and so forth. This one was new to me."

Striving to hold her impatience in check and willing herself to recollect all of Juniper's finer qualities, Sophie smiled tenderly. "It might be a new one for all of us."

"Do you think so, dear?" Juniper's expression of doubt eased, and she smiled happily. "Although I haven't studied Indian cultures extensively, I'd hate to think I'm not at least conversant with the names of most of the tribes. After all, Indians make wonderful media."

"Media?" Gabriel sounded doubtful.

Sophie enlightened him. "She means as a medium to the Other Side, Gabriel." She gave him a saccharine smile. He frowned back at her.

"Indeed. Well, there you are. I've never heard of his tribe, at all accounts. I wonder if Mr. Caine has. After all, he's traveled widely." She smiled beatifically at Gabriel.

Rapidly losing her vow to remain patient and polite, Sophie smiled through her clenched teeth. "We'll never know," she said, "if you don't tell us what it is."

Juniper blinked. "Oh! Did I fail to mention the name of the tribe?"

Still smiling, although it felt more like a grimace by this time, Sophie said, "Yes. You failed to mention it."

"Dear me, I'm getting more and more absentminded, aren't I?" Juniper gave a little giggle as if her failing memory were something of a joke.

Apparently, she recognized a lessening of control on

Sophie's part, because she quit dithering. "This gentleman's name is Flying Hawk, and in life he belonged to a tribe of people he calls the Anasazi."

"The what?" No longer peeved, Sophie peered closely at her aunt, wondering if Juniper had made it up. But no. Juniper would never do that. She respected this garbage too much.

"The Anasazi," Juniper repeated. "They're all gone now, according to Flying Hawk. Dead."

"That's happened to a lot of tribes," Gabriel opined quietly.

Sophie looked at him, then back at her aunt. "Did he say what happened to them?"

Juniper shook her head. "I'm afraid not, dear."

"Did they live in this vicinity?"

"Apparently not. Flying Hawk came from somewhere around Santa Fe, in the New Mexico Territory."

"And he's taken to riding the rails," murmured Sophie. "How energetic of him."

Juniper ignored Sophie's acidity. "Yes. He says he has a particular fancy for this train, the Pacific Express, because from Los Angeles, he can visit the ocean. He'd never seen an ocean before he died. He calls it an immense lake of salty water."

"I see."

"Say," Gabriel said suddenly, "do you mind if I tackle that thing? There's something I'd like to ask old Flying Hawk."

"Certainly, Gabriel." Juniper rose from her bench seat.

Sophie was interested to note that her aunt had finally begun calling Gabriel by his Christian name. Juniper generally maintained a certain formality in her speech, no matter how well she got to know a body. This was yet another bad sign, in Sophie's estimation.

"I go, too," said Dmitri, also rising. "Miss Sophie sit here." He patted the bench seat.

"What a grand idea. And Gabriel can take my place. How delightful it all is, to be sure." Virtually glowing with happiness and joy at promoting a match she desired—Sophie would have bet Tybalt on it—Juniper handed the planchette to Gabriel.

Sophie herself wasn't thrilled to be talking to a spirit board with Gabriel Caine. She knew good and well that neither the board nor the professed spirit of Flying Hawk—in which she didn't believe for a second—held any intrinsic power.

She wasn't sure about the combination of Gabriel Caine and herself, however, and she'd just as soon not find out today. Today had already been very stressful. She didn't want to have a bout of precognition or another one of those sudden and frightening psychic visions because she was in close proximity to him. He worried Sophie more than any other man she'd ever met in her adult life.

At the moment, he was exhibiting no such qualms as hers. He was grinning like Mr. Carroll's Cheshire cat, as a matter of fact. Sophie put on her stoniest expression and sat. Dmitri didn't stick around to see what transpired. Sophie expected he'd be glad to get back to the baggage car, since the smoking car was filling up rapidly.

She settled her skirt around her, frowned at Gabriel, set the planchette on the board, and became still. A funny sensation of prickles had begun to tiptoe up her fingers and arms. Blast. It was going to be bad; she hoped she wouldn't do anything embarrassing under the influence of whatever power it was that she and Gabriel generated together.

Gabriel gave her the broadest grin in his repertoire. "All set, Miss Sophie?"

She gave him a curt nod.

"All right, then. Here goes."

The tingles Sophie had started to experience very faintly suddenly turned on her and burned up and down her body. They didn't hurt, but they were excessively strange, and she wished they'd go away. In truth, she felt like jumping up and throwing the blasted spirit board and planchette out the window. She looked directly into Gabriel's eyes because she didn't want him to know how much his nearness bothered her. He winked at her, and it was all she could do not to jump to her feet and run away.

"Here's my question, Mr. Flying Hawk," he began genially, enjoying Sophie's discomposure. "I want to know if the prediction Miss Sophie made about my life ending on this trip is true or not."

Sophie gasped. So did Juniper. They all watched, fascinated, as the planchette quivered for a moment in the middle of the board, then made a sweeping circle of the numbers and letters painted thereon. Just when Sophie was thanking her lucky stars that Mr. Flying Hawk didn't seem inclined to answer Gabriel's question, the planchette took a powerful lunge and came to a stop. On the "Yes."

Gabriel murmured, "Shoot."

Juniper pressed a hand to her cheek and whispered, "Oh, my!"

Sophie was absolutely horrified.

Chapter Twelve

Midnight had come and gone, the train chugged relentlessly westward, and Sophie and Gabriel still sat in the smoking car. Juniper had gone to bed a long time ago, Dmitri had appeared once since he'd left them together with the spirit board, and had taken Tybalt to the baggage compartment to do his doggie duty. Sophie was about at her wits' end.

"Come on, Sophie, ask it one more question."

"I can't think of anything else to ask it," she lied. What she meant was that she couldn't think of any more inconsequentials to ask it. She had huge, whopping gaps in her life that she'd love to ask somebody about. Tonight, as every night, she couldn't seem to open up and ask about them. Besides, it was stupid to believe in things like this spirit board. Only fools who didn't have enough to occupy their minds, or were too stupid to think of their own answers, depended on such devices.

While Sophie could admit to herself that supernatural phenomena existed on the earth, and especially in her family, she still scorned fripperies like spirit boards and crystal balls. True psychics didn't need such nonsense. And besides all that, her own experience with magic and other such phenomena had led her to the conclusion that they didn't manifest themselves in concrete ways, but rather in odd, peripheral sensations and visions that only served to confuse her, and she resented them for it. Life was hard enough without puzzling visions complicating it further.

So why, oh, why couldn't she tear herself away from this thing? Or was it Gabriel from whom she couldn't tear herself away? She had a sinking feeling it was the latter, and she wished it weren't so.

Gabriel wasn't buying her lack-of-questions excuse. "Balderdash. You're dying to ask old Flying Hawk questions. You just don't want me to hear them."

She frowned at him for hitting upon her reason for reticence with such abysmal accuracy. With a lift of her chin and a huffy sniff, she said, "I've told you before that I want you to know nothing about me. Why should you be surprised now that I won't reveal my innermost secrets to Flying Hawk?" She sipped from her cup of tea that had just been brought by a porter who looked as though he needed his own bed. "Not," she added significantly, "that Flying Hawk exists in spirit on this train. Or ever did exist, for that matter."

"Better watch out, Sophie," Gabriel said with a sly wink. "I understand these Indian spirits can be mighty feisty when they feel like it."

"Fiddlesticks."

"All right, then, I'll ask it questions." His face clouded momentarily. "Although I'm not sure I want to hear any more predictions."

Sophie, feeling quite guilty about burdening Gabriel with that stupid prediction, muttered, "Don't be silly.

There's no such thing as reading the future." Which didn't explain her own recent visions and sensations of precognition when she was in Gabriel's presence.

She went on quickly, wishing she believed what she was going to say. "Anyhow, you don't need to ask Flying Hawk any questions. For heaven's sake, Gabriel, we both know this is all hooey."

An odd half smile lifted his lips. His beautiful lips. Sophie swallowed. Tonight, as they sat alone together in the smoking carriage, Sophie experienced a strange sense of isolation from the rest of the world. There seemed to be no one in the entire universe, save Gabriel and Sophie. "Well, it is," she said without much show of assurance.

"I'm not so sure about that."

Feeling beleaguered, Sophie pointed out what she considered an unjust attitude on Gabriel's part. "Anyway, *you* don't seem awfully eager to bare your soul to this idiotic board. *You've* managed to avoid asking it anything at all since your first question. What secrets does *your* past hold? I've always assumed your background to be as black as ink, but perhaps you're a saint in disguise." She gave him what she hoped was a wicked smile. "How about *you*, Mr. Gabriel I-Want-To-Know-Everything-About-Everyone-Else Caine? Why don't *you* reveal something about yourself?"

He cocked his head to one side and gazed at her, that half smile still in place. Sophie wished he'd stop smiling at her like that. He looked so perfect, so exactly what her insides told her she needed, that she felt a mad impulse to unburden herself of all her secrets, to tell him everything, to ask him to hold her while she cried her heart out on his shoulder. Again. Oh, dear.

She held the urge in check by reminding herself that the majority of the male sex were lower than snail slime, and that Gabriel Caine in particular—because he appealed to her so much—was the last person on earth to whom she should reveal herself. The possibility for being hurt was too great, as she well knew.

But, oh, dear Lord, was he going to stare at her all night? Sophie, feeling shaky ever since the "Amazing Grace" incident, couldn't stand much more of this.

At last he spoke, and she nearly sagged with relief. "I have to admit you've got me there."

She goggled at him, astonished. "You mean you actually admit you're being unreasonable?"

"I suppose so."

"And you *will* tell me something about your past?"

He shrugged. "There really isn't much to it. I was the only child of a very nice man and a very nice woman. They possessed a revivalist leaning. My father traveled the country, preaching grace and salvation through the good Lord's intervention. My mother and I went with him, of course. We acted as a musical accompaniment to his sermons." His expression took on a wistful, almost regretful cast which Sophie was astonished to behold.

For years now, she had been in the habit of considering religious folks, especially those who were rabid in their beliefs, akin to her own family of charlatans. Revivalists and Spiritualists were, to her mind, predatory knaves, who played upon people's worst fears and most exalted emotions to get them to hand over their hard-earned money. Gabriel's simple explanation of his parents' lives, stripped of any hint of ridicule or censure, didn't fit her picture. "I see." She didn't see at all.

"We traveled all over the place, so I got to see the United States and most of her territories before I was twelve. It was interesting."

"Did—did you enjoy being on the road all the time?" Her own family's constant traveling had left Sophie feeling rather empty inside, as if she needed something only permanence could provide. But there had been no permanence in her life as a child, and there probably never would be as an adult. She'd believed she'd found it with Joshua—and then Joshua had been taken away from her by Ivo Hardwick's stray bullet. She commanded herself to stop thinking about it.

"Oh, I don't know. It wasn't bad, I guess. I didn't get to have any friends that way. My mother taught me my lessons, so I probably have at least as much book-learning as anybody else."

Sophie digested that one. She'd never been able to have friends, either, because her family traveled. That, and the fact that no respectable woman would allow her child to associate with a child of the Madrigals. The ostracism she'd been the victim of as a child still rankled. Sophie felt heat crawl up the back of her neck. Shame. It was pure shame, and Sophie wished, not for the first time, that she'd been gifted with a thicker hide. But she hadn't been, and the insults had hurt her terribly.

"I don't suppose the children of the folks who went to your father's revival meetings despised you."

He eyed her keenly. "No, they thought my old man was a good fellow. And they were right. I'm sure nobody would have refused to let me play with their children, if we'd stuck around anywhere long enough."

"Lucky you." Her voice sounded about as dry as the desert outside. Irked with herself for wallowing, she asked, "And did you believe as they did? Regarding religion, I mean. I suppose it would have been difficult not to, since they were your parents and all." Which was a stupid thing for her, Sophie Madrigal, who had rejected almost every single thing her parents had believed in, to say.

Again Gabriel shrugged. "I tried. I really did try. But I never felt that kind of calling." He looked at her steadily, and his eyes held an intensity that surprised her. "I do believe in callings, though. I'm sure my mother and father felt compelled by a higher entity to preach their version of the Gospel. They were honest folks, and they loved their God with passion and dedication."

"But you didn't feel so compelled or dedicated."

"Not in the least."

"That must have been—difficult."

"It was. And it hurt. It hurt me, and it hurt my folks."

For the first time in almost a year, Sophie felt genuine empathy for another human being. Not, naturally, that she felt sorry for Gabriel Caine as he was now. But she knew from her own experience how badly the little boy Gabriel must have hurt, and she felt amazing compassion for him.

"Did—" She paused, unsure how to phrase the question. After mulling it over for a moment, she plunged ahead honestly. "Did you break from them, or did you just sort of drift away?"

"Oh, no. There was no drifting involved. It was a big, ugly break." He looked away from her for the first time in several minutes, and took to staring out the train's window.

Even when the sun shone directly overhead, there wasn't much to see out there, as the train passed through what seemed like an eternity of barren desert. Tonight, since the sun had long since set, the landscape was all black and forbidding. When Sophie turned her head to look too, her sense of isolation trebled.

Without looking at him, she spoke what was in her heart. "I'm sorry, Gabriel."

He turned to gaze at her again. "What for?"

"For enduring such unhappiness in your family."

He was silent for a minute or two, turning once more to stare into the blackness outside, then murmured, "It's over now, I guess. I'm only sorry I didn't understand it all sooner. I could have made amends to them. They died thinking I'd deserted not merely God, but them. I feel bad about it."

"I'm sure they understood," said Sophie, who was sure of no such thing. If it hadn't been for her personal tragedy, her own parents would have died thinking she despised them both. Her heart squeezed painfully.

When Gabriel turned to look at her, his grin was as near to evil as Sophie had ever seen it. "Don't lie to me, Sophie Madrigal. You're no good at it. You know damned well my folks didn't understand—not any more than I understood them. Not any more than Miss Juniper understands you."

"Oh, but she does understand me."

She wished she hadn't said that when Gabriel's expression sharpened. Because she wanted to skirt the issue of her past, she said quickly, "Why don't you tell me why you're chasing down Ivo Hardwick?"

"I've already told you that. Several times, if my memory serves."

Drat. He was right.

He went on. "Why don't you tell me why *you're* chasing the black-hearted Hardwick."

A chunk of ice invaded Sophie's heart. She said, "No."

Gabriel stared at her for a moment, and then gave up. "Dammit, you're not being fair."

"I'm sorry you think so."

The atmosphere in the smoking car was almost as dusky as the night sky outside. Sophie didn't understand why that should be, since there were no smokers left in it. Because Gabriel kept watching her, and because she was beginning to get an eerie sensation in her bones, she licked her lips and said, "Well, why don't we play with the spirit board some more?"

His grin lifted the corners of his mouth again. It was all Sophie could do not to stare at his mouth. From the

Join the Love Spell Romance Book Club
and **GET 2 FREE* BOOKS NOW—
An $11.98 value!**
Mail the Free* Book Certificate
Today!

Yes! I want to subscribe to the Love Spell Romance Book Club.

Please send me my **2 FREE* BOOKS**. I have enclosed $2.00 for shipping/handling. Every other month I'll receive the four newest Love Spell Romance selections to preview for 10 days. If I decide to keep them, I will pay the Special Members Only discounted price of just $4.49 each, a total of $17.96, plus $2.00 shipping/handling ($20.75 US in Canada). This is a **SAVINGS OF $6.00** off the bookstore price. There is no minimum number of books I must buy and I may cancel the program at any time. In any case, the **2 FREE* BOOKS** are mine to keep.

*In Canada, add $5.00 shipping and handling per order
for the first shipment. For all future shipments to Canada,
the cost of membership is $20.75 US, which
includes shipping and handling.
(All payments must be made in US dollars.)

NAME: _____

ADDRESS: _____

CITY: _____ STATE: _____

COUNTRY: _____ ZIP: _____

TELEPHONE: _____

E-MAIL: _____

SIGNATURE: _____

If under 18, Parent or Guardian must sign. Terms, prices, and conditions subject to change. Subscription subject
to acceptance. Dorchester Publishing reserves the right to reject any order or cancel any subscription.

all too brief encounter they'd had in Tucson, she knew those lips of his were soft and warm and inviting. If she were a different sort of female, she might just give up fighting her attraction to him and accept one of his thinly veiled invitations. She'd never experienced physical love as an adult. Her body yearned to discover what it was missing. Her brain, thanks be to God, was holding her treacherous body in check.

"All right. What do you want to ask it?"

She breathed a sigh of relief, not of a physical nature, but of a psychic one. She'd managed to evade, yet once more, being pressed to reveal herself. She wondered how long it would last. "Um, let me think." She feigned thought. Her nerves were vibrating so hard that her brain refused to function, and she hoped he'd come up with a question soon, or she might break from the tension.

As if he were on her side, which she knew good and well he wasn't, Gabriel said suddenly, "I have a good one."

Profoundly relieved, Sophie said, "Good. Ask it."

They'd removed their fingers from the planchette during their conversation. Now they both placed their fingers on the triangular disk once more. Their hands didn't touch, but Sophie felt the magnetic pull of Gabriel's body. Every time she got close enough to see him, the same thing happened. She feared she'd weaken one of these days. That would be worse than terrible; it might be catastrophic.

"What I want to know, Mr. Flying Hawk—" Gabriel said with assumed reverence. Sophie knew it was assumed, because he winked at her. Her heart almost stopped. "—is, will Sophie find Ivo Hardwick before I do, or will I find him before she does?"

She should have anticipated something of the sort, but hadn't, and she felt the shock career through her body. Instantly, she snatched her fingers from the planchette. "That's not fair, Gabriel."

He looked honestly surprised. "What's not fair about it? It's a good question, and it's of interest to both of us. Why not?"

Sophie couldn't think of an answer, blast it. The best she could do was point out the confusion such a question might produce in the spirit of the board. "You should ask a yes-or-no question, I think, if you're going to pursue that subject." She'd rather drop the question entirely, but she knew better than to expect Gabriel to do so.

He beckoned to her. "All right. Put your pretty little fingers back on the planchette, and I'll rephrase the question."

She huffed, annoyed, but did as he'd asked. "Very well. But I don't like it."

"I'm sure you don't."

He chuckled, and Sophie wished she could beat him over the head with the planchette. It wouldn't do any good. For one thing, the blasted thing was too light. For another thing, his head was too thick.

Gabriel spoke again. "All right, Mr. Flying Hawk, will I find Ivo Hardwick in Los Angeles?"

The planchette, which had been placed in the center of the board, zipped up to the "No."

"Damn," he said.

"What about me?" Sophie asked, interested in these proceedings again.

The planchette vibrated for a moment, made a quick little v-shaped dip, and darted back to the "No."

Gabriel chuckled. "At least I won't be the only one."

"Blast." Sophie felt an irrational sense of ill-usage. "It's all bunkum," she said to make herself feel better.

"All right, spirit, I want to ask another question. This one's personal."

Sophie's eyes thinned. She wasn't sure she wanted to hear a personal question issue from Gabriel Caine's mouth. She didn't trust him not to involve her in his stupid personal questions.

"Will Miss Sophie and I ever achieve some kind of mutual peace pact?"

Without a hint of hesitation, the planchette dashed across the board to the "Yes."

"Fiddlesticks," said Sophie, trying not to reveal how much Gabriel's question had alarmed her. "It sounds as if we're going to negotiate a treaty or something. Like the government with the Indians."

She was surprised when the planchette quivered once, then stopped, still on the "Yes."

"Ha!" Gabriel's grin was wicked again. "You know, of course, that the government's the one who's always broken the treaties. Which one of us do you suppose is the government in this instance?"

She glared at him. "You."

She'd forgotten her fingers still rested on the planchette until it took off across the board and came to rest on the "No."

Gabriel looked smug. "There. You see? You're the one who's the problem here, not me." He sounded smug, too.

Sophie resented it. "This is all folderol," she declared, rising from her bench seat.

"Aw, Sophie, don't be a spoilsport. At least sit with me for a while longer. It's not often we get to chat alone together."

Squinting down at him, Sophie said, "I don't trust you, Gabriel Caine."

He held his hands up, and adopted an expression of pure innocence. Instantly, Sophie's brain was filled with an image of a small Gabriel—a little boy Gabriel—looking just so at a tent full of people longing to be rescued from their humdrum lives. She felt the little boy's worry and tension, too, and knew at once how difficult Gabriel's childhood had been for him. The vision shocked her so much, her legs gave out, and she landed with a plunk on the bench she'd just vacated. "Oh, my." It came out in a breathy whisper.

"What's the matter?" Gabriel leaned over and reached out to touch her.

She drew away from him as if afraid of contracting a fell disease. He sat back, and Sophie read hurt and confusion on his expression. She could hardly blame him, but she couldn't trust herself. If she allowed him to touch her, she feared she'd succumb entirely, and then she knew not what would happen, but she feared her goal might become diluted. She wouldn't allow it.

Nevertheless, she had to come up with some kind of excuse. "I—I felt faint suddenly. It's nothing. It's passing."

"Are you sure?"

Damn and blast, why must he look so worried on her behalf? If she didn't watch her emotions with the vigilance of a prison guard, she'd fall in love with him, and then she'd be doomed. She was relatively certain she'd never be able to live through another crushing blow like the one she'd endured when she was young.

Because she was so unsettled, Sophie silently rattled off the credo by which she'd lived since her sixteenth year. For the most part, and regarding most women, men were hateful and manipulative and only wanted one thing. For the most part, and regarding most women, men were liars and cheats. They used you and thrust you away—or abandoned you—when you needed them most. The majority of men cared for nothing but their own pleasure. Most men, when it came to dealing with most women, were vile, unspeakably awful, vicious, and underhanded snakes in the grass. Sophie wanted nothing to do with men, because she chose the wrong ones. Because she didn't trust herself not to make another horrible mistake, she wanted nothing to do with any man.

"And particularly not you," she said aloud, much to her surprise. She hadn't meant to speak.

"And particularly not me, what?"

Gabriel looked genuinely befuddled. If she were granted the world on a silver platter, Sophie wouldn't enlighten him, either. She shook her head. "I beg your pardon. I—I felt lightheaded for a minute. That's all."

"That's not all." He rose from his own bench and came to kneel before her.

Desperate for him to keep his distance, Sophie whispered, "Please don't do that. I'm fine. Really, I am."

"You are not."

"Oh, please, Gabriel. Leave me alone for a minute. I'll be fine in a minute."

He put a hand on her shoulder and looked deep into her eyes. She shut them immediately. She couldn't take much more of this. "Please, just go away."

"I'm not going away. I'm worried about you."

She was worried about herself, for that matter, but his closeness wasn't going to cure her. If anything, it was going to be her ruin.

"All right. I can tell you don't want anything to do with me." He rose from his squatting position and looked down at her.

Sophie squinted up at him, wondering if the hurt she detected in his voice was genuine, or if it was merely another masculine ploy to weaken her defenses. Her own thoughts were so fuddled, she couldn't decide. It must have been confusion that made her say, softly, "I'm sorry, Gabriel. I didn't mean to be rude."

He lifted his eyebrows until they were two incredulous arcs over his brilliant dark eyes. "My, my, perhaps we should use the spirit board more often, Sophie, my sweet. It's made you turn polite all of a sudden."

A spurt of fury was immediately quenched by humor. Sophie could hardly believe it when she burst out laughing. Gabriel grinned and held out a hand for her. "Here, let me help you up. I promise not to ravish or otherwise corrupt you."

Still laughing, Sophie said, "You couldn't." She allowed herself to be helped up by him.

"Bet I could."

He didn't step back when she rose, and she was standing so close she could smell the essence of him; leather and soap and Gabriel Caine. She recalled that the other man, the one she'd believed herself to be in love with, had possessed a scent all his own. Gabriel's was much nicer. She'd stick a needle in her eye before she told him so.

"You couldn't," she repeated, with a smile to match his.

"And why not? I'm pretty adept with the ladies."

"I have no doubt about that." She tried to brush past him, but he wouldn't move. She gave him a stiffish look. "But you won't get me, Gabriel Caine, and you might as well stop trying."

Finally, he stepped aside. "I don't give up easily, Sophie."

"What a pity."

She turned to walk down the aisle and realized that while they'd been playing with each other, the atmosphere in the smoking car had thickened. Stopping short, she gaped into the swirling mists. Good Lord, it was happening again.

Gabriel lifted his head and sniffed. "Say, what's that sweet smell?"

The sweet smell was that of magic, although Sophie didn't believe it would be prudent to say so. The phenomenon put to rest any lingering doubts, however, about the potency of the connection between herself and Gabriel. Good heavens, whatever was she going to do about this?

Since she guessed she couldn't just ignore this physical manifestation of the magic they made together, she cleared her throat and dove in with a practical statement of fact. "It smells like a combination of aromas to me."

He looked at her. "A combination of what aromas? It's bewitching."

It certainly was. Striving to maintain her composure, Sophie said, "Well, let's see." She lifted her head and sniffed again, although she didn't need to. She knew exactly what it was. "I think I detect sandalwood, jasmine—and something else. Um—orange blossoms, I think."

"And look, there's a mist in the air, swirling around like a whirlpool. How queer it is."

It was queer, all right.

"Wonder where it came from."

Sophie knew exactly where it had come from. It had come from the Other Side, and it had been created by Sophie Madrigal and Gabriel Caine, who made magic together. Good Lord, this was awful. "Um," she said. "I don't know."

Gabriel appeared to be fascinated by the phenomenon. "You don't suppose old Flying Hawk sent it down from where he's living—or dying, rather—to impress us, do you?"

"Perhaps." She wanted to get back to her sleeping compartment right this minute. She feared what might happen if she didn't. Her control hadn't been this loosely contained since her first debacle as a dreamy adolescent girl who still believed in things like love and honor. And magic. "Um, I'd better get to bed now."

Her feet wouldn't move. Blast and damn. Her wretched feet were going to betray her. They were going to refuse to work until they sensed that some kind of conclusion between Gabriel and herself had been reached. Not a permanent solution; that was too much to ask, even for feet.

As if tugging himself back from a trance, Gabriel started slightly, then smiled at her. "I don't suppose you'd like company."

"Company?" Sophie remained puzzled for no more than two or three seconds. When she caught his drift, she used it to break the spell. "How dare you?" She sharpened her tone and stabbed him with her next words. "You know something, Gabriel Caine? Every time I get to feeling even slightly charitable toward you, you go and do or say something completely outrageous to aggravate me."

"Didn't realize I was so talented."

"Well," Sophie huffed, "you are. You have an unerring talent for infuriating me."

Gabriel sighed. "I'm sorry about it."

"I'll just bet you are." And, sniffing one of her best, most superior sniffs—which gave her a head full of the magical incense wafting about and made her dizzy—Sophie marched to the door of the carriage.

Gabriel didn't follow her. Sophie didn't know whether to be grateful or to burst into tears.

Chapter Thirteen

There was something mighty peculiar in the air, and Gabriel wished he knew what it was. He also wished he hadn't asked the spirit board about Sophie's prediction. Actually, he wished he could just forget about the damned prediction. He didn't believe in precognition or magic or any of the other spiritual idiocies being touted throughout the country these days.

Still, he couldn't stop thinking about that damned prediction. He didn't want to die. Hell, his life might not be worth much, but it was his, and who knew? He might win a big stake someday, or be bequeathed a huge fortune by some relative he didn't know about. Or be seduced by Sophie Madrigal. He grinned at that one.

What really rankled was that Sophie, the first woman Gabriel ever met whom he actually respected, had been the one to make it. "Damn," he muttered as he waited at the door of the carriage for the train to pull into the station in Los Angeles.

"What's the matter, Gabriel?" Juniper asked in her twittering, birdlike voice. "Is something amiss?"

Only then did he realize he'd sworn out loud. He turned and gave Juniper one of his lady-killer smiles. They worked on Juniper. They didn't on Sophie, which was one more thing that bothered him. "Sorry, ma'am. Didn't mean to swear." He didn't mean to answer her question, either.

"Tut, you know very well I'm accustomed to hearing much worse than that." Juniper giggled like a little girl.

"Especially since we've been keeping company with you, Gabriel."

Leave it to Sophie, Gabriel thought glumly, to splash him with the acid of her virulent tongue without any kind of provocation. Dammit, it had never taken him so long to get into a female's drawers in his life. What was worse was that his desire for Sophie Madrigal, far from waning as their association became more intimate—if intimate was the word for it—had increased so that he spent most of his waking hours thinking about how to get her into his bed. She was in his bed in his dreams, though, and they were about to drive him crazy. This fascination with her was apt to ruin his health if it kept up.

"May I see?"

Gabriel felt a tap on his shoulder and backed up to allow Sophie to move forward. Because he didn't want her falling out of the train—and because he took every opportunity he could find or manufacture to touch her—he put his hands on her shoulders to hold her still. She frowned at him, but didn't object. Juniper stood on her tiptoes and peered outside, too. "My goodness," she said. "It's awfully brown out there."

It was, indeed. "Summertime," muttered Gabriel. "I

reckon they don't get a lot of rain out here in the summertime."

"It's better than Tucson." Sophie said the words, but they didn't carry much conviction.

"I understand that there are some lovely homes in Los Angeles," Juniper said doubtfully.

"Not around here there aren't," Sophie said tartly.

"No," said Juniper with a wistful air. "But perhaps the scenery will improve when we go to that oddly named street for the seances we've booked."

"Bunker Hill," Sophie supplied.

"Yes. That's it. Now why do you suppose they named it Bunker Hill?"

"I don't know." Sophie sounded bored. "Pretensions of grandeur? Silliness? I suspect they were putting on airs, trying to make Los Angeles sound more important than it is."

"You're a real grouch, you know that, Sophie?" Gabriel squeezed her shoulders, but she didn't react.

"However it got its name, I understand there are some magnificent homes there. We're going to be conducting our seances in a lovely setting. At least," Juniper added with her customary honesty, "I hope we are."

Sophie grunted something Gabriel assumed was agreement.

"Seances, eh? That sounds interesting." Gabriel wondered if a seance was conducted like a revival meeting. Probably not. There was a lot of hollering in revival meetings; Gabriel imagined seances were much quieter affairs. They both served the same purpose, as far as he could see, each being, in its own way, a conduit to the spiritual side of life. Or death. Whatever it was.

"Oh, you must come to at least one of our seances, Gabriel!" Juniper exclaimed.

"He doesn't have to if he doesn't want to." Sophie stiffened under Gabriel's hands.

He chuckled. "Oh, but I do want to, Sophie."

"You would."

He wanted to let his hands slip down her arms, cross over her stomach, and pull her against him. He wanted her to feel the reaction he had to her nearness, to know she affected him, to understand how much he desired her.

Although, come to think of it, he didn't understand why he wanted her to know those things. She'd only laugh at him. He pointed. "Look over there. I think we're coming into the station."

He was right. He took Tybalt's basket down first, then assisted Sophie and Juniper. He was pleased that Sophie seemed to have given up rejecting his attempts to assist her.

Dmitri, who left the train after the rest of them, stood frowning at the people milling about, greeting friends and relatives who'd arrived on the train. "Crowded," he said, succinctly summarizing Gabriel's own thoughts.

"Yes. I hear this area is attracting more people every day."

"I can't imagine why." Sophie wrinkled her pretty nose. "It smells funny."

"I believe that's only the train, dear." Juniper, bright-eyed with interest, seemed to be swallowing huge gulps of Los Angeles atmosphere whole. She pointed at a man, clad in a loose-fitting white garment, leading a donkey. "Oh, look, Sophie! Isn't that quaint?"

"It certainly is."

"Do you suppose that gentleman is a Spanish man?" Juniper sounded as though the idea thrilled her.

"I suppose he is. Mexican, maybe. This used to be a Spanish colony," said Gabriel. "I suspect there's still a lot of the Spanish influence prevailing."

Sophie sighed. "I suppose so."

Gabriel was in the process of picking up the ladies'

bags when he noticed a small, thin, rugged-looking individual limping toward the Madrigals. Dmitri took two quick steps forward to meet the man and glanced back over his shoulder at Sophie. He appeared to be anxious about the man's approach.

Sophie murmured, "Mr. Huffy," as if she wasn't pleased to be seeing him. "I thought he was going to come to the hotel."

"Who's Mr. Huffy?" Gabriel looked first to Sophie, who ignored him, and then to Juniper, whose expression had changed from one of excitement to one of worry. Sensing he'd have better luck in that direction, he said, "Who's that man, Miss Juniper?"

Juniper shook her head. "Oh, dear, I'm sorry, Gabriel, but I can't tell you."

Sophie frowned at her aunt. "He's an acquaintance of ours, Gabriel, and his name is Mr. Huffy. Emerald Huffy. That's all." She took off striding and reached the newcomer before he could get within talking distance of Gabriel.

Gabriel watched, unsettled, as they seemed to carry on a spirited conversation. Now who the hell was that, really? Sophie didn't want him to know, obviously, and since Sophie was the most single-minded female he'd ever met in his life, he'd wager the man had come here to bring her information about Ivo Hardwick. This was the first time in days he'd spared a thought for Hardwick. Now he wondered how he could have allowed himself to be so lulled.

It didn't take Sophie long to conduct her business with Mr. Huffy. As soon as she turned to come back to her aunt, Gabriel knew his supposition was correct. Nothing but Ivo Hardwick could put that determined—almost exultant—expression on her face.

Damnation, he wished he knew what her story was. It had something to do with a little boy named Joshua who had died, but Gabriel didn't know who Joshua had been. Sophie's brother? A cousin? The child of a friend? Her own child?

The last notion stopped his thought processes cold in their tracks.

Good God, could Joshua have been Sophie Madrigal's son?

If he was, Gabriel guessed he'd have to find out on his own. He could tell from Sophie's demeanor that, while she might have condescended to enjoy Gabriel's company on the train, she was all business now.

With a sigh, he decided not to allow her mood to affect his. He put on one of his best smiles. "I'm seeing you to your hotel, Sophie, and I don't aim to allow you to argue with me about it."

For a second or two, he expected her to take him to task. A rebellious expression clouded her face, and she opened her mouth—to rake him over the coals, Gabriel presumed. But she didn't. Almost as soon as it had come, her mulish expression softened, and she smiled. Gabriel damned near fell over backwards.

"Thank you, Gabriel. I must say, you have your uses."

"Sophie!" Juniper twitted and tutted and Sophie paid not the least bit of attention to her.

After a moment of shock, Gabriel laughed. A man had to keep on his toes around Sophie Madrigal.

The four of them checked into the Melrose Hotel, and then Sophie and Juniper went shopping.

"For you know, Gabriel, there's a big new department store in Los Angeles. It's called the Broadway, and I've read about it in magazines and newspapers."

"A department store, eh?"

"My, yes." Juniper was as happy as the proverbial lark again. In Gabriel's estimation, it was a good thing she didn't possess the capacity to brood, or Sophie would drive her into a black depression in no time at all.

"Sounds like fun to me."

The look Sophie gave him made him grin. "Don't worry, Sophie. I won't darken your shopping spree with my infamous presence."

"Good."

He tilted his head and peered at her, and she had the grace to blush. Maybe she wasn't impervious, after all. Until he found Ivo Hardwick and placed him under arrest, he aimed to keep testing. "After all, I have some catching up to do."

"Catching up?" Juniper blinked inquisitively.

"Yes, ma'am. Can't let Sophie's hired spy get to Hardwick before me."

Sophie gave him one of her blackest scowls.

Sophie felt far from impervious when they left Gabriel at the Melrose Hotel. She felt, in fact, as if the protective walls she'd erected with such a monumental effort of will were crumbling around her. This couldn't continue or she'd be lost. Again. She wasn't sure she could survive another emotional blow. She was, after all, mere mortal flesh and blood. How many severe shocks could one person take and live? And Sophie knew better than most folks that love was but a transitory illusion. She had to keep reminding herself how much she had to lose, or she'd have fallen in love with Gabriel before now.

Strong. She had to be strong. She had to withstand Gabriel's lures and her own body's subversion. It wasn't fair.

"Bother," she muttered as she and Juniper descended the really quite grand staircase of the Melrose.

"What's the matter, dear?"

For the tiniest space of time, Sophie contemplated telling her exactly what the matter was. But Juniper didn't deserve that. She also wouldn't understand. Juniper would be ecstatic if Gabriel and Sophie got together. She said, "Nothing, Juniper. I thought I'd forgotten my—my parasol, but I have it right here." She lifted the pretty paisley item in question and showed her aunt.

"Yes. I see it, dear." Juniper carried her own favorite parasol, a black-and-white striped number that went very prettily with Juniper's lightweight summer gown of black gabardine. She looked quite fashionable. "I hope the clerk was correct and that we won't have trouble finding a cab."

"I'm sure he was."

Sophie was right. Several cabs were lined up in front of the Melrose, and the handy liveried footman employed by the hotel hailed one for the Madrigal ladies in no time at all. Soon Sophie and Juniper were rolling toward the Broadway Department Store behind a high-stepping horse that looked much healthier than most of the cab horses Sophie had seen in other cities. Perhaps the dry air in Los Angeles had a wholesome effect on the people and animals who lived here.

Sophie started to feel better. Before the week was out, she'd have accomplished her purpose in life by slaying Ivo Hardwick. Emerald Huffy had done a good job of tracking Hardwick down. All Sophie had to do now was wait until she had the free time to finish her job.

And, she thought as her bright mood darkened, she also had to circumvent Gabriel's interference. She'd not let him thwart her this time. She silently cursed herself for thinking about Gabriel again.

She was more pleased than not about the jobs Dmitri had lined up for them in Los Angeles. They wouldn't have to rent any more hotel parlors, because three of Los Angeles's richest and silliest matrons had hired the Madrigals to conduct seances in their homes. Sophie preferred seances to the reading of palms and crystals on an appointment basis because seances didn't take as much out of her.

Her thoughts reverted of their own volition to Gabriel Caine, who was still determined to prevent her from exacting retribution for Joshua's murder. She frowned as the cab headed down a street lined with palm trees. She knew they were palm trees, because she'd seen pictures of them.

"My goodness, Sophie, will you look at those trees." Juniper was obviously more impressed by the tropical palms than was Sophie, to whom they looked like rather large mops standing on end.

"Mmmm." Sophie didn't have a thought to spare for anything but her quest.

What could she do to muzzle Gabriel Caine? She already knew he wouldn't be persuaded by reasoned, or even unreasoned, argument. She might be able to talk him around to her way of thinking, but not unless she told him the truth about Joshua. Since her heart felt as though she were stabbing it with poisoned darts every time she even thought of talking about her personal tragedy, she couldn't do that.

She'd be hanged before she'd accept sympathy from Gabriel Caine or any other man. While she knew, in her mind, that not all men were evil, her heart couldn't rid itself of the feeling that men were the enemies of her entire life. It was ironic, she supposed, that had Joshua been allowed to grow up he would have been a man, but Sophie's heart acquitted him of being one of *those* men; the kind who hurt people without giving them a thought.

"Oh, Sophie, will you look at this building. Isn't it something?"

Shoving her problems aside for the moment, Sophie glanced at the building. It looked exactly like a building to her. Perhaps she lacked a proper appreciation of modern architecture. "I see, Juniper. Very impressive."

"I'm so looking forward to seeing what they have to offer. I've only seen one other department store."

"That one in New York City?"

"Yes."

The cab pulled up in front of the huge building situated on the corner of 4th and Broadway, and the cab man got down to assist the ladies out of his cab. Sophie paid the man and gave him a good tip, for which she received an amiable thanks and a big grin. Wouldn't it be nice if all of life's problems could be settled with cash?

"I've so wanted to see this part of the country." Juniper's voice fairly vibrated with excitement as the two ladies entered the portals of the Broadway.

"I understand the weather is wonderful here," murmured Sophie, striving to keep up her end of a conversation in which she had no interest.

"Temperate," Juniper said with a happy nod. "Wouldn't it be fun to see a real orange grove?" Without waiting for her niece to reply, Juniper cried, "Oh, look at that, Sophie!"

Sophie saw with dismay that Juniper was headed like a fly to honey toward the infants' department. Following slowly, Sophie commanded herself to buck up. Joshua had outgrown baby things years before his death. This interest of Juniper's was predicated upon Juniper's sweet-natured fondness for babies of all sorts. As for Sophie, she hardened her heart, knowing that if she didn't, she'd fall apart, which would be not merely mortally embarrassing, considering they were in a huge, fancy department store, but also weak. Sophie wouldn't let herself show any sort of weakness.

"Oh, Sophie, isn't this darling?"

Juniper held up a lacy white christening dress. It reminded Sophie of Joshua's, and she swallowed hard and nodded, striving to smile at her aunt.

Fortunately, Juniper's attention span was a variable commodity and today, as Juniper contemplated the further amazements in store for herself and Sophie at the Broadway, she soon tired of the infants' paraphernalia. Sophie breathed a sigh of relief when her aunt tripped on through the infants' wear, from which Sophie averted her eyes, and ended up in a part of the store where it seemed as if thousands of ladies' handbags were displayed.

After much indecision, Juniper finally bought a pretty embroidered reticule. "For you know, Sophie, one can never have too many pretty purses. I can use this with the lavender satin. Won't it look well?"

"It will indeed, Aunt. You have wonderful taste."

"Tosh." But she was pleased, and that pleased Sophie.

Juniper and Sophie ate lunch in the elegant little dining room in the Broadway. Sophie was glad to sit and rest her feet. Juniper had been dragging her willy-nilly through the store, stopping here and there to investigate the laces, hats, shoes, and notions. The store was a paradise for shoppers, Sophie thought wryly. Unfortunately, that let her out, since she hadn't been interested in shopping since Joshua's death. She'd been used to shopping for him, and she'd taken immense pride in his dress and deportment. These days, there didn't seem to be any reason to shop. She didn't care about buying things for herself.

"I don't know about you, Sophie, but I am going to indulge myself and have a dish of ice-cream for dessert." Juniper nodded, as if she'd just made an earth-shaking decision about a matter of life-and-death significance.

Tickled by Juniper's strong stand on the subject of ice-cream, Sophie laughed and said, "I do believe I'll

Emma Craig

join you, then. After all, how many times does one get to eat ice cream?"

Obviously pleased that Sophie aimed to have a treat, too, Juniper beamed at her. After their waitress, clad in a prim black dress and white apron, had brought the ice cream, Juniper said, "I want to look at the foundation garments next, Sophie. I need a new corset cover. Of course, I should make one for myself and not waste money on buying one, but I think it would be exciting to purchase one here, in this wonderful store."

Sophie wished her life were so simple that she could get excited about buying underwear. She wouldn't say so to Juniper for worlds. "Don't be silly, Juniper. You work hard for the money you earn. You should be able to purchase a corset cover without feeling guilty about it." Hoping to make Juniper feel less extravagant, she added, "Maybe I'll look around, too. I could use a new chemise."

"And hosiery, too." Juniper's eyes were bright with anticipation. "I'm sure we can both use some hosiery."

"I'm sure you're right."

So after they'd polished off their ice cream, the two ladies made their way to the department featuring foundation garments and sleep wear. Sophie's attention snagged on a lovely chemise. The fabric was soft and silky, and the neckline was scandalously low. The borders were trimmed with pink ribbons and lots of lace. With a sly smile, she wondered what Gabriel Caine would make of such a pretty undergarment. Short work, unless she was entirely wrong about him.

"Oh, my!" A thought struck Sophie so suddenly and so hard that she spoke the words aloud.

Juniper, mistaking her exclamation as one regarding the pretty chemise, hurried over to see what Sophie held. "What a nice chemise! It's just beautiful, Sophie, but . . . well, do you think it's quite appropriate for an unmarried lady?"

With a genuine smile for her darling innocent of an aunt, Sophie said, "Probably not. I think I'll continue looking, though. I'm in the mood for something frivolous."

She only hoped the Broadway, a respectable department store, carried the type of undergarment she sought, actually. Maybe something bright red. No. Red was too obvious.

"That's nice, dear. It's about time you pampered yourself a little bit. After all, you can't stay unhappy forever." Realizing what she'd said, Juniper put a hand to her lips as if to stuff the words back in and cried, "Oh!"

But Juniper didn't have the power to poison Sophie's mood today. She'd just been attacked by a perfectly marvelous scheme for neutralizing Gabriel Caine. She ignored Juniper's reference to her grief over Joshua. "Have you noticed any black chemises, Juniper?"

"Black?" Juniper eyed her doubtfully from across a table stacked with pantaloons of various sizes and degrees of ornamentation. "I don't know. Let me see. . . ." She commenced poking through racks of clothing. "Are you sure you want black, dear? It's an awfully somber color."

"I don't necessarily need black," Sophie answered. "Perhaps pink or green would do." As long as it was outrageously revealing. She picked up a pink satin corset cover, bedecked with satin ribbons. "This isn't quite what I'm looking for, but if you see anything like it in my size, let me know, please."

Juniper's eyes bulged in shock. "Good heavens, Sophie, do you mean it?"

"Of course I mean it. Well, not this exactly. I'm too

229

large for anything this frilly. I'd look like a packaged pig."

Juniper giggled. "Don't be silly, Sophie. You're a beautiful young lady. As your dear papa used to say, if a lady is largish, there's more of her to love."

Good old papa, the barefaced liar. Sophie had loved him, though, for trying to make her feel better about her size.

"Um, perhaps green would be better than pink," Juniper suggested timidly.

"You're undoubtedly right." Sophie had always acknowledged Juniper's flair with clothing and accessories. "But I want something kind of—well—fancy. Fancier than the things I usually wear."

"I see." Juniper was watching her as if she expected Sophie to begin raving any minute now.

Sophie understood why Juniper was worried about her. She'd never once expressed the least desire to clothe herself in a fashionable manner. In fact, she generally let Juniper pick out her underthings and gowns because Juniper enjoyed doing it, and she did a good job. Today, Sophie aimed to choose for herself, sensing that Juniper was singularly ill equipped to select underclothing with an eye to seduction. She lifted her chin and lied like a true Madrigal. "I feel like finding something deliciously feminine."

"All right, dear, if you think so."

It took almost an hour for Sophie to select the proper garments—but they were perfect. Not only did she purchase a chemise, fashioned out of dark green satin and trimmed with black ribbons, but she also bought a dark green French sateen corset that barely covered her breasts as it lifted them, so that she appeared to be even more well-endowed than she was. The corset, too, was trimmed with lace and black ribbons. She inspected herself in the dressing-room mirror and very nearly laughed out loud. In this getup, she looked as much like a saloon whore as she was ever likely to look.

"Perfect," she murmured, satisfied. "Absolutely perfect."

Juniper wasn't as happy about Sophie's purchases as Sophie was. Since Sophie knew her aunt would disapprove entirely if she knew what had motivated Sophie to make the purchases, she didn't enlighten her. She was humming happily, however, when the ladies stopped in the hosiery department, where they each bought new stockings. Juniper's were serviceable but comfy lisle. Sophie's were silk.

"Are you sure you want silk?" Juniper ventured to ask.

"I think so." She knew so.

"Oh. They're rather dear, don't you think?"

Since Sophie felt guilty about what she aimed to do—after all, it was unkind to Gabriel and certainly outrageous—and since Juniper seldom ever questioned her, Sophie didn't snap back at her aunt. She said mildly, "I think they'll make me feel feminine, Juniper."

Juniper gazed solemnly at the soft silk hosiery in Sophie's hands. "I'm sure they will. How could they fail to do so?"

"Exactly," said Sophie with a smile. She folded the hosiery and thought for a minute. Garters. She needed seductive garters. She turned to find them, and started when Juniper cried out suddenly.

"Oh!" She grabbed Sophie's arm and an expression of elation settled on her face. "Oh, Sophie, don't tell me you're dressing up for Mr. Caine!"

She certainly was dressing up for Mr. Caine. She said, "Perish the thought."

"Oh." Juniper's smile faded and her voice sounded sad. "I was rather hoping you were. He's such a wonderful man."

Sophie rolled her eyes. "We'll just have to disagree on that point, I fear."

"But he is, dear. The cards say so. I'm sure the two of you would be perfect together."

"Good heavens, you almost frighten me, Aunt Juniper." Ah, there they were. She hurried over to another table with a molded ceramic leg sporting a garter and hose atop it. Dark green. She wanted dark green. Or perhaps black. Pink was too babyish, and Sophie wasn't interested in looking like a child. She aimed to look like a wanton temptress.

"Let's visit the ready-made dress department," she suggested. She'd found the garters and had the underthings, and they were both beautiful and alluring. Now she had to get an outer garment that would inspire Gabriel with the irresistible urge to remove it. She was going to distract him with sex. Then, when he was sated and sleepy, she'd sneak off and rid the world of Ivo Hardwick.

Offhand, she couldn't imagine why she hadn't had this brilliant idea sooner. He'd never tried to hide his desire to debauch her; he was now going to get his chance.

A faint, faint echo of the voice of rational thought tried to assert itself by telling Sophie she was playing with fire, but she thrust it angrily aside. Of course, there were dangers to this course of action. There were dangers attached to almost anything one did in this life.

"I don't believe I've ever been in a ready-made dress department before," Juniper ventured, staring about with fascination. "My goodness, I do hope these department stores won't put all the seamstresses in America out of business."

Frowning at the seams of a dress, Sophie said, "I don't think they will. Not if all of the goods are this shoddily made." She showed Juniper the offending seam, and Juniper tutted appropriately.

Not all of the costumes for sale at the Broadway were shoddy, however. There were plenty of lovely gowns to choose from, in a variety of styles and fabrics, from day dresses to wrappers to walking costumes to evening wear. Sophie knew exactly what she was looking for, and she almost found it. The dress she ultimately selected differed from her mental image in only one important detail: The neckline wasn't as low as Sophie had hoped for. It was plenty low enough for Juniper, who appeared a good deal shocked by Sophie's selection.

"Don't worry, Aunt Juniper," Sophie said with what she hoped was a reassuring smile. "I know exactly what I'm doing."

Juniper shook her head uneasily. "I hope so, dear."

So did Sophie.

Chapter Fourteen

Sophie was up to something. Gabriel didn't know what it was, but he figured it was something he wouldn't like. She'd never, in the weeks he'd known her, flirted with him. Tonight, she was flirting like a dance-hall queen.

Gabriel kind of liked it. He'd have liked it a lot more if he believed she meant it.

Or maybe she did mean it. How far would Sophie go to distract him from his avowed purpose of thwarting her intention to kill Ivo Hardwick? If he knew why she wanted to kill him, he might have an answer to that question. In the meantime, he knew she was plotting, but he didn't know what, or how far she intended to go.

He was not, however, a man who'd turn down dessert when it was offered, even if he expected to get a stomachache from it. And if Sophie aimed to take her flirtation to its logical—to him—conclusion, he'd partake, no matter how much he suffered for it later.

"You look good enough to eat tonight, Sophie." Gabriel had already assisted Juniper into the waiting carriage, and was now holding his arm out for Sophie. Tybalt had been left in the hotel room. Gabriel had brought him a nice steak bone to keep him company during the long evening. Sophie had gone so far as to kiss him on the cheek in thanks.

Now she took his arm and gave him a flirty look out of the corner of her glorious eyes. The dress she wore was one Gabriel had never seen before. A deep, forest-green satin, it brought out the color of her eyes with a vengeance. If ever a woman was crafted for the mystical arts, Sophie looked the part this evening. Bewitching, is what she was. Gabriel wanted to rip that dress off of her right this minute and spend the rest of his life naked with her.

Silly Gabriel.

Still, she was up to something. And while he didn't know what it was, and probably wouldn't like it when he found out, he figured he might as well take advantage of it. He knew he'd pay later, but Gabriel never played without paying.

"Thank you, Gabriel. I'm glad you approve."

"Sophie bought that dress at the Broadway Department Store today, Gabriel," Juniper offered happily. "It's ready-made. I didn't think I'd like ready-made clothes, but some of them are really quite nice and well-made."

"This one certainly is," he agreed, ogling Sophie in a manner he figured she'd hate.

She didn't take the bait. Rather, she gave him an enigmatic smile and said, "Thank you."

Eyeing her niece with a trace of uncertainty, Juniper went on, "You don't think it's too low-cut, do you, Gabriel? We shouldn't want to shock our patrons."

"I'm sure it isn't," Sophie said, a trifle crisply.

"It doesn't look too low-cut to me." In fact, Gabriel

would like to see his Sophie in greater décolletage, if he were doing the picking-out of gowns for her. She had a substantial bosom, after all. Might as well show it off. He helped Dmitri into the carriage and climbed in behind him. Dmitri had had the common sense to sit beside Juniper, so Gabriel took his place beside Sophie. She didn't move farther away from him, which was most unlike her. Interesting behavior on her part. Gabriel's cynical antennae, already up, quivered with intrigue.

As the carriage rumbled off, carrying its passengers to an address on Bunker Hill, he made an effort to keep the conversation alive. "So, what do you ladies do during a seance? Do you try to contact spirits from beyond this life?"

"Sophie acts as the medium," Juniper said. "And I contact the Other Side."

"Does it always work?" In spite of Flying Hawk and the spirit board, he didn't believe in spirits from beyond communicating with the living any more than he believed in elves and fairies. He'd come to value Miss Juniper too much to ridicule the work she believed in so wholeheartedly, however. Sophie smiled at him, which made his effort to restrain his disbelief worthwhile.

"Not always," admitted Juniper. "It depends on how sincere the people asking are regarding making contact. Often people think of seances as a mere game."

"I see." Made perfect sense to Gabriel.

"If we don't make contact," Sophie went on, taking over for her aunt, "we still give them a show. Read palms, look into the crystal ball, that sort of thing."

Gabriel pursed his lips. "I thought you didn't believe in the occult, Sophie."

"I don't really believe in making contact with spirits from beyond the grave—the Other Side, as Juniper calls it—although there are certainly phenomena in life that are beyond our mortal ken." Her smile was faintly wintry. "However, I know which side my bread is buttered on. I never mock the clients."

"Sophie," murmured Juniper, unhappily.

"I beg your pardon, Aunt."

"Well," said Gabriel in an effort to settle the atmosphere, which had become a trifle bumpy, "I'm looking forward to this seance. I must admit I've been curious about them."

"I'm sure you'll find it interesting," opined Juniper.

"Fascinating," Sophie agreed, and her tone of voice grated on Gabriel's nerves.

It was clear to Gabriel that Sophie didn't believe in anything she and her aunt did—not really; not with conviction or strength of purpose. She was contemptuous of their work and treated it lightly, as if she were ashamed and embarrassed by it. This evening, for some reason, he wished she *did* believe in what he'd come to think of as Aunt Juniper's calling, as the ministry had been his father's. He wanted Sophie to have some sort of consoling belief system, to have *some* kind of refuge from the pain of the world.

He wasn't accustomed to thinking of Sophie Madrigal as a mere mortal woman who needed support and solace but, tough as she was, she did. Hell, everybody did. Even he, Gabriel Caine, cynic extraordinaire and hardened man of the world, could use a soft bosom to rest his weary head upon every now and then. Actually, he'd like to use Sophie's soft bosom for any number of reasons and for any number of purposes.

Besides, Sophie wasn't near as tough as she tried to make people think she was. With a pang, Gabriel recalled the episode with "Amazing Grace." He still wished he knew what terrible memories had caused her reaction. And he was still itching with curiosity about the little boy Joshua. He'd spent hours in conjecture, and would be willing to venture a guess at this point, but he'd like to hear the truth from Sophie's mouth. For some reason unknown to him—and deplored by him—he wanted Sophie's trust.

But if he couldn't earn her trust, he'd sure as the devil like to have her body. Eyeing Sophie out of the corner of his eye, he wondered if his latter desire would be fulfilled tonight. He hoped so, no matter how much he doubted it.

He sighed, pondering the evening ahead of him. He was in for more frustration, probably. He was too honest with himself to believe Sophie's flirtatiousness was aimed at any sort of consummation. She'd been avoiding him ever since they met; he didn't imagine for a minute that she'd suddenly decided she was madly in love with him and wanted to share his bed. Not a chance.

Still and all, she was up to something.

He got itchy, contemplating what it might be.

Silence prevailed in the cab for several long minutes. All parties peered out the windows with great curiosity, and Gabriel was glad they were in Los Angeles in the summertime, when daylight lingered. The City of Angels was something to see. The temperate climate of Southern California evidently drew a variety of people. He saw folks who looked to him like Mexican peasants rubbing elbows with elegantly clad ladies and gentlemen strolling along as if they had nothing better to do in life but take the air of a balmy summer's evening.

"Merciful heavens, will you look at that mansion," Juniper cried when the cab turned a corner and the horse began pulling them up a steep hill.

"My word," murmured Sophie, sounding genuinely impressed, "It's—huge. And beautiful."

"There's more than one of them, too," added Gabriel as the cab drew them farther along the street climbing Bunker Hill. "Looks like your seance is going to be held in a mighty fashionable neighborhood, ladies, if this is Bunker Hill."

"I should say so."

Dmitri said nothing, but glared at the street as if he disapproved of such conspicuous displays of wealth. Gabriel grinned inside when he discovered himself chalking up the little man's attitude to his being a Russian. Maybe some of Juniper's fanciful ideas were rubbing off on him.

A few minutes later, the cab turned right, entering a drive that looked as if it aimed to go on forever. The cabbie stopped at a huge wrought-iron gate and was approached by a uniformed man, who had been guarding it. Gabriel wondered if his services were really needed, or if a liveried guard was only another ostentatious manifestation of this particular Californian's wealth. Whatever his function, he opened the gate as soon as Dmitri told him who was in the cab, and the cab horse trotted them down a twisting drive.

"What do you suppose those trees are?" Juniper asked at one point. "Don't they smell queer, though?"

"I rather like the smell," said Sophie.

"I read somewhere," said Gabriel, "that somebody's been importing trees from Australia. I wonder if these are eucalyptus trees."

"Australia," murmured Juniper.

"Really?" Sophie gave him a quizzical glance.

Sweet Lord have mercy, if she was only toying with him, Gabriel wasn't sure he'd survive the night. He wanted her so badly by this time, he ached with unfulfilled lust.

"That's what I've read."

"My goodness." Sophie leaned forward so she could

get a better look at the tall trees. Doing so thrust her bosom up, and Gabriel had to swallow a groan of frustration. "It must be nice to be wealthy and to be able to import Australian trees if you feel like it."

"Oh, my, yes." Juniper giggled, as if she considered such talk as part of a game.

Gabriel didn't think Sophie thought it was a game. The better he got to know her, the better he realized that much, if not most, of her life was spent in doing things she cared nothing about, or even actively hated. A niggling sense of compassion began to fight for space with his overwhelming lust. Lord, when had this happened?

He could understand the lust part. Just looking at her tonight, in that new dress of hers, brought out the beast in him. Her skin was always lovely. Tonight, with goodly portions of her chest and arms exposed, she was ravishing. The dark green of her gown made her skin look pearly.

Damn, Gabriel wanted her. He tried with limited success to tamp his desires. If she followed through with her flirtations, he might get those desires fulfilled yet. He wondered what torturous price Sophie would exact from him. As much as he hated to admit it to himself, whatever her price, he was willing to pay it. And more, probably.

And if that wasn't a lowering admission as to how far and how hard he'd fallen for Sophie Madrigal, he didn't know what was.

The eucalyptus trees gave way to a path lined with deodars, and Juniper seemed unable to do anything more than shake her head and stare in wonder. Sophie wasn't so impaired. "Good Lord, these people must have more money than God. We ought to have charged them more than we did."

"Sophie!" Juniper was scandalized.

Gabriel wished he could paddle Sophie's perfectly splendid rump. He didn't understand why she seemed compelled to say things to shock Miss Juniper.

To her credit, Sophie said, "I'm sorry, Juniper. I didn't really mean it to sound so callous."

She did, too. Gabriel knew it, and he knew Sophie knew he knew it when she glanced at him, then turned away quickly, flushing as she did so. Damn. If she didn't stop looking so tasty, Gabriel feared he might perish from unrequited lust.

"Well," said Juniper, as if she'd given the matter serious thought, "actually, you may be right, Sophie. I mean, why shouldn't people who can afford it pay more than those who can't?" Her glance slid between Sophie and Gabriel as if she felt guilty for having voiced so revolutionary an idea.

Gabriel smiled at her. "I think you're right, Miss Juniper. Why not, indeed?"

Sophie nodded. "Yes. After all, the more we soak rich people, the more poor folks we can help for less."

Gabriel poked her with his elbow to get her to stop being so spiteful. Sophie merely turned her head and scowled at him. He felt as though nothing had changed—and never would—between himself and Sophie, and the idea made him feel empty, unless that was hunger gnawing at his innards.

Juniper, however, all but glowed at her niece, completely missing the sarcasm in Sophie's comment. "Exactly!"

The conversation was mercifully ended when the cab drew up at a massive, pillared porch. The cab's passengers stared at the house connected to the porch, speechless.

"I don't believe we've ever worked in such a grand home. Can you think of any venue to rival this, Sophie?"

"No. I think this is the highest we've climbed so far." Again, her tone was acerbic.

"These folks spared no expense when they built, that's for sure," Gabriel ventured. He'd seen people from all walks of life in his day, and wasn't usually impressed by great shows of wealth, but these Westerners really liked to put on an exhibition.

"I wonder if it has to do with the climate," Sophie muttered.

Gabriel grinned. "Maybe. Or maybe if you make your own fortune, say, in gold or railroads, you tend to be of a more expansive disposition than if you inherited your wealth from your forebears, as so many Easterners have done."

"Easy come, easy go?"

He chuckled. "Well, not exactly."

Sophie heaved a big sigh as she stepped out of the carriage. "I wish my forebears had left me money instead of occult powers. Money is so much more useful."

"Sophie!"

Sophie said primly, "I'm sorry, Aunt Juniper."

"You should be," grumbled Gabriel.

Dmitri, as was his custom, spoke not a word, but led the way up the steps of the gigantic front porch and up to the gigantic door of the gigantic house, a white stuccoed monster with an alarming excess of rococo decorations set all over the place. Plaster lions greeted them at the door, plaster gargoyles grimaced at them from the roof, and plaster flowers frolicked up the columns supporting the porch's roof.

Gabriel glanced around with interest. "I'm glad we got here while there's still daylight. I'd hate to have missed this."

"Oh, I agree, Gabriel," Juniper whispered as if she were intimidated by the grand surroundings.

Not so Sophie. "And I. Florid excess is so interesting."

Without a pause, she twisted the doorbell. She did it hard, too, as if she wasn't going to kowtow to anybody, no matter how much money they had.

It occurred to Gabriel that one of the reasons he admired her—aside from her overt feminine charms—was that she had a world of fight in her. The quality was irritating as hell sometimes, but overall, he'd rather a woman have guts than the timidity and reserve so admired in females by the general run of society.

A uniformed footman opened the door and bowed them in. Gabriel heard a titter of voices, and a couple of excited exclamations. Before the footman had finished taking their wraps, a small, beautifully dressed woman darted out of a room and hurried toward them with her hands outstretched. "Oh, my goodness, are you the Madrigals?" Her eyes were bright and dark, and reminded Gabriel of the eyes of an eagle. Predatory, is what they were.

Sophie smiled a splendid smile and bowed slightly. "Yes, indeed. And you're Mrs. Millhouse?" She shook the woman's hand as if she were a queen greeting a commoner who'd said something witty. Gabriel was as impressed as hell.

"Oh, yes, and I'm so glad you could come. My friends and I have been dying to meet you and to begin the seance!"

"Apt phrasing," Sophie murmured, but Mrs. Millhouse didn't hear her.

Gabriel dug his elbow into her ribs again in a vain effort to get her to stop being sarcastic. She didn't so much as look at him, but spoke to Mrs. Millhouse. "Please allow me to introduce you to our party, Mrs. Millhouse. This is my aunt, Juniper Madrigal."

Sophie presented Aunt Juniper with impressive formality and clear fondness. Gabriel almost forgave her for being sarcastic earlier.

"How do you do?" Mrs. Millhouse shook Juniper's hand. "We've heard so much about you and the Madrigal family, Miss Madrigal."

Juniper, every bit as elegant as Mrs. Millhouse, although not so expensively clad, smiled and bubbled something Gabriel didn't catch. It was interesting to watch the Madrigals work, because they complemented each other perfectly. Juniper was everybody's friend and companion; Sophie was above them all. Both poses were absolutely appropriate to their line of work, and created an impression that wasn't easily forgotten.

"And I am Sophie Madrigal," Sophie went on. She towered above the tiny Mrs. Millhouse, but she didn't look at all awkward. In truth, she looked regal and made Mrs. Millhouse, who would, Gabriel thought, normally be considered small and dainty, appear inconsequential, as if she might be swatted like a troublesome fly and thus removed from the splendid Sophie's majestic orbit.

"It's so wonderful to meet the two of you. I've heard such wonderful things about your work. I think your work is wonderfully interesting." Mrs. Millhouse could almost rival Juniper in the twittering and bubbling arenas, although she seemed kind of silly as she did it. Juniper had never, not since that first day in the Laredo train station, appeared silly. It occurred to Gabriel to wonder how she managed it. It was probably natural. She possessed a larger vocabulary than Mrs. Millhouse, too.

"And this," Sophie continued, not allowing anybody's twitters or bubbles to waylay her, "is our very good friend and companion, Dmitri Sokolov. He is a great help to us in our work."

The way she said it cast all sorts of mysterious connotations onto the word *work*, as if they might be in the

habit of conjuring any number of ghosties and phan-
tasms in the course of a typical day and Dmitri was used
to corral them or something. Gabriel hid his smile behind his hand with a pretended cough.

"Charmed," Mrs. Millhouse said. After hesitating for a
moment, she held her hand out to Dmitri. The latter,
however, clicked his boot heels together and bowed,
looking for the first time in Gabriel's association with
him, every inch a Russian. More than every inch, actually, since he was so short.

Mrs. Millhouse, a trifle disconcerted by Dmitri's performance, muttered, "Oh, my."

Sophie turned next to Gabriel. He was curious as to
how she aimed to introduce him. "And this," she said
without the tiniest hint of discomposure, "is our friend
and associate, Mr. Gabriel Caine. Mr. Caine," she continued, directing a frosty smile at Gabriel, "has been
learning the mystical arts from my aunt, and he sometimes assists us in our work." She didn't say how.

Gabriel shook Mrs. Millhouse's hand and murmured,
"Very pleased to meet you, ma'am." He used his best,
revival-tent, southern-gentleman manners on her, and
she blushed. Out of the corner of his eye, he saw Sophie
grimace and cast her gaze to the ceiling in disgust.

"Oh, Mr. Caine, I'm so pleased—it's so wonderful—
oh, we just can't wait!" And with that, Mrs. Millhouse
took off down the hall at a trot.

After glancing at each other, the Madrigal party set
off after her, perceiving this as their duty. It turned out
they were correct in their perception. Gabriel was interested to note that their hostess led them to a formal
dining room. Nine exquisitely dressed women sat
around an enormous table. Gabriel guessed the fashionable ladies of Los Angeles didn't have a whole lot
of useful work to do, then chided himself for being
damned near as sarcastic as Sophie.

"I hope this room is all right," Mrs. Millhouse twittered. "It's the only room with a large enough table."

"I see," said Sophie, with a hint of her old dryness. "Yes, this table is ample."

Actually, it was gigantic. Gabriel suspected fifty could dine at it if all the leaves were added. He caught Sophie's eye briefly, and was relieved to see humor gleaming therein. She never disappointed him.

She didn't disappoint him during the seance, either. Dmitri, after setting a red-globed oil lamp in the middle of the table and lighting the wick, took a chair in a corner of the room, as if he were going to oversee the goings-on. Juniper and Sophie sat at the head of the table, and Sophie directed Gabriel to sit at the table's foot. From this vantage point, he had a perfect view of the breathtaking Sophie's truly remarkable bosom as she presided over the seance.

Gabriel had half expected Juniper to be the main focus of the evening. He'd imagined she'd be the medium through whom the spirit spoke—he could hardly believe he was thinking these things—but she wasn't. Sophie dominated the entire evening.

And what a presence she was. Gabriel was more impressed than he'd dare admit, at least to her. Not only did she appear beautiful and aristocratic in all of her bounteous splendor, but she bore herself with an aura he'd never seen her display before. *Perfect control* was the phrase Gabriel settled on to describe her demeanor. If he hadn't met her before this evening, he would have presumed her to be an ice princess, merely condescending to visit these earthly planes and share her wisdom for a brief time before returning to her true domain in some mystical kingdom beyond the reaches of mortal man.

It took Mrs. Millhouse quite a few minutes to settle in at the table. She flitted and darted about the room, speaking to her guests and asking questions. At last, though, she sank into the chair next to Sophie, on her right. She appeared nervous, in spite of the kindly look Sophie bestowed upon her. Or maybe because of it.

If so stately a being as Sophie had gifted him with such a smile, Gabriel's guard would have shot up in expectation of a knife in the back or something. Mrs. Millhouse, obviously a more innocent specimen of humankind than Gabriel, only blushed once more.

Sophie spoke. "It's time to still our hearts and voices, so that the spirits may be heard." The words were spoken mildly, as if she were only offering a suggestion, but they had the effect of making everyone in the room start slightly, go still, and stare at her. She smiled at them. "Thank you. My aunt, Juniper Madrigal, will now commence the seance."

When the last rustle of nervousness and anticipation had subsided, Juniper spoke. "We are very happy to be here tonight, and to offer ourselves as a conduit to the celestial plane, to the spirit world that exists on what we call the Other Side of life." Her voice, which Gabriel had always thought of as light and pleasant, seemed to be absorbing and reflecting the atmosphere in the room. It sounded slightly enigmatic this evening. Interesting.

"If you will please join hands," Juniper said.

Gabriel found himself suddenly seized on either side by bare-handed women. Since he knew it was proper for ladies to wear gloves, he assumed they'd been instructed ahead of time to remove them. Evidently the spirits couldn't travel through kidskin. He told himself to stop being derisive, or he'd rival Sophie in no time at all.

"Our assistant, Dmitri, will turn off the electrical lights," Juniper continued. "We will then be left with only the one red lamp on the table. The red lamp, as

247

you may know, will serve as a soft medium through which spirits can arrive."

Hmmm. Red lamps, eh? Red lights were used in other professions, too, although Gabriel was pretty sure Juniper wouldn't know about that. Sophie would. He'd bet on it.

Whatever the function of the red lamp, the glow it cast on Sophie almost made his mouth water. Her fair skin took on a tawny cast, her hair gleamed dully, and shadows played on her features, giving her an otherworldly appearance. She looked to him like a fairy princess. His chest swelled oddly with pride for her. As if he had any business being proud of her. If she knew of his arrogance, she'd certainly slap his face.

He watched with rapt attention as the evening progressed, seldom taking his gaze away from Sophie. He heard Juniper's voice, lullingly soft and sweet. It damned near lulled him into believing what was happening. Juniper's voice took on the quality of a gentle humming in his ears, and when Sophie's eyes began to close, it seemed natural for them to do so.

When Sophie's head drooped slightly forward, he wasn't surprised. When Sophie spoke, in a sepulchral voice he'd never heard from her before, he started in his chair, and very nearly cried out in alarm. He stopped himself in time, thank God, or Sophie would never have forgiven him.

Juniper, her eyes closed as if she were in a mystical trance of her own, whispered, "Is my control here with us?"

Sophie—it didn't sound like Sophie in the least, but the words came out of her mouth—said, "I am here."

Sweet Jesus, that voice made Gabriel's skin crawl. His respect for the Madrigals soared. They were damned good at this nonsense. He shuddered and wished their performance weren't so blasted potent.

"You are the Princess Sabrahar?"

"I am she."

Gabriel felt the oddest compulsion to rush over to Sophie and shake her, thereby dislodging the blasted spirit that had taken over her body. He knew he was being stupid. This was an act. He told himself so at least a hundred times before the seance concluded, and he ended up not quite believing himself.

"Thank you, Princess Sabrahar, for deigning to visit with us tonight."

Sophie inclined her head as if in condescension.

"There is someone with us tonight," Juniper went on, "who desires to establish contact with a dear one now existing on the Other Side. Are you able to see into the hearts of those who desire contact this evening?"

"Yes," intoned Sophie.

Someone—Gabriel couldn't tell who—gasped. He couldn't fault whoever it was, as he pretty much felt like gasping himself.

"Philip wishes to assure Amanda that he is waiting for her," Sophie said in that same crazy toneless spirit voice that made Gabriel's insides rebel.

"Oh!" cried the woman on Gabriel's left. "Philip!"

"Amanda," said Sophie. "Be at rest. I am well. You will join me when the time is right."

"Oh," whispered the same woman. "I'm so glad."

And so it went. Gabriel didn't have the slightest idea where Sophie had secured the information she used in the seance, but he was positive—almost—that she'd used earthly means. She was good, though. Damned good. Frighteningly good, actually. If he weren't such a hardened cynic, he might even have believed she was acting as some sort of conduit from earth to heaven— or wherever the Other Side was located. He wasn't altogether sure he wanted to know.

The seance lasted almost an hour, and when it concluded with Sophie's supposed spirit possessor leaving her body and hieing itself off to parts unknown, Sophie sagged in her chair, as if debilitated by the experience. Gabriel had to curb a mad urge to leap out of his chair, race over to her, and hold her in his arms until she recovered. Damn, she was good.

The lights went on all of a sudden, making the guests at the table, including Gabriel, but excluding Juniper and Sophie, jump a little and blink. Gabriel had forgotten all about Dmitri.

The seance participants glanced avidly around at each other in total silence. Then noise erupted like a volcano in the room.

Since he perceived no reason to remain in his chair, Gabriel got up and walked around to Sophie, whose head still lolled strangely. He squinted down at her, wondering if this was part of the act. When she cricked her eyelids open a hair and sparkled up at him, he knew it was. He wanted to pick her up and kiss her in sheer relief.

It took nearly another whole hour for the Madrigal party to escape from the stately Millhouse mansion. Mrs. Millhouse and her friends lavished praise upon Juniper and Sophie, and pressed food and drink—and money—upon all of them.

"Thank God," muttered Sophie, eyeing a plate of caviar on toast points. "I'm starving to death."

"Being a conduit for spirits whets the old appetite, does it?" Gabriel popped a toast point into his mouth and grinned at her.

"It certainly does." Sophie smiled, too, as if she enjoyed sharing the joke with him.

Gabriel's heart went all gooey, and he told himself to stop being stupid. "Who the hell's Princess Sabrahar?"

She shrugged and sipped champagne. "We liked the name, and it's sort of neutral, so we use it."

"Neutral?"

"Oh, you know. It's not a real name or even a name that might be real. I made it up. I mean, I'd hate it if somebody who spoke, say, German, told us that Sabrahar is a German name and expected me, as the princess, to know German or something."

"Ah. Clever."

"As it is, Sabrahar's supposed to be from ancient Assyria, so I figure we're safe. Even if we met somebody from Assyria, if there even is such a place anymore, he wouldn't know the ancient tongue."

"I see."

"Do you?"

There was a particularly devilish light in her eyes that made Gabriel uneasy. He'd been on edge all evening long, knowing as he did that she was up to something. As the party wound down and Mrs. Millhouse herself, in all her expensive glory, saw them to the waiting cab, he braced himself. Whatever Sophie was up to, he anticipated she'd be springing it on him soon.

He didn't know whether to be elated or scared to death, so he settled for both.

Chapter Fifteen

During the seance, Sophie had been interested to note that she and Gabriel didn't generate any magical mists or auras. Thank heavens. If the air had begun smelling of orange blossoms and jasmine, or if the mystical incense had fogged the atmosphere, she wasn't sure she'd have been able to perform as well as she had.

Fortunately, Dmitri had done his advance scouting to perfection, and unearthed all sorts of juicy tidbits about the seance's attendees. Sophie had taken it from there. It was all such rot.

Although, she had to admit, there was probably *something* unusual about her abilities. And Juniper's. It was undoubtedly only through long practice that the two of them were able to touch so many people's hearts so deeply.

However they'd done it, they *had* done it, and Mrs. Millhouse was as happy as if she had good sense. The seance had gone exceptionally well, but Sophie was anticipating the rest of her evening with mixed feelings. If Emerald Huffy was right, she'd achieve her goal in a very few hours. If she'd been reading Gabriel correctly, any threat he posed to her scheme would have been nullified before that.

Her nerves jumped like live wires, but she didn't allow her anxious state to show. She knew Gabriel was on edge as well; she'd confused him completely with her coquettish demeanor this evening. She hoped he'd fall into her trap—that is to say, comply with her plan. She was pretty sure any other man in the world would. After all, most men weren't accustomed to questioning their libidos, and the important element in her evening's plans was the certain knowledge that he wanted her. He'd made his desire for her plain on a number of occasions.

"Here we are, ladies and Dmitri," Gabriel said, startling Sophie out of her musings. "The Melrose Hotel."

"Ah," said Juniper, putting a hand to her mouth to stifle a yawn. "I'm ready for bed."

"Seances always wear you out, Juniper," Sophie said mildly. "I feel quite perky myself." She cast a sly glance at Gabriel, making sure he caught it.

"That's because you're young, dear. When you're my age, you'll find them wearying, I'm sure." Juniper bestowed a lovely smile upon Gabriel, who helped her out of the carriage. "Thank you very much."

Gabriel smiled and nodded. Sometimes he was so much the well-mannered southern gentleman, Sophie almost believed the pose herself.

"I'm sure you're right, Juniper," she agreed. She bent at the waist as she edged out of the cab, hoping in that way to expose as much of her bosom as possible to Gabriel's eyes. From the expression on his face and the convulsive way he swallowed when she stood next to him on the drive outside the Melrose, she'd succeeded.

It was the first time in her life she'd been glad she was well-endowed.

Neither Juniper nor Dmitri noticed the play between Sophie and Gabriel. Sophie hoped they'd remain oblivious until she'd fulfilled her purpose. Beyond that point, actually, or she'd be quite embarrassed. To Dmitri, she said, "I'll see you in a little while."

The small man nodded, and assisted Juniper up the steps of the hotel. The Melrose's lobby blazed with lights, although it was past eleven. While Los Angeles was no New York City, and certainly slept sometimes, Sophie was glad to note that it didn't roll up the streets at dusk. She needed some night life in order to accomplish her aims for the evening.

She gazed straight at Gabriel. "Would you care to have a drink before retiring, Gabriel?"

He squinted at her as if he didn't trust this new act of hers. She held her breath, praying he wouldn't decline her invitation.

After a moment, he said, "Sure. Why not?" and Sophie would have breathed a sigh of relief except she didn't want him to be any more suspicious than he already was.

"I believe there's a bar in the Melrose," she murmured. If they stayed in the hotel, the last part of her plan would be easier to accomplish than if she had to get back here from another hotel.

"You're up to something," he said.

Sophie made her eyes go wide in startled innocence—at least that's what she was aiming for. "Whatever can you mean? I only want to have a friendly drink before going to bed. What can I be up to?"

"I don't know, but I'll bet it has to do with Ivo Hardwick."

Blast him. He was right. "You're too distrustful for words, Gabriel Caine," she said with asperity. "There's nothing I can do to stop you from arresting Ivo Hardwick, no matter how much I wish you wouldn't."

"You're right there, Sophie, my sweet. There's a lot I can do to keep you from killing him, though, and I plan to do it."

You would, she thought sourly. She only gave him another flirtatious smile.

He took her arm and guided her across the lobby to the dimly lit bar. She placed her other hand on his arm, too, thereby mashing her bosom against his shoulder. Her heart started hammering, and she swore at herself to remain calm. Every single solitary time she touched him lately, that tingling sensation began dancing through her. The sensation, caused as it was by whatever kind of magic she and Gabriel generated together, was disconcerting, and even rather frightening. A niggling voice in the back of her mind told her she was treading on dangerous ground, and she'd better be careful. But she wouldn't turn back now. She couldn't.

The Melrose Bar had very few visitors this late in the evening. Sophie saw a couple of men seated at the long polished bar. It was an elegant place, if any drinking establishment could be deemed elegant, with a dusky red carpet, hunting prints on the wall, and a long gold-framed mirror above the bar area where it looked as if hundreds of bottles stood in tidy rows. There were no other women in the room, but that didn't bother Sophie. She was accustomed to doing things other women wouldn't do.

Their shoes made no sound at all on the thick carpeting as Gabriel led her to a dark table in a corner where they wouldn't be conspicuous. Sophie considered this a good sign and smiled at him, aiming for a winning, seductive smile this time, even as she knew it might make him wary. She wished she could check her appearance in a mirror, but she didn't want him to think she was preening for him, even though that's exactly what she'd have been doing. Without comment, Gabriel went to the bar and returned with two drinks.

"Thank you." Sophie watched him sit across from her as she sipped her drink. His every movement was fluid and graceful. She hadn't observed many men who possessed such natural ease of movement. She suspected he'd learned early in life how to present himself effectively, since he'd been involved in show business of a sort different from that in which she participated. "My, this is delicious. I don't believe I've ever had anything like it before. What is it?"

"It's called a Manhattan cocktail."

"Mmmm." She smiled again. "Yum."

He tossed back a good third of his drink and set the glass on the polished maple table with a clink. "All right, Sophie Madrigal, what are you up to?"

She lifted her eyebrows in a show of naive incredulity. "Whatever do you mean?"

He frowned at her. "You're being coy. You're never coy. You'd kill yourself before you'd be coy. You're too damned sharp to be coy. What's up?"

She shook her head. "That's not fair, Gabriel. We've known each other for weeks now. I enjoy your company—"

"You could have fooled me," he interrupted, sounding more than a little bit grumpy.

Sophie hoped to heaven that this evening's abrupt departure from her usual behavior wasn't going to backfire on her. She scrambled frantically for a way to mitigate his suspicions, and decided to add a trace of vinegar to her voice. "Nonsense. We're two strong-minded people. Strong-minded people are always going to rub against each other sometimes." When she got to the *rub against* part, she slanted a flirtatious glance at him, hoping as she did so that the vinegar would wash some of the oddity out of her attitude.

"Hmmm."

"You look dubious, Gabriel," she murmured. "I'm hurt."

"I doubt it."

She sipped more of her Manhattan. "It's the truth. I've been attempting all evening to make amends." She lowered her eyes and fingered her glass, hoping she presented an affecting picture of true contrition—and erotic craving. "I know I've been somewhat unkind to you."

"You can say that again."

She decided to ignore that one. "But in spite of our differences, I find you attractive." She lifted her gaze and let it drop almost immediately, playing the demure young virgin to the hilt. "*Very* attractive."

He didn't speak for a moment, but swallowed more of his drink, eyeing her hard the whole time. She was beginning to feel like a butterfly pinned to a specimen board. When she couldn't stand the silence another second longer, she said, "You're a very handsome man. You must know that."

"So I've been told." His voice was as dry as Tucson, Arizona.

Damn him. He had to say that, didn't he? As if her opinion didn't matter because women prettier—and thinner—than she had fawned over him for years. She made an effort not to purse her mouth in annoyance, fearing any show of anger would give her away. After a moment, she said softly, "I'm sure you're accustomed to women falling for you."

"Falling for me?"

She turned away, hoping he would take the gesture as one of confusion. The Melrose's wallpaper was quite nice, she noticed, sort of a reddish-maroon with flocked cabbage roses blossoming on flocked stems. Annoyed with herself for concentrating on trivia, she commanded her attention back to the farce she was perpetrating. At least, she thought it was a farce. She hoped it was.

If she were to be brutally frank with herself, something she disliked being because it was so uncomfortable, she'd have to admit that she truly was attracted to Gabriel Caine. Wildly, impossibly attracted.

Good Lord, she couldn't think about that, either, or she'd be sunk before she set sail. She heard Gabriel shift in his chair, and peeked at him. He was glaring daggers at her, his dark eyes flashing. He looked quite dangerous, and a thrill of anticipation shot through her.

"I don't know what your game is, Sophie, but you're going to regret it in a minute or two. I'm not made of stone, you know."

Ahhh. Sophie's heart swooped crazily. It was working. She turned her head and gazed at him, trying for wide-eyed innocence again. "I beg your pardon?"

"I said," he said, "I'm not made of stone."

She fluttered her eyelashes a bit—not too much, because he'd be on to her like a cat on a mouse. "I—I don't think I understand what you mean."

"The hell you don't." He drained his glass, pushed his chair back, and headed to the bar.

Sophie stared after him uncertainly. She hoped she hadn't gone to far. If she'd driven him off, she'd be furious with herself. Worse, she might have jeopardized her plans.

But no. He was coming back to the table again, holding two fresh drinks. He hesitated before he put one of them before her. "I don't want you to drink too much. Not if you're planning what I think you're planning."

She was still dawdling over her first Manhattan. She didn't want to drink too much, either, because her goal for the evening depended on a clear head. With what she hoped was a sultry pout, she said, "And what's that, pray tell?"

He sat with a plunk and frowned at her. "My seduction."

She blinked, this time without premeditation and in honest surprise. "Mercy, you're blunt."

"Why not? We've been sparring with each other for weeks now. If you expect me to swallow this new act of yours, you're way off base."

Whatever that meant. Sophie presumed it was an expression borrowed from the sport of baseball. She didn't, however, quite know what to say next. She licked her lips, noticing as she did so that Gabriel watched her like a lion stalking a fatted calf. So, he was interested, even though he didn't trust her. That was good. She could work with that.

"I think you're being unkind, Gabriel," she said softly. "I'm trying to be ladylike about this. It's not fair of you to doubt my intentions. Even if we don't see eye to eye on most subjects—"

"I'll say," he muttered gloomily.

"—we can still find each other—well—physically attractive."

He eyed her hard for a minute. Sophie was reminded of a Gila monster she'd seen in Tucson. It had appeared to be a lazy, stout, and happy lizardly creature, but underneath its porcine languor, it was deadly. Suddenly she hoped to heaven she'd get through this night with her heart untouched. She was willing to offer up her body on the altar of her vengeance, but her heart had been too badly damaged already.

"So you're telling me you find me physically attractive?"

She snapped, "It's really irritating of you to be so explicit about this, Gabriel Caine. Have you no refinement at all?"

"No."

Bother, she thought peevishly. Leave it to Gabriel to tarnish the gleam on her well-laid plot. Any other man would be panting with lust by this time, and his brain would have ceased functioning ages ago. "In that case, yes, I find you physically attractive."

Expelling a long breath, Gabriel continued to eye her closely. Before he spoke, he sipped some more of his drink. He was frowning. Sophie didn't think he ought to be frowning. Not if he was falling for her plot. Blast him. She ought to have expected him to react differently from other men.

He surprised her when he reached across the table and touched her hand, very lightly, smoothing his thumb across the back of her hand. Sophie felt hot little sparks begin to race through her body from the point of contact. Her nipples tightened immediately. Pressure began to throb in her lower belly. Her head swam. Good God, this was terrible. How could she keep her senses in check if this was going to happen when he even touched her hand? She sucked in a breath and the faint scent of sandalwood, orange blossoms, and jasmine permeated her senses. Oh, dear.

"You're not a virgin."

She blinked at him in confusion. What? What had he asked her? Or had it been a question? It had been a statement. Good Lord, was he going to tell her he had reservations about making love with impure women? She didn't know what to say, and stammered, "I—I— what?"

A smile curled his mouth. "I'm not complaining, you understand."

"I—I—no. I don't understand. What difference does it make if I'm a virgin or not?"

He lifted her hand and carried it to his lips. When his soft, full lips brushed her knuckles, Sophie had to grab the table with her other hand or slither onto the bar-room carpet in a boneless heap.

"The only difference it makes is how gentle I have to be." He pressed her palm to his cheek. She expected to feel bristles, but he'd evidently shaved before the seance. Had he been anticipating this?

Sophie felt her eyes widen and then slowly close when he turned his head and kissed the palm of her hand. That felt so good. So warm. So wonderful.

"I don't want to hurt you, Sophie."

Forcing her eyes to open again, she saw that he was gazing at her with remarkable tenderness. She swallowed what felt like a boulder that had lodged itself in her throat. "Good." That wasn't enough, and she knew it. "I mean, thank you, Gabriel."

She didn't want him to hurt her, either, although she had a feeling they meant different things by the word *hurt*. She anticipated no physical pain from any encounter with Gabriel Caine. She wasn't so sure about her emotional health.

But she couldn't think about that now. She'd formulated her plan this afternoon, and had gone about achieving it with, if not cold-blooded determination, at least with determination. Sophie was pretty sure she could never be cold-blooded about physical intimacy.

"Finish your drink, Sophie. Let's go upstairs." He pressed tiny kisses into her palm.

Sophie's body was tingling and humming as if a pixie had sprinkled magical dust over her. "I—I need my hand back if I'm going to finish my drink." Her voice had sunk to a whisper, and she tried to clear her throat, but it wouldn't be cleared. Wonderful. If she cried in front of Gabriel Caine—tonight of all nights—she'd be humiliated forever.

He sighed. "All right. I like holding your hand, Sophie. It's warm and soft, but it's also beautiful and capable."

Good Lord, he sounded sincere. The doubt that had become second nature to her since her first disastrous love affair surged up again in Sophie, momentarily vanquishing the thrilling sensations Gabriel had implanted in her. Thank goodness. She didn't feel like drinking all of her Manhattan, but she took a substantial swallow, then eyed Gabriel with renewed humor. If she could keep her sense of humor, perhaps she wouldn't lose herself entirely. "Thank you, Gabriel. I don't believe you've ever offered me such a pretty compliment."

He grinned. "I'm sure I haven't. You'd have thrown it back in my face if I had."

"Probably." She laughed, glad she'd come through that first swamp of emotional quicksand relatively unscathed. She rose from her chair and held her hand out to Gabriel, willing to let him lead her to his bed—and her own doom.

Lord, she had to stop thinking of it in that light. This was to be her salvation, not her doom.

He took her hand and tucked it under his arm, keeping her close to him as they walked from the barroom. Sophie noticed the men seated at the bar watching them, looking both gloomy and envious. Good. She might be heavier than the fashion magazines deemed appropriate, but she could still turn the heads of men. She hoped Gabriel wouldn't find her too plump when—

No. She wouldn't second-guess herself. He wanted her. He wanted her as she was. If he didn't care for plump women, he'd have found a skinny one. Instead, he'd stuck to her and Juniper since they'd met in that wretched train station in Laredo.

Thus trying to keep her spirits up, Sophie climbed the stairs of the Melrose Hotel, her body tingling with anticipation, her mind a jumble of dark thoughts. Electrical lights burned here and there on the walls as she and Gabriel walked slowly down the hallway. Sophie felt not unlike a prisoner who, trying to escape his fate, was caught now and then by searchlights.

She chastised herself for the thought. She was doing this on purpose, because she had a plan to fulfill. She needed Gabriel Caine to be distracted tonight, and she knew—she *knew*—that this was not only the best, but perhaps the only way to distract him.

An arrow of guilt shot through her, and she suppressed it ruthlessly. She was only doing this because she perceived no other course of action. Surely Gabriel would understand why she had to do what she was going to do. Eventually. Probably. She hoped he'd understand after he thought about it for a while, at any rate. He wouldn't feel used and abused, would he? Heavens, no. Not Gabriel Caine.

Lord, she was being wicked.

She told herself to stop thinking like that.

"Here's my room," Gabriel said in a low voice.

A sickening jolt shot through Sophie. This was it. She would have prayed for strength, except that she couldn't force herself to be such a hypocrite. She managed a smile.

Gabriel hesitated. Sophie feared her jumbled emotions might be written too plainly on her face, and she attempted to keep any expression of doubt confined to her heart.

"Are you sure about this, Sophie?"

His voice was kindness itself, and it very nearly made Sophie burst into tears right there in the Melrose hallway. Good heavens, what was the matter with her? Intentionally thrusting all doubts aside, she said, "Yes, Gabriel, I'm sure." Wonder of wonders, her voice was as strong as ever. He paused for another moment. It was fully long enough for Sophie's smile to fade and for panic to begin to fill her.

Dammit! He couldn't back out now!

He didn't. "I've been waiting for this too long to back down now. If you're sorry later, I'll apologize then. If *I'm* sorry later, well . . ." He let the end of the sentence dangle unspoken.

Sophie had to force herself not to slump with relief. "I won't be sorry," she said. And she meant it, too, for the most part. She only hoped her emotional side wouldn't overwhelm her sensible side once the deed was done. She knew beyond certainty that Gabriel Caine wasn't a man to pin one's future hopes on. He was a rambler and a gambler and not the sort to stick around for the long run. She knew the type, unfortunately, very well. "I don't think you will be, either." She would be, but she couldn't afford to think about it.

"I hope you're right." He turned the key in the lock, pushed the door open, and stepped aside so Sophie could enter before him.

The moment of truth had arrived. Without so much as a stutter to her step, Sophie walked into Gabriel's hotel room. She caught sight of herself in the mirror above the dresser and was surprised that none of the mayhem wreaking havoc on her emotions showed in her face. Actually, she looked wonderful. The dusky green of her gown made her skin appear almost opalescent in the light of the one electrical lamp Gabriel turned on.

She hoped to goodness he wouldn't turn any more lamps on. It had been years since she'd made love to a man. She'd been a pretty young girl then, as lively as a colt, and as slender as a reed. The reed had grown considerably since then and, although her shape was curvy and womanly, she'd just as soon not have lights blazing on it for Gabriel's inspection. Goodness only knew how many women, thinner and far more experienced than she, he'd romped with through the years. She didn't fancy hearing—or fearing—negative comparisons.

Because she didn't want him to suspect how nervous and unsophisticated she was, she reached up to unfasten the decoration from her hair. She knew this to be a classic pose—female raising arms above head, thereby displaying her body and presenting a vulnerable picture to the predatory male.

Stop it, Sophie!

The hair decoration was a necklace, really, but she liked to wear it in her hair during seances. The garnets and gold glimmered in the low red lamplight and contrasted nicely with her blond hair.

Gabriel, who had gone to the bedside table to turn on the lamp, turned and gazed at her. She couldn't read the expression in his eyes, but they were as beautiful as ever, and warm. Sweet heaven, she hoped he liked the way she looked! This was going to be harder than she'd first thought, she realized, because all of her insecurities had chosen to rise to the surface.

Damnation, why couldn't she be cold and calculating? She *looked* cold and calculating. She was forever putting men off with her frigid presence. It wasn't fair that her insides and her outside should tell such different stories.

But that was stupid thinking. As Sophie had known for years, nothing in life was fair. She did manage what she hoped was a small, winsome smile for Gabriel's sake.

He shook his head, as if in wonder. "You're a beautiful woman, Sophie. I suppose you already know that."

Actually, she hadn't known anything of the sort. Rather than say something that might commit her either to vanity or naivete, Sophie said, "I'm glad you think so." True. That was true. Perhaps if she stuck to the truth, she'd be all right.

Stupid. Of course she wouldn't be all right! If she were to tell the truth, she'd admit to being scared to death—and guilty for using Gabriel in an underhanded manner!

She saw him swallow. Good. She didn't want to be the only one disconcerted this evening.

"May I help you? I've always wanted to stick my fingers in your hair."

She lifted her eyebrows. The mirror reflected a cool, calm, collected—and quite lovely—woman, offering a vaguely flirty expression to someone she couldn't see in the mirror. Maybe she'd better move, before she took to staring into the wretched mirror to critique her performance. She took a step away from the chair where she'd been standing. "Of course. I'd like that."

He came to her with the grace of a stalking panther. Sophie didn't shrink back and was proud of herself. Instead, she held out the gold-and-garnet necklace she'd just unwound from her hair. The chain dripped through her fingers, and flung light from the lamp against Gabriel's dark coat. The way the lamplight played on the jewels brought flickering starlight to Sophie's mind. Sparkling dots played over his face and body. *Magic drops*, she thought.

He didn't take the necklace, but laced his fingers through hers so that the necklace twined around them both. As soon as he touched her, the magical sensations began again. Sophie resigned herself to them.

"Let me help you take the pins out." His voice was husky.

Tilting her head slightly, Sophie murmured, "Of course."

"Your hair's like silk."

She didn't respond.

He didn't release her hand, but worked with his other one, searching for hairpins, which he withdrew carefully and set on the night table. Slowly, he moved from in front of her, to beside her, to in back of her, making sure he didn't twist her arm unpleasantly. When he stood behind her, he kissed the back of her neck.

Sophie wasn't expecting it, and she nearly swooned in rapture. She heard her own sharp intake of breath, and wished she'd controlled herself better.

But this was astonishing. Sophie didn't remember feeling like this the other time. But then, she'd been so young—and so scared.

"Here, let me put this thing down." Gabriel released her hand and consigned the necklace to the night table. "Ah, that's better."

It certainly was. He'd taken out all of her hairpins, and now thrust both of his hands into the mass of her hair and brushed it out with his fingers. "Your hair is gorgeous, Sophie. Not many women have blond hair, you know. Not naturally blond, like yours."

"Is that so?" Her voice remained steady, which surprised her a lot. The rest of her was quivering like jelly in an earthquake.

He didn't answer, but pressed kisses onto the exposed flesh of her shoulder. Sophie's heart filled with elation so suddenly, she nearly fainted. This felt so good. Gabriel felt so good. She belonged here, in his arms. With him. They made magic together. Already, the room was filling with the strange mystical incense that only they could create together. The sweet, spicy fragrance of their magic hung in the air. Sophie, no stranger to magical phenomena, recognized it for what it was, and gave up the last fragment of her iron restraint.

Whatever lay in store for her—and she knew in her bones that her life would never be the same after tonight—she wasn't going to hold back. Not now. She turned in Gabriel's arms, took his face between her hands, and drew his lips to hers. He groaned softly, and her entire being throbbed with longing.

Chapter Sixteen

Gabriel was a more skillful lover than Sophie's first, long-lost love. Or perhaps she was simply old enough to enjoy this activity now. Back then, she'd been too young and too worried to give herself up to enjoying her body. And his.

His lips possessed hers with a passion Sophie had dreamed about but never expected to experience. Her hand slipped into his hair and she ran her fingers through it much as he'd run his through hers. She loved his hair. She loved his body.

God help her, she loved him.

She knew she'd better not dwell on that particular truth, or she'd be done for. Worse, she might allow her love for him to hold her back from what she planned to do tonight. It was possible that Gabriel would never forgive her, and that notion almost made Sophie change her plans. Almost. She didn't; she'd waited too long for vengeance.

"I've wanted you from the moment I saw you," he whispered as he brushed kisses down her throat and chest, to where her bosom swelled above the dark green satin of her gown. She would forever consider this dress one of her wisest purchases.

Because she didn't have any idea what to say, she murmured, "Mmmm."

"When you came through that station door and marched across the lobby, I thought a queen had come to Texas. You looked so damned out of place there."

How fascinating. "Did I?" She hoped he'd continue along these lines. She'd never been told what kind of impression she made on the general public. Not that Gabriel was the general public. At the moment, he was making magic on her body with his lips and hands, which had found their way to her back and were stroking her slowly, slowly.

"You did. You scared poor old Henry to death."

"He's a stupid man." It was becoming difficult for her to concentrate on the conversation. His hands were now fumbling with the buttons on the back of her dress. Thank God.

"Very stupid. Not like us."

"No," she whispered. "Not like us."

"Why do they make these buttons so damned small?"

"You're doing fine. Keep going."

"Don't worry. Nothing less than a bullet to the brain could stop me now."

Sophie was very glad to hear it, although she wished he hadn't brought bullets into the conversation. The word shattered the atmosphere momentarily and dispersed the magical aura, like a sudden breeze dissipating a fog. She had to fight to get her mental balance back. Fortunately, it didn't take long, and soon the small tear in the magical spell they were weaving had mended itself.

"Ah." Gabriel sighed happily when the last button slipped through its hole and the creation Sophie had worn this evening with his seduction in mind slid away from her shoulders. "That's much better."

Carefully, he pushed the satin down her arms. Sophie watched him watch her, and her heart thumped out a fantastic cadence in her bosom. He wanted her. Oh, he really, really wanted her. This was no heartless joke on his part. He desired her body.

The heartless part was on her side.

She told herself to cease that line of thought, to focus on physical sensation. It wasn't hard to do.

Thank you, thank you, thank you, buzzed like a chant in Sophie's brain. Perhaps this was a new beginning for her.

No. Her new beginning would happen after Ivo Hardwick lay dead.

Stop thinking this instant, Sophie Madrigal, she commanded herself severely. *If you think, you'll ruin everything*.

"I've dreamed about this," Gabriel said in a gravelly voice. "And I've daydreamed about it. You're on my mind day and night, Sophie. Day and night. You're so damned beautiful."

He had pushed the dress down so that it now lay puddled around her feet. She stepped out of it and stood before him in her corset, pantaloons, and chemise. She should be embarrassed, but Gabriel's words of patent adoration—of her sexual allure, if nothing more—helped to relax her. She had planned and prepared for this, and it was happening now. Her plan was working beautifully. Better than she'd anticipated, actually, because she hadn't been so sure she'd enjoy it.

She'd been wrong. Making love with Gabriel, so far, was a thrilling experience. She stooped to pick up her dress and lay it over the back of a chair. When she turned again, she heard Gabriel suck in a breath.

"You're even more beautiful than I thought you'd be."

Since she had no experience in these matters, at least not as an adult, she merely stood before him, feeling exposed and vulnerable. But Gabriel Caine, who, she feared, was one of the few men in the world who could hurt her if he chose, didn't seem to be in a critical mood this evening. His eyes had gone from warm to hot and hungry, and he licked his lips like a starving man being presented with a succulent steak.

He walked slowly over to her, lightly gripped her arms, and stared at her until she got fidgety. Was he finally realizing she was too fat? Was he deciding that she wasn't so much to look at without her clothes covering all of her flaws? Sweet heaven, she wished he'd do something; she was going to snap right in two if he kept staring at her this way.

"Perfect," he murmured so softly she almost didn't hear him. "You are absolutely perfect."

Good Lord, really? Did he mean it? Or was he only suffering from an excess of sexual frustration? The bulge in his trousers was enormous; Sophie spared a moment to be grateful she was no longer a virgin. She didn't want to go through *that* again; it had hurt.

One thing she knew for sure, and that was that the longer she stood here undressed and he kept his clothes on, the more nervous she was going to get. She whispered, "You have far too many clothes on, Gabriel," and began unbuttoning his jacket.

"Let me." He took a step back, and kept his greedy gaze fixed on her as he ripped his jacket and shirt off, flinging his collar, cuffs, and tie onto the floor as if he didn't care a bean about them. The undershirt went next, and Sophie's lips parted when she saw his naked chest and arms.

"My goodness." He was built like a Hercules—or, at any rate, what Sophie thought a Hercules should be built like. He'd done some hard physical work in his life, or he'd not have those wonderful muscles on his arms or that flat, corded belly. His broad chest was a work of art.

Through the delicious magical incense, Sophie walked to him. She wanted to feel his skin. She wanted to feel the hairs on his chest. She wanted to join with him, to become one with him.

She didn't want to hurt him.

Oh, but that was silly. He might be annoyed with her, but surely he wouldn't be hurt. Again, she told herself to stop thinking or she'd spoil everything.

"You're a very handsome man, Gabriel Caine."

"Glad you think so." He pulled her into his arms and kissed her deeply, playing with her tongue, and pressing his engorged sex against her thigh. She rubbed against him, thrilled that she should have caused this reaction in him. He was no innocent, like her. He was an experienced man of the world. And he wanted her.

Of course, you fool. Any man will go to bed with any woman who lets him. Men are like that.

Again, she had to tell her cynical side to shut up. It wasn't difficult to stifle it, what with Gabriel kissing her to within an inch of her life, and the magical incense of their joint making wafting around them.

"Sophie, I can't wait any longer. I have to see you."

Oh, dear. She hoped he wouldn't be disappointed. She'd find out in a very few seconds, since he was now lifting her chemise over her head.

"Let's get this thing off."

"You already did." She smiled, because he was so eager.

"Yes. I did." He shook his head in what appeared to be genuine wonder. "God, you're gorgeous."

273

Sophie peeked down at herself. The corset she'd bought today lifted her breasts and barely covered the nipples. The dark fabric contrasted starkly with her pale skin. It was rather a revealing number, probably not much purchased by proper females. It was the first corset Sophie, who generally loathed corsets, had liked. She saw Gabriel lick his lips again, and decided he liked it too.

In a voice that was remarkably unsteady for so experienced a man, Gabriel said, "Now the corset."

"You can unlace it for me," she murmured, turning so her back was to him. She'd intentionally not laced it tightly. She didn't want Gabriel to think she'd tricked him into this by using artificial means to change her shape.

"God, my hands are shaking."

"Are they?"

"Yes." He lifted them and showed her. "See what you've done to me, Sophie? You ought to be ashamed of yourself."

She smiled over her shoulder at him as he worked on the corset laces. "Probably." She actually was ashamed of herself, not for the reason Gabriel expected, but for using him. It was underhanded—but Sophie reminded herself the end would justify the means.

As the corset fell to the floor, Gabriel's hands smoothed their way from her back to her naked breasts. He pulled her to him and kissed the sensitive hollow behind her ear as his hands covered her bosom. Sophie figured she ought, by this time, to be prepared for the exquisite sensations he created in her body, but she wasn't. A low moan escaped her. This felt so good.

Very gently, Gabriel turned her so that they faced each other again. His gaze practically ate her up. For the first time in her entire life, Sophie felt a lick of gratitude that her breasts were firm and well-shaped. She'd been so used to thinking of her sexual attributes as detrimental to her mental health, that this surprised her.

"Good Lord, Sophie, you're perfect. Perfect." His tongue flicked her left nipple, and Sophie almost died then and there. Then he took as much of her breast as he could into his mouth, and she decided she'd already died, and this was heaven.

With a movement so quick it startled her, Gabriel hooked his hands under her pantaloons and tried to tug them off.

"Wait," she said, her own voice unsteady. "You have to untie the tapes."

"Damn. Where are the damned tapes?"

His excitement and clumsiness made her laugh. "Here. I'll do it."

"Thank God. I'll take these off."

He was referring to his trousers, and Sophie watched the revelation of his legs with great interest—at least as much interest as he was displaying to the revelation of her own legs. His legs were long and thickly muscled, dark brown, and hairy. Hers were long and plump and soft and white, and Sophie hoped he wouldn't think them *too* plump.

"You know what you look like, Sophie?" His voice wobbled.

She shook her head, feeling—not embarrassed, but exposed, she guessed. "No."

"You look like a painting one of those old masters did. You look like somebody decided to create the perfect woman, and you're it."

Good heavens, did he mean that? She didn't ask, considering such restraint a matter of self-preservation under the circumstances. If he didn't mean it, she didn't want to know. "Thank you." She almost added that she'd been afraid he'd believe her to be too fat, but

275

some merciful strain of common sense dissuaded her before the fatal words could leave her lips.

His underwear slid down his hairy legs next, and Sophie gaped at the masculine tool thus revealed. It was as long, thick, and strong as Sophie might have expected had she dared to expect anything. But she hadn't. And she was amazed.

He must have caught a hint of her sudden uncertainty, because Gabriel came to her, with his hand held out. "Don't be afraid, Sophie. This is going to be a grand mating. Trust me."

Oddly enough, she did. Almost. She took his hand and went with him to the bed. He yanked the covers back.

"I'm going to make this special for you," he promised. "And for me. God, it's going to be special for me."

It would be special for her, too. It would be the first time in almost a decade she'd made love with a man. Gabriel sat on the bed and pulled her onto his lap. He kissed her as he fell onto his back, and she followed. This was it. She was going to know how it felt to be loved as a woman.

She could pretend, just this once, that she was with a man who loved her. Sophie knew she was treading on dangerous ground with that particular pretense, but she couldn't seem to help herself. It sometimes seemed to her that the only thing she'd ever wanted in life was someone to love her and someone she could love back.

The gods of something-or-other had given her Joshua for a few short years, but that had been the unkindest joke of all. Sophie's life had been complete for a very tiny span of time, and then Ivo Hardwick had blown a gaping, bloody hole in it. She'd lost her fragile peace in the blink of an eye. Ivo Hardwick had snatched it from her as carelessly as if he'd swatted a fly.

And now, this evening, she had a chance to pretend

that Gabriel loved her; that he was taking her to his bed not because he was a man and men were indiscriminate, but because he cherished her. As she cherished him. Surely, as long as she knew she was pretending, this couldn't hurt her.

At the moment, he acted as if he cherished her. "Ah, Sophie, you can't even imagine how long I've waited for this." His hands were surveying her body in a way Sophie hadn't dreamed was possible. Everywhere he touched her seemed to glow with pleasure and warmth.

"It couldn't have been too long," she said as she used her hands to good effect, too. "We haven't known each other very long."

"Long enough." He had begun feathering kisses over her breasts as his hand stroked over her stomach.

"Long enough," she agreed. Because she was intensely curious, she allowed her hands to wander over his body. His skin was warm to her touch. And hairy. He was ever so much hairier than she—which made sense. She loved the differences.

"You're as soft as a ripe peach," he murmured.

She hoped that was a good thing, but decided not to ask. It was a good thing for her that he thought so, at least for now. His lips had replaced his hands, and kissed their way across her abdomen. His tongue dipped into her belly button, and she moaned. With her eyes half closed, she watched him explore her body. What he was doing felt wonderful to her. It was almost as if he were worshiping her body.

His tongue stroked along one of her stretch marks, and everything inside of her froze for an instant. All of her instincts blared an alarm, her eyes flew open, and she stared intently at Gabriel. He glanced up at her, caught her eyes for no more than a second, and returned to practicing his sorcery on her body. Sophie relaxed. The episode hadn't lasted for more than five seconds, but it had set her heart to banging like a drum and bugle corps.

Then Gabriel did something that shocked her so much, she forgot to be worried that he might have discovered her secret. He had traveled to the blond curls between her legs, and he stroked her most private place with his tongue. Every conscious thought in her head flew away instantly, and she cried out, "Oh!"

"Don't be afraid, Sophie," he said, his voice quavering. "I've been dreaming of this."

Merciful God, had he really? Sophie hadn't known people did these things to each other. It felt—perfect. His warm tongue stroking the seat of her pleasure was the most intensely erotic sensation she'd ever experienced. Her hips rose and fell rhythmically as pressure built within her. She bunched the sheets between her clenched hands as the pressure mounted, and wasn't even embarrassed by the gasping moans coming from her throat.

And then everything inside of her splintered and came apart in a burst of delight so powerful, she wouldn't have believed it if she hadn't experienced it. Wave upon wave of fulfillment shook her. This had never happened to her before. Surely she'd have remembered something this astounding.

Her heart raced and her body was damp with perspiration when Gabriel lifted himself to her side and kissed her. She threw her arms around him and kissed him with all the love and passion she dared not express in words. She could taste the essence of herself on his lips, and she all but devoured him. She had his full cooperation.

Eventually, she realized he'd maneuvered her onto her back. Oh, yes. She guessed it was his turn now. She was more than happy to oblige him. He was an overtly happy man when he propped himself above her. She'd never seen anyone look so pleased with himself and felt a wisp of tenderness. So even Gabriel Caine could feel pride in a job well done, could he? She smiled at him.

"Thank you, Gabriel. That was—splendid."

"It was splendid for me, Sophie."

She reached out and stroked his stiff sex. He shuddered and groaned. An awareness of her power as a woman struck her for the first time. She decided to use it. "I want to feel you inside me, Gabriel." Again, she stroked his shaft. It was warm and large and felt oddly silky.

He moaned again, shut his eyes, and looked for a moment as if he was in pain. "Oh, Lord, Sophie."

Evidently, he was pleased with her. Good. She was pleased with him, too. And herself. Sophie so seldom had cause to feel good about herself, that she knew she'd venerate this moment forever. She guided him to her waiting passage, wet and throbbing with recent fulfillment.

"Oh, God," Gabriel groaned. Then he plunged home.

"Ahh." The oddest thing, Sophie thought, was the completeness she felt now that they were joined. The magic in the atmosphere, which she'd forgotten all about during the past several incredible minutes, also reacted to it. The incense pulsed and throbbed in the air, making the fragrance of orange blossoms and jasmine and sandalwood whirl about the two of them.

Gabriel seemed to have progressed beyond words. As he plunged in and out, creating in Sophie new sensations of pressure for the same fulfillment he craved, his breath came in gasping sobs. As he drew closer to his own climax, he drove her to the pinnacle as well. Her second crescendo struck her as suddenly as the first one had, and her body convulsed beneath him.

With a wild cry, Gabriel joined her in release, his body shuddering time and again in delighted consummation.

With arms that shook, Gabriel lowered himself to Sophie's side. She turned to face him and was interested to note that his eyes were closed, he was drenched in sweat, he was panting as if he'd run a mile, and his heart hammered like a piston. Intriguing. So it wasn't only she who'd been affected by this.

She stroked his lovely dark, dark hair back from his sweaty brow. If Sophie were to describe her idea of the model male specimen, she didn't think she could come closer to her ideal than Gabriel Caine.

He wasn't perfect. His jaw was too square, she guessed, although she liked it. It declared his strength of character. And his mouth was perhaps too full to be considered absolutely manly, but she liked it because it gave him a touch of humanity. His eyebrows, while matching splendidly with his truly magnificent eyes, were too straight, she supposed, for perfection. They suited him, though. Absolutely. His complexion was slightly weather-beaten, although it gave him an air of ruggedness that Sophie found attractive.

Oh, Lord, who was she trying to fool? She loved the man. Madly and, she feared, forever. And all too soon she was going to practice a perfidious deceit upon him.

Upon that lowering reflection, she returned her attention to Gabriel's eyes, and discovered they'd opened. She smiled at him. He smiled back. She had no idea what to say. She recalled that in her youth, the man who'd taken her virginity had always talked after they made love. Said he'd loved her and all that. In other words, he'd fed her hopeful heart a bushel full of lies. She hoped Gabriel wouldn't lie.

He began brushing her hair back from her forehead as she'd smoothed his. "Your hair is so pretty, Sophie."

"Thank you."

"Did your mother and father have blond hair?"

"My mother. Her family was from Denmark, and I guess a lot of people are blond over there."

He nodded. "I see." He kissed her, tenderly, softly, lovingly—perfectly. Sophie nearly melted into the sheets.

"You're quite a woman, Sophie Madrigal."

She eyed him slantwise. "Thank you, I think."

He chuckled. "It's a compliment. Believe me."

"Then, thank you."

They lay in silence for another few minutes. Gabriel continued to fondle her hair, twining locks of it around his finger as his breathing slowed. She enjoyed the attention and tried not to allow herself to fall into the mistake of hoping Gabriel would stay with her forever. She reminded herself that she wasn't the sort of woman whom men cherish, and that if she kept that fact in mind, she'd less likely be crushed when he went away.

His hand eventually left her hair and began another gentle tour of her body. He acted as if he truly valued her body—all of it—and Sophie was glad of it. Since she felt moderately bold, she said, "You're quite a man yourself, Gabriel Caine."

"Thanks." His mouth twisted into a smile that looked a shade wry to Sophie.

But that was all right. He wouldn't be Gabriel if he wasn't a skeptic. "You're welcome." She gave him a smile that was all smile.

Apparently, Gabriel recognized it, because the wariness left his expression, and Sophie thought she detected plain, unadulterated happiness take its place. She was glad.

"You know," he said after another moment or two. "We're pretty good at this."

"Indeed." She wasn't sure what to say, although she agreed. Wholeheartedly.

"Maybe we can do it again sometime."

"Maybe." Her heart took the opportunity to swoop painfully when she realized that after she'd done what she aimed to do, Gabriel would probably change his mind about their continuing relationship.

He was quiet again for so long, Sophie turned to see if he'd gone to sleep. He hadn't. He was fondling one of her nipples and gazing at her body as if he couldn't believe she'd actually shared it with him. Sophie could hardly believe it, either.

"You're—perfect," he said at last. "Perfect."

No, she wasn't. But some nymph of feminine wisdom wouldn't let her say so, and thereby disparage herself. She said instead, "Thank you, Gabriel."

"It's true."

How nice he was when he wasn't worried about her stabbing him in the back with a verbal barb. Sophie almost felt guilty for having been so difficult early in their relationship. Almost.

He continued to stroke her body. The attentions didn't seem particularly sexual at this point, but as if they were offered as a token of his esteem. Sophie accepted them as such, however they were meant. His big, rough hands felt like heaven as they caressed her.

She hadn't understood before tonight how women could enjoy sexual coupling. Her prior experiences with that first man had been hurried, fumbling acts and, while he'd seemed to enjoy them, she hadn't much.

But there was no comparison between Gabriel and that man. Gabriel was ever so much more—more—real, somehow. Also, he was older, and undoubtedly wiser. Sophie grinned to herself, knowing she'd never say the latter to Gabriel. No sense in allowing him to get swell-headed, after all.

Oh, but he was really something special, was Gabriel Caine. Sophie knew without knowing how that Gabriel would never trick a naive young girl into serving as his sexual toy, and then leave her. Gabriel was too honorable to do anything underhanded and nefarious. Why, if Sophie didn't watch herself, she might just—

"Did your little boy have blond hair like yours, Sophie?"

In a heartbeat, all of her tender thoughts exploded into dust. She felt as if he had stabbed her in the heart.

Chapter Seventeen

Shoot. Maybe he shouldn't have said anything. Gabriel reached over to Sophie, who was curled up in a ball of misery on the other side of the bed. He wanted to comfort her, to hold her, to give her whatever strength he possessed. Dammit, he wanted to help her heal.

She thrust his hand away. "No!"

He sighed. What he hadn't meant to do was precipitate a tantrum. "I hate to see you unhappy, Sophie," he pleaded. "Why won't you let me help you?"

"You? Help me?"

Her scorn hit him so hard, he reeled back as if she'd struck him. For a moment, he sat, stunned. Then he got mad. This time when he reached out, he took her upper arm and yanked her over onto her back. Her face was blotchy from crying, and her green eyes looked like drowned marbles—only they snapped fire.

"Yes, dammit!" he said, angrier than he could recall being in a very long time. "What's so odd about me wanting to help you? Christ, Sophie, people help each other every day."

"I don't need any help."

She had sense enough not to try to jerk her arm away from him. She furiously mopped her cheeks with the back of her other hand and glared at him as if he were the devil and the bogeyman and Ivo Hardwick all rolled into one.

"That's bullshit, and you know it, Sophie Madrigal. If anybody in the world needs help, it's you."

"It is not!" She'd taken to shrieking.

All things considered, Gabriel guessed he'd rather face her anger than her grief. "Like hell. You let Dmitri help you. He goes out and scouts out jobs for you, doesn't he? So you'll know whose aunt or uncle to pull from beyond the grave in your seances."

"That's different."

"Yeah, it's different. It's work. And Joshua was probably your life. But coming to terms with your little boy's death is more important than any work ever could be."

"Don't you dare talk to me about Joshua."

Her voice had fallen to a barely audible growl, and she sounded dangerous. If they both weren't buck naked, Gabriel might have searched her for weapons.

"I *will* talk to you about Joshua, dammit. He's the most important thing in your life, and always will be. Alive or dead, he'll always be the most important thing. That's why you're after Hardwick, isn't it? Because he killed your little boy."

The seconds crawled by like centuries, and Gabriel had just about decided she wasn't going to answer him, when she surprised him. "Yes."

He couldn't stand it any longer. He didn't know about Sophie, who seemed to have some sort of inner core of stone, but Gabriel Caine was a soft-hearted gent. He needed human companionship and compassion,

285

and even hearing about a small child's death made his heart ache. Knowing it had been Sophie's child who'd died made him feel like crying himself. He pulled her into his arms, and she resisted all the way. Once he had her snugly in his embrace, however, she seemed to collapse. He petted and caressed her as he would an injured kitten.

"Ah, Sophie, please don't pull away from me. I want so damned much to help you. I really do."

Her body felt like heaven pressed against his. She had the most magnificent body he'd ever seen. He loved it that she had lots of flesh to hold onto. Since she wasn't talking yet, he decided to ramble on for a while on his own. Who knew? He might break down her barriers yet.

"It was the stretch marks." He kept his voice low and gentle. He didn't want to spook her. "And I just put two and two together, and realized it must have been Hardwick who was somehow responsible for Joshua's death. I—well, I can't imagine how it must feel to lose a child, Sophie. I don't blame you for wanting to kill the bastard who killed your son." He elected to refrain from preaching at her. She'd obviously thought about the consequences of killing Hardwick, and had decided the act of vengeance itself was more important than consequences. "I'm sorry, Sophie. I'm so damned sorry."

He went on in that vein for several minutes, wondering if she'd ever allow her barriers down far enough to allow him into her life. Gabriel wanted in, although he didn't know exactly why. Hell, if he got really and truly involved with Sophie Madrigal, it would be a life sentence. Gabriel wasn't a fool; he knew the difference between a romp in the sack and love. He very much feared the latter had roped and tied him, and he was buckled up as tight as a man could be.

Might as well resign himself to it, he guessed. It didn't

look as if there was any denying it, and a gracious admission might ultimately be more satisfactory than fighting against the inevitable. Hell. A man had to be on his toes every damned second, or life would get him in the back, sure as check.

He was getting pretty sleepy when Sophie's voice finally interrupted his soft flow of endearments.

"He was drunk."

Gabriel stopped talking and stiffened. Who was drunk? Oh, yeah, Hardwick. Not surprising, if all Gabriel had read about him was correct. He didn't speak because he didn't want to jar her, but he murmured, "Mmm?"

"I guess he'd been drinking all day. We were in San Antonio, playing in a theatrical house there. Juniper and I had done a couple of seances. I'd taken Joshua to see the Alamo." Her voice quavered and she paused to swallow and get her emotions under control.

Gabriel hugged her and murmured, "I'm so sorry, Sophie."

After a moment, she went on. "Joshua was seven years old. He'd just had his seventh birthday. Ivo Hardwick had evidently gotten into an argument with some other man in a saloon."

Damn. Gabriel wasn't sure he wanted to hear this, but he knew he had to. If he loved Sophie—and he did—he had to share her burdens. He only wished they weren't quite so heavy. He wasn't sure he was up to their weight.

"He and the other man had gone outside to settle their differences by fighting it out in the street, I guess. It was about two in the afternoon. A lovely day. Perfect. Warm and bright, with puffy clouds overhead, and only a little breeze. Joshua and I had been singing together as we walked back to our hotel, when Ivo Hardwick got tired of fighting and decided to shoot his opponent.

He missed the other drunk and shot Joshua through the heart. He died instantly."

"Christ."

Sophie buried her head against Gabriel's shoulder. He felt her tears, hot and bitter, against his skin. "I didn't even have a chance to say good-bye to him."

"What about the law? Didn't they arrest him?"

He felt her head shaking back and forth against his skin. "They called it an accident. I think—" She had to swallow and suck in a breath in order to continue. "—I think they confiscated his gun and fined him."

"Jesus."

There wasn't a thing in the world to say, and Gabriel knew it. He held her and rocked her and let his own tears trickle down his cheeks. If this wasn't Sophie, and if he didn't care so much, he might have felt silly, crying like this. But he didn't. Sophie's Joshua was worth all the tears anybody cared to shed for him. And her.

Aw, Sophie, Sophie, Sophie. For the first time in his life, Gabriel wished he could sacrifice himself for another person. He'd give his life for Sophie, if it would do her any good. But there was nothing he could do to help her—unless it was to save her from her own vengeance. No matter what she believed, killing Ivo Hardwick wouldn't solve her problems. Since Gabriel knew she'd not listen to him—or believe him if she did—he didn't bother telling her so. She'd heard it all before, and rejected it.

After what seemed like a decade, she stopped crying and sat up, propping herself against the pillows next to him, her body pressing against his. He wiped her tears from her cheeks and kissed her. "I'm so damned sorry, Sophie."

"Thank you." Her voice was rough, as if all of her crying had hurt her throat. She sucked in a deep breath. "I wasn't married to Joshua's father, you know."

Oh. Well, hell. "Um, no, I didn't know that." It didn't matter a hill of beans to him, but he wasn't sure how to say so without making her defensive.

She gave him a smile that was far too sardonic for a woman of her youth and beauty. "It's the truth. I was sixteen when a man named John Horn took up with my family's road show. I guess John was in his late twenties." A low, contemptuous laugh crept from her throat, and Gabriel went cold. "He said he loved me."

Aw, hell. Sometimes Gabriel purely hated his fellow men. Predatory bastards. "And you believed him." He heaved a defeated sigh.

"Yes. And I was stupid enough to believe him."

"Now, wait a minute, Sophie," Gabriel said with as much severity in his tone as he dared use on her tonight. "That's not fair. You were a kid. He was a grown man. You were his victim, not stupid. His kind prey on young girls, the damned bastards."

He would have gone on to explain his further thoughts on the issue, but he realized Sophie's huge hazel eyes were staring at him. He drew her closer and said, "What? You don't really blame yourself for falling for that swine's pretty words, do you?"

She didn't answer for a minute. Her mouth opened and closed twice before she said, "Well, yes. I always have done so. I think I was stupid."

"Don't." He was feeling a particle savage by this time. "If I had John Horn here, I'd shoot him in the balls for what he did to you."

She smiled. "Why, Gabriel Caine, if that's not the nicest thing anybody's ever said to me, I just don't know what is."

He laughed, too. "Well, he was scum, Sophie." He eyed her shrewdly. "And I have a sneaking suspicion you weren't the happiest sixteen-year-old girl in the world, to begin with. I'll bet you were ripe for the pluck-

289

ing. I can imagine you, young and beautiful and lonely. I know good and well how hard it is to travel with a parental tent show, believe me. I'll wager you were just longing for somebody to love you and take you away from it all."

She looked surprised for a minute. "Yes. Yes, that's exactly the way I felt."

"I thought so. I remember feeling the same way, but I was a boy. When I grew up, I could just take off. Women don't have that privilege."

"No. We don't." She began fiddling with the sheet that covered their legs. "I—I didn't know until then that my mother had been disowned by her family when she married my father. Her family was rich—I think they'd made a fortune in lumber or something. They disapproved of my father and his line of work, and they refused to acknowledge my mother after she married him."

"Criminy, I don't understand people like that."

"I don't, either, but they did."

"You'd think people would consider their family members akin to gold. How many other daughters did these people have, that they could afford to throw one away like that?"

She graced the air with a little laugh. "I don't know. I do know that my mother and father had a hard time of it during their marriage. They never seemed very happy to me, but I didn't know why. My mother had, in effect, sacrificed everything for my father, and I have a feeling he didn't think he lived up to her hopes." She heaved a huge sigh. "Oh, I know he didn't think so. And I'm afraid she didn't either."

"It must not have been awfully comfortable in your home."

"It wasn't." She gave him another wry grin that made his heart do funny things. "If you could call our living quarters a home. It was a trailer, actually, pulled by a big old raw-boned horse named Ginger. Except when we were stopping with my uncle Jerome in Kansas City. I used to pretend Uncle Jerome's house belonged to us. It was a nice house. Nothing special, like the Millhouse mansion—but it was permanent."

He nodded. "That's probably another reason you were ready for that Horn character when he showed up."

She sighed. "Probably." She didn't continue.

Gabriel waited for a few minutes, then said, "When he found out you were carrying his child, I suppose he didn't offer you marriage or anything."

"Good heavens, no. He was horrified, although I didn't understand why at the time. He took off in the middle of the night. Didn't even leave a note or anything."

"Bastard." And after he shot the son of a bitch's privates off, he'd shoot other parts of him. He'd try to prolong Horn's agony for as long as he could before he put an end to his miserable life. Gabriel had never experienced violent urges of this nature; showed what love could do to a man. "You must have been—hurt." And if that wasn't an understatement, he didn't know what was.

This time she nodded. "I was. I was—crushed. Literally, I felt as though he'd taken my heart out of my body and stamped on it under his boot heels. It was pretty awful. I felt like such a fool."

"I can imagine." He held her for a moment in silence, trying to give her some of his strength. Not that she didn't have plenty of her own. "Was Miss Juniper in the picture then?"

"Oh, yes." Sophie smiled a lovely, uncynical smile. "Juniper Madrigal is the most genuinely good person

I've ever met, Gabriel. Honestly, I think she's some kind of living saint. Or something."

"I believe it." He did, too.

"She was wonderful. Never uttered a word of blame to me, and went on and on about how wonderful it would be to have a precious little baby in the family, and about how long it had been since she'd been able to care for a baby. I think she might have saved my life. I—I thought about ending it more than once."

"Yeah. I'm not surprised." He shuddered at the thought of his beautiful Sophie ending it all before she'd had a chance to live. "And I'll value Miss Juniper even more from now on, if she kept you from killing yourself."

"She did. And she helped me tell my parents what had happened, too."

"That must have been hard."

"Oddly enough, it wasn't, although I was dreading it before I did it. It was the strangest thing, but when I told my parents about the fix I was in, they seemed to recall the bond that had drawn them together to begin with. They—they sort of fell in love all over again."

"Really?" He pulled away a little and peered down at her.

"Really. It was sort of an unexpected benefit. Oh, they were sorry it had happened, but it was sympathetic sorrow. It wasn't as if they were ashamed or angry with me or anything. They were mostly sorry that I'd been deceived and hurt. And what I considered as my own tragedy seemed to draw them together in a way I'd never seen before. For the first time, I realized how much they loved each other. They must have, when you consider it, because they'd gone through hell to be together."

Gabriel thought about it for a minute and realized his

heart felt much lighter. "That's a very nice story, actually."

She laughed. "You think so, do you?" Shaking her head, she shivered all over, as if the recollection was too vivid for her own comfort. "It was really horrible."

"Well, yes, I can see that it would be, for you. At the time. But then your parents kind of found each other again, and that's nice."

"Yes. And I had Joshua."

Gabriel heaved a huge sigh. "And you had Joshua."

"He was a wonderful little boy from the very beginning. He was a perfect baby. He had big, big eyes and dark eyebrows and eyelashes from the day he was born. He looked older than he was when he was a tiny baby because of his lovely dark eyebrows and lashes. He didn't look all squishy like some babies do, either."

Gabriel cleared his throat. "Um, I have to admit that I'm not familiar with very many babies."

"Ha!" She laughed again. This one sounded genuine. "I'm sure you're not."

"Not that I don't like kids or anything, you understand. It's only that I, ah, haven't been exposed to very many of them."

"Of course not. A big, bad bounty hunter like you—"

"I'm not a bounty hunter, dammit." He gave her beautiful bottom a very small smack.

"Oh, that's right. Well, a big, bad—um—apprehension agent like you—"

"That's better." In fact, he liked it.

"—surely doesn't have much to do with children."

"Not on an everyday basis."

"Well, you can take it from me that Joshua was a beautiful boy. Inside and out. He had big blue eyes, sort of like Juniper's, and shiny brown hair. And he was no trouble. He was never any trouble at all."

Feeling inadequate for the situation, Gabriel tried to

convey with his embrace how much he cared for and sympathized with her. He could tell she was close to tears again because her breathing was deep and rough; he admired her for being able to talk about it at all.

"My parents died in the influenza epidemic of '94."

"I'm sorry." God, that meant she'd lost her parents and her son within a very short span of time. Gabriel winced internally.

"I was sorry, too. We'd become close by that time, my parents and me. I loved them very much, and they loved me. And they loved each other, which I think is probably the biggest miracle of all."

"You might be right." Interesting statement, too. Gabriel had met very few long-married couples who still valued each other. Good for the Madrigals.

"It was hard, losing them. It was hard for Joshua. He was only six at the time."

"You mean you lost your parents and your son in a single year?" Good God, that was even worse than he'd feared.

He felt her nod before he heard her tiny, "Yes."

"Ah, Sophie, life's not fair, is it?"

"No, it isn't."

He drew her down with him until they were both lying beneath the sheets, and held her close. "I wish I could bring Joshua back to you, sweetheart. I know that's a stupid thing to say, but I mean it."

"I know you do. Thank you."

As if the angel of good sense had suddenly entered the room and whacked him with its wand, enlightenment regarding a particularly puzzling aspect of Sophie's personality struck him. "Shoot, no wonder you seem to hate men."

"Most of them," she agreed after a moment's hesitation. "I guess that's not really fair. My father was a nice man, and my uncle Jerome is wonderful. And

Joshua—" She had to stop talking and swallow. "Well, Joshua would have been a good man. I know it."

"I do, too, sweetheart. You would have made sure of it. And we're not all like John Horn, Sophie. Honest to God, we're not."

"Oh, I know it, really. Or the infamous Mr. Patterson of Tucson, Arizona Territory."

"Crap, I forgot all about him."

She chuckled against his chest. "I could name a million more, if those two examples aren't enough. I meet some true rats in my line of work. I'm not considered respectable by decent society, you understand. I am, however, considered fair game by many otherwise respectable husbands and fathers."

"That's hogwash. You're more respectable than most of the women I've met in my day."

"Why, thank you. I'm sure you'll disregard our present circumstances when evaluating my relative respectability in the future."

"Don't get sarcastic on me, Sophie. You know what I mean."

"I guess so."

He'd been lusting after her for so long, and their first sexual encounter had been so remarkable, that it wasn't too long before Gabriel was ready for another go-around. He held himself back because he didn't believe it would be appropriate under the circumstances. The very notion of little Joshua Madrigal being gunned down on a San Antonio street by the disgusting Ivo Hardwick made him want to wash himself. He didn't want to taint the evening with his lust.

Dammit. When had he, Gabriel Caine, managed to develop such inconvenient compunctions? He couldn't recall. But he had developed them, blast it, and there was no getting away from them now. Anyhow, it was delicious simply lying here with his arms around her.

Sophie was an armful and then some. He wanted to make another survey of every inch of her glorious flesh soon, and hoped she'd oblige.

Somehow or other, he was going to have to figure a way to remain in Sophie's company after he'd arrested Ivo Hardwick and taken him back to Abilene. First, of course, he'd have to smooth her ruffled feathers. She was sure to be as mad as fire to have her scheme to kill Hardwick overthrown. But Gabriel had faith in himself. Besides, he'd just cross that bridge when he came to it.

It was the next part he couldn't figure out, the staying-with-Sophie part. How did people generally accomplish things like that, anyway?

Holy smoke, they married, didn't they?

The thought of marriage was too much for him. He went to sleep under the influence of it.

She'd told him. She'd sworn she'd never tell Joshua's story to anybody, least of all a man. But she'd told Gabriel Caine. What's more, she'd told him everything. Even about John Horn, her own stupidity, and her parents.

Lord, she could hardly believe it. Love could make a woman turn simpleminded, and Sophie was beginning to feel resentful of the fates for making her fall in love with this particular man at this particular time. Love wasn't fair. Life wasn't fair. At least Gabriel had admitted the latter.

The true irony was that she wanted nothing more than to cuddle up in his strong arms and sleep her troubles away. She was sure she could sleep sweetly and completely tonight, next to Gabriel, in his bed.

But that behavior would go directly counter to her plans. What's more, if she succumbed to the temptation, she would be abandoning Joshua. She'd never abandon her little boy. She had retribution to exact on

Ivo Hardwick before she could even think about herself and her own happiness—if there was such a thing in the cards for her.

In the cards. What a remarkable expression to think of at this moment.

Feeling more than usually ironic and jaded, Sophie carefully extricated herself from Gabriel's embrace. The magical incense had dissipated, the world had returned to its mundane orbit, and the night air was cold on skin that had lately been warmed by Gabriel's arms. A sharp pang of longing struck her, and she thought about postponing her plans for the evening. She could just as well kill Hardwick tomorrow, after all. She didn't necessarily have to kill him tonight.

And that, as she well knew, was a pernicious devil trying to weaken her resolve. She would act tonight, for tonight she knew where her target lay. If she waited, Hardwick would get away—and she might not find the strength to try again.

Also, she'd planned this evening carefully in order to negate the threat of Gabriel's interfering with her. If she didn't act now, she might never have another chance. If what she planned seemed ignoble and unsavory, it was because . . . because . . . Well, she didn't know, but she hoped the feeling would go away.

Her heart constricted when she considered what Gabriel's reaction would be when he realized what she'd done. She decided such thoughts were too depressing. She should dwell on happier matters. Eliminating Ivo Hardwick from the world, for example.

She dressed, thanking her stars for the little bit of light shining in the room. After she'd gathered up all of her things, and all of Gabriel's clothes, including two pairs of his shoes, she tiptoed to the bed one last time and gazed down at him, wishing she could kiss him goodnight. She didn't dare take the chance.

A notion that this wouldn't happen another time, that she'd never experience his love again in this life, weighed heavily on her. Why, oh, why, had this happened now? Why did she have to find the right man now, of all the inconvenient times? She shook he head, angry with herself for getting sentimental.

Then she told herself it didn't matter, that Gabriel was probably just like all the rest, and that he'd leave her, too. She told herself that all men were like that. There were no good men in the world. Men always left. Or the men in her life did, at any rate. She knew good and well she was lying to herself, making excuses for doing something beastly.

And, with tears trickling down her cheeks—tears for Joshua, and tears for Gabriel, and even tears for Sophie—she silently left Gabriel slumbering like a child in their bed of love.

Chapter Eighteen

Gabriel awoke with such a sensation of well-being tickling his innards, he wondered for a minute if he was sick. But that didn't make any sense.

Then he remembered Sophie. Yes, indeed. Ah, Sophie. The woman he loved.

But he probably shouldn't think about that part of his good mood, or this happy feeling would go away. He turned over, keeping his eyes closed. He was as hot and hard as a man could get, and he wondered if she'd be amenable to another tumble. They'd made magic together last night; he wouldn't mind starting this day right.

He reached out for her, thinking to draw her close to his body. He needed her right smack next to him in order for him to feel right. With a chuckle, he wondered how that had happened so fast. His arm flopped on the bare sheet.

Hell, she must have gotten up. He hoped she hadn't

been embarrassed and tiptoed back to her own room. Blast.

"Sophie?" His throat was dry, and her name sounded as if a randy bullfrog had croaked it.

Silence answered him, a big, hollow silence.

Damn. Maybe she was gone. He wondered if Juniper would be shocked. He tended to doubt it. For such a sweet, elderly lady, she was remarkably sensible about some things. His heart twanged when he recalled Sophie's tale of Joshua, and how wonderful Juniper had been.

He tried again. "Sophie? Are you still here? I hope you're still here. I need to tell you something."

Would she laugh at him when he told her he loved her? Somehow, he didn't think so, although she was an odd duck, his Sophie. He never knew how she'd react to anything.

Again, Sophie's sweet voice answered him not.

Aw, hell, it looked as if he was going to have to wake up. He opened his eyes and blinked into the somber grayness of his room. It had looked sort of nice last night—it had even seemed to be filled with some sweet-smelling vapor or something. This morning, it looked empty. Astonishing how the absence of one lovely blonde could affect a room's overall aura of hospitality.

Heavy curtains hid the day outside from his eyes, and prevented the sun from dispelling the gloomy atmosphere now pervading the room. Gabriel didn't like the room this morning. He frowned into it, blinking his eyes in an effort to bring everything into sharper focus. Dammit, he wished she'd stayed with him until morning.

But she hadn't. And the first thing he needed to do was open those blasted curtains so the sunshine could get in. This cavernous, empty room was giving him the willies. Naked, he strode to the windows and flung the curtains aside. Since he was on the third floor of the Melrose, he didn't think he'd shock any Los Angelenos who happened to be strolling by on the street below.

He turned and frowned. The day was sunny, but the sunlight didn't seem to be helping his room—or his mood—any. He turned and grimaced at the furniture, trying to figure out why he felt so suddenly incomplete.

It must be because Sophie'd gone away. His frown deepened. He wished she'd at least awakened him to say good-bye. Her clothes were gone; she probably hadn't wanted to let Juniper wake up all alone in the room they shared.

Damn, this room looked bare. He scanned it for a moment, wondering why that should be.

"Shoot." Narrowing his eyes, he squinted around the room again, surveying it closely. He didn't see his clothes.

Maybe she'd tidied up. He'd been pretty excited last night; he guessed he'd flung his clothes everywhere.

But this morning they weren't anywhere. Gabriel hurried to the closet. Nothing. He checked the bureau. Nothing. He looked under the bed, in the bed, threw the chair cushions around, and even stuck his head out the window and stared at the sidewalk beneath the room. Nothing.

Sophie Madrigal, the conniving little harpy, had stolen his clothes!

"Now why in the name of gracious did she do that?"

The truth hit him like a blow to the heart, and he sank onto the bed, for the first time in his life reeling from something a woman had done to him. "She's going after Hardwick. God damn."

She'd used him. *That's* what she'd been up to last night. She'd lured him into bed and seduced him, lulled his senses, played on his softer emotions with her little boy's story, and tricked him. She'd taken his clothes with her when she'd absconded to give herself time.

301

Without anything to wear, he sure as hell couldn't follow her right away.

Gabriel glowered around the room and cursed savagely. How the devil was he supposed to get more clothes? He couldn't very well stroll over to Sophie's favorite store, the Broadway, damn her soul to perdition, buck naked, now could he?

"Damn her!"

The worst part of it—the absolutely worst possible part of it—was that he was even more hurt than he was angry.

Damnation, the wench had suckered him in like a pro. Even made him fall in love with her, which was a notion so outrageous as to be incomprehensible—yet she'd done it.

Trapped between rage and heartache, Gabriel buried his face in his hands for several agonizing minutes before he sucked in a gigantic breath, filling lungs that hurt almost as much as his heart did. Then he rose from the bed, replaced the cushions and drawers he'd yanked around in his panic, wrapped himself in a sheet, pulled the bell cord, and waited for a bell man to answer his ring.

It took two hours for someone from the hotel to go out, buy ready-made goods in his size, bring them back to the hotel, and for Gabriel to dress. Inquiries he'd made as he'd waited in screaming impatience for his new clothes to arrive had been answered as he expected them to be: The Madrigal party had already checked out of the hotel.

No big surprise there. It wasn't a surprise, either, that they hadn't given the hotel desk any indication of where they intended to go now. He was almost certain they wouldn't stay in Los Angeles.

He thought about a newspaper partway through the

first hour of his imprisonment, and sent for a daily.

Thank God Los Angeles was big enough to warrant a daily newspaper. He scanned the headlines first, looking for news of a murder overnight. He didn't see any, although there might not have been time for one to be reported and written up.

After his first quick perusal, he roamed more carefully through the paper, searching for the names Hardwick or Madrigal. He told himself he was glad when he didn't see them printed in the paper, because that meant he, Gabriel Caine, could most likely still accomplish the job he'd been hired to do. Hell, he'd almost lost sight of his purpose, thanks to Sophie. The she-devil.

He hated the fact that he was relieved Sophie's name wasn't in the paper. It probably meant she hadn't yet accomplished murder. And hadn't been killed. Or locked up. Not that he cared at this point. He only wanted to arrest Hardwick before Sophie got him.

Or Hardwick got Sophie. The idea made his blood run cold, which made him want to kick himself down the stairs—and maybe back up them again.

"Hell, she's a doxy and a no-good cheat. You know better than to care about someone like that. You cut your eyeteeth years ago."

In total disgust, with himself, with Sophie, and with life, Gabriel slapped the newspaper onto the bed. "Who the hell are you trying to kid, Caine?"

He couldn't think of an answer to save himself.

"Are you sure, Sophie?" Juniper looked at her niece with her big, blue eyes fairly radiating doubt.

"Of course I'm sure." She was also hurting, miserable, and enraged, but she didn't want to tell Juniper so. At the moment, she was deriving some very slight comfort from petting Tybalt, who was curled up like a cinnamon bun on her lap and snoring contentedly. Which made one of them.

Juniper shook her head. "I don't like it."

Sophie glared at her. "Nonsense. I know what I'm doing." She was taken aback to see Juniper's lips pinch into a tight line, as if she were angry. Juniper seldom got angry.

"I don't like it that we just took off, Sophie. We should at least have left a message for Mr. Caine."

"Fiddlesticks." Sophie's heart gave such an enormous spasm, she was surprised she didn't faint.

Juniper's head wagged back and forth. "That's not right, Sophie. He's been our good friend this last month or so. We should never have just left without even leaving a note or something to explain our abrupt departure."

If there was one person in the universe about whom Sophie didn't want to talk, it was Gabriel Caine. She stared out through the window and pretended not to hear her aunt.

"Sophie?"

Still, Sophie watched the buildings of Los Angeles slip past the train's window and didn't speak.

"Sophie."

Silence.

Juniper muttered something under her breath, and Sophie hoped she'd give up the subject. Her luck, however, was running universally bad today, for Juniper went on with relentless persistence. Sophie's free hand formed its fingers into claws. She kept stroking Tybalt with the other hand as if she hadn't a care in the world.

"And Dmitri. I don't like leaving Dmitri to make excuses for us. It's not the way the Madrigal family has been used to doing business, Sophie. We've always been punctilious about keeping our engagements and giving the people who hire us a solid reading."

"A solid showing of bunkum and rot," Sophie muttered, feeling more than ordinarily beleaguered.

"That's not fair! You're being perfectly awful, Sophie, and you ought to be ashamed of yourself! This insane obsession of yours is going to be the ruination of the business, and that's not even the worst of it! The worst of it is that it's turning you into a creature I don't even know anymore. In fact," she said with uncommon spirit, "I don't even *want* to know the creature you've become, because she's a spiteful, single-minded, detestable person."

Sophie turned her head and stared, stunned, at her aunt. Never, in all the years she'd known Juniper Madrigal—which added up to all the years of Sophie's life—had she heard Juniper scold another person. That it should be she, Sophie Madrigal, already overburdened by life's tragedies, who was the recipient of this particular reproof, seemed to Sophie to be the crowning injustice. She wanted to cry. She wanted to drum her heels on the floor and jam her fingers in her ears and stick out her tongue and throw a temper tantrum.

"And furthermore," Juniper went on, shocking Sophie still more, "I think you've treated Mr. Caine abominably." She huffed again, and Sophie almost heard her aunt's unspoken, "So there."

"Leaving him at the hotel without a word. And you know he cares about you, Sophie!" The accusatory look in Juniper's eyes was almost more than Sophie could bear.

Unfortunately, Juniper was correct. Little did she know the extent to which Sophie had hoodwinked Gabriel.

And it had all been for naught. She wanted to shriek and scream every time she thought about the farce her last night in Los Angeles had turned into. First she'd been thoroughly and enchantingly loved by Gabriel—

and it had been enchanting. If Sophie had doubted it before, last night had expelled any lingering reservations about the two of them belonging together. They did. And she'd ruined it through base deception and flummery.

The irony didn't escape her. She, who had spent years accusing her family of being frauds and cranks and charlatans, had perpetrated the most egregious deception of them all. And she'd done it to a man she'd come to love.

Her throat tightened. She tried to swallow and couldn't because a huge obstruction, throbbing and aching, wouldn't let her. Her eyes burned. She kept petting Tybalt, who seemed in that moment her only connection to the life that was slipping away from her.

Then, after she and Gabriel had made beautiful love and become a unit that might, if she'd let it, have grown into something rock-solid and perfect, she'd tricked him. She and Gabriel had a chance there, for one evening, to lay the foundations of a life together; to forge an enduring bond; the sort of bond that seldom occurs in life. As a rule, people ran around as if in blindfolds, aimlessly careening here and there, bumping into this person and that, never knowing what they wanted and, therefore, never finding it. The Universal Mind, as Juniper preferred to think of God, was to Sophie a devious, cunning intelligence. It had thrown her and Gabriel together—undoubtedly as a cruel prank, Sophie thought bitterly—and given them a chance at happiness.

But the time wasn't right. Sophie had a job to do first. It was another connivance of that same Universal Mind that had made Sophie's and Gabriel's objectives diametrically opposed to each other. She couldn't achieve her goal without destroying his, and he couldn't achieve his without ruining hers.

It wasn't fair. Nothing was fair.

The most unfair part of all was that she'd lured him, seduced him, deceived him, and left him, thereby ruining the very tiny chance they'd had for achieving a unity of souls. And she'd done it for nothing. Ivo Hardwick had already fled by the time she stole Gabriel's clothes and stranded him, sleeping peacefully under the delusion that she would be there for him when he awoke.

Offhand, Sophie couldn't recall ever hating herself as much as she did this morning.

Thank God for Emerald Huffy. A taciturn, relatively unpleasant individual, and one whom Sophie didn't personally care for, he was good at his job. He'd told her where Hardwick had gone.

A twinge of self-mockery made Sophie's mouth twist. Of course, Huffy would never do anything to impede Hardwick's progress. That, as he'd be the first to tell Sophie, wasn't his job. The longer Hardwick continued to escape his doom at Sophie's hands, the longer Huffy would get paid. But Huffy kept a good watch on Sophie's prey, and hadn't yet failed to keep her informed of his various destinations.

Juniper was right in that she might be jeopardizing the Madrigal family business, too. Sophie'd left Dmitri to make her excuses to Mrs. Crenshaw, who had hired them to conduct a seance this evening. But Sophie couldn't conduct a seance this evening because Ivo Hardwick had eluded her again, and she'd sooner disappoint a client than allow Hardwick to escape death at her hands.

This time he'd run to San Francisco. She thought grimly that he was taking shorter and shorter hops in his effort to escape his fate. Maybe he was running out of money or something. Sophie didn't care. She'd find him in San Francisco and kill him there. It didn't matter to her where she accomplished the deed, as long as she wiped Ivo Hardwick off the face of the earth forever.

If he escaped her reprisal in San Francisco, she'd track him down again. If the family business folded, she'd be sorry to see it go. Even though she considered the family business one of knavery and deceit, the Madrigals were, for the most part, a good-hearted lot. They never hurt anyone.

Not like Ivo Hardwick. Or Sophie herself.

"Oh, Sophie, I wish there were something I could do or say to make you understand what you're doing to yourself."

Sophie had been so engrossed in her own black thoughts that Juniper, who had been silent for several minutes, made her jump. Tybalt jumped, too, opened his eyes, and glanced up at her in mild rebuke. She said, "I'm sorry, Tybalt." Accepting, as usual, Tybalt sighed, closed his eyes, and drifted off to sleep once more.

With reluctance, Sophie allowed herself to look from her dog to her aunt. It occurred to her that she was used to Juniper behaving much as Tybalt behaved. Until today, Juniper had not protested Sophie's acting out her plan for vengeance except in the mild, ineffective way Tybalt protested being suddenly awakened from a sound sleep.

She supposed she shouldn't be surprised that her aunt had finally turned against her. She probably ought to expect to be bitten by Tybalt one day soon.

"I'm sorry you don't approve," she said coldly.

"No, you're not. You're not sorry in the least. You don't care about anything or anybody but yourself."

Sophie's mouth dropped open. Never, in the whole history of the world, had Juniper said anything so downright straightforward.

"You've taken Joshua's death and twisted it until you're determined to become as bad as the man who killed him. Joshua. Precious little Joshua. It's awful, what you're doing, Sophie Madrigal. Awful." Juniper snatched a handkerchief from her handbag and blew her nose defiantly. She'd also started crying, probably from terror at her own boldness.

Breathing hard, Sophie ground out, "I won't talk about it with you, Aunt Juniper. I won't talk about it with anyone."

She could scarcely believe it when Juniper, her cheeks burning fire and her dripping blue eyes crackling, declared, "How convenient for you, to be sure! It doesn't matter how many other people you hurt in your determined pursuit of self-destruction, as long as they don't talk to you about it. Well, I don't want to talk about it, either. In fact, I don't want to talk to you at all!"

Juniper Madrigal, a woman whom Sophie would have sworn didn't have a cross bone in her body, flung herself out of her seat on the train and marched away from Sophie. Sophie didn't know where she was going, and she didn't ask. She didn't dare ask, actually.

As she watched Juniper's retreating back, which at this moment looked as if it were strapped to a poker or some other steely implement, every cell in Sophie's body cried out in regret and confusion.

Gabriel knew she'd have gone to the train station, so that's the first place he headed after he paid his shot at the Melrose Hotel. Damnation. He wasn't hurting for money, but he hadn't expected to have to buy new clothes on this journey.

"Damn her."

He'd been damning her ever since he'd realized what she'd done. It felt better to damn her than to consider

309

the tremendous wound she'd dealt him. His insides felt as if they'd been scooped out with a serrated trowel, tramped on with hobnailed boots, twisted into knots, and then thrown, indiscriminately, back into his body. He'd never hurt so much; not even when he was a kid.

Hell, when he was a kid, the worst thing that had happened to him was realizing his father and mother weren't flawless. Sophie had torn his heart in two—and, until he'd met her, he hadn't even believed he possessed a heart.

"Damn her."

He had no idea how he was going to find out where the Madrigals had headed, but judging from their past performances, Gabriel figured he could do worse than start at the train station.

The man at the ticket window looked bored. "Tall woman, short woman, midget, and a white wicker basket? Mister, this is Los Angeles. It maybe ain't New York City, but it's no one-horse town. I can't remember everybody who buys a ticket."

"You'd remember these people. At least the tall blonde. She's somebody you can't easily forget."

The ticket man obviously didn't believe him. He sneered. "I've seen all kinds of women, friend. I don't recall a one of them."

Crap. Gabriel gave up on him and went to the next window. He wished to heaven Sophie had performed this stunt in a smaller city. Los Angeles, although not a booming metropolis, was too damned big for Gabriel's comfort, and its train station had too damned many ticket windows.

"Yeah? Lemme think." The second ticket man scratched his chin. Then he scratched his head. "I dunno, Mister. I mighta seen 'em. This is a busy station, though, and things get crazy sometimes."

"Thanks." Gabriel moved to the third ticket window,

waited in line, and asked his questions again.

This ticket man at least appeared interested. "What you lookin' for 'em for? They done something?"

"It's a family matter," said Gabriel. He didn't want to get into explanations that wouldn't make sense to this man. Hell, they didn't make sense to him.

"Family matter, eh?" The man looked skeptical.

Gabriel didn't care how skeptical he was as long as he answered his questions. "Yes. She might have asked about taking a pet on the train."

"A pet, eh? Cat or dog?"

What difference did that make? Keeping his impatience in check with difficulty, Gabriel said, "Dog."

"Dog." The man closed his eyes, tipped his head back and, Gabriel presumed, thought about it. When he began shaking his head, Gabriel knew what his answer would be before he said it. "Nope. Can't say I recall such a group."

If there was one thing Gabriel didn't need added to the mix of misery and pain roiling around inside him, it was discouragement. He was feeling mighty discouraged anyhow when he got in line at the fourth and last ticket window. Hell, for all he knew, the Madrigals had fled in the middle of the night. Maybe the shifts in the train station changed at some weird hour of the morning. Maybe none of these ticket men had been here when the Madrigals had bought tickets.

Maybe the Madrigals hadn't left.

Lord above, he'd never find them.

But he couldn't allow himself to think like that. Wherever Ivo Hardwick had gone, the Madrigals were sure to follow. What was that man's name that Sophie used to keep tabs on Hardwick? Huffman, was it? Or Huffy?

"Hell, it doesn't matter," he muttered. A stout woman standing in line in front of him, dressed in crisp black,

311

turned her bonneted head to frown at him. He wanted to tell her to mind her own business. Instead, he tipped his hat, smiled, and said, "Sorry, ma'am." God forbid he should sully her respectable ears with such language.

She sniffed and turned away from him again. This line was moving even more slowly than the other three had. His nerves jumped, and he had the unreasonable sensation that the longer he dallied here in Los Angeles, the less likely he was ever to find Sophie. Or to find her in time.

He had to get to Hardwick before she did. He didn't give a hang about *her* any longer, but he had a job to do. He'd be damned if he'd allow one woman's crazy insistence on personal revenge to thwart him. He wished he believed he didn't care about her any longer.

"Damn her," he muttered, then braced himself for the stout woman's disapproval.

Before she could get her tightly whaleboned torso to complete its rotation so that she could give him a glare, Gabriel spotted somebody in the crowd. His heart nearly jumped out of his chest. Bounding out of the line, he ran over to where he'd spotted his quarry, shouting at the top of his lungs. "Dmitri! Dmitri, wait up!"

For a moment, Gabriel feared his fevered brain had conjured the little Russian out of whole cloth and a crowd of unwary Los Angelenos. He saw nothing but normal-sized men and women who had, moments earlier, been milling about. They were all now turning to stare at him, probably thinking he was some kind of lunatic.

But then, reminding Gabriel of his father's description of the Red Sea parting for Moses and the Israelites, the crowd separated. It disgorged a little man in overalls and a cloth cap, who looked for all the world like a peasant who ought to be hoeing in an Eastern European turnip field. Gabriel could have wept with joy.

He grabbed Dmitri's shoulder, startling the poor man into a yell of fright. "Dmitri! God damn, I'm glad to see you!"

Dmitri clearly did not share Gabriel's joy. He looked, in fact, fairly glum. "*Das vedanya,*" he muttered.

Gabriel didn't care about Dmitri's mood. "Listen, Dmitri, you've got to tell me where Miss Sophie and Miss Juniper went. They're in danger, and I've got to help them." So what if he lied? Actually, it wasn't much of a lie. If Sophie achieved her aim, she'd assuredly be arrested for murder. If that wasn't danger, Gabriel didn't know what was.

Dmitri's head shook stubbornly. "Miss Sophie, she don't want you to find her."

"I know she doesn't, dammit. But if you care about her, you'll tell me."

Gabriel could see that his comment hadn't made a dent in Dmitri's restraint. He kept shaking his head, unmoved. Lord, he had to think of some argument that might sway the man. Clearly, the loyal and trustworthy Dmitri thought he was right in doing Sophie's bidding. Gabriel knew he was wrong. Dead wrong.

"Listen," he said, feeling frantic, "you've helped her before in this scheme of hers to kill Hardwick, haven't you?"

With his eyes thinned almost to slits, Dmitri nodded.

"You must have figured out by this time that her plan is crazy. She's carrying it to impossible lengths. Why, she almost got you killed in Tucson."

"She don't mean to."

Loyalty, trustworthiness, and flat stupidity, Gabriel thought angrily. "She might not have meant to, but she did it. You'd be just as dead if I hadn't intervened as if she had meant to."

313

Dmitri shrugged.

"Dammit, if you don't care about yourself, think about her, then. She's crazy to think she'll be able to do it and not get caught."

"She don't care about getting caught."

Aw, hell. Gabriel shook him hard. "Dmitri, *think!* It will kill Miss Juniper to have Sophie locked up in prison for murder. Think what it will do to the family business. Even hiring a lawyer will drain the family's resources." Actually, he had no idea what the family's resources were, but he knew how much lawyers cost.

Dmitri seemed to waver. Gabriel pressed his advantage.

"I know Hardwick is a bad man. Hell, I'm after him, too, because he shot a man in Abilene. He's at least an irresponsible swine, and at most a total loose screw and an agent of Lucifer. He needs to be locked up. Maybe he needs to be put to death, but it's the law that has to do it. If Sophie does it, they'll lock *her* up."

"He killed Joshua."

Pain squeezed a sigh out of Gabriel. "I know he did. And I don't blame Miss Sophie—or Miss Juniper or you or anyone else in the world—for wanting Hardwick to pay for that."

"Ya."

"Dammit, Dmitri, she's going about it all wrong! She's only going to ruin her own life."

Dmitri shrugged, as if to let Gabriel know that Sophie's life was, to all intents and purposes, already ruined. Frustrated and furious, Gabriel thrust his fingers through his hair, dislodging his hat. He bent, swept it up off the dirty station floor, and slapped it against his thigh.

"Listen, Sophie's a young woman, and her life isn't over yet. I'm sure she thinks it is. And I'm sure she'll mourn the loss of her son forever, but what she's doing isn't honoring Joshua's life or avenging his death. It's making a stupid sacrifice for nothing. She might do any number of things to make Joshua's short life mean something. Instead, she'd got her mind set on something that's only going to cause everyone involved terrible grief. What happened to Joshua was a senseless tragedy. Hardwick is a diabolical ass. Sophie's working on becoming no better than he is. Can't you see that?"

He'd begun shouting without being aware of it. When Dmitri glanced around, and Gabriel did, too, he saw that several people were eyeing him as if, while they might have only suspected it before, they were now convinced he'd lost his sanity. In a harsh whisper, he went on. "Please tell me where she went, Dmitri. You'll be doing her a favor if you do."

Dmitri stood like a stone. For a little guy, he harbored monumental resolve. Juniper would probably have told Gabriel it was because he was a Russian. Gabriel didn't know about that, but he was very nearly at his wits' end with the man. He was on the verge of lifting Dmitri up and shaking the teeth out of his head when at last he spoke.

"I don't know . . ."

Afraid he might actually damage him in his present state of near-frenzy, Gabriel turned around, gritted his teeth, stamped his foot, didn't yell—which showed monumental self-control—slammed his hat against his thigh again, sucked in a huge breath, swiveled again, and said, "I do. If you don't help me, I can't help Sophie."

For a full minute, Dmitri thought and Gabriel stewed. His insides were twisted up like a skein of yarn, his blood raced, his heart battered against his rib cage like a Gatling-gun, and his head had begun to ache. He was pretty sure that either he or Dmitri were destined not to survive this encounter. If Dmitri refused to help him,

Gabriel wasn't sure he could keep from heaving him in front of a train. If Dmitri didn't give him some kind of answer damned soon, Gabriel himself was going to suffer an apoplectic stroke and die right here in the train station.

"I help you."

The tension left Gabriel so fast, he staggered backwards. As quick as spit he straightened. "Thank God. Where'd she go, Dmitri?"

"San Francisco."

"Ah. Do you know where she's stopping there?"

The little Russian nodded. "I go with you." He held up a ticket. "Train leave at noon."

Thank God, thank God, thank God. For the fifth time that day, Gabriel got into a line in front of a ticket window in the Los Angeles train station. Dmitri stood beside him, stolid, composed, and absolutely Russian.

Chapter Nineteen

Emerald Huffy met their train, a circumstance for which Sophie blessed Dmitri. She'd not have been able to maintain this pursuit if Dmitri weren't so efficient.

"There's that man again." Juniper frowned out through the window as the train pulled into the station.

Juniper had rejoined Sophie an hour or so after she'd stormed away from her, but there remained a good deal of restraint between them. Sophie thought Juniper might apologize to her, but she didn't. It didn't occur to Sophie to apologize to Juniper.

"I see him," she said noncommittally.

"I suppose there's no talking you out of this idiotic plan of yours."

Jerked out of her contemplation of Emerald Huffy's uninspiring countenance by the coldness of Juniper's tone, Sophie turned and saw that Juniper's expression matched the ice in her voice. All at once she wondered if she was doing the right thing. Had she become obsessed with something that was, at most, a very bad idea?

She shook her head hard, dislodging the errant thought. Of course she wasn't wrong. It was her duty, as the mother of precious Joshua, to rid the world of Ivo Hardwick. In a voice as frigid as Juniper's, she said, "I suppose there isn't."

"Fine." Juniper snatched up her handbag and headed for the exit door.

Sophie stared after her for a moment before, with a feeling of doom weighting her every movement, carefully settling Tybalt into his blanket-lined wicker basket. She picked the basket up and headed toward the exit herself. She hoped Dmitri would arrive on an early train. Her heart, already hurting, quailed at the notion of wandering the streets of San Francisco all by herself.

Huffy gave her a salute as she stepped off the train. Since Dmitri had remained in Los Angeles—to tidy up the mess Sophie had made by their abrupt departure, according to Juniper—the Madrigal ladies had to fetch their own baggage. Sophie saw Juniper head for the platform at the end of the car, where the porter would sling their bags, but she herself headed for Huffy. First things first.

Oh, sweet heaven, *was* she being a single-minded lunatic about this whole thing? *Was* she wrong?

She silently screamed at herself to stop the second-guessing. She'd set her course long ago. The death of Ivo Hardwick had become the only thing she lived for; without her plan for revenge, her life held no meaning. Before she could question the depressing nature of such a purpose to life, she called out, "Mr. Huffy!"

He walked slowly in her direction. He was the most careful and methodical man Sophie had ever met. As a rule, Sophie found such attributes in a person tedious in the extreme; in Huffy, she applauded them. He was excellent at pursuit. She didn't need him for scintillating conversation. For that, she'd had Gabriel Caine—until she'd deceived him.

Stop it!

Impatience gnawed at her, and she asked a question before Huffy had reached her. "Do you know where he's staying?"

Huffy, unimpressed and unmoved by Sophie's impatience, waited until he stood before her before he answered. Then he only nodded.

Accustomed by this time to Huffy's ways, Sophie withdrew a small notebook and a pencil from her handbag. "All right. I'll take the address, if you please."

Huffy gave it to her. Sophie peered at the notebook, frowning. "Washington? Near Brennan Place? Isn't that in Chinatown?" The Madrigals had played venues in San Francisco many times and Sophie was familiar with the city and many of its streets.

Another nod answered her. Huffy didn't waste words. A body might think they were precious, the way he horded them.

She looked up at him, still frowning. "Where are you staying?"

"A little place near there. Fellow name of Wong Ching. On Grant."

"Yes. I know it. I may have to call upon you to accompany me if Dmitri hasn't arrived by this evening."

Huffy shrugged. "That ain't what you paid me to do."

Irked by the man's too-literal understanding of his job, Sophie snapped, "I'll pay you more."

Huffy squinted, frowning in his own right. "Don't rightly know as I care to do that, ma'am. Not here in San Francisco. The law's tighter here than it is in Tucson. Don't fancy gettin' arrested as accessory to murder. I ain't eager to spend no time at the city's expense."

She slammed her notebook shut. "Very well. If Dmitri

hasn't arrived by the time I set out, I shall go alone."

If she had hoped to shame Huffy into accompanying her, she'd misjudged her man. He only gave another shrug—a one-shouldered one this time. She wasn't even worth two shoulders to him. "Anything else?"

Upset and angry, Sophie said, "No. I suppose not. Go on. If I need you again, I know where to get in touch with you."

He tipped his hat. "Reckon I'll stay at Wong's for a couple days before headin' back to Texas."

Sophie thought for a moment. She didn't like to contemplate failing to complete her business yet again, but she supposed she'd better. Anything might happen, although if she failed tonight, it would be hard on her. "Very well. If I need you again, I should know by tomorrow morning at the latest."

Huffy nodded, turned, and walked slowly away from her. Watching him go gave her an unsettled, sick feeling in her middle, so she turned and headed toward the baggage heaped on the platform next to the train she and Juniper had lately exited. Juniper was standing next to her bag, watching her. As she approached her aunt, Sophie felt much as she'd felt when she was a child and had done something naughty.

Without speaking to each other, the two ladies hailed a cab and had themselves, their luggage, and Tybalt carried to a small but tidy hotel called the Gondolier on Market Street. The proprietor was a friend of the Madrigals from years back, and specialized in renting rooms to traveling theatrical folks. At least, Sophie thought with unwarranted irascibility, he had her family pegged properly.

Gabriel was all but gnawing his knuckles by the time the train he and Dmitri were riding neared San Francisco. "You're sure you know where they're staying?"

Dmitri rolled his eyes. He'd answered the question approximately seventy-five times since they'd boarded the train in Los Angeles.

"All right, all right," Gabriel said. "I'm sorry. I'm worried, is all."

Dmitri didn't bother to answer, but headed to the baggage compartment, where he picked up both of their bags and brought them to where Gabriel, too edgy to sit, stood fidgeting near the door to their car.

"Thanks, Dmitri. That'll save time."

Dmitri nodded. He already knew that. Gabriel considered apologizing again, but knew it was useless. Hell, in his present state of nerves, *he* was useless.

Gabriel's bag was pretty light, since he hadn't bothered to purchase more than one set of duds. There would be time for that after he found and horsewhipped Sophie, and then strapped her to a bed and hollered at her until her pink and shell-like ears turned red and fell off.

Sweet Jesus, he had to find her before she killed Hardwick.

Gabriel had stopped even pretending to tell himself that he didn't care about Hardwick's fate except insofar as his own job was concerned. He knew that was a lie, and he couldn't keep it up after the first flush of his outrage faded.

He didn't want Sophie to kill Hardwick because if she did, she'd ruin her life. That's what he cared about. That's all he cared about.

She was a faithless, ruthless, conniving, manipulative jade. And he loved her with every cell in his body. Which just went to show that her be-damned prediction had already come true. His life as he'd known it for thirty-three years—happy-go-lucky, carefree, jolly, unencumbered years—had come to a crashing end the moment he'd met Sophie Madrigal. He ought to have had sense enough to run in the opposite direction the moment she walked through that door of the Laredo train station. But he hadn't. Now he was stuck.

"Damn her."

Dmitri glared at him, and he shrugged. "Sorry. Can't help it." He cracked his knuckles, kicked the door, and tried to will the train to go faster. He had a feeling that if he and Sophie were to get together and will for something to happen, it would happen. They made magic together.

Thinking about Sophie and him together depressed him, so he tried to stop and couldn't.

"*Damn* her."

Dmitri walked to the other end of the car, where he sat, crossed his arms over his chest, and stared out the window. Gabriel wished he'd been able to control himself better. He needed Dmitri. If Sophie wouldn't listen to him—and he knew she wouldn't—maybe she'd listen to Dmitri.

"Don't be an ass, Caine," he advised himself mercilessly. Sophie Madrigal wouldn't listen to anyone when it came to Ivo Hardwick.

It was five-thirty in the afternoon when he finally left the train, feeling as though he'd shed a six-thousand-pound burden—only to pick up another one. "Where did you say they're staying?"

Dmitri lifted his head as if praying for patience to some esoteric Russian saint, and said, "Gondolier. Market."

"Right. Right. I remember now." Gabriel raced out of the train station and hailed a cab, and only then discovered that Dmitri wasn't with him. So he had to waste five minutes rushing back into the station, finding him, and then rushing back to the cab, dragging Dmitri by the arm. It was his own fault. Dmitri had little tiny legs. He couldn't keep up with Gabriel's long pins. Knowing that, it was all he could do to keep from yelling at Dmitri for being slow.

He was losing his mind.

"Damn her."

Dmitri rolled his eyes for approximately the hundredth time that day. Gabriel knew he was being irrational—and couldn't help it.

Sophie couldn't stand sitting in a hotel room with Juniper, who was still behaving in a totally atypical manner. She'd tried pacing, but found Juniper's icy observation of her passage around the room extremely off-putting. She'd tried reading, but that lasted only seconds.

Too nervous to read, she strode to the window, pulled the curtain aside, and peered out onto the crowded street below. Ah, this was better. She would survey the street. That's what she'd do. San Francisco was an interesting city. She'd always enjoyed visiting San Francisco. Joshua had adored it.

At this particular time, it would be best if she didn't think about Joshua's last visit to San Francisco, Sophie decided after she'd begun to breathe again. She made a resolution that she would only consider the scenery and not think about Joshua at all, for the preservation of what was left of her sanity and composure.

So, naturally, she could think of nothing but Joshua.

Looking out at the scene below, she saw a woman holding a little boy's hand. The little boy was skipping at his mother's side—Sophie felt sure the woman was his mother. She imagined he was singing, as Joshua used to do. He'd loved to sing. So had she, when she could do it with him.

"Blast," she whispered and pressed her fingers against her eyelids, trying to blot out the memories.

"You know in your heart that what you're doing is wrong."

Juniper's hard, crisp voice startled Sophie so badly that she whirled around. Oh, good God, she was dealing out the cards. If she started lighting candles or praying, Sophie would surely go mad.

She took a deep breath and commanded herself not to shriek at her aunt. Juniper loved her. Juniper had loved Joshua. The fact that Juniper didn't understand Sophie's compulsion—indeed, her clear duty—in this instance was too bad, but there wasn't anything Sophie could do about it.

Slap, slap, slap. Sophie's nerves jumped every time Juniper placed a card on the table. She never dealt the cards with that fevered intensity. Whatever was wrong with her?

Lord, she was laying them out in the Celtic Cross pattern, too. That meant Juniper was reading the cards for Sophie—and Sophie didn't want to know anything Juniper saw depicted therein. She didn't believe any of it, anyway, and today she really, really didn't want to hear Juniper preach cards at her. Sophie couldn't bear it. Not today.

Juniper slapped an ace of spades on the table, and Sophie couldn't watch anymore. *Don't say anything*, she silently begged her aunt. *Just don't say anything at all*. She felt more fragile than she had since the day Joshua died. She had a feeling that if Juniper said one little word, she might shatter into tiny, prickly shards of pain.

She crossed her arms over her stomach and hugged herself, wondering again what ailed Juniper, who was normally the gentlest, most loving creature in the universe.

But that was silly, and Sophie knew it. *She* was what was wrong with Juniper. *She* was the problem here. Her very presence was disturbing to the calm atmosphere that pervaded any space into which Juniper inserted herself. Now Sophie, with her hate and anger and determination, was ruffling Juniper's peaceful waters.

Very well. Sophie knew Dmitri's train wouldn't arrive in San Francisco until later in the afternoon. If she waited for him here, she'd only upset Juniper and frustrate herself. Therefore, she would—she would take a walk.

"I'm going out, Juniper."

Juniper frowned at her. This was the first day in her whole life in which Sophie couldn't recall Juniper smiling once. She said nothing.

Sophie grabbed a lightweight summer coat and slipped it on—San Francisco's famous fogs could render evenings cool even during the summertime—and donned a plain chip hat. She changed her footwear because she knew she'd be doing a lot of walking and didn't want her feet to hurt.

Before she left, she opened her handbag and withdrew her Colt Lightning revolver. When she glanced up, she saw Juniper, her lips set, watching her.

Lifting her chin, Sophie said, "I want to be prepared for any eventuality."

Juniper sat silent for a moment, the knave of hearts and the queen of spades clutched in her fingers. Then she said, "No, you don't. You want to murder another human being."

It was too much. Sophie's temper flared out of control like a skyrocket gone wrong. "That's not fair! I'm going to achieve justice for Joshua." The words burst from her in a white-hot rage.

Juniper said quietly, "You may lie to yourself, Sophie, but you may not lie to me. Joshua no longer has anything to do with this craze of yours." Her comment seemed to float on air still pulsing with Sophie's fury.

The words reverberated in Sophie's ears, overpowering her own furiously shouted declaration. Or was it a lie?

God, she was losing her mind.

"I don't care what you think." She opened the cartridge and made sure the gun was loaded before carefully replacing it in her handbag. She lifted her small notebook and flipped to the page containing Ivo Hardwick's San Francisco address.

"I know you don't care what I think, Sophie." Juniper's voice held a world of sorrow. "There's no room in you any longer for anything but your own hate."

"Nonsense." She snapped her handbag closed, made sure her hat was securely pinned to her French knot, and headed for the door. With a tug so hard, the knob almost came off in her hand, she opened the door and was about to walk away from Aunt Juniper without another word.

Compunction struck her, hard, in the heart, and she turned at the last minute. She saw tears standing in Juniper's eyes and realized how difficult this was for her aunt. She licked her lips, feeling terrible.

"Listen, Juniper, I don't want us to be at odds. Won't you please give me your blessing?"

Juniper wiped her eyes. "I—I can't, Sophie. I can't bless what you're going out there to do. I can wish you love and happiness and respite, and I can pray that you'll find peace somehow, but I can't bless your present endeavor, because it's wrong."

Sophie tried to recall another time when Juniper had remained obdurate in the face of a family member's request for a blessing, and couldn't. For all of Juniper's seemingly flighty mannerisms and frivolous ways, she was a woman grounded in pure goodness. Juniper didn't lightly refuse a request. Sophie's chest hurt like fire, but she wouldn't let her aunt know it. It took all of her self-will to smile. "Fine, then. Will you at least wish me well?"

"Of course. I do wish you well, Sophie. Always."

Before she could start crying and ruin her exit, Sophie said, "Thank you, then," and left. Her eyes blurred the street in front of her when she got to it, and she walked blindly forward for almost a mile before her emotions steadied and she managed to contain her tears.

Striding like a soldier going off to war, she sucked in heaps and heaps of San Francisco's distinctive smells. Baking bread, incense, fish, salt water, chocolate. Uniqueness was San Francisco's stock in trade.

She marched to the wharf, past ships that lay to, with fish drying on ropes strung across their decks. She strode past coils of cord smudged with creosote lying in seemingly haphazard piles. She passed crab sellers, fish sellers, oyster sellers.

On and on she walked. She didn't care where she walked, as long as she walked. She thought about Joshua. He'd loved to come to the wharf, eat crabs, and watch the birds. Pelicans and seagulls perched here and there and dove into the water. They'd seen an albatross once. Joshua had particularly loved the seals that would float in the water, begging for food from people standing on the pier. They'd tossed fish to the seals. She could almost hear Joshua's squeals of glee.

"Oh, please stop it," she begged her errant mind. Why did it dwell on Joshua? Her heart throbbed with missing him. Why couldn't people really die of broken hearts? It wasn't fair that she'd had to go on living after Joshua's death, with her heart torn in two but still beating.

Somehow, though, the notion of killing Ivo Hardwick didn't soothe her today as it always had before.

Juniper. It was Juniper's scolding that had tainted her purpose. Sophie drew herself up and tried to convince herself that this was a momentary bump in her road. A hitch. A—what did people who liked to hike up mountains call them?—a switchback?

Yes, this was a mere switchback, and when she'd walked long enough, she'd be back on course again.

Gabriel Caine thundered into her brain as if on a white charger, and Sophie knew she'd been lying to herself. Again. She'd treated Gabriel horribly, and he would be perfectly right never to speak to her again. The man she loved. The one man in the world who might possibly have been able to help assuage the ache of Joshua's loss—and she'd ruined any chance they'd ever had of creating a life together.

Momentarily unable to go on, Sophie leaned on the railing and stared out into the bay. Gabriel. She'd lost Gabriel as surely as she'd lost Joshua, only she'd done it herself this time. Ivo Hardwick hadn't wrenched Gabriel away from her as he'd done Joshua. She'd shoved him away all by herself.

She watched a pelican flutter to rest a few feet away from her on the railing. The bird eyed her as if assessing her ability and willingness to feed it. She'd have been glad to throw it a fish, but she didn't have one handy.

"So you ruined it, Sophie," she told herself, frightening the bird. "You might as well at least do one good deed."

Her handbag seemed to weigh down her arm. When she'd finished with Ivo Hardwick, she wouldn't have to carry a revolver around with her anymore. Maybe she'd come back here and toss it into the bay. With a nod, and feeling as if the weight of the world were on her shoulders, Sophie turned and walked away from the wharf. Her feet knew the way to Chinatown, and she let them take her there.

Chapter Twenty

Gabriel feared his heart would burst before the hotel room door opened and Miss Juniper's familiar gray head peeped around the jamb. "Oh! Mr. Caine!"

That was all he heard before Tybalt bolted out from behind Juniper and leaped up on Gabriel's leg, yipping with joy and recognition. The dog was making too much noise to allow anyone else to speak, so Gabriel bowed to the inevitable.

Bending and petting Tybalt, he crooned for a moment. As soon as Tybalt had proffered a sufficient greeting, he trotted back into the hotel room with his curly tail lifted, pleased with himself for doing his job well. Gabriel watched him, then turned his attention back to Juniper.

He couldn't tell if she was pleased or not. Removing his hat, he said, "How-do, Miss Juniper. I'm glad I found you."

Juniper brightened when she spotted Dmitri. "Oh,

Dmitri, you made it. Was everything all right in Los Angeles?" Her smile tipped a bit, and Gabriel realized she was uneasy about something to do with Los Angeles. He probably should ask, but was too rattled about Sophie.

"Uh, Miss Juniper, I really need to find Miss Sophie. Do you know where she is?"

As soon as Juniper directed her pretty blue eyes at him, Gabriel knew something was wrong. His heart hitched, reeled, and staggered about for a moment. "What?" he almost shouted. "What did she do?"

Heaving a big sigh, Juniper said, "Nothing yet, I hope, but you know she will."

Damn. "Yeah. I know. Do you know where she aims to finish this job of hers?"

"Oh, dear, I wish I'd not been so angry with her. I might have got her to tell me. Won't you come in so we can discuss this, Mr. Caine?"

He didn't want to. Every nerve in his body was primed for action, not sitting around and talking. The truth of the matter was, however, that he didn't know where to go. It would accomplish nothing to hare off, as he felt like doing, since he hadn't the least idea even which direction to take. He tried to sound at least moderately gracious when he accepted Juniper's offer. "Yes, thank you."

Dmitri walked into the room as well, and sat on the edge of a chair. Juniper sat in the other chair, leaving Gabriel the bed, so that's where he sat, and cleared his throat.

"So, you have no idea where she went?"

Juniper gave a hopeless shrug. "I only know she's determined to kill Mr. Hardwick, but I don't know where she aims to accomplish the fell deed."

"Right." Gabriel turned to look at Dmitri, who gazed

stolidly back at him. "She didn't give you any hints, did she, Dmitri?"

As it had been doing all day long, the little Russian's head shook back and forth. Damn. Gabriel cudgeled his brain, trying to think of something cogent to ask. "Uh, did she happen to mention that man she hired to look for Hardwick?"

"Mr. Huffy?" Juniper thought for a moment, then shook her head, too. "I'm afraid not, Mr. Caine. She didn't speak of him to me."

Damn. He glanced at Dmitri, who still shook his head.

"I did, however," Juniper continued, making Gabriel jerk his head around, "hear them speaking together at the train station when we arrived here in San Francisco."

Gabriel surged up from the bed. "You heard them talking to each other?"

Juniper winced.

"Sorry," said Gabriel. "Didn't mean to shout." Hell, he hadn't meant to do nine-tenths of the idiotic things he'd done today.

Juniper gave him one of her sweet smiles. "I understand, Mr. Caine. You're worried."

That was putting it mildly. He smiled back at her, sure his own attempt wasn't nearly so sweet. "Right."

"Yes, well, I did hear them begin to speak, at least. I didn't stay to listen, because I wanted to get to the baggage. And, I must admit, although it's not to my credit, that I was by that time very put out with Sophie."

It had taken her long enough. Gabriel couldn't say it. "You were?"

Juniper nodded sadly. "Yes. I finally lost my temper and told her I thought she was dead wrong about this determination of hers to kill Ivo Hardwick. I told her I didn't think that was any way to honor Joshua, but it was putting her on the same level as Hardwick." Her head snapped up, and she looked at Gabriel as if she'd committed high treason. Slapping a hand over her mouth, she cried, "Oh!"

Gabriel, touched by Juniper's tremendous love and patience with a niece who'd been through insufferable grief—and had, as a consequence, started behaving insufferably herself—said, "It's all right, Miss Juniper. I know all about Joshua."

Juniper slumped for a moment before she sat upright again. "Sophie told you?" She sounded as if she didn't quite believe it.

"Under protest. I—guessed a good deal of it first." He opted not to mention the stretch marks, as that would open a whole new can of worms.

"Oh, dear. I had hoped she'd told you of her own free will. If she'd done that, you see, it might signify a softening of her heart."

This time it was Gabriel's turn to shake his head. "She's too blasted stubborn for that, I'm afraid."

"Yes." Juniper heaved another sigh. "I fear you're right."

"But you said you overheard some of Sophie and Mr. Huffy's conversation?"

"Yes."

"Did either one of them mention a hotel or a meeting place or somewhere that sounded like a location where Sophie might be headed?"

"Well, I'm not sure." Juniper tapped the side of her nose with a slender forefinger. "I can't remember if it was—oh, dear, what was it? I know she said something about Chinatown."

"Chinatown?" Cripes, she wasn't going to try to hire a bunch of tongs to slice Hardwick into bacon, was she?

"Yes. Washington Street and—oh, dear." Juniper

scowled, giving her the appearance of a child pretending to be angry. "It began with a B."

"What began with a B?" Gabriel was getting confused.

"The street."

"I thought you said it was Washington."

"Well, yes, but it was near another street that began with B."

That was a big help.

"Oh, dear, I can't recall."

"But you think it begins with a B?"

"Yes."

"And it's in Chinatown?"

"Yes."

Gabriel glanced at Dmitri, who looked as confused as Gabriel felt. Well, a B was better than nothing. "Thanks, Miss Juniper. I'm going to do my best to intercept Sophie before she can get herself arrested." He thought for a moment before he added, "Or killed."

"Killed?" Juniper gazed up at him with huge, frightened eyes.

"I'm afraid Ivo Hardwick isn't your basic model citizen. He's killed before, and he's not got any morals. At least none that you can point to and say to yourself, 'that's a moral,' if you know what I mean."

Juniper pressed a hand to her cheek, and her face drained of color. Gabriel wished he'd kept his last observations regarding Hardwick to himself. "But I'll do my best, ma'am." He started toward the door, but Juniper's voice stopped him in his tracks.

"She loves you, Gabriel."

He turned around, sure he'd misunderstood. "I beg your pardon, ma'am?"

Juniper's eyes had begun to leak, and she drew a handkerchief from her pocket and dabbed at them. "She loves you. She won't admit it, even to herself, but she does."

Unable to speak for a couple of seconds, Gabriel gaped at the little lady perched on the chair. Juniper nodded, and Gabriel found his voice. "I—ah—I love her, too."

She gave him the sweetest, saddest smile he'd ever received from anyone. "Of course you do. I've known it for weeks. Every time the two of you are together, the magic is palpable. I've seen it in the cards from the moment we met in that awful little train station in Texas."

"Laredo," Gabriel murmured, feeling a trifle numb.

"Is that where it was?" Juniper peered at him, but didn't seem to see him. "I'd forgotten." To Gabriel, it looked as if she was staring into the past. She rose from the chair. "You know, I've been too unhappy recently to read the cards for you and Sophie, but I believe I will now. Maybe they'll give me some hope."

If they didn't, Gabriel didn't want to know about it. "Well, ma'am, I reckon I'd best be off, then. I—well, I'll find her. Somehow, I'll find her." He hoped to hell he'd find her before she found Hardwick. Or, if he was too late for that, he prayed he'd get to her before the police did.

"I go with you."

Dmitri hopped down from the chair, stuck his soft cap back onto his head, and marched to stand beside Gabriel, who said, "I guess that's all right."

"I go," Dmitri repeated, obviously not caring if Gabriel wanted him along.

"Please be careful, both of you." Juniper rose and clasped her hands in a beseeching gesture at her waist. "I'll be praying for you. And for Sophie."

Gabriel supposed a prayer or two couldn't hurt any. He tipped his hat. "Thank you, Miss Juniper." And there, he thought as he closed the door behind himself and Dmitri, is a genuinely good woman. He wished he could get hold of Sophie and make her study her aunt for a few decades; she could learn a lot from Miss Juniper.

"Try Wong's," Dmitri said as soon as they'd reached the staircase leading to the street.

Gabriel squinted at him. "Wong's? What's Wong's?"

"Hotel. Grant Street. Chinatown. Huffy stay there once. I remember."

"Thank God somebody can remember something," Gabriel muttered. "Can we walk, or should we get a cab?" San Francisco was an admirably walkable city, but Gabriel's legs were so much longer than Dmitri's, he hesitated to suggest walking.

"We walk," said Dmitri, thereby further securing Gabriel's approval and appreciation.

"Do you know the way?"

Without wasting lung power on an answer, Dmitri set off at a fair clip down Market street. Gabriel followed, also without wasting breath. Uphill and downhill they walked, and it wasn't long before they reached Grant Avenue. Gabriel recalled when he first visited San Francisco, some fifteen years before, the street hadn't yet been renamed in honor of the former president, but had struggled along as Du Pont Avenue. The change in its name hadn't altered anything else about it, from the looks of things.

He had a particular fondness for San Francisco, probably because of its exuberance. He wondered if he could talk Sophie into settling here.

"Criminy, what's the matter with me?"

He realized he'd spoken aloud when Dmitri turned and said, "You want me to say?"

"No. Sorry. I, uh, stumbled," he muttered, wishing that were all that was wrong with him.

Hell. Now why in the name of thunder was he even thinking about settling down with Sophie? Anywhere?

Unless he was even more of a fool than he already knew himself to be, he had no business thinking about Sophie at all, except as a problem to be taken care of.

He and Dmitri fairly sprinted up a long, steep hill, and he decided it would behoove him not to think about Sophie at all. He could think about—what?

Cigars! Yes, indeed. He could think about how extremely glad he now was for his father's strict edicts against smoking and drinking. He'd chafed under those rules as a lad, but he appreciated them now. Why, if he'd taken to smoking, Gabriel was positive he'd be winded long before he'd reached the crest of this hill.

Dmitri paused at the peak of the hill and pointed. Gabriel paused, too, and looked. Chinatown. There it was, spread out below in all its mysteriousness and inscrutability. Although, Gabriel thought acidly, he doubted that the Chinese were any more inscrutable than any other race; it's only that white people weren't accustomed to the Chinese culture.

Not that any of that mattered. "Glad it's summertime," he murmured as he and Dmitri set out, trotting down the hill.

Dmitri nodded. "Light."

Succinct, but accurate. It was almost seven o'clock in the evening. As difficult as finding Sophie was sure to be this evening, if they'd tried to do the same thing in the wintertime, they'd not only have ignorance and uncertainty, but darkness working against them.

The smells of Chinatown always made Gabriel feel a little wistful, although he couldn't have said why. Perhaps they rekindled boyhood fancies about traveling to exotic ports. The odors of fish and rotting vegetable matter mingled with incense, roasting meat, ginger, sandalwood, and other intriguing scents. Combined with the singsong of Cantonese being spoken, shouted, and sung from all directions, the overall effect jarred a person out of the humdrum. Pleasantly. He wished he could enjoy it. Perhaps he could. Later.

"Where's this Wong's that you talked about?"

"Follow me." Dmitri didn't even turn around, but kept marching down Grant Avenue.

Gabriel followed, dodging pushcarts, vegetable stands, boys with long poles balanced on their shoulders, old men, young men, and even a securely guarded woman. Gabriel tried not to stare. She looked so—so—well, she didn't look American. Surrounded by bodyguards, she must be some rich Asian gent's special honey, because she was dressed to the teeth in embroidered satin, and her face was as perfect and impassive as a doll's. He knew her life probably wasn't a bed of roses—she was a slave, after all—but the vision she conjured in his mind's eye was remote and romantic.

He chided himself. Romance was for fools, and he had a job to do here and now.

Wong Ching's hotel was a small affair, inconspicuous and well kept. Gabriel sucked in a deep breath and prayed hard before he knocked at room number ten, which, he had been assured by the front desk clerk, was at present being rented by Emerald Huffy.

The front desk clerk had told the truth, and—glory be to everything Gabriel had ever not prayed to before in his wasted life—Huffy was in. He squinted from the dim interior of the room at Gabriel's face, looking almost as impassive as the singsong girl had.

Gabriel didn't hem and haw. "Where's Sophie Madrigal?"

Huffy tried to close the door, but the flat of Gabriel's hand prevented him from doing so. The click of Gabriel's gun dissuaded him from attempting any further obstructive behavior. He said in a voice like sandpaper, "Who the hell are you?"

"Never mind who I am. Where's Sophie?"

Huffy's squint traveled from Gabriel to Dmitri and back again. He seemed to relax a little bit, evidently taking comfort from seeing the Russian in Gabriel's company. "How the hell should I know?"

"Don't be coy, dammit. Where's Hardwick? She's going to be where he is."

Still squinting, Huffy frowned at Gabriel and didn't answer. Gabriel shoved his gun into Huffy's gut.

Huffy shrugged. "Hell, she don't pay me to get kilt for her. Hardwick's at Chang's. On Washington and Brennan."

Juniper had been right. It did begin with a B. Gabriel let the hammer down on his Colt, nodded once, and turned abruptly. He didn't wait to see if Dmitri followed him, but strode away from Huffy's door. He heard the door click behind him and realized Huffy could have shot him in the back if he'd been of a mind to do so.

But Huffy wasn't the sort to run risks or to shoot people for no reason. Gabriel suspected about the only incentive that would move Huffy to action would be cold, hard cash.

Sophie's cash had paid for information, but it hadn't bought her Huffy's loyalty. He felt sort of sick as his stride ate up the sidewalks of San Francisco, Dmitri's much smaller boots tapping out an accompaniment at his heels.

"Dammit, it's getting dark. Why can't she do these stupid stunts of hers in the morning?"

Gabriel didn't expect Dmitri to answer him, so he wasn't disappointed when the little man kept his own counsel. They'd been roaming the streets for what seemed like his whole life. The long summer evening was fast fading into night, and they hadn't found her yet. Nor had they found Hardwick, who wasn't in his room when they'd knocked. Nobody knew where he'd gone.

Maybe that was lucky. Maybe Sophie hadn't found him, either.

Gabriel didn't much believe in luck, however, and Sophie had been in San Francisco hours longer than he and Dmitri had. She could have found and killed Hardwick and right now be languishing in some shabby San Francisco police station. Gabriel wondered if she'd tell the police anything if she did get arrested.

He had to stop thinking about Sophie being arrested. For all he knew, Juniper was right and people's thoughts could affect the universe. Damn, he really was going crazy.

Strings of Chinese lanterns swayed above the streets over their heads, and odd music drifted out of a Chinese theater as he and Dmitri passed by. Gabriel had been in San Francisco a few years ago during the Chinese New Year's celebration, and he was grateful now that there were no firecrackers going off. If he had to put up with firecrackers as well as his current state of nervous anxiety, he'd probably crack and kill somebody.

"We'd better check the alleyways," he muttered to Dmitri. "You know how much she loves to take Hardwick down dark alleys."

Dmitri nodded and darted between two buildings. Shoot, was that an alley? Gabriel followed, and realized that Chinatown was truly a maze of bizarre walkways. This one was barely wide enough for him to pass along, but he could tell it was used regularly. A sickly sour-sweet odor that he recognized as opium drifted out of a window, and he grabbed Dmitri's shirt back. "Wait up. I don't think she'd go to an opium den, do you?"

The Russian shrugged. "What about Hardwick?"

Right. Hardwick was a low-down, scum-sucking son

of a bitch. He drank like a fish. Who could say he didn't also smoke opium when he had the chance? And if Hardwick went there, Sophie would follow if she could. Crap. Gabriel didn't want to go into an opium den. And he sure as the devil didn't want Sophie to go into one.

"I go," said Dmitri, either sensing Gabriel's reluctance, or realizing one could do the deed more quickly than two.

Gabriel silently blessed him as he waited in the dark walkway, feeling creepier and creepier as the minutes crawled by. But Dmitri rejoined him eventually—probably not more than ten minutes after he'd left him—shaking his head. Well, good. They didn't have to spend any more time in this foul place. He felt more comfortable walking down Grant, even though he knew Sophie would surely take Hardwick someplace considerably darker and less populated.

The street was crowded, and Gabriel noted with interest that there were very few white people still out and about in this neighborhood after dark. Probably afraid of the tongs or the so-called Yellow Peril. Gabriel wasn't worried about that. His own race generated plenty enough peril without borrowing trouble from the Chinese. All he had to do was look at Sophie, if he ever doubted it.

He'd give his eyeteeth to look at Sophie right this minute. But he didn't see her anywhere. He and Dmitri tried every dark alley and space between buildings they passed by, and still she eluded them. Gabriel's fear that she'd been arrested began to gnaw at his innards like a termite on dry wood.

Fighting off despair, he forged ahead, looking, peeking, peering, hoping, even praying. Fog had begun rolling through the streets, making Gabriel think of some kind of unholy miasma as it curled around his feet and fuzzed his vision.

Damn it all to hell, he didn't need fog *and* darkness. Sophie was crazy enough on her own. She didn't require help from above to make his life miserable.

He had followed Dmitri down a foul-smelling alleyway to where a wall blocked their passage, and had turned around to head back to Grant when he nearly jumped out of his skin. Dmitri had grabbed the back of his jacket and was hissing at him.

"Wait."

Gabriel spun around, his heart pumping wildly. "What is it?"

Dmitri held a finger to his lips. "Shh. I think I hear her."

God, God, please let him be right. Gabriel told himself to calm down and take it easy. "Where?"

Instead of answering, Dmitri went to the wall, which was about four feet high and made of crumbling blocks, and pulled himself up. He grunted as he flopped onto his stomach on top of the wall, and his feet stuck out like those of a puppet. Gabriel squinted into the darkness and strained his ears to hear what Dmitri had heard.

By thunder, he was right! At first all Gabriel could detect were a couple of voices; no words could he distinguish. And then Hardwick's voice, whining and unhappy, penetrated the fog, the darkness, and Gabriel's black worry.

"God dammit, it wasn't my fault!"

"No? My son is dead, Mr. Hardwick, and you shot him. Whose fault is it?" Sophie's voice was as cool and collected as if she were asking about train schedules or the price of cabbage.

"Nobody's!" Hardwick cried. "It was an accident."

"Oh, no, Mr. Hardwick. I don't think so. It was your drunkenness, capricious nature, and heedlessness that killed Joshua. I, on the other hand, am going to kill you

341

on purpose." Gabriel's skin crawled to hear her sound so pleased with herself.

"Hell, lady, you're crazy."

Gabriel couldn't see them, but they were there. Somewhere. He vaulted over the wall and left Dmitri to scramble over on his own as he raced toward the voices.

"I'm not crazy, Mr. Hardwick. Merely determined to put your worthless life to an end."

"No." Hardwick began to blubber. "Please no."

Gabriel was running full tilt when he realized there was a gap in the buildings, and Sophie and Hardwick were at the end of another short walkway opening onto Grant. How had he and Dmitri missed it? Traffic rumbled by on the busy thoroughfare not ten yards away. The activity and light of Grant didn't penetrate to where Sophie and Hardwick stood, though. Gabriel could hardly make them out as he grabbed the edge of a brick building and hurled himself around the corner, making a powerful lot of noise.

Sophie spun around and saw him, her eyes huge. Gabriel thought she swore, but only heard her say, "Stay back, Gabriel."

"Like hell I will."

"I mean it. I'll shoot you, too, if I have to."

"Damnation, Sophie, maybe you *are* crazy."

Weeping in earnest by this time, Hardwick whimpered, "She is. She is."

"Shut up," Gabriel told him savagely. "You deserve to die, but not like this."

"Yes, he does. I'm going to kill him. Now."

And turning to face Hardwick once more, Sophie lifted her gun. Hardwick screamed and covered his head with his arms. Gabriel dove for Sophie.

He didn't see what happened, but he heard the gun go off, sounding like a cannon blast in the confined space. He heard another scream which he thought came from Hardwick. Then he went down hard, an excruciating pain searing his upper arm.

God damn. Had she shot *him*? That would be just like her, dammit.

"Gabriel!" Sophie sounded panicked.

He stayed down, unsure of what to do, and not sure he could do anything anyway. He heard heavy, unsteady steps pounding by him as he lay facedown on the pavement. Where the hell was Dmitri?

"Stop!" Sophie screamed.

Cripes, what now? Cautiously, Gabriel lifted his head to see what in blazes was going on. Hardwick was running, staggering a little, toward Grant, and Gabriel thought he saw blood dripping from him somewhere.

Oh, there was Dmitri. About time. As Gabriel tried to shove himself to his feet, the little Russian barreled into Hardwick, sending him reeling out onto Grant. Sophie had by this time knelt beside Gabriel.

"Oh, Gabriel, what did I do? Oh, Lord, please don't die! Please don't die. I love you so much!"

Oh, yeah? Well, that was pleasant news, although he wasn't sure he'd live to appreciate it.

He lifted his head higher, squinting at the lights on Grant and trying to perceive what was happening with Hardwick and Dmitri. Hardwick backhanded the midget and lunged forward. "Oh, shit," Gabriel whispered, realizing what was going to happen about a second before it did.

"What?" Sophie asked, her voice shaking. "What is it?"

Too horrified to speak, Gabriel pushed himself to his knees and pointed.

He heard a soft cry from Sophie as she, too, watched the coach, pulled by four matched and beautiful blacks, roll into Ivo Hardwick and knock him flat. Two of the horses clattered over Hardwick's body, followed by two of the carriage's wheels.

Gabriel turned and saw that Sophie, still kneeling on the filthy pavement, was staring with horror at the accident site. He tugged her into his arms, and she buried her head against his shoulder. There. That was better.

Dmitri, who had been flung aside by Hardwick, struggled to his feet. He, too, watched the awful scene on the street.

Gabriel shut his eyes. "Well, Sophie Madrigal, you got your heart's desire. I guess it wasn't exactly the way you'd planned it."

Sophie didn't say a word because she was too busy crying. That was all right with Gabriel. He still wasn't sure about his own physical condition. He thought she might have shot him in the arm, although if she had, why had Hardwick been bleeding? He didn't much want to release Sophie, but he did squint down at his arm. Well, hell, he didn't see any bullet holes. Actually, his arm didn't hurt much anymore, either. He wiggled it experimentally. Not a twinge. Hmmm.

"Did you shoot me?" he asked, keeping his tone conversational. They had a lot of things to discuss, but he figured they should take care of first things first.

"I—I don't know."

She lifted her head. Her eyes streamed tears, and she wiped them, leaving a smudgy dark streak across her cheek. Gabriel used his thumb to clean the streak. Then he kissed the spot. He couldn't seem to help himself. "Well, I felt something. A big pain in my arm."

Nodding, Sophie said, "Yes. I—I don't know what happened."

"You didn't see?"

"No. Yes. Well—I don't know. I was—everything happened so fast. And there was this huge flash of light."

"A flash of light?"

344

"Yes."

Dmitri limped over to them. "Magic," he said.

Sophie and Gabriel stared at each other for a long time. Then, slowly, Sophie nodded.

Well, hell. Gabriel struggled to his feet and helped Sophie to rise. "I reckon we'll have to figure it out later. We'd better see what's happening with Hardwick now." He turned to Dmitri. "Would you mind looking for the gun? Sophie seems to have dropped it."

Sophie peered at her empty hands and shuddered. Gabriel took her firmly by the arm, prepared to lead her out onto Grant. She was going to face the result of her quest for vengeance here and now. Then maybe they could get on with the rest of their lives. Together.

Chapter Twenty-one

The tall Chinese gentleman shook his head. "Sorry, Mr. Caine. You won't find a Chinese in San Francisco who'll touch a white man."

Several other Chinese men crowded the accident scene. When Gabriel glanced around at them, they shook their heads, too, confirming the tall man's pronouncement.

"Not even to take him to save his life? Take him to a hospital or something?"

"Sorry," the tall Chinese gentleman said. "We've had too much experience with such things. It's not good for a Chinese to have anything to do with white men."

"But I don't think he's dead yet," Gabriel pointed out.

Hardwick, who clearly wasn't going to hang onto life much longer, groaned. Sophie, standing at Gabriel's side, stared at the injured man, her face as impassive as that of any Chinese.

The tall Chinese gentleman, who was dressed to the

nines in a Western-style evening coat and tails, smiled. "He will be soon." Philosophical race, the Chinese.

"I reckon."

"You see, if he dies after we try to help him, we will be blamed. If he lives after we try to help him, the police will arrest us for hurting him."

"I see."

All things considered, Gabriel didn't feel much sympathy for Ivo Hardwick. He might be suffering, although he was probably unconscious, but his present misery was no greater than the suffering he'd put others through in his misspent life.

"Um, but we can't just leave him there, can we?"

The well-dressed gent said, "I suppose someone's already run to get the roundsman on the corner of Grant and Washington."

Gabriel nodded and turned to see where Dmitri was. He'd probably found the gun by this time.

Things became even more confusing shortly thereafter. A policeman rushed up, took in the scene, and dispatched an eager Chinese boy to fetch an ambulance. He had to call him back not more than a second later, because Hardwick had expired. Revising his request, he sent the boy for the undertaker.

Sophie sipped hot, sweet tea and decided she might survive the evening. This was especially true since Gabriel hadn't released her hand once since he'd tackled her in that awful alleyway.

The building in which she sat was pretty seedy, but the policemen had been uniformly polite and nice to them all. They'd even driven Dmitri to the Gondolier so he could tell Aunt Juniper that everyone was all right. Sophie knew, although they hadn't discussed it in front of the police, that Dmitri would also inform Juniper that Sophie hadn't been able to accomplish her purpose.

347

Now that it was all over, Sophie was glad of it. She had enough on her conscience without adding the death of even so slimy a specimen as Ivo Hardwick to its load.

"I think that's about all, Miss Madrigal." A chubby policeman with a lovely handlebar mustache had been taking notes in the station house. He was the one who'd given her the tea. He'd offered Gabriel whiskey. Sophie wished he'd poured some into her tea, but she didn't ask. She felt drained; too tired to be elated or depressed or anything but tired and empty.

And still Gabriel held her hand. Did that mean he didn't hate her after all?

Dmitri hadn't found the gun. Sophie had an idea about what had happened to it—and to Gabriel's arm—but she didn't offer it to the San Francisco Police Force. She was sure they wouldn't understand. Actually, she wasn't sure *she* understood, but she was willing to give it a chance. Juniper would know. She'd been longing to see Juniper ever since Hardwick had breathed his last under that enormous carriage. She shuddered, and Gabriel squeezed her hand.

"Can either of you think of anything we've not included in this report?" The chubby policeman smiled first at Sophie and then at Gabriel.

She shook her head. Her hat had fallen off, and she guessed it was gone for good—maybe it and the gun had run off together. "I don't think so." She was so weary, it was all she could do to push the words out of her mouth.

"No. That should do it." Gabriel sounded more energetic than she. She wanted to fold up on his lap, throw her arms around him, and sleep for a hundred years.

"Well, then. Since you folks are from out of town, I'll ask you to come back here tomorrow to read and sign your statements. Will that be all right with you?"

"Certainly," Sophie murmured, wondering if she'd wake up tomorrow. Oh, surely she would. A body couldn't sleep through an entire day, no matter how exhausted she was.

"Sure," said Gabriel. "Any particular time?"

"No." The policeman rose from behind his desk and held out his hand for Gabriel to shake. "I'm sorry about your man, Mr. Caine, but the Pinkertons should understand."

That's another thing. Gabriel was a Pinkerton man. Sophie had gaped when he'd informed the policeman that he'd been in pursuit of Ivo Hardwick, and had been commissioned to bring him to Abilene, Texas, to stand trial for murder and injuring another man. He'd even pulled out an identification card and showed it to the policeman. Peeking over his shoulder, Sophie saw the card and recognized the always-open eye printed on it, so she guessed it was true. He hadn't told Sophie anything at all about the Pinkertons. The beast hadn't been honest with her.

Integrity tapped on her mental door and begged entry, reminding her that she'd been totally wicked to Gabriel. Integrity was such a pest sometimes.

"Right. I'll cable them first thing tomorrow. I don't suppose there's a cable office open tonight." It was the first time Sophie had ever heard Gabriel sound tentative.

The mustachioed policeman smiled a man-to-man smile and winked at him. "You don't want to go out of your way to do that tonight, Mr. Caine. I'm sure you want to take care of Miss Madrigal."

"Right." Gabriel squeezed her hand again. "You're right, of course."

Thank God. Sophie didn't say so, because she still wasn't sure about Gabriel. For all she knew, he was

Emma Craig

hanging on to her hand so she couldn't get away before he could beat her.

"I'll see if the police car is back from taking your little man to the Gondolier."

Their "little man." Sophie resented the policeman's words for Dmitri's sake, but didn't say anything.

"If Saunders has returned, I'll ask him to take you home," the man continued.

"Thanks. That's very kind of you." Sophie smiled at Mustache and held out her hand. Good Lord, her glove was terribly soiled. Mustache didn't seem to mind. In fact, he gave her a very warm smile as he took her hand. He even bowed over it. Sophie thought cynically that he'd let his mustache go to his head. So to speak. Then she told herself to stop being mean.

"Appreciate your help," Gabriel said.

"It was a terrible accident," said Mustache, shaking his head as if he regretted it. "I'm sorry Miss Madrigal had to see it."

"She's tough. She'll get over it."

Sophie decided it wouldn't be prudent to smack Gabriel on the arm. Especially since she still wasn't entirely sure she hadn't shot him.

Both Gabriel and Mustache helped her into the police carriage, which waited for them outside the police station on the outer edge of Chinatown. The San Francisco Police Department tried not to interfere much in Chinatown's everyday business. Sophie considered such a practice intelligent and prudent, and was surprised the police had thought of it.

As soon as the door closed and the horse had jerked the carriage into motion, Gabriel turned to her. "All right, Sophie Madrigal, what the hell happened in that alleyway?"

Sophie, wanting to stave off the moment of truth for as long as she could, since she figured Gabriel would only disbelieve her when she told him, lifted her hand to his arm. "Did I shoot you? I hope I didn't. I didn't mean to."

"No." He frowned down at his arm. "I don't know what happened, but I'm not shot."

"Good. I—I didn't want to shoot you." A shiver rattled her bones at the thought.

"Nice of you, I'm sure," he said dryly. "Now, tell me: What happened in that alleyway? I was diving for you and didn't see a damned thing."

Sophie breathed deeply and let it out slowly. Then she shrugged. What the hell, as Gabriel himself might say. She looked him square in the eye. "It was magic."

He blinked at her. "Beg pardon?"

She shrugged again. "It was magic."

His eyes began to narrow, and she hurried to forestall an eruption of anger. "I'm serious, Gabriel. It was as if time stopped for a second when you jumped at me. I saw a huge bolt of light materialize out of nowhere. It struck your side—I guess it hit your arm—and you went down like a sack of cement. I thought at first the light had come from the gun, because I know I pulled the trigger, and I heard the sound of a gunshot."

"Yeah. So did I." He'd started frowning.

"But I guess the bullet didn't hit you."

"Didn't hit Hardwick, either, according to the coroner."

She shivered again. "I guess not."

Silence slid into the carriage along with the fog seeping in through the windows. Sophie repeated, "It was magic."

"Hmmm. Right."

"It was." She tried to think of some way to convince him, but was unable to come up with anything brilliant. Or even dull. It had been magic, and that was that.

His brow furrowed as if he were pondering difficult

questions, he asked, "Did they find the gun?"

"No. Dmitri didn't find it, and I guess the police didn't find it, either."

"They weren't looking for a damned gun," Gabriel all but snarled. "Which was lucky for you."

She sighed. "I suppose so."

"You suppose so." He sounded disgusted. "You, my dear, have no idea how damned lucky you were tonight."

"I have a notion." Whether her luck was good or bad all depended, of course, on what happened now.

Gabriel glowered into the darkness for a minute before he turned to face her again. "You said you loved me when I was lying there in that damned alley. Was that a lie? Did you only say it because you thought you'd killed me?"

Good Lord, did he believe that? Sophie shook her head. "No, Gabriel. I said it because it's the truth. I love you. Dearly."

"Do you treat all the people you love like hell, or did you single me out for special treatment?"

Oh, dear, he was going to be difficult. "I—"

He held up a hand. "Wait. I forgot. You also treat your aunt like hell. I guess I'm not so special after all."

Sophie felt her lower lip tremble, and clamped her teeth on it. She couldn't cry. She wouldn't cry. That would be a sly and manipulative thing to do. Sophie deplored such tactics used by females to twist the wills of men.

"And then there's Dmitri. You damned near got him killed in Tucson. And tonight. Shoot, Hardwick might have smashed him like a fly if he hadn't been in such a hell of a hurry."

"But—"

"I guess you treat your dog kindly. That's something."

"Gabriel!"

"And I guess you love old Tybalt. Probably because he never argues with you or tells you what a damned ass you're being."

"Gabriel!" Why was he saying these horrible things to her?

Because they were the truth, her conscience reminded her. Blast. Sometimes Sophie purely hated the truth. Nevertheless, now that she took the time to peer back over the last ten or eleven months, she could see where she'd been a trifle—oh, very well, *quite*—difficult.

"Dmitri and I went to see Miss Juniper when we set out to find you, and she was feeling guilty because she'd finally lost her temper at you. Ha!"

Sophie winced.

"The woman's a saint. How anybody could put up with you and your insane obsession—"

"It wasn't!"

"It was, too. Your insane obsession, for so long, passes my understanding."

"You're being mean." Honest, perhaps, but mean.

"Mean, my ass. I just want you to know, Sophie Madrigal, that I'm not going to put up with any more nonsense like what you've put Miss Juniper and Dmitri—not to mention me—through again. Never. If you so much as *look* like you're getting obsessed about something, I'm going to throw you over my knee and spank your beautiful bottom."

Sophie tried to read his face, but the carriage was too dark. A faint scent of jasmine, sandalwood, and orange blossoms kissed her nostrils, and she almost jumped out of her skin. Good Lord, was this a love scene they were enacting in this godforsaken rattletrap police carriage?

"Um, how are you going to do that?"

353

"Want me to show you here and now?" He sounded ferocious.

"No! What I meant was—well, aren't you going back to Abalone?"

"Where? Oh. Abilene. No. I'm going to cable Franklin and the Pinkertons tomorrow."

"But—don't you have to go back to your job?"

"I'm thinking of going into another line of work."

"Oh."

"And I think San Francisco's the best place to do it."

"You do?"

"Yeah. San Franciscans love all sorts of strange stuff. They'll love what I have planned."

"Really?" Sophie's heart had started teetering back and forth, like a seesaw, and she was feeling a little sickish. The scent of orange blossoms, sandalwood, and jasmine was stronger.

"Sure. I understand a lot of mystics and mediums are moving West. I'm sure my show will top them all."

"Your show?" Wonderful. Now her voice was quivering like aspic.

"Sure." Keeping one of her hands in his, he lifted the other, splayed his fingers out, and passed his hand in front of her as if he were displaying a banner. "I can see it now. We'll have our own theater, and the marquee will read *Madrigal*. I think just the one word will be good. Dramatic. Folks like their occult spirits served up with drama, you know."

Sophie's mouth fell open. She couldn't find a word in it to save her life.

He smiled all at once, revealing his perfect white teeth in his perfect tanned face. "So, what do you think, Sophie? Think it'll go over big in San Francisco?"

She had to swallow and clear her throat before she could get her tonsils and tongue to coordinate. "I—I'm not sure what you mean, Gabriel."

"No? I thought I was being pretty plain. I'm great at managing businesses. Been doing it all my life until I took up with the Pinkertons after my folks died. My uncle wanted me to keep managing the preaching side of the family, but I couldn't stand the hypocrisy. On my part, not his. He believed in what he was doing. But I figure it doesn't matter if I believe in magic or not. Hell, you're a spiritualist, and you don't believe in it. Why should I?"

Oh. Sophie understood now—and her heart sank into her sensible shoes. "I see. You and Juniper worked something out."

"Juniper and me? Now when in hell could we have worked anything out? I've been looking for you all damned day."

Sophie opened her mouth. Finding it empty, she closed it again.

"By the way, that was a really dirty trick you played on me in Los Angeles, Sophie. You're going to have to work some to make that one up to me."

She couldn't take any more. With as much force as she could, she whacked his chest. "Damn you, Gabriel Caine! What are you talking about! You're trying to drive me crazy, aren't you?" Big fat tears started rolling down her cheeks, and she was utterly humiliated.

"Trying to drive *you* crazy? I like that. You've already driven me nuts, damn you. If you hadn't, would I be talking about spending the rest of my life with you?"

"*What?* What are you talking about?"

"God dammit, I'm going to marry you! I'm going to marry you and keep you on a damned leash. You're too dangerous to be allowed out without a keeper, and I can't feature anyone else being fool enough to take the job." He reached out to grab her other hand before she could hit him again. "Can you?"

He needn't have grabbed her. She was too stunned

355

to hit him again. "You want to marry me? Me?"

"Well, as to *wanting* to marry you . . ."

"Gabriel."

"Oh, all right." He brought both of her hands to his lips and kissed them. "Have I told you how much I love you?"

She shook her head.

He sighed heavily. "Well, I do. I tried not to, God knows, but I can't seem to help myself."

"Oh."

She could barely make out his eyes twinkling at her out of the dark. She licked her lips. "Oh? Is that all you can say? Oh?" He chuckled, one of those deep, dark chuckles that curled through her like a river of fire, heating her blood and making her heart bump crazily.

"I—I—" It was no use. She couldn't speak.

He drew her into his arms. She folded up like a concertina and all but melted against him. "Ah, Sophie, I love you so much it scares me sometimes. And I know I'll never be able to make up to you for what you've lost. Nobody will ever be able to replace Joshua. But you know, I really like kids, and if we were to have a couple, it might make you feel better." He drew back and looked down at her. She was too moved to do anything but swallow and try not to bawl like a baby. "What do you say? Will you marry me? If you say no, I'll kidnap you and run off with you."

Making a monumental effort, Sophie managed to tilt her head back and look up at him. "Yes." It was only a whisper. She wanted to shout the word to the world. "Oh, yes."

"Good." As if he feared she might change her mind, he tightened his embrace. He didn't let her go until they reached the Gondolier. Even then, he kept holding her hand all the way up to Juniper's room.

*　　*　　*

"Our dog snores." Gabriel, replete after loving Sophie completely and with absolute honesty—not to mention the sweet incense of sandalwood, orange blossoms, jasmine, and magic—thought Tybalt's snoring was kind of cute, actually.

"I know he does." Sophie, her breathtaking body gleaming white in the moonlight and damp with the sweat of their lovemaking, smiled at him, and Gabriel's heart overflowed. It had been doing that ever since they'd returned to the Gondolier.

"This was a brilliant idea of yours, Sophie," he said, deciding not to prolong the snoring conversation. "Taking a room together next to Juniper's, that is."

"It was, wasn't it? You see? Not all of my ideas are maniacal."

"Thank God for that. If you ever decide to kill anybody else, take it up with me first, all right?"

"Of course, Gabriel."

She sounded intolerably submissive, and he didn't believe it for a minute. He decided to subdue her in his own way, propped himself on an elbow, and leaned over to suckle one of her perfectly spectacular breasts. She sighed happily and reached for his sex, which was stiffening up satisfactorily.

"We're really good at this," he mumbled around a nipple.

"We certainly are."

When he slipped into her warm, moist sheath the second time that night, Gabriel realized Sophie's prediction had come true absolutely and beautifully. And he was glad of it.

Their first child, Martin George Caine, was born ten months after their marriage, in the bedroom of their lovely San Francisco home. The family business, being carried out in a theater owned by Gabriel and a friend of his, was prospering better than any of them could have predicted—except, perhaps, Sophie, although she didn't much go in for predictions any longer.

Gabriel knew the Madrigal family magic had carried over to another generation as soon as he saw his son in Sophie's arms. Nothing but the magic of love could have transformed his magnificent Sophie so completely.

Juniper agreed, although she still dealt the cards, lit candles, and prayed a lot. That was all right with Gabriel. Life could be rough sometimes. Anything that helped a body get through it was aces up with him.

So he was happy to let Juniper have her magic. Personally, he preferred love. Fortunately for him, he had plenty of both.

EMMA CRAIG
Cooking Up Trouble

Heather Mahaffey is a beauty, true, and clever, but her father has a tendency to run off at the mouth. And that can be a problem—especially when he is praising her to the wealthiest rancher around, telling him that she can out-cook anyone in the New Mexico Territory. The whole situation is mortifying, especially when Heather knows she has difficulty boiling water. Worse, the wealthiest man in the territory is also the best looking. Philippe St. Pierre has a face women would die for . . . and a body to match. And then there's the devilishly handsome man who offers to assist her—one Mr. D.A. Bologh. Is he on the up and up, or does he have a purpose far more sinister? Either way, with one kiss from Philippe, Heather is in the kitchen and cooking up trouble.

___52398-1   *$5.99* US/*$6.99* CAN

Dorchester Publishing Co., Inc.
P.O. Box 6640
Wayne, PA 19087-8640

Please add $2.50 for shipping and handling for the first book and $.75 for each book thereafter. NY, and PA residents, please add appropriate sales tax. No cash, stamps, or C.O.D.s. All orders shipped within 6 weeks via postal service book rate.

Canadian orders require $2.00 extra postage and must be paid in U.S. dollars through a U.S. banking facility.

Name _____
Address _____
City_____ State_____ Zip_____
I have enclosed $_____in payment for the checked book(s).
Payment <u>must</u> accompany all orders. ❑ Please send a free catalog.
CHECK OUT OUR WEBSITE! www.dorchesterpub.com

Enchanted Christmas
Emma Craig

Noah Partridge has a cold, cold heart. Honey-haired Grace Richardson has heart to spare. Despite her husband's death, she and her young daughter have hung on to life in the Southwestern desert, as well as to a piece of land just outside the settlement of Rio Hondo. Although she does not live on it, Grace clings to that land like a memory, unwilling to give it up even to Noah Partridge, who is determined to buy it out from under her. But something like magic is at work in this desert land: a magic that makes Noah wonder if it is Grace's land he lusts after, or the sweetness of her body and soul. For he longs to believe that her touch holds the warmth that will melt his icy heart.

___52287-X $5.99 US/$6.99 CAN

Dorchester Publishing Co., Inc.
P.O. Box 6640
Wayne, PA 19087-8640

Please add $1.75 for shipping and handling for the first book and $.50 for each book thereafter. NY, NYC, and PA residents, please add appropriate sales tax. No cash, stamps, or C.O.D.s. All orders shipped within 6 weeks via postal service book rate. Canadian orders require $2.00 extra postage and must be paid in U.S. dollars through a U.S. banking facility.

Name_____
Address_____
City_____State_____Zip_____
I have enclosed $_____ in payment for the checked book(s).
Payment <u>must</u> accompany all orders. ❑ Please send a free catalog.

A Gentle Magic

EMMA CRAIG

When cattleman Cody O'Fannin hears a high-pitched scream ring out across the harsh New Mexico Territory, he rides straight into the heart of danger, expecting to find a cougar or a Comanche. Instead, he finds a scene far more frightening—a woman in the final stages of childbirth. Alone, the beautiful Melissa Wilmeth clearly needs his assistance, and although he'd rather face a band of thieving outlaws, Cody ignores his quaking insides and helps deliver her baby. When the infant's first wail fills the air, Cody gazes into Melissa's bewitching blue eyes and is spellbound. How else can he explain the sparkles he sees shimmering in the air above her honey-colored hair? Then thoughts of marriage creep into his head, and he doesn't need a crystal ball to realize he hasn't lost his mind or his nerve, but his heart.

___52321-3 $5.50 US/$6.50 CAN

A GAMBLER'S MAGIC
EMMA CRAIG

Gambler Elijah Perry is on a winning streak, until he is shot in the leg and fears his good fortune is at an end. Then he awakes to find the straight-laced Joy Hardesty scowling at him and he sees he's been dealt another tricky hand. But as the lovely nurse tends his wounds, he discovers a free, joyful spirit beneath her poker face and a straight flush that bespeaks an enchanting innocence. There is magic in the air, and Elijah realizes that it is not a sleight of hand that has brought him to New Mexico, but Lady Luck herself. As he holds the beauty in his arms he knows that in winning the love of a lifetime he'll more than break even.

___52358-2 $5.50 US/$6.50 CAN

Dorchester Publishing Co., Inc.
P.O. Box 6640
Wayne, PA 19087-8640

Please add $1.75 for shipping and handling for the first book and $.50 for each book thereafter. NY, NYC, and PA residents, please add appropriate sales tax. No cash, stamps, or C.O.D.s. All orders shipped within 6 weeks via postal service book rate. Canadian orders require $2.00 extra postage and must be paid in U.S. dollars through a U.S. banking facility.

Name_____
Address_____
City_____State_____Zip_____
I have enclosed $_____ in payment for the checked book(s).
Payment <u>must</u> accompany all orders. ❏ Please send a free catalog.
      CHECK OUT OUR WEBSITE! www.dorchesterpub.com

Midsummer Night's Magic

Four of Love Spell's hottest authors, four times the charm!

EMMA CRAIG
"MacBroom Sweeps Clean"

Stuck in an arranged marriage to a Scottish lord, Lily wonders if she'll ever find true love—until a wee Broonie decides to teach the couple a thing or two about Highland magic.

TESS MALLORY
"The Fairy Bride"

Visiting Ireland with her stuffy fiancé, Erin dreams she'll be swept into a handsome stranger's enchanted world—and soon long to be his fairy bride.

AMY ELIZABETH SAUNDERS
"Whatever You Wish"

A trip through time into the arms of an English lord might just be enough to convince Meredyth that maybe, just maybe, wishes do come true.

PAM McCUTCHEON
"The Trouble With Fairies"

Fun-loving Nick and straight-laced Kate have a marriage destined for trouble, until the fateful night Nick hires a family of Irish brownies to clean up his house—and his love life.

___52209-8 $5.50 US/$6.50 CAN

Dorchester Publishing Co., Inc.
P.O. Box 6640
Wayne, PA 19087-8640

Please add $1.75 for shipping and handling for the first book and $.50 for each book thereafter. NY, NYC, and PA residents, please add appropriate sales tax. No cash, stamps, or C.O.D.s. All orders shipped within 6 weeks via postal service book rate. Canadian orders require $2.00 extra postage and must be paid in U.S. dollars through a U.S. banking facility.

Name_____
Address_____
City_____ State_____ Zip_____
  have enclosed $_____ in payment for the checked book(s).
Payment <u>must</u> accompany all orders. ❏ Please send a free catalog.

Winter Wonderland

**Emma Craig,
Leigh Greenwood,
Amanda Harte,
Linda O. Johnston**

Christmas is coming, and the streets are alive with the sounds of the season: "Silver Bells" and sleigh rides, jingle bells and carolers. Choruses of "Here Comes Santa Claus" float over the snow-covered landscape, bringing the joy of the holiday to revelers as they deck the halls and string the lights "Up on the Rooftop." And when the songs of the season touch four charmed couples, melody turns to romance and harmony turns to passion. For these "Merry Gentlemen" and their lovely ladies will learn that with the love they have found, not even a spring thaw will cool their desire or destroy their winter wonderland.

___52339-6 $5.99 US/$6.99 CAN

Look for this title in
December 2001
from

JANEEN O'KERRY
SISTER OF THE MOON

In the sylvan glens of Eire, the Sidhe reign supreme. The fair folk they are: fairies, thieves, changeling-bearers, tricksters. Their feet make no sound as they traipse through ancient forests, their mouths no noise as they weave their moonlight spells. And so Men have learned to fear them. But the Folk are dying. Their hunting grounds are overrun, their bronze swords no match for Man's cold iron. Scahta, their queen, is helpless to act. Her people need a king. And on Samhain Eve, she finds one. Though he is raw and untrained, she sees in Anlon the soul of nobility. Yet he is a Man. He will have to pass many tests to win her love. At the fires of Beltane he must prove himself her husband—and for the salvation of the Sidhe he must make himself a king.

_52466-X $5.50 US/$6.50 CAN